199

THE NOBEL

PRIZE

Yuri Krotkov

TRANSLATED FROM THE RUSSIAN BY DR. LINDA ALDWINCKLE

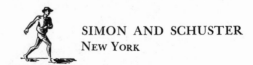

SIMON AND SCHUSTER
NEW YORK

Copyright © 1980 by Yuri Krotkov
All rights reserved
including the right of reproduction
in whole or in part in any form
Published by Simon and Schuster
A Division of Gulf & Western Corporation
Simon & Schuster Building
Rockefeller Center
1230 Avenue of the Americas
New York, New York 10020
SIMON AND SCHUSTER and colophon are
trademarks of Simon & Schuster
Designed by Jeanne Joudry
Manufactured in the United States of America
1   2   3   4   5   6   7   8   9   10

Library of Congress Cataloging in Publication Data

Krotkov, Iurii, date
The Nobel Prize.
1.   Pasternak, Boris Leonidovich, 1890–1960,
in fiction, drama, poetry, etc.   2.   Khrushchev,
Nikita Sergeevich, 1894–1971—Fiction.
PZ4.K9377No   [PG3482.8.R66]   891.7′344   80–10374
ISBN 0–671–24255–5

The author is grateful for permission to reprint
the following excerpts:
From Eugene M. Kayden's translation of the poem
"Summer 1917" in *Boris Pasternak—Poems* (page
75); reprinted by the permission of
The University of Colorado.
From Henry Kamen's translation of the poem
"It's unbecoming to have fame" in *In the Interlude,
Poems, 1945–1960* by Boris Pasternak (on pages 164,
181, 209, and 216); reprinted by permission of
A. D. Peters & Co., Ltd.

Contents

PART ONE

CHAPTER ONE

The Corn Czar

1.

"There's something I forgot to mention to you, Nikita Sergeyevich," Serov said as they drove through the Moscow suburb of Odintsovo. "Last night a message came through from our man in Stockholm. It appears that this year's Nobel Prize for Literature is going to Boris Pasternak . . . for *Doctor Zhivago* of course."

"What's that?" Khrushchev, lost in his thoughts, had not caught the general's meaning. The Chairman of the KGB repeated his news.

"Pah! Goddam sonofabitch!" Nikita cursed. "That Pasternak!" But otherwise he betrayed no hint of concern over the

9

KGB chief's report. Serov, aware that the Pasternak situation was a thorny one, puzzled over Khrushchev's uncharacteristic reticence.

Mikoyan nonchalantly broke in. Half opening his left eye and yawning, he muttered in Armenian-accented Russian, "We don't give a damn about Nobel prizes, Ivan!"

They were on their way to the government hunting reserve in Borodino, a village about an hour from Moscow. Dawn was just starting to break, and the outlines of forests and rolling fields shrouded with mist were gradually taking shape.

Khrushchev, short and pot-bellied, wore an aviator's jacket lined with red fur. He also wore galoshes and a hat with earflaps that was pulled down over his forehead. His lower lip protruded, giving his face an air of petulant determination. He sat, as usual, next to his driver, Mitya, who had been with him for more than twenty-five years. The others had made themselves comfortable in the back. The dark, wrinkled Mikoyan wore a quilted jacket and an astrakhan hat. He napped as they rode, stirring only to scratch his mustache occasionally. Serov, with clearly defined blue-gray circles under his eyes, was dressed in breeches and a heavy sweater. He stroked his angular knees with the palms of his hands, a habit he found soothing. The KGB colonel who was Khrushchev's chief bodyguard looked somewhat like his charge, but was more vain about his appearance. Gouty swellings on his trunklike legs marred the smooth lines of his box-calf boots. He scrutinized the plump neck of his master.

The headlights of the black limousine and of the two cars carrying security officers cut through the autumnal gloom and lit up the asphalt, uneven in places, of the Minsk highway. Mitya was not using the Kremlin "cuckoo" siren, because the road was almost empty; in forty minutes of driving they had encountered only two battered trucks and a police car.

Khrushchev whistled under his breath. Huddled against

the early morning chill, with a double-barreled Sauer shot-gun in a solid case gripped tightly between his legs, he was trying to concentrate on hares. Every Sunday on the way to Borodino he forgot about the affairs of party and government and thought only about hares. When he had been a young farm boy he'd been amazed to discover that their back legs were longer than their front ones. The funny creatures still fascinated him.

Swearing at potholes in the road, Mitya began telling a story about his son who worked in the crab industry in Kam-chatka. Annoyed by his chatter, Nikita flared up: "Always running on about your boy. I'm bored stiff. You'd do better to speed up and stop crawling along like a tortoise. Didn't you sleep last night? Your wife wear you out?"

"No . . . I, well . . ." Mitya stuttered in confusion, his poor complexion becoming noticeably blotched.

"We're keeping to the legal eighty-five kilometers an hour, Nikita Sergeyevich. By resolution of the Politburo," the chief bodyguard interjected on behalf of the driver.

" 'By resolution of the Politburo'!" Khrushchev mocked him. "We're all law abiders around here. Eighty-five kilometers an hour!" He turned to Mikoyan. "See what a life I lead? I'm First Secretary of the Party Central Committee and Chairman of the Council of Ministers. I'm respected and feared all over the world. But here, in my own country, the people around me don't give a damn about me. I'm con-stantly corrected and corrected. Nothing's sacred. Before a speech of mine appears in *Pravda*, all sorts of theoreticians and academicians from the Central Committee rush to edit it this way or that, smoothing sharp angles, so to speak. They distort and criticize every statement. Soon I'll be able to ex-press myself freely only when I'm visiting foreign countries. There, thank God, so far they don't correct me."

"But, Nikita Sergeyevich, I—" the chief bodyguard began in self-justification.

"Shut your trap!" Nikita interrupted.

2.

When the hunt was over, Mikoyan had bagged five hares, Serov two, and Khrushchev three—he missed a fourth from close quarters, and then, ignoring the protests of the security officers, had clambered into a swamp after it and got his boots full of cold water.

Nothing had gone well, Khrushchev thought as they rode back to Moscow, and it was all Serov's fault—Serov with his damned message from Stockholm. That idiotic *Doctor Zhivago!* Tired and morose, he began to dwell on the questions that plagued him. Was he not recognized as the initiator of a new international policy, as the originator of "peaceful coexistence"? Had he not been hailed as a "peacemaker"? Had he not relaxed government control within the Soviet Union? What was the upshot? The West thought he could be pushed around. The West, damn it, was squeezing him. This business with Pasternak was outrageous! Had such a thing ever been heard of before? A Soviet writer, without so much as a nod, had gone and published a novel in Italy. And an *anti-Soviet* novel into the bargain! And the most sickening part was that *Doctor Zhivago*, whatever its complaints, was just the tip of the iceberg. But what could he do? Start throwing people in prison again? Banish them to labor camps? Technically, he had not abolished the proletarian terror, but he had tried to limit it—which, he recalled now, had prompted Serov to declare, "Comrade Khrushchev, you have tied the hands of the security forces." (How Serov longed to go back to the hard line!)

Goddam sonofabitch, Nikita thought, that Pasternak should have been stepped on long ago! The incident called into question his whole political philosophy. Like Stalin, he was determined to make the Soviet Union a true communist state, but he had repudiated the other man's methods. Had he been wrong? He knew that some people in high party circles—so far only in private—were accusing him of "liberalism," of permissiveness, of trying to arrange a marriage of convenience between capitalism and communism. He was reproached for his trips abroad, for tinkling glasses with the leaders of bourgeois states. And he was blamed as well, damn it, for the troubles with China. It was like being trapped in a Turkish bath. Goddammit, no matter! But he'd deal with his opponents and he'd lead the Soviet people out of the wilderness—to a secure, unrepressive, decent existence. And he'd continue the "liberalism" and "peacemaking"—lull the West to sleep . . . and then smash it to bits.

Suddenly emerging from his depression, Nikita turned to Mikoyan and charged, "You don't give a damn about Nobel prizes, Anastas, but I do."

Mikoyan winked surreptitiously at Serov. "Is it my fault, Nikita, that I've got five hares for my Ashkhen and you've got only three for your Nina?"

Khrushchev seized on the hares' blood still on Serov's hands. "You're always bloodstained, Ivan. A KGB man to the marrow!" Then he burst out laughing.

Khrushchev could rely on Mikoyan, his first deputy in the Council of Ministers, and on Serov as well. They wouldn't sell him out, he knew. Mikoyan had supported him in the confrontation with Molotov, Malenkov, Kaganovich, and Voroshilov—in short, with the whole pack of Stalinist wolves —when they had rebelled against him. Khrushchev knew that in his heart the Armenian hated Stalin. And he knew that Mikoyan admired him because he was not and did not try to be Stalin. As for Serov, Nikita would never forget how the two of them had mercilessly established Soviet power in Bukovina after the Red Army (with Hitler's assent) had occupied the Western Ukraine in 1939. And although he had been Marshal Beria's deputy in the Ministry of Internal Affairs, Serov had signed the order for Beria's arrest, thus helping to eliminate the dangerous Georgian and the threat that he posed of a new dictatorship after Stalin's death. Moreover, Serov also had been completely loyal during the confrontation of Nikita with Molotov, Malenkov, Kaganovich,

Voroshilov, and the rest. At the Central Committee plenum, where the battle had broken out, all the entrances and exits of the building had been guarded by army officers. The Chairman of the KGB, General Serov, remained "neutral," knowing that the Defense Minister, Marshal Zhukov, was on Khrushchev's side. (When Zhukov was later dismissed, he was nicknamed the "rocket launcher," because he had fired Nikita into orbit and then burned himself out.)

3.

That night Khrushchev developed a sore throat and a fever. He stayed in bed the next morning and started sucking lemons. His favorite remedy did not help, and at midday his wife, Nina, called the Kremlin doctor out to Barvikha. Nikita had already telephoned Suslov, the Central Committee Secretary for Agitation and Propaganda, on the hot line. Despite his raspy throat, he talked with him for about thirty minutes, the phone growing sweaty in his hand. The conversation was naturally about Pasternak and his *Doctor Zhivago*. In Suslov's opinion, the report from Stockholm was most probably accurate.

"So are we going to sit around groaning, with our arms folded, or what?!" Khrushchev bellowed into the telephone.

4.

Two days later came the official announcement from Sweden: Boris Pasternak had been awarded the Nobel Prize. The news was broadcast all over the world—in Russia by the numerous services of the Voice of America—and word of it spread through the Moscow intelligentsia, causing joy, envy, and indignation.

The spark had been ignited. . . .

5.

Nikita lay in bed with tonsillitis for the next three days. But as soon as he was up and about he told Lebedev, his assistant, to summon Suslov, Polikarpov, and Alexei Surkov, the General Secretary of the Union of Soviet writers, to Barvikha.

Khrushchev's state dacha, which had once belonged to a wealthy factory owner, was a two-story log house with carved decoration and a long wing extension. Servants' quarters, a garage, and the bodyguard's house stood off to one side. The dacha had a billiard room and movie theater and, on the grounds, a volleyball pitch, tennis court, and shooting range. The whole complex was surrounded by a high wooden fence topped with barbed wire. Just inside the fence was a deep trench, patrolled at night by Alsatian dogs—left over from Stalin's day.

On the walls of the living room, finished in walnut paneling, hung painted revolutionary scenes, Khrushchev family photographs, and portraits of world Communist leaders, not including Stalin. Beneath them, bookcases were filled with academic publications. A round mahogany table, polished to a high gloss, stood in the center of the room, while the rest of the furniture, including a piano, was arranged helter-skelter under dust covers. A television set with a large screen— evidently foreign-made—occupied a corner.

Suslov, Polikarpov, and Surkov arrived together at the appointed hour of eight in the evening. Khrushchev received them in a heavy jersey warm-suit, which made him look even stockier than usual, and bedroom slippers. The chief bodyguard lingered for a minute or two and then slipped away.

Suslov, at about fifty, was tall and thin, with a sallow complexion and a scrawny neck. A pince-nez bit into his long, beaklike nose. He rarely smiled, perhaps because he had false teeth, and spoke pedantically (in the Central Committee he was called "the theoretician"). Khrushchev was not fond of the secretary and in fact was a little afraid of him. He had once remarked that Suslov was the mainspring in the Central Committee building on Staraya Square not because he was "the theoretician" but because he made it his business to know everything that went on there—even which light bulbs had burned out in which washrooms. Khrushchev also joked about Suslov's fanatic dedication to classical Marxism, maintaining that he carried a copy of *Das Kapital* everywhere, even to the toilet. Both remarks had reached Suslov's ears, but nevertheless their relations were normal by Central Committee standards. Suslov, following Mikoyan's lead, had supported Nikita at the memorable Central Committee plenum that initiated Khrushchev's rise, although, to be sure, Nikita had already gained prominence with his "anti-Stalinist" speech at the Twentieth Party Congress, which some said was the turning point of his career.

Polikarpov, tall and good-looking, had a pleasing voice and a self-assured though wary gaze. Khrushchev had had few dealings with him, but he knew that the head of the Central Committee Department of Culture was a Suslov man and that he had had considerable experience in working with the intelligentsia. For several years Polikarpov had been the leader of the Union of Soviet Writers, and had later been the Chairman of the All-Union Radio Committee. In his early fifties, Polikarpov had twice been in the Kremlin hospital with angina pectoris, but now seemed well. Like Suslov, he was dressed in the Central Committee style: dark-blue baggy suit, white shirt with starched collar, orange tie, and the short boots also favored by ministers and KGB generals.

Surkov, who was also in his early fifties, had an open, handsome face. His fair hair, streaked with silver, fell across his forehead, making him look like the poet Sergei Yesenin. Well built, he was of medium height and moved easily. His poetry, much of which had been set to music, was widely known. He stressed his *o*'s and, like most poets, prolonged his words as if he were singing them. But there was something of the common man in him which attracted people to him—he still seemed like the boy next door. Having risen from the ranks, he had advanced quickly, and had recently been elected a candidate member of the Central Committee and a deputy of the Supreme Soviet. In the last years he had acquired a certain elegance: he often wore well-tailored suits and fine Italian shoes and had even tried polishing his nails.

Krushchev and his three guests sat down at the round table, and Nina, his plump, good-natured wife, set it for tea, putting out cheese tarts she had just baked. Nikita disliked being served by the civilian KGB staff. He much preferred Nina to the maids with their little white caps perched on elaborate hairdos. And despite her busy life (she was a teacher), Nina liked putting on an apron and keeping house.

Nikita did not touch the tea but picked up thin slices of lemon from the plate he had moved toward him. He licked each slice, wrinkling his face from the sour taste, and then, like a seal eating a flounder, swallowed it whole without chewing it. After drinking their glasses of tea, Polikarpov and Surkov complimented Nina on the cheese tarts. Suslov nodded in agreement, then blew on the lenses of his pince-nez and began polishing them with a handkerchief.

After Nina left, Khrushchev pushed the lemons away and, pursing his lips, said: "Well, then, comrades, let us all together, the whole congregation, confess our sins. We've been foolish. Lost our Bolshevik vigilance. Blundered. Idiots, that's what we are. If *Doctor Zhivago* hadn't come out in Italy, there wouldn't have been all this stupidity with the Nobel Prize. Am I right, Comrade Surkov?"

"I did everything I could have done, Nikita Sergeyevich." Surkov turned pale and, after asking whether Khrushchev objected, lit a cigarette.

"No, go ahead, smoke. . . . I know that Comrade Polikarpov packed you off to Rome and you met the publisher to whom Pasternak gave his manuscript. What's his name?"

"Feltrinelli," Polikarpov prompted.

"He's a member of the Italian Communist Party, the lousy swine. And he twisted you around his little finger, Surkov." Nikita scowled. Then, recollecting himself, he addressed him more politely: "He twisted you around his little finger, Comrade Surkov. He simply put aside his political philosophy and went ahead and printed *Doctor Zhivago*. And made himself a bundle, the sonofabitch. In the West they all live off treachery. It's money first, last, and always. Now this book has been circulating about the world for two years, telling everyone what bloodthirsty scoundrels we 'reds' are."

"The fight is over, Nikita Sergeyevich. What's the point in brandishing fists?" Suslov twisted a pencil in his long bony fingers.

Khrushchev turned toward the Central Committee secretary and met his gimletlike eyes. "I agree with you, Comrade Suslov." He got up and rested his elbows on the back of the chair. "But remember that under Stalin not even a mouse could have slipped across the Soviet border. We've flung the window wide open. Tourism, cultural exchanges, festivals, and all kinds of nonsense. Look, we say, what great fellows we are, there's no one finer than us! Then both sides play every dirty trick in the book. No, old man Stalin knew what he was doing when he kept Soviet writers on a tight rein. They didn't dare squeak when he was around. But I, or rather we, fuss over them like a child with a new toy."

Surkov, still nervous, was about to smile but decided to frown instead, and the result was neither one nor the other. He lowered his head, inhaling a little more cigarette smoke.

Khrushchev felt like telling Suslov everything, everything that had been building inside him since he'd first addressed the basic issue: Was a dictatorship not only necessary but inevitable in the Soviet Union? Was it possible for him to dissociate himself from Stalin? Time and again he had been forced to go back to the harsh methods of dictatorship, notwithstanding his public declaration that a dictatorship of the proletariat was no longer necessary in the Soviet Union. Was true liberalization possible? His critics were becoming more and more outspoken. He knew from Serov that Polikarpov had told friends, all of them scoundrels, "Nikita vilified Stalin for nothing." He knew that many party officials, particularly those in the upper ranks, the *nomenklatura*, had never forgiven him for his anti-Stalinist speech. Yes, and he had to admit that, although he had knocked the villain down, he had stood at attention with the rest when Stalin was alive. He knew also that even though his popularity had grown among the Russian people, he still did not hold the reins of government in his hands. He still had to depend on others— on Suslov, for example, and the other members of the Politburo. He knew he would never acquire absolute power.

But instead of unburdening himself, Nikita suddenly blurted out: "I've got a domestic conflict too. It's my daughter Rada, the 'intellectual.' She's a hundred percent modern in everything. And she's got a degree. When she's staying here at the dacha we do nothing but quarrel. She raises hell and I raise hell. Nina's the only one who can calm us down. And what's it all about? I'll tell you. In the morning, when I'm shaving, I like listening to marches on the radio. Yes, marches. They set me up for the day. But Rada storms into the bathroom, and off goes the march and on comes some symphony. Then she gives me a lecture on music appreciation. She says I should listen to 'real' music. But for me real music is marches. For her it's Beethoven and Grieg. Well, how can you help raising hell?"

Polikarpov smiled, Suslov remained inscrutable, and Surkov, still determined to be serious, burst into laughter. Then Khrushchev burst into laughter as well, like an actor who has delighted his public and so decides to join them.

"Nikita Sergeyevich," said Surkov, "I'm afraid that all our problems are inevitable as long as the capitalist encirclement continues to exist—"

"What? Capitalist encirclement? But where did you get your hands on such a fine suit, Comrade General Secretary of the Union of Soviet Writers? In that 'capitalist encirclement,' I'll bet. Well, stand up, then, I want to get a good look at it. Go on!"

Surkov shrank with embarrassment, but, responding to Khrushchev's request, rose from the table, walked to the middle of the room, and even turned around twice to satisfy Nikita's baiting.

"What a fine collar! I must have one like that made for myself. And with pants like drainpipes. I travel around the 'capitalist encirclement' too, you know, Comrade Surkov."

"I can give you the address of the tailor," Surkov said cheerfully. "Paris. Boulevard des Capucines."

Surkov had done what Nikita liked doing himself—said something that left uncertain whether it was a joke or not. Khrushchev was not pleased. He appreciated irony in himself but not in others.

"It seems, Comrade Surkov," he remarked with a twitch of his lower lip, "that you also have an 'intellectual' daughter. I've heard that she's learning to play the piano and you've hired a music teacher for her. A private tutor comes to your house. Isn't that true?"

"Yes, it's true. I've hired someone to give her private lessons." Surkov sat down at the table. "My daughter has her heart set on entering the Moscow Conservatory next year. She's a talented girl."

"Aha, so she'll be demanding all sorts of symphonies too?"

"Actually, I don't see anything wrong with Beethoven, Nikita Sergeyevich."

Khrushchev was sitting quietly with his belly against the edge of the table. Suddenly he banged on the table with such force that the glasses and spoons rang in their saucers. No, of course this whole Nobel Prize mess had nothing to do with Beethoven or Surkov. It was something else altogether. Nikita flushed violently, his moist jowls trembling like an angry dog's. "The swine! The scoundrels! The bastards!" He bellowed so loudly that his voice cracked. "They didn't give the prize to our Mikhail Sholokhov for his novel *And Quiet Flows the Don*, but to that lousy Jew Pasternak—"

Khrushchev suddenly stopped. A five-year-old girl had wandered into the room unseen carrying a bowl of pudding. When the child saw Nikita's furious expression her chin quivered and she burst into tears.

Khrushchev rushed to her, swung her off her feet, and beamed at her, completely changing in an instant without the slightest effort.

"Now, don't be afraid, my little pet. I was joking. I'm not a nasty grandpa, I'm a nice grandpa. Come, little one, let's try the pudding. Show these gentlemen what a clever girl you are. Come on, now! It's tasty, mmm, tasty."

He lowered himself onto the sofa, set his granddaughter on his knee and began feeding her expertly with a spoon. The little girl changed as quickly as Khrushchev had. She calmed down, began to eat the pudding, and regarded her grandfather's guests with grave curiosity.

Khrushchev turned amiably to Surkov. "I remember your songs from the front, Alexei. By the way, what's your patronymic?"

"Alexandrovich. But only the poems, the words of the songs, were mine. Someone else provided the melodies."

"Yes, yes, of course, Alexei Alexandrovich. In any case, we felt better during the war because of them. The soldiers liked your songs. And you became famous because of them, Alexei Alexandrovich." Khrushchev stressed Surkov's patronymic twice.

"Thank you for the compliment. You can see I'm for marches too," Surkov said with a smile. "But all the same I'm not against symphonies."

"I see. So you worship in all the temples." Nikita laughed. "Do you hear that, granddaughter, what our Surkov's like? He wants to please everyone. But I'm asking you, comrades, why didn't those people in Sweden give the prize to Sholokhov?" He answered his own question. "Because, my little one, in our life *everything* is politics. Do you understand? Uncle Stalin taught us that. Yes, yes, he taught us that. Mikhail Sholokhov, you see, is a Communist, a man who shares our ideals. That's it, ideals. Eat your pudding, my little wide-eyed flower. While Pasternak, you see, is drawing us toward . . . Christianity, toward symphonies, 'real' music. Ah, my little pet, you see how things are turning out. Should I, and these gentlemen here, should we all waste our time on this baptized Jew and his novel? I've got more important things to do. Our country's facing serious economic tasks. Am I not right, comrades? Yes, I'm right. Task number one, for instance, is to catch up with and overtake the United States in per capita production of milk and meat. And we must begin sowing corn in northern districts. Yes, granddaughter, corn."

Hearing the word "corn," the little girl began to laugh and started chanting it teasingly to her grandfather.

"You little chatterbox!" Nikita glared at her with mock severity. "I'll give you a smack. You'll get one from me." Lowering her to the floor, he added affectionately, "Come on, my little doll, let's go see Grandma."

Khrushchev stood up and led the little girl out of the room. She walked obediently beside him, looking back at his guests and still chanting the word "corn" as they disappeared.

Surkov turned to Suslov. "Mikhail Andreyevich, our First Secretary has gotten to the heart of the matter. Pasternak's ideals are totally opposed to our own. We'll have to deal with him firmly and quickly and then get on to more important business."

Suslov said nothing, and his expression gave no hint of his reaction to Surkov's remark.

Returning to the living room, Nikita sat down at the round table, put yet another slice of lemon in his mouth, sucked it, and swallowed it.

"Well, then, Comrade Suslov," he said. "Now let's listen to you. What's on today's agenda? Report to us, please." (Khrushchev always tried to be polite with the secretary.)

Suslov spoke in an impassive but businesslike tone. "The day before yesterday Pasternak sent a telegram to Stockholm that read: 'Eternally grateful, moved, I am proud, astonished, unworthy.'" Suslov's memory for quotations and texts was phenomenal.

"Pity they didn't just send the word 'unworthy,'" Nikita commented, and added with a sigh, "I wish the priest had drowned him in the font . . . eh?"

Suslov continued: "When the Western news correspondents swooped down on the writers' colony at Peredelkino, like flies making for a honeypot, they asked him about his reaction to being awarded the Nobel Prize. Pasternak repeated these same words. Yesterday newspapers throughout the world ran articles about him on their front pages. He's caused a great stir. His photographs have been printed everywhere. Some of the Soviet writers of the older generation, Pasternak's neighbors in Peredelkino, congratulated him in person."

"Who exactly?" Khrushchev asked with interest.

"Vsevolod Ivanov and Kornei Chukovsky," Surkov replied for Suslov.

"Chukovsky? That old chap—isn't he the one who writes for children?"

"Yes, that's he." Surkov nodded.

"I'm amazed." Khrushchev shook his head. "What's he got in common with Pasternak? A month or two ago I read my eldest granddaughter his book *From Two to Five*, and I enjoyed it myself. I laughed till I cried. It's a marvelous book, great. Here, for example: An old woman tells her grandson that Christ was nailed to the cross, but he suddenly slipped away. And the young one, the grandson, answers back: 'Fools, they should have *screwed* him to the cross, then he wouldn't have gotten away!' " Khrushchev burst out laughing, slapping his thigh.

Suslov continued. "Pasternak has already received a number of telegrams from abroad. We couldn't stop them from being delivered. That would have been going too far. All the telegrams congratulated him of course."

"The swine! Pouring fat on the fire, the vermin!" Placing his hands on the table, Nikita began drumming his fingers.

Suslov went on. "Yesterday, as you know, Nikita Sergeyevich, *Literaturnaya Gazeta* carried a statement by the editorial board of the journal *Novy Mir*. Pasternak submitted *Doctor Zhivago* to *Novy Mir* for publication, and the board refused, giving its reasons."

"What a character!" Khrushchev broke in. "So he hoped his anti-Soviet novel would be published in a Soviet journal. And he even sent the manuscript to *Novy Mir*. Isn't that incredible, Comrade Surkov? He's either as stupid as a new-born babe or he's certifiably crazy."

"No, he's not crazy, Nikita Sergeyevich," Surkov replied. "We just don't think the way he does."

Suslov intervened. "Yesterday *Pravda* condemned Pasternak. Today a similar article appeared in *Literaturnaya Gazeta*. As you can see, we're not sitting on our hands, Comrade Khrushchev."

"I trust not, Comrade Suslov." Nikita scratched the back of his neck energetically. "I trust not. Only . . . how's that beauty—Olga, isn't it?—how's she behaving? How do things stand between her and the poet? Is Pasternak sleeping with her, Comrade Suslov?"

"She's his literary secretary, Nikita Sergeyevich. And friend. She's a poet herself and a translator. And, yes, they are lovers."

"So he's betraying his wife?"

"His wife has known about it for years. It's no secret."

"And she's done nothing about it? She's not threatening to poison herself?"

"She suffers in silence, as far as I know. She's proud by nature. And however Pasternak acts with Olga, Nikita Sergeyevich, he's no Don Juan."

Nikita turned to Surkov. "You're a liberal, Alexei. What do you think of this? General Serov told me that Olga, de-lightful little Olga, is turning Pasternak against the Soviet system. It seems she's involved in all sorts of shady deals. She speculates in currency and is very friendly with a number of foreigners."

Surkov nodded. "According to my information, she's a bad influence on Pasternak."

"Under Stalin the little charmer would have been serving time in Kolyma long ago," Khrushchev remarked sharply.

"Under Stalin the little charmer did serve time in Kolyma, or somewhere out there, Nikita Sergeyevich," Surkov said. "Has she been rehabilitated? Well, there you are. The damned 'thaw.' Khrushchev's 'thaw.' Now we're knee-deep in muck again. All the petty-bourgeois rabble have crawled out of their holes. I was an ass to allow it. I repent. I gave freedom. Well, not just me, I had your support. You, Comrade Suslov, and you—"

Nina entered the living room. "Shall I bring some more tea?"

"We've had enough, Nina. Don't bother us. They've drunk their fill, and we're talking business now." Khrushchev hesitated. "On second thought, come over here and sit down." He took his wife by the hand and drew her down next to him on the sofa, his arm around her shoulders. "Now, then, old girl, answer my questions truthfully, as your heart dictates. They have to do with our conversation. We've talked about this before, but I want them, these people here, to listen to you."

"Why to me?" Nina smiled broadly. "I'm just a simple Russian woman."

"Stop that. In the first place, it would be good for us to listen to a simple Russian woman—her mind is a treasure," Nikita stated firmly. "And in the second place, you're not simple. You've got a higher education, you teach English in a military academy, even if you have got a Pskov accent."*

"He's laughing at me again." Nina nudged her husband in the stomach.

"Listen now, Nina. First of all, tell them—did I tell you to read *Doctor Zhivago*?"

"Yes, and I read it. You know that."

"But this is for them, for them. It's all for their benefit. An act. Do you understand? Now answer the following question: What's the novel about?"

* Pskov is a provincial Russian city.

25

"About life."

"Of *course* it's about life. But what else? Give us a bit more detail. About life!"

"Well, it's about the upheaval in Russian society in the nineties, how it led to the October Revolution and the Civil War. And it's about Yury Zhivago, who was a member of the intelligentsia, how his family fell apart and how he lost his way during those stormy years and died."

"Yes, Yury Zhivago died; that was his fate. And so, isn't Pasternak saying that the revolution was a catastrophe for the Russian intelligentsia?"

"Yes, if you like."

"Well, Pasternak got it all wrong. Wrong, do you hear? Hundreds, no, thousands of the old Russian intelligentsia sided with Lenin at that time. Did he mention Lenin in the novel?"

"No, not that I remember. There's a lot about Christ."

With a shrewd expression Nina went on: "Here's my advice, comrades. All this fuss over *Doctor Zhivago* is doing us no good. The right thing to do now is to print it here. Just two or three thousand copies. That's all that will sell—only the elite will read it. There's no reason to worry about this book. It won't reach the masses, because it's too obscure, too intellectual. It would put ordinary people to sleep."

"You see what a *simple* Russian woman thinks," Nikita exclaimed with delight. "Simple, but not as simple as all that. The wife of the First Secretary of the Party Central Committee and the Chairman of the USSR Council of Ministers thinks that *Doctor Zhivago* should be published in Russia. That's what the 'thaw' has done. Things have really gone that far. Hear how the woman talks. But, comrades, perhaps she's right. What about it, Surkov?"

"I'm against it, Nikita Sergeyevich," Surkov said decisively. "In my opinion, we don't have the right to take the pressure off this book. It's an obvious ideological attack. In fact, the novel is being used by the West as a subversive weapon against us."

"Did you hear what the poet Surkov thinks, old girl?" Nikita said, again with a gleeful note.

"Yes, but we must put everything in order in our own country, in our own house. That's what's most important. We have to get rid of all this controversy, all these rumors," Nina retorted.

Khrushchev's lips quivered and he snapped at her: "You're a fool, Nina, that's what you are! There's no way to just wipe away a problem. I've told you over and over, there are no easy answers in this life. Do you understand? Now, the poet Surkov—there's a brain for you. I agree with him. The West regards *Doctor Zhivago* as a sort of bomb that can be used against us. We have to defuse this bomb. That's right, Comrade Surkov. All right, you've had your say, my love. Your words are exquisite. Now go back to your own business."

"Well, you're the one who sat me down here. I didn't push myself on you. He's always calling for me and then insulting me." She got up and walked toward the door without looking at her husband.

"Wait a minute, old girl," Nikita called after her, as if there had been no sharp words between them. "Look at the suit that Surkov laid his hands on in Paris. It's great! Please, comrade poet, stand up again."

"With pleasure, Nikita Sergeyevich." Surkov got up for the second time, walked to the center of the room and turned to both sides, like a professional model.

Glancing at Surkov's suit, Nina observed, "Western cut . . ."

"Shall I get one like it, Nina? What do you think?"

"We'll find you one."

"Where will you find one like this? In our country? No, unfortunately they don't know how to make any like this in our workshops. They sell sacks instead of jackets in the government shops."

"Sacks? Nikita, you're exaggerating."

"Honestly, Nina, they're sacks."

"What a dandy we've become! All right, I'll write a letter

to Paris saying the corn czar needs a suit with drainpipe pants." Nina laughed and left the room.

"Listen to her! Just answers me back," Khrushchev said, smiling. Then, frowning, he went on: "Calls me the corn czar. The whole family, every one of them, calls me the corn czar. I know lots of people call me that; even abroad they joke about Khrushchev and his corn. I ask you, comrades, have I done anything to deserve this mockery? Stalin never gave a thought to the Russians who were starving. I want our people to have full stomachs, to have money. And it's corn that will save us. It will solve our food problems once and for all. Corn's cheap, a nourishing cereal, and it's hardy and easy to grow. I'll sow it over the whole of northern Russia. The Americans aren't fools, and they think highly of corn. Mark my words, corn's the answer."

Khrushchev picked up another slice of lemon and began to suck it, smacking his lips. Surkov took a gulp of cold tea and lit a second cigarette, after asking Khrushchev's permission. Suslov twirled a pencil in his fingers and remained inscrutable. Polikarpov sneezed several times and fell silent. The wall clock in the corner of the living room—probably a relic of the first inhabitant, the factory owner—ticked loudly. Somewhere in the house a door slammed.

Polikarpov rubbed his nose with a handkerchief and said, "Nikita Sergeyevich, have you heard that black marketeers are selling *Doctor Zhivago* on Kuznetsky Most, right in the center of Moscow?"

"Lousy swine! They wouldn't have dared to under Stalin! How much?"

"One hundred rubles a copy, it seems."

Nikita's whistle expressed his thoughts: What a price! What a swindle!

"They're in Russian. Emigré editions, printed in West Germany and the United States," Suslov explained.

"Should we arrest them all, eh?"

"The émigrés?" Polikarpov asked with a smile.

"The black marketeers on Kuznetsky Most," Khrushchev

replied dryly. After clearing his throat he went on simply and calmly: "Well, comrades, enough idle chatter. I think it's obvious what we have to do. We have to show the imperialists, their stooges, and this troublemaker Pasternak with his *Doctor Zhivago* that we know how to stick the knife in when we need to. Comrade Suslov, tell this Pasternak character, through your channels, that I, Nikita Khrushchev, the 'corn czar,' the First Secretary of the Party Central Committee and the Chairman of the USSR Council of Ministers, am giving him a simple choice. He must refuse the Nobel Prize immediately and send a telegram to Stockholm to that effect, and he must also write a letter of repentance—no, two letters, one to me and another to *Pravda*. Or else . . ."

"Or else?" Surkov repeated, staring hard at Khrushchev and feeling his heart miss a beat.

"Or else we shall take *strong* administrative measures," Nikita snapped.

"Right. I agree," said Surkov. He spoke coolly, with no hint of the emotions racing through him. Images from Pushkin's verse drama *Mozart and Salieri* crowded his mind, recalled from his high school days: the composer Salieri, envious of Mozart's genius, poisoning a goblet of the master's wine. Surkov had always known that he would never reach the heights attained by Pasternak, and the knowledge tormented him. But he was proud that at least he understood Pasternak's poetry, even liked it. As a poet, he would have preferred not to speak out in public against Pasternak, but in the company of Khrushchev and Suslov he had to embrace orthodoxy.

Nikita, anticipating that Suslov might use this whole incident to undermine his authority, asked with a touch of irony, "But don't you think, Mikhail Andreyevich, that it might be better to raise the 'Pasternak affair' for discussion by the full membership of the Politburo?"

Although Khrushchev had made a show of consulting his comrades, of paying lip service to collective leadership, he was, Suslov knew, in charge. And because Khrushchev's decision clearly suited Suslov, Suslov replied without hesitation, "We'll deal with Pasternak as a routine matter without consulting the Politburo."

"Many hands make light work," Khrushchev observed, again with irony.

6.

After the three bureaucrats had left Barvikha, General Serov dropped in to visit the "invalid." They went to the billiard room for a game of Pyramid, notwithstanding the doctor's advice to Nikita to abstain for a week. As they played they chatted about Pasternak. Serov declared that he should have been brought to trial immediately after it became known that he had handed over the manuscript of *Doctor Zhivago* to Feltrinelli. Altogether, he was for ostracizing the poet.

Chalking his cue, Nikita said offhandedly, "You know, Ivan, it seems to me that Suslov is digging my grave. He's scheming."

"Not really."

"It seems so to me. I can't make him out at all. I've been working with him for years, but I still don't know what sort of a man he is. Is he a red Jesuit, or what?"

Serov stared at Nikita for a few seconds, then realized that he was not joking, was really disturbed by Suslov. He pulled his nose and said in a meaningful way, "Nikita Sergeyevich, we all have our weaknesses."

"What's his?" Khrushchev looked up sharply.

"Well, do Jesuits play cards?"

"Play cards?"

"Yes, he likes playing whist. For money."

"Huh . . ." Nikita clearly was disappointed. "I thought you had something substantial. I need a land mine, my friend. A bombshell. Your information wouldn't hurt a fly. What Central Committee member doesn't like playing a few hands of cards? You can't just drink vodka, goddammit!"

7.

After returning to Moscow that evening Suslov and Polikarpov, who both lived in the government house on Granovsky Street, organized a small game of cards. Half an hour later two of their regular partners arrived—Professor Boris Ponomarev, the round-faced and balding specialist on foreign socialist parties who was Suslov's right-hand man, and the young, red-faced Baranov, a recent graduate of the Academy of Social Sciences, who worked for the Central Committee as an expert on propaganda in capitalist countries.

They played whist for three hours. The stakes were high—ten kopecks a trick. Ponomarev distinguished himself, as always. He was a master at whist and played misère with special skill.

Before Polikarpov left, Suslov invited him into his study. "So who will be the one to take Khrushchev's ultimatum to Pasternak, Dimitry Alexeyevich?" Suslov asked. "I don't think it should be anyone associated with the party, but someone from his own circle, someone who's about the same age as he is."

"Another writer?"

"Yes, I think it would be better if it were a writer. Someone well known, with authority."

"Not Surkov?"

"No, no, he won't do. Alexei is too direct. And a bit of a lout, a bit too simple. Do you know what I mean?"

"Yes . . . someone from . . . I've got it!"

"Who?"

"Konstantin Fedin. They were close friends once. And they're from the same generation. He's not a party man and he's famous. Will he do?"

"Fine. Since basically he's on *our* side."

"There's no doubt about that."

"Isn't he from the Volga, like me?"

"Yes, he is, and his mother was a teacher's daughter, if I'm not mistaken."

Suslov yawned, sat down on the leather sofa, and took off his shoes. "Good. So have a talk with him tomorrow, Dimitry Alexeyevich."

"I'll see to it."

Thereupon, as if he had cast aside a mask, Suslov laughed out loud, showing his porcelain teeth. His laughter seemed forced, even theatrical, but it was laughter nonetheless. "Nikita certainly is muddleheaded," he said.

"My younger son, who's in the Pioneers, recently watched him give a speech on television and said that the whole thing was a 'circus,' " Polikarpov replied cautiously. They had both lowered their voices.

"We've had more than enough clowning."

"Isn't it nonsensical, Mikhail Andreyevich? He seems to be turning into a megalomaniac."

"There's nothing to worry about," Suslov reassured him. "We won't let him join the Communist monarchy."

"What if he tries to force his way there?"

"Well, we'll have to deal with that. But right now, can't you see, there's no one to replace him. Do you have a better man in mind, Dimitry Alexeyevich?"

Polikarpov looked at him curiously, but Suslov, the eternal number two, didn't respond. "Khrushchev's liberalism and voluntarism are not without danger, Mikhail Andreyevich."

"Let's wait and see," Suslov replied vaguely. He did not understand why at decisive moments he spoke up for Khrushchev, for whom he had never felt any personal sympathy. Perhaps he could not separate himself from the party machine: as one of its main cogwheels, he influenced and was influenced by the whole mechanism. And when a dogma subjugates a man, who in turn subjugates a group of people, a self-sufficient control mechanism is inevitably created, something like a perpetual motion machine, a peculiar octopus that enslaves its creators. Suslov's whole life seemed to have been computer-programmed, his individuality worn away by dogma. No longer did he need to refer to the classics of Marxism-Leninism; the "red Jesuit" had long ago absorbed them and thus always kept his bearings when dealing with party problems. He did not make mistakes. On the question of Pasternak his opinions and those of Khrushchev coincided. Here they were bound together by their traditional class hatred of the intelligentsia, an anomaly, since they were of the intelligentsia themselves. (Both of them had graduated from institutions of higher learning, and Suslov had edited *Pravda* under Stalin.) Publicly they both professed solidarity with the intelligentsia, but, having risen from the ranks, both were hostile toward a group historically regarded as an elite. In the present instance they were striking at Pasternak because they saw in him a social evil inherited from the past.

Suslov had advised Polikarpov to wait and see, because for the moment the party machine was turning in a Khrushchevian direction—or rather, not going against it. Suslov, however, had already noticed some ominous creakings in the mechanism. Perhaps Nikita was beginning to move too far from the party line.

"Do you know, Dimitry Alexeyevich," he said at length, "why Nikita has taken a personal interest in the Pasternak affair?" He stretched and looked at Polikarpov intently.

"Because he wants to demonstrate his Bolshevik vigilance to us, thus tempering the so-called Khrushchevian liberalism."

Suslov smiled thinly. "A tightrope walker."

CHAPTER TWO

Narcissus

1.

Nina Tabidze was sitting at the dining room table, which was covered with a plastic cloth. Although she was well past fifty, her face was still lively and beautiful; her hair had turned gray and she had made no attempt to color it. She was plump, and her youthful shapeliness and elegance had become blurred. She wore a plain brown dress with a woollen shawl wrapped around her waist. Nina was smoking—she was a heavy smoker and had a chronic cough. The reading glasses balanced on the tip of her nose made her look slightly comic, like an old granny. She was reading *Pravda*. Several other newspapers and a pile of letters were lying on the table next to a bunch of autumn flowers, some fruit and bread, a small carafe of vodka and an earthenware jug of wine.

She still could not believe the words in *Pravda*: "... Yury Zhivago, a mean, narrow-minded, petty-bourgeois dreamer, is as close to Soviet people as is the author himself, the snob Pasternak. He is their enemy, and the friend and ally of those who hate our country and our way of life. This is borne out by the acclamations of the West. Pasternak has put a weapon into the hands of the enemy; he has given them an anti-Soviet book. This weapon is slander of the USSR."

"My God! What viciousness!" Nina exclaimed, pronouncing the words with the trace of a Georgian accent.

She had flown to Moscow from Tbilisi the day before the announcement of the prize. Pasternak's younger son, Lyonya, had driven her straight from Vnukovo Airport to Peredelkino in his Moskvich, and she had been staying with the Pasternaks at their dacha for about a week.

The writers' township at Peredelkino is about twenty-five kilometers from Moscow; it lies along the Moscow-Kiev railroad, a little to one side of the Minsk highway. It is a rustic place with small groves, clearings, gullies, and a sluggish, narrow river. A hostel belonging to the Writers' Union, where forty or fifty second-rank Soviet writers spend working holidays, is located there. The hostel, the so-called House of Creativity, is reminiscent of a boardinghouse, and some humorist wrote an epigram about it:

> Be quiet, be quiet! Be still as the night!
> Somebody somewhere is trying to write.

Famous and honored men of letters have dachas in Peredelkino, either their own or ones rented from the Literary Fund. (Most of them also have apartments in Moscow.)

There Boris Pasternak spent most of his time. The dacha he had rented for the last twenty years was the fourth from the corner on Pavlenko Drive. Surrounded by a fence, from which several of the planks were missing, the house stood on about an acre of land, a large part of which was used as a vegetable garden. A few cherry and apple trees, as well as some gooseberry bushes and strawberry plants, had also been planted. The garden was skirted by a path that began at the decrepit wooden gate, which was always open. The dacha was a two-story frame house; behind it, among tall, spreading pine and fir trees, was a garage, and on the right a guesthouse, where Yevgeny, Pasternak's elder son (by his first wife), spent the summer with his family.

As Nina sat in the dining room reading and rereading *Pravda* she heard Pasternak pacing in the room above and Pasternak's wife, Zina, and the maid, Tatyana, arguing in the kitchen next door, where they were making pies. Nina was reading everything that had been published about Pasternak in the previous day's papers. But having read the articles several times, she still could not grasp the meaning of it all, feeling only that every line was sharper than the blade of a guillotine. She was seized by a familiar nervous tremor: her jaw became numb and a momentary torpor overcame her. This had first happened to her in the unforgettable year of 1937, when Stalin's arrests had started throughout the country and her husband, the Georgian poet Titsian Tabidze, one of Pasternak's closest friends, had been detained.

Nina remembered every detail. One night Titsian was summoned to the "Chief Bolshevik of Transcaucasia," Lavrenty Beria, who suggested that he speak out in public against another Georgian writer, Paolo Yashvili, a great poet who was Titsian's contemporary, and accuse him of being a Turkish or Polish spy. When Titsian refused, Beria said: "You are an enemy of the people yourself. Go home and wait. They'll come for you." And the next day they came. They searched the whole apartment, sealed up Titsian's library, and arrested him. Nina expected that they would both be arrested, and she had rolled up two bundles of pillows and blankets (at that time prisoners brought their own bed linen with them). But she was allowed to remain free, although as the wife of an "enemy of the people" her "freedom" meant a life of total deprivation, loneliness, and fear. Seventeen years

36

passed in this way. Seventeen years. After the death of Stalin, when his innocent victims were rehabilitated, Titsian was also posthumously vindicated. And after seventeen years Nina was given a new apartment in place of the one that had been taken away, and the poetry of Titsian Tabidze was published again in Georgia (and in Russia, in translation).

Nina looked out of the window. It was still light, and she could see the scarecrow in the middle of the garden, dressed in an old checked jacket and gray cap belonging to Pasternak.

Was a terrible disaster really approaching for the second time? Staring blankly at the scarecrow, Nina found her thoughts coming to her in rapid, jerky succession. When Khrushchev had come to power, people seemed to sigh with relief. And the arrests had stopped. Nina had been ready to shower Nikita Khrushchev with kisses for revealing Stalin's atrocities. Pasternak, however, had said to her yesterday: "My dear Ninochka, at the bottom nothing has changed. Khrushchev takes one step forward and two steps back." Was he right? After Titsian's arrest, ominous articles had appeared in the papers—in fact, the same things had been written about Titsian as were now being printed about Pasternak.

Nina's gaze wandered over the dining room. In the corner stood two tall leafy plants; neither she nor anyone else in the household knew what they were called. The alcove straight ahead contained a large old-fashioned sideboard, on which a whole battery of homemade liqueur bottles was lined up. On the left stood a refrigerator, and on a small table to the right was a television set with a blown tube that no one had yet succeeded in repairing. Everything was unpretentious, simple, and comfortable. This house was Nina's second home. In her mind's eye she went into the hallway and saw the door leading into what was still called the music room, where she slept when she came to visit. Beyond it she saw the door into Zina's room, in which stood the black upright Bechstein, and opposite it the door into Lyonya's room. Next to the dining room was a steep staircase leading to Pasternak's spacious room on the second floor, where he worked and slept. Everything in the house was familiar to her. Her gaze lingered on numerous framed studies and drawings by the poet's father, who had been a renowned artist—a nude in crayon, a pen-and-ink sketch of the artist's daughter, and many others. It was both pleasant and unsettling for her to acknowledge that she belonged there.

From the kitchen she heard more sharp comments from Zina and machine-gunlike bursts from Tatyana, who conceded nothing to her mistress and gave back as good as she got. Zina's voice was dear to Nina; their friendship dated from the early thirties, from the day Titsian had met Pasternak. Nina's youth, her tragedy, and now her old age were all bound up with Zina's voice.

Overhead Boris continued to pace, taking giant strides and making the liqueur bottles on the sideboard bounce up and down.

Nina felt her breath catch in her throat. He meant so much to her. It was he who had really drawn her into Titsian's poetic world by helping her develop what he called her "poetic eye." This had happened after Titsian's arrest, when for seventeen years she had received a letter every week from Pasternak in Moscow. And what letters they were! She had been intoxicated by them, her heart beating faster as she tried to understand his fantastic imagery. She read his letters so often she knew them by heart. Boris had written even during the war. Undeterred by Stalin's terror, he had openly written to the wife of the proscribed poet. He not only cultivated Nina's poetic taste but also inspired in her a sense of the higher meaning of life and gave her strength to survive and to bring up her daughter. Nina believed that Pasternak had been sent to her by God. Each of her visits to Peredelkino—in the last few years she had flown there twice a year, in the spring and in the fall—was an occasion for celebration.

And now suddenly fear arose again, fear for the person

dearest to her. Impulsively she got up from the table and moved toward the hallway, intending to go up to the second floor. But when she opened the door, Pasternak was standing in front of her.

At first glance his features seemed far too large, even deformed. His overdeveloped lower jaw stuck out farther than it should; the sockets of his intense brown eyes were unusually deep, and his nose was clearly Semitic. (When the Nazis came close to Moscow, Pasternak had said that thanks to his nose he would be the first to be thrown in a gas chamber.) His thick, almost Negroid lips, sometimes gentle and perplexed, appeared momentarily severe and aloof. Dressed in a checked shirt with rolled-up sleeves, old, patched trousers, and worn-out felt slippers with rubber soles, he looked awkward, although tall and solidly built. He spoke melodiously.

"Ninochka! Where were you off to? To see me?" Pasternak's smile disarmed her.

"No, no . . . I just wanted to get something from the music room."

"I can tell from your eyes you're not telling the truth." He put an arm around her shoulders and led her back into the dining room, immediately glancing at the table.

"Hasn't today's *Pravda* come yet? No . . . I see you are still poring over yesterday's papers. You must forget about it, Ninochka."

"I'm trying to." She tried to defend herself with a gentle reproach. "But you are pacing up and down in your room waiting for today's *Pravda*. The liqueur bottles are about to fall off the sideboard."

"Really? Yes, these wooden houses do vibrate."

"Titsian liked to pace about the room too when he was composing his poetry. Are you writing something, Borya?"

"No. I don't feel up to it. My dear Ninochka, if only you knew how important it is for me that you decided to fly here. Particularly now. It turned out incredibly well. You must have felt in your heart that I needed you. Did you feel that?"

"Yes, Borya."

"And the wine you brought is excellent, as always. It's Kakhetian, isn't it?"

"Yes, from Telavi, the town where I was born, where I went to school."

They paused while Pasternak recovered the thread.

"Ninochka, you said that Titsian paced out his verses. No, I think he took it more gently than that. An epic poem is paced out. Vladimir Mayakovsky paced his out—he had a gigantic stride. But while you were occupying yourself with these trashy newspapers, I was merely strolling and reciting verse. It calms me down and transports me to the world of beauty. The world of beauty really does exist, you know."

"Of course."

"And whose verse do you think I was reciting? Your Titsian's."

"Borya, that means you were reciting yourself, because you translated most of his poetry into Russian."

"No, Ninochka, it is entirely his. Verses aren't just words, they are inspiration, thought, and image in magical harmony. I just brought Titsian's verse closer to the Russian reader. Ninochka! How wonderfully he wrote! If I only could . . ."

Nina laughed. "Whenever Titsian recited your poetry, he said, 'If only I could . . .'"

"Yes, we loved each other. That doesn't happen very often between poets." Pasternak threw back his head and went on almost pathetically. "Ninochka, my own dear one, Titsian is the supreme modern Georgian poet. Yes, yes, yes. In his poetry nature eclipses the world of fantasy, his simple, magical combinations of words turn what is ordinary in life into something eternal and unique."

Nina did not interrupt him, because she understood that he had to talk about Titsian, about poetry, about Georgia, in order to take his mind off what was being written about him in *Pravda*, in order, perhaps, to dispel his anxiety. It occurred to her that for him poetry was not only a form of attack but also a means of defense.

His jaw quivered as he closed his eyes and recited a verse of Titsian's that Nina, too, often repeated to herself as a sort of prayer before going to sleep:

"Though tears are hopeless,
Your sobs do not cease.
A melodious pipe
Sings to you of love.
You reach out toward it.
Thus a poet is born."

Nina rested her head on Pasternak's chest, and her shoulders trembled; he smoothed her hair just like a father and kissed her hands, saying, "Ninochka, my dear sweet Ninochka . . ."

She looked up, her eyes filled with tears. "Borya, when you sent me the manuscript of *Doctor Zhivago*, I hid it in the woodshed and allowed only those who were completely trustworthy to read it. And when I had read it myself I said to my daughter: 'This novel will belong to the world.' Wasn't I right? Doesn't *Doctor Zhivago* belong to the whole world now?"

"Ninochka, Russia, alas, is not yet a part of the world."

Nina took her cigarettes from the table and lit one, coughing after she inhaled.

"When are you going to give up smoking?" Pasternak exclaimed. "It's so harmful. Listen to that cough. It's terrible. You and Zina smoke like chimneys. If only you would spare Lyonya and me. Tatyana has gotten used to you."

He opened the window from the top.

"I started to smoke on the night of Titsian's arrest. And I swore I'd quit on the day of his release, which . . . never came."

Pasternak frowned, passed the palm of his right hand over his forehead, and sat down at the table, oppressed by her allusion to Titsian's death.

"Borya, I'm counting on a miracle!" Nina said suddenly in

a cheerful voice. "A miracle that will clear up all this fuss about your book. I'm counting on Khrushchev's wife. She's called Nina too, and in Tbilisi they say she is a good woman with some influence over her husband."

Pasternak gave Nina a melancholy smile. "You and Zina are naïve children. . . . But why do you have a shawl tied around your waist?"

"Old age is no joy, Borya. It's arthritis. My bones are aching."

The embittered voices of Zina and Tatyana could be heard from the kitchen. They had started to argue about something and it was apparent they were both about to come into the dining room. Pasternak quickly got up from his chair.

"Ninochka, when today's papers come, have Tatyana bring them to me, yes?" he said hurriedly. "They're having a battle in there over the right way to bake pies. Let them get on with it. I'm going."

And he went back upstairs.

Nina walked over to the window. Night was falling and she could barely make out the scarecrow in the garden. The lights of neighbors glowed in the distance.

She thought about Titsian, remembered how he had once been an enthusiastic supporter of Stalin. He had been proud that the Soviet leader was a Georgian, and he had admired his reforms. In fact, both Titsian and Pasternak had always been drawn to the new and the revolutionary. Writers, writers of genius, were always liberals. But everything had ended in a bloody farce. Stalin was a Georgian and Nina was a Georgian, although he was a man of the people while she was a princess. But Nina had always hated Stalin: she did not understand much about politics and was guided by the dictates of her heart. She hated him. Perhaps she was mistaken, but she had never been able to forgive the Bolsheviks in the Civil War for shooting her beloved brother, who had been an officer in the czar's army.

At length Pasternak's wife burst in from the kitchen dressed in a lace-trimmed dress and an apron. A large, round-shouldered woman, with dark, dyed hair, penciled eyebrows, and bulging eyes, Zina conveyed a first impression of being temperamental and cold at the same time. Once beautiful, she now had an air of remoteness and suffering. But as soon as she smiled, revealing an even row of large white teeth, her whole face became kinder and more attractive. She held a packet of Belomorkanal cigarettes, which she was never without, matches, and a plastic ashtray.

Tatyana followed her in, wearing felt boots and a pinafore over her cotton print dress. About fifty, small, bright, with a round face and tiny nose, she triumphantly bore a tray of freshly baked pies.

"Either I bake them, Zinaida Nikolayevna, or you bake them!" she declared emphatically, setting the tray on the sideboard. "That means either you look after the house or I do. Make up your mind. That's all. My patience has run out. I don't know where I stand. I'll leave, that's what. I've had a very good offer, by the way. Maids are worth their weight in gold now. The country is full of engineers and academicians, but there aren't enough maids! I'm in a rut here, that's what."

Zina noisily pulled out a chair. "Do you hear how she talks to me, Nina? And it's been like this for twenty years, since the day Lyonya was born. Dictator! Tyrant!"

"Tyrant yourself," Tatyana snapped.

Nina moved away from the window. The argument between Zina and Tatyana distracted her from oppressive thoughts about both the past and present. She stubbed out her cigarette and said: "You should give in, Zina. Tanya can manage the pies without you."

Tatyana gave an obsequious smile. "There you are, Zinaida Nikolayevna! There's a clever person talking."

"I can't give in. Today's my name day—Saint Zinaida's day."

Tatyana would not be put off. "Well, fine. Then have a rest, enjoy life. You could go to the movies. Why not? *Tarzan* is being shown again in Bakovka. Or you could play some cards with Nina Alexandrovna. You're both good at that sort of thing. Thank God you came, Nina Alexandrovna. But pies are my job. And that's that." She rubbed her nose with the edge of her pinafore and returned to the kitchen, shutting the door firmly behind her as if to emphasize her victory and her rights.

Zina lit a cigarette and began to count on her fingers. "There's an apple one, a strawberry one, this one's got cabbage in it, and now she'll put a meat one in the oven."

"Why so many?" Nina was amazed.

"So many? Have you forgotten how it used to be? In the old days we baked ten for my name day. Now no one comes by. A few days ago some friends dropped in to have a glass of vodka and congratulate Borya on the Nobel Prize. But today not a soul. They don't even remember my name day. That's friends for you. After the uproar in the papers they're probably afraid to set foot in our house. We're like lepers." She shivered. "Aren't you cold, Nina?"

"No."

Zina noticed the open window, went over and closed it, touched the radiator with her hand, then sat down at the table. "Has Borya been down?" Nina nodded, and she went on. "I suppose he was looking for today's *Pravda*. I can't believe what I've read in the papers. It's as if everyone's gone mad."

Nina joined her at the table. "Do you think they're acting on Khrushchev's orders?"

"I don't know. One thing is strange, though—he hasn't been to see her. Usually Borya goes to see her sometime during the day. It *is* cold in here. Yury Mikhailovich hasn't stoked the furnace enough. Yes, everything's the same between them." She sighed deeply. "I told you—everything's the same between them. Between Borya and Olga." Nina did not respond, and, putting down her cigarette, Zina picked up a piece of pie from the plate and began to eat it. For the last few days she had been irritated by her friend's complete absorption in Borya's difficulties. At the same time she was annoyed at herself, because she realized that this was how it

44

should be. But Nina was the only woman who knew everything about her life, and Zina felt that only she could understand her pain. On the very day of Nina's arrival she had told her how Borya was continuing to see Olga, who had settled in Peredelkino and was renting two rooms in Masha Sergeyeva's cottage near the dam.

Nina was watching the liqueur bottles on the sideboard. They were dancing again, which meant that Borya was pacing up and down in his room.

Tatyana's cheerful singing could be heard from the kitchen.

Zina went on. "She spreads rumors, one that she's pregnant again. By Borya."

"Nonsense," Nina said. This was the same word she had used when Zina had told her about this on the day she arrived.

"Nonsense or not, last week Borya told me, 'If we are fated to be rich, we shall live as we have always lived; we shall give away our money to the poor.' "

"What's wrong with that?" Nina shrugged in bewilderment. "What does that have to do with Olga?"

"It has everything to do with her. He has put his financial affairs in her hands. She holds the purse strings."

Nina hesitated. Poor Zina! she thought. So much has fallen on her shoulders. Olga. Money. The Nobel Prize. And she hasn't even been congratulated on her name day. No one wants to get mixed up with Pasternak and his Swedish award. She spoke compassionately. "Zina, forget about Olga! Put her out of your mind. You have more important things to think about. Tell me instead what will happen to Borya."

"What will happen?" Zina usually admired Nina's energetic, matter-of-fact way, but this evening her friend's common sense was a barrier between them. She nibbled at her pie, reached for a cigarette, and said, perhaps wearily, perhaps indifferently, "Nothing good. You've read everything that's been in the papers the last few days."

"Deliberate distortions. Filth. The reply of the *Novy Mir*

editorial board is an example of the worst demagogy and treachery!"

"What they wrote in *Pravda* today was even more threatening. I threw it in the trash can."

"Today's *Pravda*? You mean you threw it away without Borya's seeing it?"

"Why should he? What's already been printed is bad enough." She got up and, opening the door to the kitchen, called out, "Tatyana, stop singing, please."

Tatyana replied affectionately. "Sorry, Zinaida Nikolayevna, I won't anymore."

Zina returned to the table. "Our pies are cold," she said with a smile. "They'll be stale soon."

2.

Polikarpov meanwhile was just sitting down in a rocking chair in Konstantin Fedin's study. He had already told Fedin about Suslov's instructions. The distinguished prose writer now had to say yes or no.

Fedin was slim, of medium height, with intelligent blue eyes. Although his thin gray hair was combed straight back, two strands fell across his high forehead. The regularity of his features was striking. Like a Persian, from time to time he fingered the string of amber beads he always held in his white elegant hands. He looked no more than sixty, and his confident, energetic gait and unstooped body gave him a youthful air. His suit was well cut, and he wore the red badge of a Deputy of the Russian Supreme Soviet in his left lapel.

Leaning against the corner of a pedestal supporting a bust of Voltaire, Fedin stared silently at Polikarpov. His guest stared back as if they were engaged in a duel. Polikarpov gave a friendly smile. Fedin went over to his large writing desk and moved one of the many bibelots that lay between the gilded pen set and the foreign-made telephone. (He was the only writer in Peredelkino who had a direct line to Moscow.)

46

Then he tapped twice on his Hermes typewriter and sat down in an armchair.

"I've never seen these portraits before." Breaking the silence, Polikarpov nodded toward the wall, where signed photographs of Maxim Gorky, Romain Rolland, and Barbusse were hung.

Fedin broke his silence too. "But why did you pick on me, Comrade Polikarpov? I'm not General Secretary of the Writers' Union. Why not Alexei Surkov?"

"In the first place, you live next door to Pasternak," Polikarpov replied, rocking back in the chair.

"That's not a good enough reason." Fedin smiled wryly. "The writer Vsevolod Ivanov lives on the other side. Why didn't you choose him?"

"I said, in the first place. Second, you're a close friend of Pasternak's—or rather, you *were*. You belong to the same generation and you both began your literary careers at the same time. There was a lot that bound you together, although I know all that is in the past. Third, you're a famous novelist and your books are popular abroad as well as here. You've devoted yourself to describing the struggle for what is new in our country, to the turning point in the consciousness of the old Russian intelligentsia. Fourth—this follows from the preceding point, and, in the opinion of the party Central Committee, is even more important—you are one of us, even though you're not a party member."

On hearing the words "one of us" Fedin shrugged and frowned. "What does that mean, Dimitry Alexeyevich?"

"You really don't know? I mean your convictions and that you—"

The sentence was left unfinished. Polikarpov's face had suddenly become ashen. He clutched at his chest, put his feet firmly on the floor, stopping the movement of the rocking chair. For a moment his lips turned blue and a wheezing sound came from his throat. He knew the cause of these symptoms; he had learned to live with his angina. During an attack, which occurred suddenly and without warning, his whole chest and stomach seemed to ossify. The sharp, stabbing pain stayed in that area for a second or two and then moved into his left shoulder and arm. He would sit rigidly, waiting to see whether the pain would fade or intensify, whether the attack would be mild or severe. Convulsively Polikarpov put his hand in the pocket of his trousers, pulled out a metal tin, and opened it. He took out two white tablets and hurriedly put them under his tongue.

"Dimitry Alexeyevich . . . are you all right?" Fedin stood up.

Polikarpov did not reply. His eyes were misted over and his forehead was damp with sweat. Fedin reached for the telephone to call an ambulance, but the pallor of Polikarpov's face vanished as quickly as it had come and his color returned. But his hands still trembled slightly, and he dropped a few white tablets on the floor before closing the metal tin.

"Nitroglycerin?" Fedin leaned toward Polikarpov. "Would you like some water?"

"No . . . thank you . . . it's passed," Polikarpov said quietly, and as he looked at Fedin, he thought bitterly: He won't be any help. He lives only for himself. All the rest is just a pretense.

"Perhaps you'd like to lie down on the sofa?" Fedin said sympathetically.

"No, no, it's all right. I feel better. The attack has passed. Just a momentary spasm. In fact, it wasn't that bad. My aorta plays up."

"Your heart?"

"Yes." And Polikarpov added with a faint smile, "I'll be dead soon, Konstantin Alexandrovich."

"Never! You'll live another hundred years. I was dying once too, from consumption. But the Soviet government sent me to Davos in Switzerland and I recovered. I'm alive, as you can see. Are you sure you won't lie down?"

"No, thank you. I've quite recovered. Everything's fine."

"I remember you had a similar attack at a meeting of the Writers' Union presidium."

"That was when it all started. You Soviet writers gave me angina. I often have attacks now," Polikarpov said only half-jokingly. "At my age and in my state of health, Konstantin Alexandrovich, you start to think about death. Maybe my thoughts aren't original, but I do believe that when death comes I won't be afraid. That's because I'm not absorbed in my own ego; I know that the world won't end with me. I'm sorry for people in the West. Most of them live only as individuals, and their own personal interests determine everything for them. They must be terrified of dying."

"I agree with you, Dimitry Alexeyevich. People who are obsessed with an idea, by a great mission, always die heroically."

"So you're not afraid of death either?"

"No, I'm not afraid."

"That's good." Polikarpov got up from the rocking chair and walked about the room, then stopped. "However, let's get back to business. I came to see you on business. I don't want you to forget that you were chosen by the Secretary of the Central Committee himself, Mikhail Suslov."

Fedin took out his handkerchief and blew his nose, giving himself some time for thought. He then remarked, without looking at Polikarpov, "I respect Comrade Suslov, but still . . ."

"What's troubling you? Do you disagree with us about *Doctor Zhivago?*"

"No."

"Well, then, it follows that you, the best Soviet writer of your generation, are the person to approach Pasternak at this decisive moment. His life is at stake, and he must be told. Yes, his *life*. Tell him that. The Central Committee isn't joking. Ah, Konstantin Alexandrovich, when I was young I was a schoolteacher, a simple village schoolteacher in Byelorussia. It was then I first understood how important it is to prevent a mistake from happening. And not only when you're dealing with children. A word of advice from a teacher or a friend can change the entire direction of a life, can forestall disaster."

Just as Polikarpov finished speaking, the study door flew open and an excited little boy, about five or six years old, with disheveled hair and a wide-open mouth, burst into the room on a red tricycle. With a whoop he rode around the rocking chair and the desk and vanished into the hallway as abruptly as he had entered.

"Your grandson?" Polikarpov asked with a smile.

"Nikita." Fedin nodded.

"Nikita? In honor of Khrushchev?" There was a hint of iron in Polikarpov's tone.

"Begging your pardon, Dimitry Alexeyevich, he was born before Stalin died. A year before," Fedin replied, and then added, "Would you like to know what a certain Soviet writer said about you?"

"Of course. If it's decent."

"Absolutely. He said that the American State Department should pay you a thousand dollars a month."

Polikarpov laughed and Fedin thought he winked at him.

"A tidy sum. Which means this writer puts a high estimate on the damage I have inflicted on Soviet literature. We don't put people in prison for criticism nowadays, you know. In fact, criticism sometimes makes us mend our ways. Just see how things have changed—I'm not even interested in this fellow's name."

"You should be. He does have a name." Fedin went over to the window and lifted the curtain. Close by, through the branches of the pines and birches, the outline of Pasternak's dacha could be seen, with light shining through its windows. The two houses were separated only by a dilapidated wooden fence which cats and dogs found no difficulty in slipping through. In contrast, a high, sturdy fence shielded Fedin's dacha from Pavlenko Drive and prevented curious passersby from looking in at him. His privacy was further protected by the many trees that surrounded his house. "As you like. I'll go to see him," he said after a pause. "I'll go right away. This minute. So I don't have time to change my mind."

"Splendid. If you don't mind, I'll wait for you here. Give me something to read, an adventure story."

"Will Dumas do?"

"I adore him. Especially *The Count of Monte Cristo*."

Fedin took the book from one of the shelves and gave it to Polikarpov. "Dimitry Alexeyevich, I want to ask you . . . just how far will the Central Committee go in this affair?"

Their eyes met. The reply was important, and Polikarpov chose his words carefully. Although his voice was soft, his message was not: the Central Committee was determined, absolutely determined on having its way in this matter. "To victory!" he ended almost cheerfully. But when Fedin had opened the door into the corridor he called after him, "Good luck!"

3.

As he walked up Pavlenko Drive, Fedin felt the autumnal chill; he put his arms in the sleeves of his elegant autumn coat, which he had thrown over his shoulders, and wound a silk scarf around his neck. He never wore a hat.

It was only a hundred meters or so from the gate of his dacha to the gate of Pasternak's. What a familiar, well-trodden road! To his right stretched a large field, sown in spring with rye by the neighboring state farm, and now turning to yellow. The short dry stalks had been left to rot until the first rains, which usually turned the whole field into a brown quagmire.

Fedin slackened his pace. Had he agreed to Polikarpov's, or rather Suslov's, request too readily? The thought was an unpleasant stab at his conscience. Had he found out enough about this whole complicated affair? Was he making a mistake? He knew that Polikarpov would wait for him however

51

long he was at Pasternak's. His guest had acted with discretion. He had asked permission to drive his car into the yard so that no one could see it. (His driver had then settled down for a nap.) So Fedin had as much time as he liked. He did not have to hurry; he could think everything over thoroughly, weighing the pros and cons, without pressure from the Central Committee. Ultimately, he thought, he was not subservient to those bureaucrats in Moscow, and no one had the right to force him to do anything "as a matter of party discipline."

Whether or not he was prepared to admit it, for nearly forty years Fedin had been troubled by a vague sense of guilt. He had spent most of the First World War as a prisoner of war in Germany, and by the time he was returned to Russia, the October Revolution had already taken place. He could not forgive himself for having been on the sidelines during those great events. His guilt had intensified in the thirties under Stalin when, in the course of filling in numerous forms, he had had to expose his undistinguished record. He realized that those who read the forms and who determined his civic fate might at any time find him wanting.

Fedin had reached the gate of Pasternak's dacha. He should enter and . . . but he had not yet reached a firm decision. Why should he hurry? He had as much time as he liked to think things over. He walked past the gate, moving toward the gully, then crossed the road into the field; he walked through the dry stubble, which brought to his mind his childhood and the smell of freshly mown hay.

What Polikarpov had said to him about not being afraid of dying was interesting. Fedin had lied, for he had always been afraid of thinking about death. It was true that the more sensitive a man's spirit, the more terrifying it was for him to think about death, because a developed individual was more deeply aware of his uniqueness and felt more acutely the mystery and tragedy of human existence. But did this mean that he himself was ruled by his highly developed ego? And did it mean that he was living a double life (like so many others around him)—one for show, full of confidence in the new order, in socialism, in Soviet power, and the other concealed, his inner life, full of doubts and contradictions? Hadn't he decided long ago where he stood? Had he not answered the question in his books: with whom and against whom he stood? Yes, he had described his loyalties clearly and without compromise. But had this commitment now become something of a burden? Had he lost the right to have any thoughts that differed, however slightly, from the ideology he had chosen to support? In short, had he become an artistic Pharisee and dogmatist, stifling what was alive and recalcitrant in literature? And had he as a result ended up in a world that was called progressive but was really founded on delusions?

So where did he stand? What, in the last analysis, was authentic in him? Of course, these questions had to do with individuality and independence, the act of becoming one's own man. Could the individual have a valid existence apart from society? The eternal question: Was individual freedom an absolute right? Fedin had once found the concept of artistic freedom very attractive; now he thought it was just a meaningless fancy. Maturity had brought him to the formula "Freedom is the recognition of necessity." But he often found this necessity demeaning to the individual. Wasn't he being humiliated right now? He had no desire to go to Pasternak and tell him what Polikarpov, Suslov, and no doubt Khrushchev as well wanted him to say.

Once he had dreamt of inhabiting the ivory tower and portraying life as his conscience and eye decreed. But it had been his conscience (and he was proud of it) that had brought him into the camp of the Bolsheviks, to dependence and collective obligations. No, he was not deceiving himself. He had not been taken in by meaningless rhetoric. In his books he had written about the Russian revolution, about the early years of the construction of a new life, and about the corruption that was inseparable from the capitalism and egoism of the West. In general, he had written what he believed. What about God and Christianity? He was interested in both as historical phenomena, but his mother had brought him up without God. That meant he was an atheist and a materialist. So what was holding him back? Why was he delaying his mission as messenger of the Central Committee and not going to see Pasternak?

But what if he'd gotten it all wrong? Fedin thought. Perhaps he was hurt that Pasternak had won the Nobel Prize, while he, Konstantin Fedin, could not even dream of such an honor—although what writer did not long for recognition? No, he had never envied Pasternak; he was not Alexei Surkov and he was not a poet. He and Pasternak were completely different artists. Moreover, having read *Doctor Zhivago* (in manuscript form), Fedin had concluded that from a literary point of view the novel was far from perfect. In his view it was loosely constructed and verbose, seriously flawed by its wrongheaded ideology and by what he called "historical infantilism." He was convinced that the prize had been awarded to Pasternak for something besides the literary merits of *Doctor Zhivago*. (It was significant that in its announcement the Swedish Academy had mentioned the poetical works of Pasternak as well as his novel.) Nevertheless Pasternak's name was famous throughout the world, and Fedin's was not. Only a few people had heard of him, even though Polikarpov had called him the best Soviet writer of his generation, which was, after all, no mean achievement. No, he wasn't acting out of envy. There was something greater involved—it was a matter of principle.

But why, then, had he passed by Pasternak's house? Why was he walking around and around in this field trying to collect his thoughts? This was what gave him away. Perhaps his principles were nothing but a kind of shield behind which he hid his impotence? It was true that he was no longer capable of sudden changes of direction and explosions of feeling. Others changed throughout their lifetimes. In his youth he had been flexible, but that was many, many years ago. Had Stalin and the seductions of communism deprived him of his ability to change? Was this the price he had paid for his convictions?

Over and over he tried to rationalize his mission, but each time he ended by going around in a circle, unable to find a starting and finishing point. He needed external guidance in order to draw a line.

4.

At length, however, Fedin went back to Pavlenko Drive. He strode through the gate and walked decisively toward the windows of Pasternak's dacha, knowing that since the main entrance on the veranda was closed at the end of summer he had to go in at the side.

A Ping-Pong table laden with tools and the like and covered with a tarpaulin stood near the short flight of steps. A pump that brought up well water stuck out of the ground next to it. Every morning, whatever the season, Pasternak stripped to the waist and washed at this pump. A stack of firewood and two large piles of coal—in readiness for the winter—lay behind the steps. Farther off, by the garage, stood a Pobeda sedan.

As Fedin approached the steps Pasternak's two dogs began barking at him. Tobik was a small, half-blind poodle, and Bubik a slightly younger, mischievous and pugnacious fox terrier. They didn't recognize him—he had become an infrequent visitor—and their yelping startled him.

"You silly old thing," he said. "And you, Bubik, you're a silly old thing too. What's all the fuss about? It's me, Uncle Kostya—what's all this for?" He patted the dogs.

Tatyana appeared on the steps. She had recognized who was there and she greeted Fedin loudly, as if giving a military salute. "Have you come to see us, Konstantin Alexandrovich?"

"Good evening, Tanya. Yes, I've come to see you. Is Boris Leonidovich at home?"

"Of course. Please come in, Konstantin Alexandrovich. You're always welcome here. Oh, Boris Leonidovich will be glad. I know they'll be thrilled to see you. Please come this way."

She was trying her utmost to be hospitable, smiling expansively and opening doors for him. He followed her through the small vestibule into the kitchen, and from there into the dining room, where Zina and Nina were still sitting at the table. The room reeked of stale smoke.

On seeing Nina, Fedin paled. He knew her well and once (a long time ago) had been a little in love with her. He had kept his feelings secret because he had not wanted to hurt his wife, Dora. He had known Titsian as well and when he was in Georgia for conferences and literary receptions he had spent many evenings drinking with him at his apartment. He had known them in Moscow too.

"Good evening, Zina," he said rather formally and immediately turned to Nina. "Hello, Nina Alexandrovich. I didn't know you were in our part of the world. When did you arrive?"

Nina smiled. "Hello, Konstantin Alexandrovich." She too remembered those far-off days when the young Fedin had admired her. "I flew in a week ago. How have you been?"

"Fine, thank you. Much the same."

They shook hands; then Fedin sniffed the air and said, "There's a distinct aroma of pies. Are you getting ready for a celebration, Zina?"

"Yes, Kostya, a celebration," Zina replied drily, "but not for the reason you're probably thinking of. Today is my day. Zina's name day. Have you forgotten? You used to remember."

"Oh, please forgive me. Congratulations." He shifted from one foot to the other.

"Thank you."

Nina stood up and moved a chair toward Fedin.

"Do sit down, Konstantin Alexandrovich. Give your legs a rest."

"Excuse me, but I don't have much time. I'm in a hurry and I . . . I must talk to Boris. Is he in?"

"Yes."

"I'll go up and see him."

Having decided that business should not be mixed with pleasure, Fedin made a sort of bow and left the room.

Zina's unfriendly gaze followed him. Nina shut her lips tightly and felt her jaw go numb in anticipation of some new unpleasantness. "He's changed," she said quietly.

"Kostya? He's older."

"That too."

"We were friends once. I saved his daughter, you know. There was a fire at his dacha. I climbed over the fence and dragged her out of the house."

"Yes, I remember."

"It's not like that now."

"His wife, Dora, was so nice."

"She was a good woman, God rest her soul. But in my opinion he's always been crafty. I've never trusted him; I always expect the worst from him." Heaving a sigh, Zina added, "I wonder what he wants to talk to Borya about?"

"About the Nobel Prize, of course. What else?"

Tatyana was still standing in the kitchen doorway. She heard everything that Zina and Nina said; on her face there was no trace of the welcoming, hospitable smile with which she had greeted Fedin. She suddenly took off her right boot, flung it with all her strength at the door leading into the hallway, and yelled contemptuously, "Deputy!"

5.

Pasternak's study—his workroom, as he called it—was a spartan refuge, nothing luxurious or superfluous in it. In an alcove on the left a low bed, rather like a soldier's bunk, neatly covered with a rough woolen blanket. (He thought that a man's character could be judged by the way he made his bed.) An ordinary table without distinguishing features, his writing table, stood between the two windows and was flanked by two small bookcases. The only concession to luxury was an armchair with a threadbare seat and a high back. On the wall to the right, in addition to works by his father, hung a photograph of Leo Tolstoy.

Pasternak had been pacing again, but when he heard the staircase creak he went over to the door and opened it.

"Hello, Borya," he heard out of the darkness.

Pasternak recognized Fedin's voice immediately and raised his eyebrows in dismay. There's going to be a disaster, he thought. "Kostya, is that you?"

Fedin entered the room and Pasternak closed the door. Neither extended his hand, although they usually shook hands on meeting.

"Well . . . come in, my dear friend, come in," Pasternak said in a deliberately singsong voice, stressing the word "dear." "I'm so glad to see you." He turned the overhead light on and blinked in the sudden brightness.

"I've just dropped by for a moment, Borya. I've got people waiting for me at the house. High-ranking guests. To be brief, I've come to—"

Pasternak interrupted him, taking the initiative and turning the conversation in a completely different direction. "Yes, of course, Kostya, I understand, and I'm very grateful to you. You want to congratulate me on the Nobel Prize. At last it's come to us, to Russia. I'm so happy. Vsevolod Ivanov, Kornei Chukovsky, and another writer have congratulated me already. And now you, my right-hand neighbor. Your good wishes are so important to me, Kostya. Because you're Fedin, a first-class novelist. I'm really so glad. Give me your coat."

Fedin took off his coat and placed it on the back of the chair himself. "Borya, do you read the papers? Our Soviet papers? I mean *Pravda* and *Literaturnaya Gazeta*?"

"Why? Have I missed one of your pieces?"

Fingering his amber beads, Fedin looked at Pasternak from

under his lowered brows. "Let's not play cat and mouse." He sat down on the edge of the armchair. "We know each other too well. You may act like a child, but we both know it's just a pretense. And one that's not appropriate now. So stop it and let me say a few words to you."

"Of course, Kostya, of course—only I'll sit down, if you don't mind." He lowered himself onto a chair. "I don't quite understand what you said about . . . a pretense, but first let me ask: How's your daughter, how's Nikita, your grandson?"

Fedin pulled off the scarf from his neck. "What? Oh, they're fine, thank you."

"Won't you be cold? Shall I turn the heat up?"

Fedin shook his head and said distinctly, separating each word, "Borya, I have to talk to you seriously; it has to do with your life."

"My life? What do you mean?"

"I'm talking about your survival. Forget everything else. If you want to live, you must refuse the Nobel Prize immediately."

"I . . . I don't understand."

"You must understand," Fedin continued dryly, as if he were giving an order. "You must understand that voluntarily or involuntarily you are providing ammunition for our enemy."

"But who's our enemy, Kostya?"

"Don't you know?"

"It can't be Hitler, thank God, and Stalin's dead too."

"Borya, stop playing the fool."

"Wait!" Pasternak raised his right hand. "We haven't seen each other for such a long time. That must be why we're so awkward. Let me have a look at you, Kostya, my friend. Do you remember when we were young? Arguing about literature the whole night long, always searching for the new! Where's all that gone, Kostya? Do you remember, you once preached the theory of 'art for art's sake,' and I supported you? But the powers that be criticized us for advocating 'supraclass literature.' Then we grew up a bit. A great and complicated creative life began. You moved in one direction, and I, it seems, moved in another. But we were still friends, Kostya, and we respected each other—"

"Borya, stop it! What's the point? That's all water over the dam. What is facing us now is reality, and it's inexorable. I repeat: I'm talking about your life. I came to you because as your *friend* I want you to *live*. That's the most important thing. Stop this bravado and get rid of any illusions you may still have. This is a matter of life and death, Borya."

Impulsively Pasternak got up from the chair and rubbed his forehead with his palms. He went over to Fedin and brushed his hand lightly across his shoulder. "What if we remain silent for a while, Kostya, and just look at each other like this? What if we have a talk . . . in silence?"

"If you like. My conscience is clear."

For a minute they stood looking at each other. Pasternak's eyes bored into Fedin's, but Fedin did not yield, did not lower his bright, searching gaze. To an outsider the scene might have looked comic or even absurd—two grown men staring at each other for a whole minute in silence—but they were in deadly earnest.

Pasternak spoke first. He started to pace as he did so, but his voice sounded more natural, less obviously melodious. "Why don't you congratulate me anyway, Kostya? There's only one thing that's important—the prize has been won by Russia, yes, by Russia. Aren't you a Russian?" He raised his voice. "Answer me, Kostya, aren't you a Russian?"

"I was not born a Jew," Fedin retorted.

Pasternak froze, but at that moment the stairs creaked, and Tatyana came into the room carrying a tray with two glasses of wine and two pieces of pie. She placed it ceremoniously on the table.

"Konstantin Alexandrovich, our hostess Zinaida Niko-layevna has ordered you to taste the pies. She said you like the strawberry one, Konstantin Alexandrovich. I remembered that too. This is the one with strawberries in it." Pasternak tried to hurry her out, but, nettled by his tone, she abruptly sat down. "Why are you driving me out, Boris Leonidovich? I'm a human being too, even if I am a servant. I won't go."

Pasternak kissed her forehead. "Forgive me, Tatyana, but Kostya and I have some very serious things to talk over."

"I understand." Tatyana got up. "Very well. Our pies, Konstantin Alexandrovich, are a bit better than the ones the delivery van from the Kremlin food center brings you twice a week." And, having savored her point that only a party hack would enjoy such Kremlin largesse, she departed.

"Kostya, you still haven't answered my question," Pasternak said calmly. "It's a fact that I'm a Jew and I don't dispute it. But you—are you a Russian?"

"I didn't come here to answer rhetorical questions, Borya. Our literary and ideological paths diverged long ago. And don't remind me of our youth. Youth is green. Much in people's lives has changed in the last few decades. Even when you first read me passages from *Doctor Zhivago* I commented that—"

"You commented that the novel was not historically accurate," Pasternak interrupted. "You advised me to include Stalin—"

Fedin had forgotten, and Pasternak's words took him by surprise. "Did I really tell you that?"

"I read sections of *Doctor Zhivago* to you while *he* was still alive—the 'wise father,' whom you called a 'great reformer.' Do you still call him that?"

Pasternak guessed correctly that Fedin still did. Stalin was a touchstone for Fedin, and Fedin had been shaken by Khrushchev's speech exposing him and by the process of destalinization which ensued. For Fedin, Soviet history made no sense without Stalin. The Georgian had been an integral part of it all, and if his role was discounted, the whole Soviet experience became nonsense. Fedin criticized Stalin for the mass terror, but he even tried to justify him in this, claiming that without a strong hand to tear out weeds, it was impossible to cultivate a new field. He armed himself with the slogan "You can't make an omelet without breaking eggs." This helped him to accept radical social reconstruction, which, in his opinion, was now occurring all over the globe.

"Borya, you know my position on *Doctor Zhivago*," he said, avoiding Pasternak's question about Stalin. "As a member of the editorial board of *Novy Mir*, I signed the journal's statement criticizing your novel and giving its reasons for refusing to print it. All that is clear. But the point is that *Doctor Zhivago*, alas, has ceased to be a purely literary phenomenon. Both the novel and you—yes, you yourself—have become tools in the hands of the West, and that's the main issue. If the so-called free world hadn't danced with glee over your book, I wouldn't be warning you now about the impending danger. The reactionary capitalist press has raised a hue and cry. They've put you on one side and the rest of us on the other; they're using you as a symbol of resistance to the Soviet system.

"Do you think so?"

"Yes. Don't be blinded by vanity!"

"Do you think that my novel does not deserve the Nobel Prize as *literature*?" Pasternak asked.

"Well, do *you* think it does?"

Pasternak paused, and when he answered, his voice no longer sounded confident. "No . . . I don't know . . . maybe not. But, Kostya, I was awarded it not just for *Doctor Zhivago* but for my poetry as well. And I was nominated for the Nobel Prize five years ago, before *Doctor Zhivago* had even appeared."

Fedin's blue eyes seemed to hypnotize Pasternak: there was strength, faith in them. He was not pretending or being false; he was saying what he really felt in his heart.

"Can't you see that the world is divided, Borya? There are two ways of life and, as a result, two forms of literature, two forms of art. Ours, socialist, and theirs, capitalist. This may be an oversimplification but basically it's true. It's how things stand, Borya, and there's no escaping from it. Your ideas about the civilized West are like the superficial impressions of a tourist. Your conception of the West is anachronistic and stupidly sentimental. There's a struggle going on in the world, not for life but to the death. Communism has taken the place of Christianity. Right now it is forced to be a dictatorship because it is surrounded by enemies, who are determined to destroy it at any cost. There is no weapon they wouldn't use, because they no longer have any morality—if they ever did. In these conditions the Swedish Academy can't exist as a peaceful island in a raging ocean and remain neutral. In our day, Borya, the writer has to choose a position, take a stand. Which side are you on? Remember what Maxim Gorky said. His question: 'Which side are you on, writer?' was crucial. Which side are you on, poet Pasternak?"

At this point Pasternak almost screamed, "I'm on the side of Russia!"

6.

Pasternak's voice carried to the dining room, where Zina and Nina were still sitting and smoking. The cigarette smoke hung in the air like steam in a Russian bathhouse. Wreathed in it, the woman looked like ghostly crones, but neither had gotten up from the table to open the window. Zina stared at the ceiling, while Nina followed the dance of the liqueur bottles on the sideboard. Both had been trying to guess from Pasternak's and Fedin's steps overhead whether the men were arguing. Pasternak's outcry left no doubt.

Tatyana bustled in and out, straightening up after dinner and putting out the last of the pies as they came from the oven. She stopped for a moment, looked at Zina and Nina with a sarcastic grin and shook her head, thinking to herself: Just like two old witches . . . all they need is a broomstick. Then she raised her eyes to the ceiling, gave another sarcastic grin, shook her head and repeated, "Deputy!"

Nina turned to Zina. "You know, I really don't think they'll touch Borya."

"What did you say?"

"In 1937 it was more terrifying than now because it was more arbitrary. Titsian and I didn't sleep for nights on end, waiting for a knock on the door. When they did knock, it was four o'clock in the morning. I remember it as if it were yesterday. There were three of them in civilian clothes, and witnesses of course—the doorman and a neighbor. They ransacked the whole apartment and sealed up two rooms. They left only one room for Ninochka, Mama, and me. And we lived in it for seventeen years. I remember that one of them, who was elderly and worn-out-looking, with bright red cheeks, kept breathing heavily . . ."

"Naturally," Zina said absentmindedly. She often answered without thinking about what she was saying. When she was lost in her thoughts her eyes stared dreamily into the distance and she paid little attention to those around her.

"No, they won't dare touch Borya, because it's a matter of world concern now. Khrushchev is no fool. He realizes what it would lead to—"

"I like Khrushchev," Zina interrupted, waking up from her dreamlike state.

"Do you?"

"Sometimes he rides in an open car, so he can't be afraid of getting killed. He doesn't try to avoid ordinary people, and he even appears in public with his wife."

"I agree with you, Zina. He seems human. But Borya has a different opinion for some reason, and he's cleverer than we are."

"Borya?" Zina stretched her legs, which made her look almost hunchbacked. She pressed her lips together and glared at Nina.

"What's wrong?"

"You love Borya more than you love me."

"Oh, come on, Zina. What are you saying? Don't be a child." Nina laughed, but for a moment her eyes betrayed a scarcely perceptible sign of embarrassment.

Zina noticed, and thought as she had many times before—although now without jealousy—She's in love with him too.

7.

Pasternak and Fedin meanwhile were sitting at the table upstairs eating pies and drinking wine. The ritual seemed so normal, so genial, it was hard to imagine that a heated quarrel had taken place a few minutes earlier.

"By the way, Kostya," Pasternak said in a lively voice, "don't forget that it's our family tradition to bake a ten-kopeck coin in every pie."

"Of course. I remember." But a moment later he gagged and withdrew a coin from his mouth.

"Lucky fellow!" Pasternak exclaimed. "Yes, you always were a lucky fellow."

Fedin beamed like a child, then tied the coin in the handkerchief he had pulled from his pocket. "It'll be my good-luck charm."

"Ah, Kostya, you deny that God exists but you're superstitious."

"No. I just don't want to spoil my friendship with fortune." He smiled.

They continued eating. Several minutes elapsed in silence. But when they had finished, Pasternak leaned back in his chair and said, "Here we sit enjoying pies, Kostya, while the hungry years of the thirties rise up before me. The Urals. A lake with an odd name—Shartash. Do you remember how you, one of the bigwigs of the Union of Soviet Writers, sent me on a 'creative field trip' to get my fill of socialist truth? Oh, I got my fill all right. More than my fill. How I remember that government rest home! Whenever a poet arrived from Moscow, the local authorities always knew how to treat him. I had come to 'reflect' on real life—so they stuffed me with food while the country tightened its belt. Peasant women used to beg for bread for their children beneath the windows. One day I gave one of them a bit of pie that I hadn't managed to finish at lunch and she tried to shove money into my hand. Do you know who was staying there with me, Kostya?" Without waiting for Fedin's response he went on: "The Khrushchevs. Yes, the *Khrushchevs*, Kostya, the elite, the well-fed party hogs."

"Borya, in the early thirties you actively supported the Soviet system."

"Yes, I did. I supported it even earlier than that. I wrote, 'Revolution, you're a miracle!' But what was left of the revolution, of the miracle, in the early thirties when you, yes, you, dragged me into the unreal world of banquets and government rest homes, of conferences and festivals floating on rivers of wine, where everyone praised Stalin and his 'pupils,' into a world of bureaucratic prattle and pompous, official poetry? Luckily I didn't get bogged down like most. I wasn't blinded by the glittering prizes you offered for loyalty. In the Urals, Kostya, at the new socialist construction sites, I saw how our whole nation was being deliberately and systematically poisoned—a collective psychology. I saw how *organized* mediocrity was held up as the highest good, how a humiliating anthill, with plebeian ants and patrician ants in Communist Party tunics, was planned and established. The people were herded together just as they had been under Peter the Great. But then Stalin decided to perpetuate it all through fear and commanded that people be thrown into prison. Of course he also had an economic motive—he needed millions of unpaid working hands. Then the terror set in. Bloody nights followed one after the other. You saw Nina Tabidze downstairs in the dining room, Kostya, didn't you?"

"Yes, I—"

"You know as well as I do how many years poor Nina waited for Titsian. Seventeen. She was branded as the wife of an 'enemy of the people' for seventeen years. Yet she kept hoping that Titsian was still alive. Now we know he was killed by a blow from a revolver butt during an interrogation three days after his arrest. And who knows where he's buried."

66

Pasternak went to the window. The light shining through the curtains of the house threw fantastic shapes on the ground. In the distance, beyond the field and the stream, the lights of houses on top of a hill could be seen, and in the moonlight he could just make out the tall white Church of the Patriarchal Residence, with the country house of Alexei, the Patriarch of All Russia.

"It's a sad story of course," Fedin said. "Titsian Tabidze was a very fine poet. And there's no question of his having been a Turkish or Polish spy, despite the accusations against him and Paolo Yashvili in the newspapers."

"It wasn't just Titsian and Yashvili who were lost but hundreds of thousands of others as well." Pasternak turned from the window. "Titsian was an honest man, and I'm in his debt. He paid with his life for my life. His death took the scales from my eyes and gave me the strength to start writing *Doctor Zhivago* and to see it through to the end. I started it while Stalin was still alive, Kostya. It was blessed by Titsian's blood. Yes, by his blood. At night I hear him moaning . . . do you, Kostya? At night I hear the groans of the millions of people tortured in our prisons and concentration camps. These millions were not guilty of any crime. They were guilty, if you please, of just one thing: they wanted to live, and some of them wanted to think a bit too."

Fedin lowered his eyes. "Stalin was cruel. But his mistakes have been exposed. Titsian has been rehabilitated."

"A late 'vindication' and an early death." Pasternak grinned bitterly. "Stalin was a monster, Kostya. He was thirsty for blood, but nothing grows on blood except fear. The question still torments me: Why didn't he exterminate *me*? Why did he exterminate Titsian and hundreds of other writers, yet spare me? Doesn't the question torment you, Kostya? Stalin didn't touch you either, favorite of fortune. But he could have . . . and now no one would know where our graves were to be found."

"Borya, what's the point of stirring up a past that's long gone?"

"Forgive and forget?" Pasternak darkened with anger. "But what about our new fat men, all those Stalinist 'liberals,' 'peacemakers' and collectivists, the grandees of communism, those bandy-legged village boys who were reared and educated by the 'mighty helmsman' and who still miss him? What guarantee is there that they won't plunge our country into a sea of blood again or put a new, 'liberal,' harness on our people? Where's the guarantee, Kostya? Where?"

"You're exaggerating everything as usual."

"I live from the heart. I'm not a careerist, Kostya."

"So . . . that means I am a careerist."

"You're a party lackey."

Fedin rose from his chair. Nothing Pasternak had said—and he had been right about most of it, right in a human sense, he knew—could mitigate the offense to his honor. "I believe in the ideals that I serve, as a writer and as a citizen. I'm not a solipsist, Borya. I don't measure the events of life by my emotions and appetites, calling them the dictates of my conscience. I see the world in its objective historical light." He paused to recall what Polikarpov had said to the effect that the world doesn't end with one's ego.

Pasternak continued: "When I protest against the lack of spiritual freedom I'm not acting on a personal whim, Kostya. Some things, like corruption and injustice, are simply wrong. And if we try to justify them we destroy ourselves spiritually. How long can people live on dreary superficialities, absurd double-talk?"

"It's you," Fedin protested. "It's only you, an old-fashioned Russian intellectual with petty-bourgeois prejudices, who find everything in Soviet reality superficial and false. You think you're a fabulous, unique poet. But you're a Narcissus. Like your Zhivago, you think that the universe is contained in the drops of your own tears. But the destiny of all mankind is being forged on our planet, and you can't simply dismiss political and social reality. The masses have moved into action. You've overlooked the contemporary hero for a long time now, Borya. You smell of mothballs. You're outside contemporary life. You're scared of it, you've dissociated yourself from it, you've withdrawn into your shell . . . you're a . . . a . . ."

"Spiteful petty bourgeois," Pasternak prompted, completely seriously.

"Precisely. The spiritual freedom you value so highly is meaningless because it's of no use to anyone. Forgive me, but I think your theorizing is a form of spiritual masturbation. Oh, Borya, you're a very talented poet, but you speak for only a handful of people. You'd be comfortable in snobbish, bourgeois salons, but they haven't existed for a long time in our country."

"How can I answer you, Kostya? You're right. But I keep remembering the words of the great German poet Heine: 'Under each human gravestone one can find world history.' "

"You'd do better to remember what Maxim Gorky wrote to you—that you imagined yourself as the sun, with the world revolving around you."

Pasternak sat down wearily. "Kostya, we speak different languages. For me the Russia of the future cannot exist without the Russia of the past. This continuity creates the culture of a nation. But let's put a stop to this comedy." Calmly, almost indifferently, he asked, "So what do you propose I do?"

"One: Send a telegram today or tomorrow morning to Stockholm refusing the Nobel Prize. Two: Write a letter stating the same to Comrade Khrushchev. Three: Write a similar letter to *Pravda*." Fedin threw his scarf around his neck and began to put on his coat.

"A most businesslike proposition. And what do I get in return?"

"The campaign against you, which is only just beginning, will in all probability be stopped. Gradually. It's not easy to restrain the wrath of the people."

"The wrath of the people? Hm . . . Well, and if I say no, Kostya, what then?"

"Then you'll have only yourself to blame."

"I see, Kostya. . . . So who are these 'guests' of yours? I'd guess it's that fanatic Dimitry Polikarpov. He bedeviled us writers with his party-mindedness during the year he served in the Writers' Union. Two years ago he summoned me to the Central Committee and forced me to send a letter to Feltrinelli in Rome asking him to postpone publication of *Doctor Zhivago*. It was already too late, thank God, and Feltrinelli ignored my request. The only thing about Polikarpov that's human is his angina. God forgive me if I blaspheme."

"Oh, how inconsistent you are, poet Pasternak!" Fedin exclaimed. "On the wall you've got a photograph of the great realist Leo Tolstoy, and in the bookcase—I can see from here —you've got Kafka, Proust, Joyce . . ."

"Is that all? Can't you see anything else from over there, anything 'doubtful,' 'tainted,' simply counterrevolutionary?" Pasternak jumped up from his chair, flung open the doors of one of the bookcases, and pulled out a thick, hardbound volume. "There you are, Konstantin Fedin, the most revolutionary book ever written!" He put it down on the table. "Can't you see?" he shouted. "It's the *Bible!*"

8.

As before, Zina and Nina were wreathed in cigarette smoke, although the air had cleared slightly because the door into the kitchen was open. Tatyana was standing in the doorway leading into the hallway and, her neck craned, was trying to listen to the conversation upstairs. Zina and Nina did not take their eyes off her, eagerly awaiting some information. Suddenly Tatyana started and dashed through the dining room into the kitchen. Hurried steps were heard on the stairs and Fedin appeared with a strained, perhaps offended expression on his face. He walked purposefully through the dining room without glancing at the women, muttered a goodbye in their direction and made a vague gesture with his hand. Nina removed her glasses from the tip of her nose and put them into a plastic case, while Zina said with a shrug, in imitation of Tatyana, "Deputy!"

Peals of laughter were heard from the stairs, and a few seconds later Pasternak entered the dining room. When he appeared in the doorway he was laughing so much that he did not even notice the cigarette smoke.

"What are you laughing about, Borya?" Zina asked.

"My dear girls," Pasternak said cheerfully, "did you know that our friend Kostya Fedin, the famous Russian novelist, friend of Maxim Gorky, Romain Rolland, and Barbusse, and conscientious party servant, is still as superstitious as ever? He doesn't believe in God, but he's superstitious. He hasn't eradicated that legacy of capitalism in himself, damn it. He found a ten-kopeck coin in his pie, so he took it home with him as a good-luck charm."

"Everyone hopes for good luck, Borya," Nina said philosophically and smiled.

"What did he come for?" Zina asked.

"What, Zinochka? Phew! You've filled the room with smoke, girls! It's like God knows what in here. Is it possible to smoke that much?"

He opened the top window again and walked about the room straightening his father's works. He had no intention of complaining about Fedin or, for that matter, saying anything at all about the message he had brought. Why upset Zina and Nina? Anyway, he wanted to think about something else, something completely different.

"During the war, Nina, the antiaircraft gunners on the roof of the writers' house in Lavrushensky Alley slept in our apartment and lit their camp stoves with my father's works. So many wonderful watercolors and drawings perished, all for nothing. It was my fault of course. I didn't manage to hide them in time."

"You've already told me that, Borya. You even wrote to me about it." There was a reproachful note in Nina's voice because he had not replied to Zina's question.

"Yes, Ninochka, of course I've told you and written to you about it. That's true. Oh dear, this foolish habit of repeating oneself," and he added sadly: "My mother and father died in London. They have fog there almost the whole year round. Why did they leave for Europe and not come back, just as if they'd run away from Soviet power? My mother was a superb pianist. By Fedin's standards, no doubt, my parents were petty-bourgeois Jews and philistines, if that's not one and the same thing. But my father was a friend of Tolstoy's and visited him at Yasnaya Polyana—"

"Borya, what did Fedin come for?" Zina repeated her question.

Again Pasternak did not answer her. He smiled and said dreamily, "Dear Mama and Papa, if you knew what has happened to your Borya . . ." He sat down at the table and covered his face with his hands.

"Borya?" Nina said.

He suddenly seized Zina's hands and kissed them. "Zina, my nearest and dearest, when I die, if things are hard for you, for you or Lyonya, if you need something from them, our leaders, go and see Alexei Surkov. He's simpler, but he's more honest, yes, more honest . . . but don't go to Kostya. Don't ever go to Fedin, I beg you."

Zina withdrew her hands.

"What's happened, Borya?" Nina exclaimed. "Why aren't you telling us anything?"

He looked surprised and then grave. "You want to know what's happened? Well, Nina, I'll tell you." He lowered his voice to a whisper. "There, upstairs, yet another Russian intellectual has just died."

"Fedin?"

"There might have been something of Yury Zhivago in him."

"He died long ago," Zina exclaimed.

"What? Perhaps you're right, Zina." Pasternak shrugged. "But all the same I was counting on him. I thought he was a human being, incapable of treachery."

In the yard Tobik and Bubik barked at the sound of an approaching car.

"That must be Lyonya," said Zina, although she knew that the dogs would not bark at him. Besides, her son had told her that he was going to spend the night in Moscow.

"This deceased Russian intellectual," said Pasternak, "proposed that I refuse the Nobel Prize. He stated, among other things, that the Russian people are marching into a new epoch and I'm out of step. An army saying."

"But you're flat-footed." Zina took him literally. "That's why the army wouldn't take you."

Pasternak looked at Nina in dismay, perhaps embarrassed at the mention of such an intimate detail. "Yes, you're right," he commented. "Without a doubt you're right, Zinochka. Only . . . don't stoop, please, it makes you look older."

Zina decided that her remark about her husband's feet had offended him and that he had responded in kind. His annoyance pleased her, because in her eyes it tarnished his halo of Christian perfection.

Tatyana, who had followed Fedin into the yard, hurriedly returned to the house and announced importantly: "You have visitors, Boris Leonidovich. Those—what are they?—English people again. Three ladies from the embassy and a Russian who translates for them—well, at least I think he's one of ours. Shall I let them in, or what?"

"Of course let them in, Tanya," Zina said cheerfully. "At least there'll be someone to eat our pies. Call their driver too."

But Pasternak suddenly shouted: "No, no! Send them away, Tanya! I don't want to see them!"

9.

A half-moon was shining through the clouds. It was well past midnight. Everything was quiet and almost everyone in Peredelkino was asleep. The night watchman at the writers' hostel wandered sleepily about the park and twirled his stick to warn off thieves, just as his predecessors had done for centuries. At the corner of Pavlenko Drive a transformer box buzzed quietly. The nearby houses went dark one after another. Light bulbs hanging from poles along the roadside still burned dimly. The silence was occasionally broken by an airplane landing at Vnukovo Airport, a few kilometers from Peredelkino.

In Pasternak's dacha lights shone in three windows—two on the second floor and one on the first.

In Fedin's dacha only one light burned—upstairs, behind the thick curtains in the writer's study.

Wearing a patterned silk dressing gown and an embroidered skullcap, Fedin stood in the center of the room with an open book in his right hand, reading Pasternak's poems aloud. He wanted to read them louder, at the top of his voice. He wanted to fling the window open wide, lean out, and read so loudly that his voice would carry to Pasternak's ears.

On the desk, next to an unfinished glass of tea, the ten-kopeck coin that he had found in Zina's strawberry pie lay in a handkerchief.

Why was he reading Pasternak's poems? What had made him do this? Love of poetry? Fedin remembered how Fadeyev, the former General Secretary of the Union of Soviet Writers, who committed suicide, had publicly criticized Pasternak's poetry for being excessively refined and subjective. But at home he had gotten drunk on vodka and recited Pasternak's poems, which he knew by heart, the whole night through. Had he been doing some form of penance? And was this why Fedin was reading the same poems? Perhaps he was merely laughing at himself? Perhaps he was a kind of masochist?

Fedin believed that the ethics of collectivism were the highest expression of human values. Now his whole raison d'être, the most important and stable part of him, had suddenly been completely negated by a single line of Pasternak's poetry: ". . . poet, rich in love, lives and spring seasons."

Pasternak's poems disturbed Fedin deeply, because the artistic spirit, which was not always bound by the constraints of reason, was still alive in him. He was not just an "engineer of human souls," as Stalin had once defined the writer, but also an artist.

Pacing up and down his study, Fedin stepped on a small tablet, one of those that Polikarpov had dropped; it cracked under his slipper. Fedin involuntarily looked at the rocking chair in which Polikarpov had been sitting when he had suffered his attack.

He turned over the page of the small volume and again read aloud:

> "The small rain shuffled at the door
> With the smell of wine corks in the air.
> The smell in dust, the smell in grass.
> And if one cared to learn,
> The smell of gentry copybooks
> Was of equality and brotherhood."*

Narcissus? Would Narcissus accuse the gentry of hypocrisy, of only mouthing support for equality and brotherhood? *Equality* and *brotherhood*. Didn't these concepts have a *social* meaning? What is more, didn't the Bible have a great deal to say about them?

10.

If Fedin was wracked by anxiety, if he was troubled by contradictions that he tried to reconcile in every possible way, if his doubts had led him to read Pasternak's poetry, a single line of which had made him feel guilty and even reject momentarily the "fundamentals of communism"—whatever his difficulties, Pasternak was in a far worse state that night.

* From "Summer 1917," in *Boris Pasternak—Poems*, trans. Eugene M. Kayden (Ann Arbor: Univ. of Michigan Press, 1959).

The poet was sitting at his table listening to a foreign radio broadcast. He was wearing blue-striped pajamas a size too large, which looked like hand-me-downs. His hair was disheveled and his forehead moist with sweat. The bed behind him was rumpled and littered with several dozen congratulatory letters and telegrams that had arrived from abroad during the last few days. He had read them already but was now rereading them over and over again. The dial on his old Blaupunkt radio was whining and the green tuning eye winked as the receiver picked up and lost the transmission. A sheet of paper lay on the table in front of him; he had written down some sentences in English and French: "The pure voice of this remarkable poet exposes the barbarous regime of Marxist dictators." "He is independent and proud." "This is the only free voice in enslaved Russia!" "The novel *Doctor Zhivago* is a chef d'oeuvre of the twentieth century."

There was all kinds of interference: a rumbling, screeching, and crackling din, most likely caused by Soviet jamming of Russian émigré broadcasts from West Germany. (Pasternak had seen one of the jammers nearby, between Peredelkino and Odintsovo.)

He looked at the radio angrily, then equally angrily at the sheet of paper. The praise was flattering, but *this* praise deeply offended the poet's modesty; he judged his own works more severely than any outsider.

Pasternak moved to the armchair. The frenzied publicity stirred up in the West annoyed him. Both *Doctor Zhivago* and its author seemed to be important only in an ideological context. Not a single radio broadcast had spoken about his work seriously, profoundly, from a *literary* point of view. There was no question that the radio was seething with anti-Soviet propaganda; his name was used in every sentence to "expose" those vile "reds."

Pasternak loved the West. He had translated Shakespeare, Goethe, and Schiller into Russian; he worshiped Heine and Rilke and had read them in the original German. His trips to Germany and Italy in his student years had been imprinted on his memory for the rest of his life. He felt he had been influenced by Shakespeare and Goethe, whom he passionately admired, and this made him glad.

Now, suddenly, echoes of the Soviet propaganda that claimed he had cut himself off from Communist Russia were reaching him from the West. This barrage was just like a typical Soviet campaign of ideological aggression. Furthermore, it was clearly directed at a European public, as if there were Frenchmen, Germans, or Englishmen who needed to be convinced that their sympathy for the Soviet Union was misguided, that the socialist system was indeed cruel, corrupt, and unalterably opposed to the "free world."

Did he really know what the West was? Perhaps he had gotten it wrong? He rested his head against the back of the chair and closed his eyes. Until now he had been convinced that the West had one indisputable achievement: it had reduced the power of the state over the individual to a minimum. True, money had replaced the power of the state, and the state preserved the power of money. Nevertheless he had believed that those who were not greedy, who could be satisfied with the basics, would find a clear path to spiritual freedom in the West.

Also, the West was still living under the aegis of Christianity, and this was of the utmost importance to Pasternak. He remembered what he had written about Christianity: ". . . humanity consists of two elements: God and work. The development of the human spirit breaks down into separate works of vast duration, which have been realized over centuries and have followed one after the other. Egypt was one such work, Greece was another, the prophets' understanding of God in the Bible yet another. The last such work in time, for which a substitute has not as yet been found, is the work fired by the whole of contemporary inspiration—Christianity."

He had written that ten years ago. Did he still believe it? In his youth Pasternak had dreamed of rising above the everyday world and soaring in the realms of creativity. It was because of this that he had first embarked on a musical career and, while he was a student at Moscow University, planned to enter the conservatory. Music seemed to him to be the language of that other, impossibly beautiful world, merely projecting the reality of earthly existence in its godlike sounds. Poetry was to be found somewhere beside music and was also for Pasternak a reflection of the idea of Christian love. Music was hypnotic and even terrifying; it transported one to the cosmos. But poetry, despite its sublime elements, was bound to the earth, and the earth was Pasternak's point of departure.

The October Revolution of 1917 and the early years of the Soviet state had caught Pasternak up in their whirlwind, and, although he still continued to develop as a lyric poet, he responded to the call of the times by writing the poem "Lieutenant Schmidt." Both before and after this, social themes could occasionally be glimpsed in Pasternak's intimate poems. But he was not really committed to them; in fact, his coldness toward social issues led the press to label him a "salon poet" and a Narcissus, the name Fedin had also given him.

But in 1937, when Stalin's arrests had shaken him to the depths of his being, Pasternak began to reconsider the role of literature in society and his own position as a writer. Only then did he decide to engage in an uncompromising fight to the death. The time had come to stop using art to isolate himself from political reality. Collectivist ideology had transformed Russian life and was destroying all its foundations. So when he embraced the philosophy of individualism, Pasternak placed himself firmly in the opposite camp. He gradually saw that his duty lay in defending individualism and Christianity from the "barbarians."

All this thought and change involved a profoundly private, dialectical process. By standing up for individualism and Christianity in *Doctor Zhivago*, Pasternak announced the new direction he had chosen. He was well aware that in this book he was using literature to intervene actively in politics.

And he knew that by doing this he had in a sense joined those he opposed, those who proclaimed that "socialist realism" was the only valid literary method. Of course he rejected didacticism as strongly as he always had, but more and more frequently he would quote to himself a verse from Corinthians: "If the trumpet give an uncertain sound, who shall prepare himself to the battle?"

In *Doctor Zhivago* he wanted to examine, not the chance occurrences of everyday life but those apocalyptic events during the stormy years of the Revolution and Civil War which reshaped the entire lives of millions of human beings and which threw people into agonies of fear or creative ecstasy. It was interesting that on this higher plane of literature, as he called it thereafter, Pasternak discovered immutable laws that were not dependent on the will or desire of the writer but moved and developed of their own accord, depriving the writer of choice.

All the same, why had he become angry when listening to Fedin's tirades about the place of the writer in contemporary life? After all, having once engaged in this spiritual battle, he too, for good or ill, had felt compelled to adopt a definite position in real life. Why did he expect mercy from his opponents? And why did the broadcasts from the West annoy him? Everything was in confusion, as Fedin had said. Yes, two worlds had collided in a struggle—not for life but to the death.

Pasternak reproached himself for being inconsistent. A long time ago, when he had started writing *Doctor Zhivago*, and even earlier than that, he had believed that he had rejected Soviet power, decisively, condemning it as inhuman. But despite *Doctor Zhivago*, at times he still wavered, going back to the beginning, then losing his way somewhere between Christianity and communism, conscious that Christianity *called* one to a better life while communism *dictated* a better life.

Cascades of thoughts rained down on him. He was being swamped and he had to find high ground. As this had happened to him before, he knew how to escape from the whirl-pool. He forced himself to think about something very simple and ordinary. He thought about the next day, how, early in the morning, after taking off his shirt and tying a Turkish towel around his waist (it had to be a Turkish one), he would go into the yard and start washing at the pump, snorting from the icy water. Tobik and Bubik would circle around his feet, and Tatyana would wail, "You've left a lake behind you again, Boris Leonidovich," and he would joke back, "Yes, we're all made of water, Tanya. Ask Lyonya, if you don't believe me. He's the educated one around here. He knows it all." He thought about Lyonya, his younger son, whom he called the "misanthrope" and Tatyana called "young master." Lyonya had been disappearing to Moscow for days and nights on end, and Pasternak thought that he had fallen in love. Then he forced himself to think about breakfast, well-fried eggs and potatoes. He liked to scrape the burned bits from the frying pan and eat them off his knife, even though in his childhood his mother had said this was bad manners.

Pasternak visualized the dining room table and the clay jug of wine brought by Nina. Then a miracle took place. The thought of the Kakhetian wine and this clay jug calmed him. He suddenly felt an intense desire for a glass of wine, and the desire turned his mind from higher matters to everyday ones, and made him feel happy again, as if he had just smelled freshly baked bread or slid between newly laundered sheets. Eating ice cream has the same effect on young children, and watching the sunrise on fishermen at sea. Pasternak had always been saved from unanswerable questions by simple, everyday things. Whether pondering on the meaning of life and Kant's *Prolegomena*, or earthing up a strawberry plant and chopping wood, he felt in his element.

The glass of wine—or rather, the idea of a glass of wine—filled him with optimism. Pasternak no longer wanted to think skeptically about the West; he remembered that he knew several very worthy, talented, and honest people in

London and Paris, with whom he corresponded through Olga (although it was true that the voices on the radio did not seem to share their civilized good humor). The West was not perfect, but it was stupid to deny that creative and civil freedoms existed there. Even now, even in America, writers were publishing books filled with outspoken, sometimes harsh criticism of capitalism. If there was no freedom in the West, such books would not appear, though there were not many of them, of course, in comparison with the cheap and vulgar sort.

He rose and made his way downstairs, determined to be cheerful.

11.

In the dining room a shaft of light fell through the half-open door into the kitchen. Tatyana had forgotten to turn off the switch (she was asleep, snoring softly, in her tiny room off the kitchen). On hearing Pasternak, Tobik and Bubik, who usually settled down for the night in the vestibule, got up and came into the dining room, wagging their tails and greeting him with soft cries. He squatted and patted them. Then, in the semidarkness, he went over to the table and poured a full glass of wine out of the clay jug. Slowly, with a contented smile, he drank it in short gulps, savoring the pleasure as long as possible. The wine had never tasted so good to him before, perhaps because he had never needed it as much as now.

Pasternak was not one of those poets who use wine as a stimulus to their imaginations. Wine excited him, and when he drank it he often became noisy and a bit of a fool. Sometimes it calmed him down and plunged him into a state of euphoria and even drowsiness. Usually he would first become talkative, and then suddenly his head would drop to his chest and he would nod off.

Having drained the glass and licked his lips, Pasternak considered drinking a second, but restrained himself. Groping into the hallway, he stopped when he heard Zina and Nina talking in the music room. A strip of light was showing through the crack under the closed door. Pasternak hesitated. Should he go to the door on tiptoe and eavesdrop on the conversation of these two women who were so close to him or should he listen to his conscience, which told him that eavesdropping, even in his own home, was wrong?

12.

The music room had gotten its name from the black Bechstein that had stood in it many years before. Zina's first husband, the renowned Soviet pianist Heinrich Neuhaus, had been a close friend of Pasternak's and had come here frequently to practice for his concerts. Later the Bechstein was moved to Zina's room, and her son by Neuhaus, the young and talented Stasik, used it to prepare for concerts.

It was a square room with two windows, framed by blue curtains, overlooking the garden. In the left-hand corner near the door was the couch that Nina used as a bed. In the opposite corner stood a narrow iron bedstead, like that in Pasternak's room, covered with a flannel blanket. The walls, covered with faded pale-yellow paper, were hung with works by the poet's father, and on the floor were several fabric rugs that Zina had made. A floor lamp with a brittle plastic shade, a square table from the Napoleonic era, and an antediluvian record player completed the arrangement. Although the room was sparely furnished, it was exceptionally clean and tidy.

Nina was kneeling in the far corner; she was wearing a long nightshirt, and her gray hair hung loose to her waist. Whispering a prayer, she crossed herself fervently and touched the floor with her forehead. Zina was sitting on the bed, also wearing a nightshirt, and holding a small straw basket containing three bundles of letters, two of which were tied up with red ribbon. She was smoking, flicking the ash into an ashtray, and reading one of the letters aloud: ". . . in my thoughts and dreams I turn my head and see you standing there beside me, tall, seventeen or twenty years old, my delicate wing of speed, of calm spirit, my white vision, proud knowledge of mine, piercingly clear, like lilac in the dew . . ."

Zina folded the letter in four and put it back in its envelope. Then she picked up another: "Oh, if I but loved you simply—as others would love an educated lady who comes and gives advice, full of smiles and sympathy—then I, perhaps, would overcome all this. But this love is impossible to stop. This is what happens to man when higher things are bestowed on him. Such love should not be swept aside with a brush or wiped away with a rag, but cared for with tenderness; it has unfurled its sail over life, gathered life into a single, indisputable whole, endowed it with meaning. Under its protection one can sail even unto death and fear nothing ever again. It is a breath of gentle affection, blended with the breath of life's journey. You are the one I have loved and seen, who will stay with me . . ."

Zina replaced it in its envelope, sighed deeply and, after a pause, repeated: " 'You are the one I have loved and seen, who will stay with me.' Borya wrote those words to me, to *me* . . ."

Nina went on praying.

Zina threw back her head, closed her eyes and froze for a moment. Some shattering emotion seemed about to well up in her, but this sensation passed immediately. Dry-eyed, she looked at the envelope in her hand and resisted the urge to crumple it up and hurl it to the floor. Instead she reached for another letter and, having unfolded it, again read aloud: "Work, nature and music have become part of you—you give them meaning. You are the sister of my talent. You give me a feeling of wholeness and of life. And without you my happiness is not complete. I want to make you the only one in my life. I want to clothe you in a dress of my pain, nerves, thoughts. I am materially and spiritually inseparable from you."

Zina put all the letters into the basket and moved it away from her, as if saying that its contents no longer belonged to her.

"Lord, Lord, hear my prayer . . . ." Nina murmured.

"The Lord is deaf and dumb." With a bitter smile Zina went on: "I just read you the letters Borya wrote me many years ago. They aroused love in me, love. I left Heinrich for him. And what happened? Now Olga tells people that she, *she* is Pasternak's wife, that her daughter Irina is Pasternak's daughter. She calls me a harridan, a witch, a simple-minded hausfrau, a burden. And it's not true she was arrested because of her 'sympathy' for Pasternak. She was put in prison for the dishonest way she handled the affairs of the journal *Ogonyok* when she was working there. I heard this from people I trust. Her hands aren't clean. Yet it was *this* woman Borya used as a model for Lara in *Doctor Zhivago!*"

Nina got up from the floor, went over to Zina and sat down beside her on the bed. "Zinochka, forget about it. It's not the time."

Again, when their eyes met, Zina thought without malice: She loves him too. No, she was not jealous of Nina, because she knew her, knew that her love for Pasternak would never rise to the surface and that in itself this love was irreproachable. She was glad of Nina's love for Borya, because it meant that the two of them together would outweigh Olga. "I know it's not the time, but I can't stop myself."

"Zina, Titsian was unfaithful to me too. I forgave him."

"No, no . . . I'm old, a hunchback. I can feel something welling up in me. It's true I'm just a simple housewife and a burden. And nothing more."

"Nonsense!"

"Ah, Nina . . . I was born into an intellectual family. My parents weren't rich, but we spent our summers in a dacha outside St. Petersburg, and I received a higher education."

"Why are you telling me this?"

Zina ignored her. She was really talking to herself, trying to sort out the past. "When the Civil War began, I found myself in the Ukraine. I studied music. I met Heinrich Neuhaus. He was a professor. When he looked at my fingers he said, 'They're not very musical, but they'll do if you work hard.' And he showed me his own completely unmusical fingers. We got married. I gave birth to Adik and Stasik. By then the Soviet era had begun. We moved to Moscow, and I met Borya. He and Heinrich were friends. I fell in love with him . . . and I gave up everything for him. Children. Family. I lived for him. Yes, yes, even my music. I became a housewife and an ordinary woman. Ordinary. But Olga writes poetry, does translations, gets published. She's what you might call a creative individual. But what am I? A void. The most important thing about me is that I am Zina *Pasternak*, the wife of the poet Pasternak. I'm just a wife, a woman who knows how to bake pies—and I don't even do that very well, in Tatyana's opinion. But it was Borya, he was the one who reduced me to this level. He was the one who took music away from me. At the graduation exam in Kiev I played Beethoven's 'Pathétique' and was loudly applauded."

"Zina—"

"He was the one who took away my future. Oh, how banal this all is! We lived together for almost thirty years. Then another woman appeared. He was attracted by her and chose her . . . as his queen."

"Zina, you've got it all wrong."

"No, I haven't, Nina. I'm just the mother of his favorite son. And then, I've got dyed hair, but she's a natural blonde. Lara was a blonde . . . ."

"My dear." Nina embraced Zina. "He'll come back to you. Only you must want him to. But you're like ice. You're a 'solid lump of pride,' just as Borya said. You must stretch out your hand to him and help him. Don't push him away and punish him for a mistake or weakness."

"We're strangers."

"Zinochka, all marriages have their difficulties. There were times when I was very unhappy with Titsian. Do you remember when you and Borya were staying with us in Tbilisi?

You were all very happy, but I wanted to kill myself. I'd already gotten the poison."

Zina laughed. "Nina, do you remember how Borya poisoned himself with iodine? You were there."

"I remember perfectly. You were going through one of your crises. I think you'd even decided to go back to Heinrich. I received a telegram from Borya: 'Nina, my dear, come right away.' As soon as I arrived in Moscow he drank the iodine."

"And we saved him with milk. He resisted and called out, 'Let me die!' "

"Zinochka, I think he just wanted to scare you."

"Well, he succeeded."

"Borya certainly knows how to pretend."

"You're telling me!"

At that moment there was a knock at the door, and Pasternak came into the room. He rubbed his eyes with his fists and stretched, as if he had just gotten out of bed.

"Borya!" Nina exclaimed, quickly throwing on her dressing gown.

"My sweet girls, why aren't you asleep? You don't want to sleep, so you won't let anyone else get some rest. It's the middle of the night. When I heard voices I came down to see if burglars had broken in."

Zina hid the basket of letters behind her.

"Sorry, Borya, we were just—"

"Ah, Ninochka, I'm just teasing," Pasternak interrupted. "I'm restless tonight myself. I sat for a whole hour trying to catch something on the radio about myself and *Zhivago*. And I have to say, Nina, with my hand on my heart, that they've gone out of their minds in the West. They were broadcasting God knows what about me."

"What exactly?" Nina asked.

"They've got no sense of proportion—no self-control. They're blinded by sensation. They come out with all sorts of vulgar, sentimental trash. I marvel at such lack of taste. By the way, they're making up all sorts of cock-and-bull stories

86

about Lara. When they asked Leo Tolstoy who was the model for Natasha Rostova in *War and Peace* he replied, 'I am Natasha.' That's good, isn't it? So, Ninochka, I, Boris Pasternak, state triumphantly that I am the heroine of *Doctor Zhivago*, I am Lara. No, in actual fact, she's a mixed image. She's a synthesis. A part of her is you, Nina—you're my Georgian Lara. And a great deal of her of course, a very great deal, is you, Zina. She's the woman of my century and my vision."

Nina was startled when Pasternak mentioned Lara; he seemed to be replying to Zina's comment that he had modeled Lara on Olga. It crossed her mind that perhaps he had been standing outside the door and eavesdropping on their conversation. But whatever his reasons, she was glad that Pasternak, who seemed unusually animated, had reassured Zina. "I thought so," she replied quickly. "Precisely. It's not the color of Lara's hair that's significant."

"No, of course it's not the color of her hair, Ninochka! But let me go on. When I was sitting by the radio with my earphones on, listening to all this nonsense, I could not help asking myself over and over again, 'What if our respected Comrade Fedin, Konstantin Alexandrovich, deputy of the Supreme Soviet and so forth, what if he's right?' What if I really am just a puppet in the hands of the imperialists?"

Pasternak laughed nervously, and Nina protested. "Borya, people in the West don't understand fear; they say whatever comes into their heads. What have imperialists got to do with us? Do they really exist?"

Zina cleared her throat before speaking. "If you renounce *Doctor Zhivago* I'll leave you."

Taken aback, Pasternak stared at his wife in surprise. Then his delight turned to pity, and finally to anger. "Don't talk nonsense, Zina. First, I have no intention of renouncing *Doctor Zhivago*. Second, who was terrified when I handed over the manuscript to the Italian publisher, or rather his representative? It was right here in the dining room, during the international youth festival. Don't you remember?" Zina recoiled defensively and lit a cigarette. "Weren't you the one who wanted me to demand the manuscript back?"

"I was frightened for . . . the family, for Lyonya," she muttered.

"And don't smoke, please. Let's have some fresh air at least at night."

Zina stubbed out her cigarette and lowered her eyes. Pasternak sat down on a chair and wiped his forehead with the palm of his hand.

"All the same, what if Comrade Fedin was right, Nina? What if I really am just a self-obsessed Narcissus who doesn't see what's going on around him?"

"That's not true!" Nina protested again. "You're a poet, Borya. A poet can predict a storm from the slightest movement of a blade of grass."

"You really think I have such great meteorological ability? I wish I could see into the future." He smiled wanly. "My dear girls, I want to confess something to you. Yes, I'll get down on my knees in front of you and confess. Right now." He lowered himself to his knees. "Since my conversation with Fedin I've been gabbling all kinds of nonsense, smiling one minute, brooding the next, thinking and thinking. I've been as changeable as the wind, but in actual fact the whole time I . . . I've been tormented by fear."

13.

The next morning it started raining early. Dense, tightly packed clouds covered the sky as far as the horizon. Toward ten, however, it brightened and rays of sun began to break through the clouds. The raindrops on the pine and fir needles made the trees glisten; underfoot the fallen leaves were drenched.

"We'll be in Peredelkino by one o'clock," said the driver, a man about forty, with high cheekbones and cunning eyes. He maneuvered skillfully through the heavy traffic along the

Minsk highway. The car, which belonged to the Literary Fund's medical clinic, had red crosses painted on its sides, but it did not enjoy an automatic right of way.

"I don't think it will be easy to find Pasternak's dacha," said the young woman sitting next to him. Her dark hair curled out from under a white doctor's cap, and her eyes shone like black cherries. Her features had a Semitic cast, and a trace of a mustache showed on her upper lip. She wore a light overcoat, lined with cheap fur, and high overshoes.

"We've got the address. We'll find it, Rosalie," the driver said confidently and somewhat familiarly.

Dr. Rosalie Zaak was thirty-two and lived with her mother, a retired dentist, who worried about everything, especially her daughter's marriage prospects. Rosalie had had polio as a child and walked with difficulty, dragging her left foot. She had long since decided not to think about marriage and children; instead she devoted herself to her medical work and spent her free hours reading poetry and going to the theater. Pasternak was the poet she most admired.

Just before Odintsovo the car turned left onto the road to Peredelkino. At the junction two men wearing waterproof capes were digging a trench by the side of the road. One of them, a young man with a brown sunburned face, followed the car with his eyes, shook his head, and said to his mate, "Do you see that, Yegor, someone must be dying somewhere, eh?"

14.

Tatyana was feeding Tobik and Bubik in the yard next to the Ping-Pong table. She had made them a large bowl of leftover potatoes and chicken, with some lard thrown in. It was rich food, and the dogs were quarreling, each one trying to shoulder the other away from the bowl. They growled at each other and at Tatyana when she tried to enforce some order.

"Ooh, what little monsters, Lord have mercy! Where do you think you're going, Tobik? Watch out or I'll give you fish heads instead. And you too, Bubik, what damn tricks are you up to? Where do you think you're going to push in?" She gave the dog a shove with her foot.

Engrossed in her work, Tatyana had not noticed the car turning through the dacha's gates. And the dogs, busy lapping up their food, had paid no attention either. Suddenly she turned around and, seeing the car with its red crosses, called out in surprise. Rosalie Zaak had already gotten out, followed by the driver, who lazily opened the trunk and took out two cases, a large medical one and a smaller one containing Dr. Zaak's personal belongings.

"Excuse me, please, is this Boris Pasternak's house?" Rosalie asked.

Tatyana drew herself up to her full height and placed her hands on her hips. "There's no one sick here!"

"May be, for all you know, old girl," the driver remarked with a grin.

"I'm not an old girl to you, you rude bastard!"

Tobik and Bubik joined in, barking loudly and moving toward the driver, who ignored them.

Tatyana shouted at them, and the dogs stopped barking. Bubik approached Rosalie, sniffed her, and started wagging his tail.

"Good day. I've come to see the poet Pasternak," Rosalie said timidly. "He does live here, doesn't he?"

"Yes, he lives here, don't you worry, Rosalie Naumovna," the driver said, then turned to Tatyana. "Those dogs don't look too healthy to me, old girl. You ought to give them meat."

Tatyana placed her hands on her hips again. "There's no one sick here! No one, I tell you!"

Aroused by the commotion, Zina came out of the house, wearing a dark-blue housecoat and a hairnet pulled tightly over her head. "What's going on here?" She cast a cautious and unwelcoming glance at Rosalie.

"It appears they've sent a physician for Boris Leonidovich."

"What sort of physician, Tatyana?"

"I'm not a physician. I'm a therapeutic doctor. Rosalie Naumovna Zaak, with two *a*'s. I've been sent to you from the Literary Fund medical clinic for an indefinite period. Our director said to me, 'Go to Pasternak's dacha in Peredelkino, Comrade Zaak, for an indefinite period.' "

"Very interesting." Zina scowled. "And why, may I ask?"

"You see . . ." Rosalie hesitated. "Actually, I don't know . . . maybe I'll be needed. Please don't worry, I'll eat in a café in town, I won't be a burden to you. I just hope you can find a place in the house for me to sleep."

Zina came down two steps, looked at the driver and the two cases, then said in her coldest and most uncompromising manner, "Go straight back where you came from. And take your cases with you. If the Kremlin masterminds think my husband will harm himself because of their threats, they are mistaken. Pasternak will outlive all of them put together."

"Of course, of course!" Rosalie exclaimed.

"We don't need you, madam," Zina added. "We'll manage somehow without Zaaks with two *a*'s! And besides, I have a book on medicine, a fine revolutionary book of home cures."

Pasternak had come out of the house while she was speaking. He wore a gray sweater and patched pants and smiled openly and slightly naïvely. "What's the argument about, Zinochka? May I know, if it's not a secret?" He spoke cheerfully, but a hint of anxiety showed in his eyes. "Who has come and why?"

"They've sent a doctor from the Literary Fund clinic. For an indefinite period. They're concerned about you. Do you understand? This woman is intending to live with us. Our leaders must be frightened you'll catch cold or come down with influenza."

"I am so happy to make your acquaintance, Boris Leonidovich. When I was a student at the Medical Institute I attended your literary evenings at Moscow University. At one of them you read your translation of *Hamlet*. When the director of the clinic offered me this assignment I was so happy. I said to myself: 'Rosie, this is wonderful. First, you're going to meet your favorite poet at last, and second, you're going to live in the country for a while, where you can breathe some fresh air.' Oh, I'm so tired of Moscow. At home, on Shablovka Street, the noise never stops, day or night. And the clinic is always so busy."

"Yes, that's true," the driver confirmed in a businesslike fashion.

"I dream of walking in the woods, even in the rain—"

"Go back where you came from!" Zina interrupted her. "I repeat, we don't need you. We'll do without you."

"Wait a minute, Zinochka." Pasternak scrutinized Rosalie with curiosity and sympathy. "What is your name? Rosalie . . . ?"

"Naumovna. But you can call me what you like. Just Rosa."

"Zaak, with two *a*'s," the driver added.

"With two *a*'s? Perfect. And my mother was called Rosa. Zinochka, Rosalie Naumovna, or just Rosa, wants to have a rest from Moscow. I can understand that. Moscow is exhausting. Rosa wants to breathe some fresh air. Do you really begrudge her this air? And can we really not find a spare bed in the house?"

"Oh, please don't send me back. Please!"

"Zinochka, I'll make use of the opportunity to take some treatment," Pasternak said playfully. "I have had a ringing sound in my left ear."

"Whatever pleases you, Borya." Zina shrugged. "Of course we'll find a spare bed."

15.

The fall weather is changeable around Moscow. Rainy days alternate with sunny ones, when everything is turned to gold.

Rosalie was lucky. The day after her arrival in Pederelkino

the sky cleared, the earth dried out, and the air became a little warmer. So after breakfast, which Pasternak himself prepared for her, and which she therefore did not have the strength to refuse, she went for a walk toward the village of Michurinka. Pasternak planned her route, sketching it on a sheet of paper and telling her it would take an hour and a half to two hours.

After Rosalie's departure a tragicomic scene was played at the house. Zina and Nina were sitting at the dining table with the invariable cigarettes between their lips. Rosalie's medical case sat on a chair in the corner, and Tatyana was bending over it in a demonic pose. Pasternak, as if to emphasize that he had no part in what was going on, paced about the room adjusting his father's works, first moving them slightly to the left, and then slightly to the right.

"I'll bet my life on it," Tatyana stated categorically. "Inside there she's got a, you know, a thing for recording voices . . . that miracle machine . . ."

"A tape recorder," Zina said.

"Yes, that's it, Zinaida Nikolayevna. I can see it through the side."

"I think you're right," Zina agreed.

"So you two have finally found something to agree on," Pasternak remarked sarcastically. "At long last you're seeing eye to eye."

"But if it isn't a tape recorder in there, then what is it?" Nina wondered.

"It doesn't matter. God helps those who help themselves," Tatyana snapped. "Let's open it and see. What a fuss about nothing. What's there to be afraid of? Just jimmy the lock with a pair of scissors and—lo and behold!"

" 'Lo and behold!' " Pasternak mimicked. "God knows what's going on here. With all this persuasion, Ninochka, I'm about ready to give in. But you should stand up to them. I don't know—they've gone berserk. Tatyana, don't you dare! I forbid it! It's a crime! Can't you understand? It's robbery!"

"Ah, you're such a simpleton, Boris Leonidovich," Tatyana countered. "Eavesdropping and spying on you—isn't that a crime too?"

"But Rosalie has gone for a walk, to Michurinka, while you here . . . No, the case can't be touched without her being here."

"Do you want us to ask her permission?"

"Of course. Otherwise I won't allow it. And when it comes down to it, I'm the head of this household. I can't understand why you have such a low opinion of her. Do you think she's a KGB agent? She's a sweet Jewish woman with a little mustache and a limp, who loves poetry."

"I know her sort," Tatyana interrupted. "Take my word for it, she's been sent here to sniff something out."

"Sniff something out? What's there to sniff out here?" Pasternak turned to Nina again, seeking her support. "Ninochka, do you think that's possible?"

"Oh, Borya, alas, anything is possible. Methods have become so sophisticated now. They didn't spy on Titsian, and they didn't record his voice on tape. *Then* you were just arrested and killed."

"I'm sure she's from the KGB," Zina said.

"As a rule they don't employ Jews in the KGB!" Pasternak exclaimed.

"They do, Borya," Nina said, shaking her head.

"No, no, I can't believe it. She's so charming—we talked for three hours yesterday. She knows all my poems by heart. Can you imagine a KGB agent reading poetry? There you are! And she drinks in the beauty of nature with such greed. You should trust people."

Tatyana moved the medical case from the chair to the table.

"It's heavy. Where's all this talk getting us? Anything could be hidden in here. If you're so fussy, Boris Leonidovich, go upstairs and do some writing. Go and write some poetry. Opening cases isn't your line."

"No, it's not. I can't deny that." And walking toward the hallway he added: "I've seen nothing, I know nothing, I have no responsibility for all this. You are criminals and conspirators. You too, Nina."

"All right, all right, go, then," Tatyana muttered.

Pasternak left the dining room and closed the door behind him, but changed his mind and decided to wait in the hallway. He did not feel like himself. The whole thing was shameful and disgusting. As he listened by the door he remembered how as a boy of fourteen, at a school dance, he had touched a girl's breast when he was dancing with her. She was furious, and he turned bright red and ran from the room. Thereafter he had stayed far away from her, despising himself for his "unworthy" action.

Meanwhile, armed with a pair of sewing scissors, Tatyana had skillfully used their sharp points to open the lock of the medical case. Zina got up, went over to Tatyana, and together they started rummaging through the bag's contents. Seated at the table, Nina placed her glasses on the tip of her nose and craned her head toward them.

"You'd better look out the window, Nina, in case that Zaak woman comes back unexpectedly," Zina said.

In the case Tatyana and Zina discovered a large number of phials and boxes of medicine, an apparatus for measuring blood pressure, syringes, tweezers, bandages, tampons, all sorts of unremarkable medical supplies. They looked through everything but did not find a tape recorder or anything to arouse suspicion. Exchanging a disappointed look, they carefully began to put everything back in its proper place. The only sound was from Tatyana, who was breathing heavily.

Having realized without their saying a word that they had met with failure, Nina walked away from the window, sat down at the table, and lit a cigarette, which as usual made her start coughing violently.

Tatyana closed the lid, clicked the lock shut—again with the help of the scissors—and placed the case on the chair in the corner of the room where it had been before. Then she started singing in a low voice as if nothing had happened and took herself off to the kitchen.

So there was nothing there! Hearing Nina coughing, Pasternak burst in from the corridor.

"Aha!" he cried out triumphantly. "You're very quiet now, aren't you, little birdies? Where are you off to, Tanya? Oh no, you wait a minute, my girl! Don't run off. You did the damage, so you can take the blame. You're not a child, you don't play with dolls any more. You're a big girl now. You must have some kind of a brain in your head. So you found nothing at all. Fancy that, girls! Isn't that a shame? What did I tell you? Rosa is a wonderful, sweet woman, and you . . . KGB! KGB! You imagine you see the KGB everywhere. The KGB wouldn't employ someone like her. And you're a fine one, Nina Alexandrovna! Where's your sense gone? How can I look Rosa in the eye? Did you think of that? Tell me how. You dragged me into this adventure and now you'll have to tell me how I can look Rosa Zaak in the eye."

16.

Lyonya arrived from Moscow in time for lunch. A slim twenty-year-old, he resembled his mother, although he had inherited some of the oversized features of his father. His beautiful chestnut hair had a soft wave, and a slightly ironic smile often played on his full, supple lips. His brown eyes were calm and a little sad, and there was a Pasternakian look about his chin and the line of his neck.

"How are your studies going, son?" Pasternak asked.

"*So far*, Dad, everything's the same. I haven't been called in to see the rector or given a warning that I'll be expelled from the university because my father is the author of *Doctor Zhivago*. At least not yet."

"Well, that's fine, excellent."

Lyonya laughed. His father also forced himself to laugh. But Rosalie, whom Pasternak had already introduced to his son, lowered her eyes and said nothing.

Lyonya was planning to spend two days in Peredelkino,

and Pasternak and Zina were puzzled by his visit. They knew he was in love with a girl in his class, who was apparently called Natasha, and recently he had rarely slept at the dacha, arriving only at odd hours for just a couple of winks. However, neither his father nor his mother asked him about his friend, since they were waiting for Lyonya to bring up the subject himself. Only Tatyana, who was the first to get wind of the affair of the "young master" she had rocked in her arms, made an occasional teasing insinuation.

They sat down to eat at four o'clock. For lunch there was green-cabbage soup and meat pies, the last of those baked for Zina's name day.

Tatyana handed round the plates of soup and then sat down and picked up a wooden spoon, her own special one. Pasternak poured out wine for everyone.

"Don't be in such a hurry, Tatyana," he said. "Before we start eating I want to propose a toast. Dear Rosalie Naumovna, I want to drink to your health. You are a remarkable woman. I love you. You are charming company. You are an honest and kind person. And now, addressing you in my official capacity as head of this household, I want to tell you that you are the victim, yes, the victim of unjustified suspicion."

Rosalie blushed and started blinking fast, not understanding what Pasternak was driving at. Zina and Nina, who had guessed, exchanged uneasy glances. Tatyana sat stony-faced, seemingly unfazed by Pasternak's little speech.

"Today, in this house, Rosalie Naumovna," Pasternak continued, "a crime was committed."

"A crime? What do you mean?" Rosalie asked, completely bewildered.

"What are you talking about, Papa?" Glancing at Tatyana, Lyonya added, "Tatyana must have been up to her old tricks again."

"What tricks do you have in mind?" Tatyana said sharply.

"Well, like putting pinecones in the dogs' dinner."

"No, son, nothing like that," Pasternak said. "Nothing like that. Dear Rosalie Naumovna, I must apologize to you pub-

97

licly. The fact is, I, sinner that I am, suspected you of being
. . . In short, in your absence, when you went out for a walk
this morning, I, *of my own accord*, without your permission,
opened your medical case and checked to see if you had a
tape recorder for recording my conversations."

Rosalie burst into laughter. "Splendid!" she exclaimed.
"You had the sense to do it yourself. I wanted to tell you to
do just that so I could feel at ease—that is, I could feel at ease
that you felt at ease. Such a thing . . . is not impossible, Boris
Leonidovich."

"Really? Well, I didn't find anything in your bag, alas."

"That's an old trick, Papa," Lyonya remarked. "These
days they can put tape recorders, or rather, microphones with
a transmitter device, in jacket buttons. That's how far science
has progressed.

"I'm more interested in how far medicine has advanced.
Rosalie Naumovna, would you examine me after lunch and
prescribe a course of treatment for me. I want to be cured of
suspiciousness. It's a terrifying ailment. Incidentally, Zinochka, Nina, and you too, Tanya, it might do you all good
to take some medicine, eh?"

Tatyana was not lost for an answer. "Only castor oil will
help me!"

17.

When they reached the meat pie they heard Tobik and
Bubik barking in the yard.

"Who the devil has come now?" Zina asked. Then, addressing Tatyana, she said, "Go and see who it is."

Anticipating some new unpleasantness, Nina looked at
Pasternak. The postman had already been by with the newspapers and letters, and although the news had not been good,
the basic situation had not been changed. Nina was waiting
for the next step by the authorities—a specific blow in response to the poet's inflexibility.

Two deep furrows appeared between Zina's eyebrows.

Emerging from the house, Tatyana saw a tall man with a gray mustache that almost covered his mouth. He wore a half coat, a hat with earflaps, and old-fashioned leggings, and was carrying a new leatherette briefcase.

"Who do you want, old-timer?"

The visitor answered in a powerful voice, stressing his *r*'s. "Good afternoon, comrade. Call off your dogs. Aren't you Tatyana?"

Tobik and Bubik calmed down, cowed by the stranger's firmness.

"Yes, I'm Tatyana, but—who are you?"

"Akimych. I've come to see the poet Pasternak. On important business."

Tatyana eventually let him into the house, where, continuing to stress his *r*'s, he addressed the whole company.

"Good afternoon, comrades. I hope you're enjoying your meal. Excuse me for interrupting at such a bad time. Such is my profession. I depend on the trains. They don't give me a car. Don't you recognize me, Boris Leonidovich? Your housemaid didn't recognize me either. But I remembered her name—Tatyana. The last time I was here, Boris Leonidovich, Alexei Maximovich Gorky was still alive; he was a god in our Union of Soviet Writers. I'm the messenger from the Writers' Union. Akimych."

"From the Writers' Union?" Zina repeated in a whisper.

Pasternak got up from the table. "It's good to see you, Akimych. Please come in and sit down. Make yourself at home."

"Thank you, Boris Leonidovich. Your words are sweeter than honey. I've come to see you on urgent business. Most urgent." He took off his hat, pressed it together between his knees, opened his briefcase and began rummaging in it.

"Of course, of course . . . I remember you, Akimych, I remember." Pasternak was excited. "It's true, it was ages ago. You were a handsome chap then. And your mustache was as black as tar. Everyone called you 'the hussar.' "

"Yes, that's what they called me. Now it's just Akimych. I've turned seventy. Time to retire. Old age forces you to give in."

"On that occasion, if I'm not mistaken, you brought me an extremely nasty letter from Gorky."

"Yes, you do get nasty ones. That's a messenger's lot. He has to deliver nasty ones far more often than nice ones. Right now, Boris Leonidovich, I've got a summons for you, with instructions to deliver it to you personally. You have to sign for it here." Akimych handed it to him, and Pasternak prepared to sign the receipt for it.

"Here? Like this?"

"That's right, Boris Leonidovich. Thank you. I remember your handwriting . . . just like a chicken crossing the road."

"Yes, my handwriting . . . But perhaps you'll take some lunch with us? We have a tasty meat pie. My wife and Tatyana baked it."

"Meat pie? No, thank you. I don't touch meat. I'm a vegetarian. And then I'm in the course of executing my official duties."

"Well, what about some Kakhetian wine? Won't you have a glass?"

"Kakhetian? No, thank you. I'm a vegetarian. I don't touch wine. And then I'm in the course of executing my official duties." But here Akimych added, "But if you have some vodka in the house . . . eh?"

"Of course we have," Pasternak said warmly. "Zina, where's our vodka?"

"There's a little left in the carafe," Zina responded unwillingly.

"There's half a liter in the icebox, unopened," Tatyana intervened.

"Half a liter?" Akimych smiled sweetly. "That's rather a lot, dear lady. You can take to your bed from too much drink. And then I'm in the course of executing my official duties."

Pasternak opened the refrigerator, found the half-liter bottle of vodka, took a wineglass from the sideboard and filled it to the brim.

"Won't you take your coat off, Akimych?" he asked.

"No, I'm fine, Boris Leonidovich. We manage like this, in our coats. It's chilly outside. Winter will be upon us soon." He suddenly put his hat on and pulled his earflaps down.

"Papa, you should read the summons," Lyonya urged. "What's it about?"

"There's plenty of time. Later."

"Your son?" Akimych smiled at Lyonya. "You can see he's a sharp one. Jumps into the thick of it before his old man."

Pasternak handed the glass to Akimych. "Yes, youth is incorrigible," he said.

"Thanking you, Boris Leonidovich, thanking you." And, picking up the glass in his right hand, Akimych proposed a toast: "To the Nobel Prize. No one in Russia has ever received it before. You're the first to be honored. They say it's worth sixty thousand dollars. A tidy sum. Money. Money's security. But without money you sleep more soundly. Anyway, it's not certain whether you'll receive it or not."

"I won't receive it," Pasternak remarked calmly. "And you're right. Without money you sleep more soundly, Akimych."

"That's how it is, Boris Leonidovich." He downed the glassful of vodka.

"Will you have something with your vodka? Salted cucumber?" Tatyana asked.

"Nothing. Just air."

"Just air?" Tatyana repeated.

"Yes." He inhaled audibly through his nostrils.

"Papa, what's the summons about?"

"Yes, Borya, what's it about?" Nina joined in, trying to conceal the anxiety in her voice.

"Excuse me, but who are you?" Akimych addressed Nina.

"Nina Alexandrovna Tabidze," Pasternak answered for her. "A close friend of mine. The wife of the famous Georgian poet Titsian Tabidze. Perhaps you've heard of him?"

"Of course I've heard of him. I know the name of every Russian poet as well as my own. That's my business. But this Titsian, he's one of the suppressed, isn't he?" Then, addressing Rosalie, he asked: "Who are you, comrade? Was your husband suppressed too, or your father, perhaps?"

"I'm a doctor from the Literary Fund clinic," Rosalie replied.

"Rosalie is a remarkable woman, Akimych. We're friends." Pasternak wondered why Akimych was asking so many questions. Was he determining how trustworthy the poet's circle was, so that he could, perhaps, start speaking more openly? Or was he just biding his time, waiting to be offered a second drink of vodka? "Have another glass, Akimych," he said, filling his glass to the brim.

"To your *Doctor Zhivago*, Boris Leonidovich," Akimych announced enthusiastically. He drained the glass. "True, they're cursing it in the papers like nothing on earth. But I'm telling you—I may be just a messenger—but if they're cursing it, that means it's a good novel."

"Thank you." Pasternak smiled.

Having drunk the glassful down, Akimych again inhaled through his nostrils. Then, going over to the table, he sat down, placed his briefcase on the floor, and, lowering his voice, started speaking in a conspiratorial tone.

"This is just between ourselves, comrades. Since all of you here are family or friends, I'm not worried about informers. I'm going to tell you some confidential information I've heard. I'm sure it's true; I'd stake my life on my source's honesty. So, then . . . a directive has been sent down from above. I won't sweeten it. I'll give it to you straight. To them up there other people's tears are like water off a duck's back. So, then . . . an attack has been planned. I can't tell you how many attacks I've seen in my time. Big ones and small ones. How many writers have been put through the mincing machine. Only now they're mounting a special one. So, then . . . representatives have been summoned from the national republics. To give it authority. Well, so it's on an all-union scale. They're leaning on the whole bunch. Of course the Central Committee's behind the scenes, as usual. No step is ever taken without the Central Committee. They say he's handling it himself. Nikita. The fat man. He might play the fool, but he's no idiot. And he's bloodthirsty, like Stalin. As they say, six of one to half a dozen of the other."

"Bloodthirsty?" Zina repeated, almost involuntarily.

"I'm afraid they'll decide to take this dacha away from you, Boris Leonidovich."

"What's he saying that for?" Zina was indignant. "It's not even our dacha. We rent it from the Literary Fund."

"Well, they'll terminate the lease," Akimych said. "They have simple ways of doing such things. Or they'll move some other people in. One dacha for two or three writers and their families."

"Comrade vegetarian," Lyonya asked quite seriously, "do you usually play the part of the villain?"

"Lyonya!" Pasternak exclaimed in outrage.

"And I'm telling you, Boris Leonidovich," Akimych went on, having failed to understand Lyonya's question, "the program for the attack on you has already been written and approved. The votes have been counted and the speeches have all been assigned. Everything's all settled. They've even made up a list of words that should be used to describe you. There's 'Judas,' 'serpent,' 'renegade,' 'traitor,' 'narcissus.' Why narcissus, a flower, God only knows. But that's the truth. Oh, yes, and 'parasite' as well. The attack will expose your crimes: nonpayment of member's dues to the Writers' Union for the last twenty-five years—"

"I plead guilty," Pasternak confessed.

"And withdrawal from the public life of the Writers' Union by refusing to go on creative field trips to new socialist construction sites."

"I went once and vowed I would never go again," Pasternak said, and, making a wry face, he asked hesitantly: "So, Akimych, what do you think? Will they expel me from the Writers' Union?"

"You can be sure of it, Boris Leonidovich. They won't let up. You have to be made to pay for bucking the state machine. All hell's already broken loose in the papers. And it'll get worse."

"Akimych, you and your prophecies have brought nothing but evil into this house," Nina said.

"Yes, that's true. But I'm just a messenger, and I wanted to warn you. So you're prepared, Boris Leonidovich." Akimych stood up and smiled. "I also have a request to make of you." He took a small volume of Pasternak's poems from his briefcase and handed it to the author. "It's for my nephew. Don't refuse—he's always reading poetry, and he collects autographs. Please write something in it. What will it cost you, Boris Leonidovich? I'm doing it for my nephew, on my honor. He's sick, poor lad. And if anyone tells you that Akimych trades in autographs, spit in his eye. People tell such lies."

18.

After Akimych had left and lunch was more or less over, Lyonya sat down at the piano in his mother's room and started to play a short piece by Brahms. The sound of the music seemed to bring his father relief. But it was not just the music. However paradoxical it might seem, Pasternak had been glad to receive the summons from the Writers' Union. (And he had been amused by the opera-buffa figure of Akimych.) Before the summons had arrived, Pasternak had been immobilized by uncertainty. Now he felt firmly convinced that he was right and was even looking forward to the battle; now he had the courage to go on. All the confusion of the last few days had evaporated. Events had finally acquired a specific form and demanded precise, controlled action. Pasternak had moved closer to a direct collision with the arbiters of Soviet literature. At the meeting of writers in Moscow to which he had been summoned (not invited, but *summoned*) he would be accused of all the deadly sins. And the charges against him would be brought by his fellow writers, his "brothers"—even, perhaps, some talented ones such as Fedin.

Before they had even discussed it among themselves, every member of the household felt that Pasternak should ignore the summons. And his own first reaction had been to throw the message from the Writers' Union in the garbage can. But when he had gone up to his room and sat down at his table, he suddenly thought that, all things considered, it would not be such a bad idea for him to go and speak at the meeting and tell them that they were all mindless pen-pushers, party hacks. He would tell them they had sold whatever talent they had once had for their careers, for proper Soviet literary prizes, for luxurious apartments, for special clinics and markets. They had lost their consciences, and the only voice they listened to was that of their bellies.

Pasternak's hand reached for a pen. A poem was needed. The words were forming on his lips, the meter was moving somewhere in his soul. Even the title had arisen of its own accord. The poet wrote on a blank sheet of paper "The Nobel Prize." He waited for the first stanza to come. It was somewhere nearby, hovering or hiding in his imagination. Muttering indistinctly, Pasternak got up and walked about the room, trying to speed up the birth of the poem.

Aha! The first stanza . . . here it was! But no, the lines were feeble, even banal. What was needed was an incisive poem, passionate and absolutely straightforward.

Pasternak lowered himself into the armchair. One thing was clear and unshakable: a poet had the right to be a judge, a prophet. Pasternak believed that the soul of a poet was not subject to either dogma or money, because it lay somewhere in the realms of . . . the Great Bear, for instance.

Inwardly uttering the words "Great Bear," he closed his eyes, and before him arose the dacha in Pokrovsko-Streshnevy, near Moscow, which his parents used to rent for the summer, the dacha at which he had spent much of his youth and where one evening (ah, how distinctly he remembered it all), when he was on the terrace, standing next to his mother, he, a twelve-year-old boy, had looked up at the Great Bear and asked, "Mama, what is God?" She had stroked his head and said so calmly and confidently, "God is justice, Borya." And this had stayed with him for the rest of his life.

Justice! Admittedly, he could not always answer the question of what was just in life and what was not. But the starry sky with the Great Bear in it on the warm evening near Moscow and his mother's explanation of God had, perhaps, made a poet-prophet of him.

"My own dear mama . . ." Pasternak said quietly.

He believed that if Russia had embarked on the road of justice in 1917 and had blazed the way to a new and better world, then all those laureates and deputies who had represented Soviet literature would be seen for what they were—a disgraceful parody of justice and humanity, a betrayal of the Revolution.

Yet even now he was reluctant to admit that Russia had *not* embarked on the road of justice in 1917—although, strictly speaking, this was what he had concluded in *Doctor Zhivago*.

No, the first stanza would not come to life. Except for the title of the poem, the sheet of paper remained blank.

Pasternak listened. Lyonya was still playing the piano.

In a deliberately singsong voice the poet recited lines he had written many years before: "When they play Brahms for me, I shall faint with anguish."

CHAPTER THREE

The Wrath of the People

1.

The Peredelkino railroad station had been built in czarist times, and since then it had been repaired and repainted over and over again. It was indistinguishable from all the other railroad stations around Moscow. The wooden platform was fairly long and wide and did not have an overhanging roof. The stationmaster's office and the waiting room, rudely constructed of pinewood, stood in the center of the platform. Adjacent to them was a "buffet," which was always filled with people drinking beer and surreptitiously lacing it with vodka, although this was prohibited by law. The station had been painted blue, but the color had faded and was washed away in spots. At the end of the platform, on the right as one faced the station, a dilapidated flight of wooden steps led down to a square of asphalt with a barrier separating it from the railway line, which ran toward Peredelkino in one direction and toward the village of Choboty in the other.

Two days had passed since Akimych's visit. It was windy, and toward evening clouds gathered and it started to rain. At times the rain was heavy, then it would die down. Three lights burned dimly on the platform; one globe was partly shattered (some boys had probably thrown a stone at it).

The railway police usually put in an appearance before the arrival of the train from Moscow or from Aprelovka. But at this hour the platform was almost empty. Two mangy stray dogs chased each other about, and a peasant woman stood near the buffet. As round as a ball, she was wearing a long belted khaki blouse covered by a homemade plastic cape.

Farther down the platform a couple was sitting on a bench with cast-iron legs. Pasternak had his arm around Olga, and they were sheltered from the rain by a large old-fashioned umbrella. Olga was a rather short, plump blonde, with hair hanging loose like a mermaid's. She looked no more than forty, and her Slavic features were striking, although slightly coarse. A hint of capriciousness played about her mouth, but her eyes had a warm, straightforward gaze. Her voice was throaty—rather similar to Zina's. She wore a fashionable foreign raincoat with a brightly colored scarf and had rubber overshoes with buckles on her feet.

Pasternak was wearing a shabby gray herringbone overcoat, a large black cap, and galoshes.

They were waiting for the train from Moscow.

"Want some sunflower seeds?" the peasant woman asked, approaching Pasternak and looking about cautiously.

"Hello, Agafya, what are you doing here?"

"Oh, it's you, Boris Leonidovich. Forgive me. I didn't recognize you." Either the peasant woman had really not noticed Pasternak or, seeing Olga with him, had decided to be diplomatically shortsighted. "A ruble a glass. That's a special price for you. A ruble and a half for everyone else."

"Pour them in here, in my pocket. Two glasses." The woman pulled a bag and a glass from her blouse and, after looking about again, filled Pasternak's pocket with seeds. He gave her a five-ruble note. "Buy your kids some chocolate with the change."

"Thank you, Boris Leonidovich, thank you for the kids. The police are always after us, handing out fines. They say we're a private sector. What kind of private sector are we, for Christ's sake?"

"Agafya, they're fighting capitalism in the consciousness of the masses. If I remember, your husband works at a factory in Vostryakovo. Am I right? And he makes just enough to keep you from starving. Which is why you're here, trading in seeds. To supplement the family income. But you just try telling your husband things should be like they were in czarist times. He'd put up a hell of a fight. 'I don't want to slave away for some millionaire factory owner,' he'd say. Nowadays factories belong to the state, which means they don't belong to anyone. No owners. Nowadays you can live with your head held high, even if it means tightening your belt. Right?"

"Yes, of course. The people's lot is a miserable one. But what harm is there in selling seeds?"

"Give you a free hand, Agafya," Pasternak went on, with an almost imperceptible smile, "and you'll start out with seeds. Then you'll open your own shop, and then you'll open a factory. Right?"

"What factory, for Christ's sake? I just want to get a coat for the eldest. She's got nothing to go to school in, only a knitted jacket." As if out of habit, the woman burst into tears, and rubbed her nose with her fist. Then she bowed to Pasternak—she hadn't given Olga a single glance—and moved off toward the waiting room.

Pasternak and Olga began shelling the seeds.

"The workers here adore you," Olga said, with a touch of bitter irony. "You're democratic and you talk to them as if they're your equals. You remember all their names and even their life histories. I know, I know, they'll stick in your memory for the next twenty-five years. My dead husband was a 'democrat' too—a 'populist,' you might say—but he was declared an 'enemy of the people' in 1937. No, he wouldn't give in; he hanged himself instead. What's the point of all these notions of equality and brotherhood, Borya? What's the point of the silly charade you just indulged in? We're intellectuals and they're workers. We're different. Instead of 'Proletariat of the world, unite!' our slogan should be 'Intelligentsia of the world, unite!' Borya, what do these dimwits understand about poetry? What do they need it for? All they need are drinking songs. They were raw material for Dostoyevsky, and that is as close as they've ever come to the world of art and culture."

"My God, Olga, you say such stupid things! These 'dimwits' are human beings like you and me."

"No, you're being hypocritical."

"Why do you say that? Because I gave a thought to Agafya and her husband and children? I, who chose to make Yury Zhivago, the son of one of the richest families in prerevolutionary Russia, the hero of my novel? Yes? Maybe I am a little hypocritical. But, Olga, you know, if I had to choose between condemning everyone to poverty or making some people rich and others poor, I'd choose universal poverty."

"That's stupid, stupid, stupid! You're like Prince Myshkin in Dostoyevsky's *The Idiot*. Stupid and quixotic. A parody of Christian virtue. Rich people have created all the best things in the world, Borya. They've made it civilized. Wealth makes it possible to found schools and universities, open theaters and museums, help poets. No, not in our country of course. In the West. Why does culture flourish there? Because the tone is set by the wealthy, people with position, with scope, with possibilities. Just think how many different cultural institutions exist in America only because millionaires support them. What's bad about that? Such people should be praised and not insulted! What hypocrisy! It's not that simple to be rich. You still have to work—and work hard."

"Stop it, Olga! I'm tired of this same old argument. We

have different opinions on this question. You know I believe that wealth causes envy among people and inevitably hatred."

"Now you'll tell me that Balzac and Dickens shared your opinions. But remember that both of them worshiped money. And wrote for money. You're Myshkin, Myshkin!"

"Myshkin and Don Quixote have always been my heroes."

"Myshkin and Don Quixote were idiots, absolute idiots. Their 'humanity' and 'honesty' were stupid weaknesses. Besides, Myshkin is one of the most farfetched characters in literature. I hope you'll agree with that."

"But, Olga, every *great* character in fiction has to be farfetched in a sense. The character must escape the bounds of the ordinary, the everyday, to become a generalization or symbol."

"Myshkin is a thesis. He lacks flesh and blood!"

"He embodies a dream about goodness. Every *great* character without exception personifies the writer's secret dream. I came across an English book not long ago. Its author is famous for adventure stories, but in this work, toward the end, quite unexpectedly he gets to the heart of things and starts to philosophize. His hero, Doctor Jekyll, takes a potion that transforms him from a kind and sympathetic man to a cruel and vile creature. He dies because he cannot control the evil within him. The author appears to be saying that there is both good and evil in the human race but evil is dominant. Isn't that a thesis? Yes, of course it is. A thesis or an idea. Altogether, the book is primitive, in my opinion. But in *The Idiot* Dostoyevsky proclaimed that good triumphs in man. Myshkin is a symbol of good."

"In *Doctor Zhivago* you said that evil triumphed."

"For the sake of good. Anyway, not only evil—"

"All the same, Myshkin drivels. He's so sugary sweet."

"You mean you prefer the images of 'icons and axes,' by which certain 'specialists' in the West define the Russian character?"

"Yes, the Russian is pious and a brute!"

"What nonsense! What's wrong with you, Olga? You've become so cruel."

Their conversation continued in the same vein, with Olga showing signs of irritation. She could not stop herself and even said things she did not really believe, just to contradict Pasternak. She felt like saying even nastier things to him, even though she knew that he now needed her sympathy and affection more than ever. Pasternak did not try to placate her. He was not in the habit of giving in on matters of principle, even when he was arguing with the woman he loved.

In the end Olga lost patience and abruptly, vehemently, changed the subject. "But why, why don't you cut this tangled knot? Right now, once and for all? Why don't you get rid of that hag? I know you hate her. Is it really impossible to get a divorce?"

She was obsessed by Zina, enraged that the other woman still laid claim to what belonged to her by right, even if the other woman was his lawful wife. To be loved was not enough. She was determined to become his wife, the legal wife of Boris Pasternak.

Pasternak pulled himself up slowly on the bench. Nearby they heard the wail of an injured dog, followed by the raucous yell of a man's voice. "Zina is my youth," he said. "She is the mother of my son, and I have given her so much pain." He frowned, then covered his eyes.

Olga was suddenly disarmed. She reproached herself for giving rein to her own concern, for forgetting what had happened to him during the past few days—and what lay in wait from the Writers' Union. What right had she to torment him with her demands?

"Forgive me, Borya," she whispered, lowering her head. "But you haven't been to see me for two days . . ."

Pasternak leaned toward her and kissed her cheek, on which two or three drops of rain had fallen. "Olga, don't forget," he said, "I'll soon be seventy. It's too late to start life afresh."

The low, drawn-out whistle of a train sounded in the distance. A railway police sergeant wearing a black greatcoat with a pistol on his belt appeared on the platform. A minute or two later, when the round railway clock standing nearby showed 7:35, the train approached the platform, its brakes screeching. *Moscow-Aprelovka* gleamed on the side of the first of six green metal cars, their windows spattered with rain. Heralded by the sound of compressed air escaping, the folding doors opened, and passengers began to clamber out of the cars—workers returning home and housewives coming back from a day's shopping in Moscow, their string bags stuffed with the variety of provisions available only in the capital. Most of them wore dark overcoats, which did not show the dirt, and rubber or rough leather boots.

They all moved toward the stairs at the end of the platform, while stray dogs fled from the rain of feet. A few people, mostly men, turned into the buffet before they reached the steps. Olga got up and searched the crowd.

"There he is!" she cried, catching sight of a familiar face.

A thin man of average height got out of the last carriage and moved toward her, swaying slightly, his right foot catching against his left. He wore a once smart but now threadbare velvet overcoat with the collar turned up, ankle boots with worn-down heels, and baggy trousers frayed around the cuffs. His head was bare and his face haggard, the sharply defined cheekbones emphasizing a red, swollen nose. Although probably about fifty, he seemed younger because of the twinkle in his eyes, which seemed to say, "Look at me, I'm a wonderfully drunk poet!"

"Olga, my enchantress! Light of my life! Let me kiss your hand." He spoke in a hoarse, feeble voice, stammering slightly.

"Good evening, Misha." Olga held out her hand, which he kissed in a graceful, amused manner.

"Boris Leonidovich, my respects," he continued. "We are slightly acquainted. That is, the poet Mikhail Markov has always loved the poet Boris Pasternak."

"How do you do, poet Markov." Pasternak grinned benevolently as they shook hands.

"You have abducted my enchantress, Boris Leonidovich. Olga will tell you—I've been in love with her since I was a boy. Since the Komsomol—"

"Misha, stop talking nonsense and sit down," Olga interrupted. "Why are you so late? Did the meeting at the Writers' Union drag on? We've already met two trains. I was afraid you weren't coming. Well, tell us. What happened?"

"For you I'll do everything at once. I'll sit down here, even though it's a bit damp. And I'll tell you all. How could I not come? How could Cyrano de Bergerac deceive his . . . oh, damn, I've forgotten her name . . ."

"Roxane," Pasternak prompted.

"That's it, Roxane. Anything of beauty just escapes my mind. The big freeze-up has set in for good. Actually, Boris Leonidovich, the poet in me disappeared long ago, together with the youth of Soviet power, in a single year, one might say. I ran dry. Yes, but once I sang fervently of our first five-year plans, of all the romanticism of socialist creation. And I meant it. At the time I was a poetic Cyclops—I had only one eye. Still, I managed to be a poet, and not a bad one. Remember how I sang of the last war against Hitler, when I was wounded in the stomach? I think I gave the whole bloody horror a certain glory. Who doesn't remember Mikhail Markov's poems from the front? I even glorified Stalin in them, goddammit! Yes, that's how it was. But then I lost my gift—my one eye went blind, so to speak. So now I write texts for documentary films to eke out some kind of living. It's all over with rhymes."

"Misha, how you run on," Olga reproached him. "You didn't by any chance drop into the restaurant at Kiev station and have a glass of vodka?"

"What do you mean? Of course I had a quick one, Olga, my beloved. In case you haven't heard, Boris Leonidovich, I'm an alcoholic. And I'm not ashamed to admit it. The poet Mikhail Markov—or rather, the former poet Mikhail Markov

114

—is a dedicated drinker. How can you stand this life without liquor? Tell me, Boris Leonidovich."

"I eat sunflower seeds instead," Pasternak said, smiling. "Do you want some?"

"Sunflower seeds? No, thank you. I've got some candy. 'Rocket carriers.' Do you want one? I suck them to cover the smell of vodka. I usually reek of it. Can you smell it now? Is it very offensive?"

"No, no, of course not, I can't smell a thing," Pasternak assured him.

"And just think, Boris Leonidovich, I don't smoke. I'm the only alcoholic I know who's a nonsmoker."

Markov pulled a bag of candy from his coat pocket and sat down on the bench. He took out a piece of candy, unwrapped it, and put it in his mouth. Then he unwrapped two more and tossed them to the stray dogs, who immediately swallowed them whole and took up positions a short distance away to beg for something else.

"Misha, stop stalling. What happened at the meeting of the Writers' Union?"

"At the Writers' Union? You mean in the temple of revolutionary literature? What happened was what *had* to happen. Was the poet Pasternak expelled from the Union of Soviet writers? Yes, he was—*unanimously.*"

"Which means you voted in favor of expulsion too?"

"Of course." Markov burst out laughing. "Future generations, no doubt, won't thank me for it. I was the one who shouted 'Down with narcissism!' And just imagine—my cry was taken up by the whole room. Now it'll become the slogan of a new campaign in poetry—antinarcissism. Funny, isn't it?" He fell silent.

The train pulled away toward Aprelovka. Again Pasternak heard the injured dog, followed by the yell of its master. Olga looked at him and then spoke sharply to Markov.

"There's nothing funny about it."

"What is absurd is always funny, Olga." And, resting his elbows on his knees, Markov lowered his voice and added seriously, "It is necessary for all this to reach the point of total absurdity."

"What do you mean?" Pasternak asked.

"Well, just take our corn czar with his corn renaissance and corn matzos for Soviet Jews. When it reaches total absurdity, it will all burst like a bubble. Salvation, my friends, lies in the absurd. Wasn't that the case with socialist emulation, and shock work, and compulsory political tasks, and social obligations, and wall newspapers, and the Komsomol café in Moscow? And last but not least, hasn't our dear 'socialist realism' finally become an absurdity? A creative method. The method of Maxim Gorky. The socialist reflection of reality. But what does it all mean in practice? Our creative method is the great art of *shortchanging* the reader. Do you go to grocery stores, Boris Leonidovich? Not often, I should think. Your maid does the shopping, right? But I look after myself. My wife deserted me long ago and went off with our son to her mother in Chelyabinsk. So I do the shopping. And I'm telling you—throughout the whole country the customer is *shortchanged*. It goes on right before everyone's eyes. For example, you pay for a hundred grams of butter—if you're lucky enough to find it in the stores—but you are weighed out ninety-two grams at the very most.

"And it's the same in everything. There's sleight of hand and cheating. In literature as well. The art of shortchanging, commonly known as 'social realism,' is our creative method. It's been canonized by scientific idiotism. I don't deny that shortchanging goes on all over the world, but here it is justified by the convenient notion of *party-mindedness*, which legitimizes tendentiousness and banality. Have you heard this joke: 'What is the difference between realism and socialist realism? The first is when a writer writes about what he sees, and the second is when he writes about what he hears.' "

"That's funny!" Olga exclaimed.

"It's not funny at all," Pasternak lamented. "It's sad because it really shows how far our Soviet writers are from what is genuine. The genuine creator puts himself, his own ideas

116

and feelings, his demands and fears, everything into the child that he creates. There's no room for short change. And the result is an undeniable prototype of the era, a unique reflection of the heart of life, its beauty *and* its tragedy, even in those instances when beauty and tragedy are stained with blood. The creative impulse cannot *be* suppressed. It's like the process of birth. Just try and stop a chicken from breaking out of its shell."

"It pops out if it hasn't already been gobbled up as a fried egg," Markov said laughingly. "That's yet another form of short change. Ah, Boris Leonidovich, you're an idealist, a saint, an incurable romantic. In some countries they take pride in their poets, but in ours, alas, they punch them in the face. I'm sorry but it seems that you're one of those destined to be punched in the face."

"Yes, with your help." Pasternak screwed up his eyes and called out effeminately, " 'Down with narcissism!' Like that?"

"Yes, just like that, Boris Leonidovich," Markov agreed. "I poured fat on the fire. That's my latest passion. I'm Lady Macbeth, setting fire to my own house. At least, I think that was what she intended to do."

"You talk such nonsense, Misha," Olga said.

Markov got up from the bench. "Oh, Olga, even when I play the fool I still have some sense. I know that someday the following words will be written about Boris Pasternak: 'He was a wonderful poet, and he was also the first in the land of communism to say out loud what Copernicus once said'—or was it Galileo? I can't remember which—' "All the same, it turns." He demonstrated that even if a writer lives in the land of communism he can still publish his works wherever he likes. Borders fall away. The poet Pasternak destroyed them in the minds of the Soviet people. He opened up the way to the world, to the universe. Before him, the way had been closed. Stalin had convinced the people that beyond the boundaries of the USSR the world was dark, filled with crocodiles, sharks, and other monstrosities.' "

"All right, Misha," Olga interrupted, "you've made your

point. But I'm tired of all this talk. Why are we standing here? Let's go to my place and have some tea and jam. The rain seems to have stopped."

On the way Markov told them exactly how Pasternak had been expelled from the Writers' Union that day.

"Imagine, my friends, our Moscow House of Writers. The cradle of Soviet prose, poetry, and dramaturgy, or, as I call it, 'the Muses' cradle.' The central auditorium was jammed. An execution certainly draws an enthusiastic crowd. Some of the more bestial Soviet Shakespeares and Voltaires were frothing at the mouth. In short, the members were packed together like sardines. Eight hundred literary sardines! The balconies were overflowing. People were even sitting on the stairs. On the wall was a gigantic portrait of the founder—Lenin. The presidium was glistening with the bald heads of tin soldiers, literary marshals, generals, and colonels. I'm only a lieutenant, demoted from major. Alongside them were perched the party regulars, the robots from the Central Committee. The restaurant adjoining the House of Writers—call it the 'Salvation of Souls' because so many of us have found illumination at its bar—was closed of course, on orders from the red Olympus. On such a historical occasion vodka would be dangerous. It's easier to deal with people who are sober. The first to mount the rostrum was that wormlike careerist Sergei Smirnov, a lousy prose writer and a Central Committee protégé. He blinked his white eyelashes, sniffed through his crooked nose, and began shouting: 'Pasternak did not sign the Stockholm proclamation of peace! He is a tool of the imperialists!' There were cries of 'Judas!' 'Renegade!' 'Parasite!' from the audience.

"Next that Jewish critic, that Marxist swine Zaslavsky mounted the rostrum. I've got nothing against Jews, but I despise those vipers who are determined to be more Marxist than Marx. He waved his arms about and bawled: 'Pasternak supported the French writer, the fascist Camus! He's decadent! He's a bourgeois apologist! He's a high-society Pierrot!'

and so on and so forth. There was a howl from the floor in response: 'Take away his dacha!' [Pasternak remembered Akimych's prediction.] 'Burn his furniture!' Then yet another Central Committee protégé, that fat hog Sofronov, a poet and dramatist without any discernible talent, just managed to climb up onto the rostrum. What a scrounger, what a little kulak he is! He hoards gold and uses his party card to live off the fat of the land. He built a dacha for himself here in Peredelkino and called it the 'Russian Tower.' Spraying gobs of saliva on all sides, he howled: 'Pasternak has not paid his member's dues to the Writers' Union for twenty-five years! He has not worked with the people! He has not joined an amateur dramatic or music society! He has refused to go on creative field trips! He has spoken out against the liberation of the Arab peoples!' At that point someone in the auditorium yelled, 'He's a Zionist, the swine!' And this was followed by 'Deprive him of his royalties!' 'Remove his books from libraries!' and finally, 'Take away his Soviet passport!' and 'Expel him from the Soviet Union.'

Pasternak smiled although he was close to tears. His face appeared drawn, and again he thought he heard the wail of the unhappy dog. He stopped and looked around.

"What's the matter, Borya? Do you think someone is following us?" Olga asked, squeezing Pasternak's hand in her plump, warm palm.

"That's incredible," he said quietly, whether out of tiredness or indifference. "They want to take away my Soviet passport. I don't think they've ever done that before."

It started to rain again. The drops of water running down Markov's face made his skin look strangely metallic and unreal. His ironic, almost Mephistophelian smile did not leave his lips. After putting another candy in his mouth and sucking it for a while, he continued his story.

"The short-story writer Ivan Broshka was sitting next to me. He presents a staunchly orthodox front, though they say he has portraits of Lenin, Trotsky—a recent acquisition—

Stalin, and Eisenhower in his apartment. He leaned toward me and said softly: 'Listen, Misha, this whole business is absurd. How can we expel Pasternak from the Writers' Union without having read his novel? It's indecent. After all, we are writers.' I replied: 'Stand up and say that out loud. You're clean. What have you got to be afraid of?' He nodded decisively, stood up, went to the rostrum, and howled, as if he were being knifed: 'The novel *Doctor Zhivago* slanders the Russian intelligentsia! It slanders the great October Revolution!' As it turned out, the witches' sabbath lasted all of three hours."

A car suddenly appeared from around a bend. The driver, who must have been drinking, misjudged the curve and went into a wild skid, coming dangerously close to a ditch by the side of the road. He finally managed to get the car under control, but not before it had covered the three walkers with a shower of water. None of them seemed indignant or even startled. Pasternak and Olga just clung more tightly to each other.

Markov continued with a malicious smile: "I must say I was amused at the reasons why these eight hundred sardines, these eight hundred 'engineers of human souls,' crowded into the 'Muses' cradle.' First, as I've already said, all of them were enthralled by the prospect of an execution. And second, they came because it had been announced that after Pasternak's expulsion from the Writers' Union there would be a screening of a foreign movie with that French star . . . Brigitte Bardot. I didn't stay for the film. But imagine this historic canvas: eight hundred bloodthirsty Shakespeares and Voltaires, after taking their revenge on a lyric poet, watching Brigitte shake her breasts around and run naked across the screen."

Olga meanwhile had begun to brood about what she had said to Pasternak at the station—all those careless remarks about rich people, about Myshkin and Don Quixote, and especially about Pasternak's hypocrisy. Walking at his side, she felt ashamed of the pain she had inflicted (although she had said only what she thought). Seeming to sense her regret, he stopped and kissed her on the lips.

Markov smarted and said in a hollow voice, "I started life as a foundling. No one ever loved me."

Pasternak looked at him.

" 'Russia, his incomparable mother,' " Olga recited from *Doctor Zhivago*, " 'famed far and wide, martyred, stubborn, extravagant, crazy, irresponsible, adored, Russia with her eternally splendid, disastrous and unpredictable gestures . . .' "

As he listened to her Pasternak remembered how this passage had formed in him with exceptional facility, of its own accord. He loved it because the simple combination of adjectives expressed everything he felt about Russia. While listening to the words he continued to look at Markov. The thought flashed through his mind that in speaking of Russia he had of course been thinking of people, and Markov here was one of them. He knew that Markov really did regard him highly both as a poet and as a man, that inwardly he was on his side, that he really did criticize Soviet power severely and justly. But at the same time he saw that Markov had a typically Russian trait—a passion for self-flagellation. Moreover, Markov was pleased that things were bad for Pasternak, because they were just as bad for himself, and in a way this made them equal. It was a case of misery loves company.

2.

"You're an atheist and I hate you!" Natasha stated emphatically.

"But don't you see, I can't believe in what doesn't exist. I was never made to read the Bible at home. Your crazy grandmother has put all this rubbish in your head," said Lyonya.

"Don't you dare insult my grandmother. Stop the car. I'm getting out."

"Nat, don't be silly!"

They were driving from the Byelorussian railway station

toward Tverskoy Boulevard in Lyonya's old Moskvich. It was midday and the autumn sun occasionally peeped through the clouds.

At nineteen, Natasha still had a tomboyish air. She was short and plump, with a slightly upturned nose, blue eyes, and thick reddish hair. She wore a light foreign-made coat, bought secondhand somewhere (Soviet sailors brought them back from Italy), and fashionably narrow shoes. A small gold cross hung around her neck.

Natasha believed in God, and on Sundays went secretly to the Yelokhov church, sometimes with her grandmother and sometimes alone. She lived with her grandmother in two rooms near the Dynamo subway station. Her parents had been in the Far East for five years, working on a construction site near Nakhodka Bay, and she saw them just once a year, when they came to Moscow for their vacation. Her grandmother was very devout and had brought Natasha up to share her religious faith. But granddaughter, unlike grandmother, also had a feeling for what was modern and contemporary in life. She was able to reconcile her belief in God with the teachings of the chemistry department of Moscow University.

Their studies had brought Natasha and Lyonya together, and they had fallen in love at first sight. Their only quarrels had to do with religion. Lyonya did not understand her belief in God, and Natasha often attacked his atheistic philosophy.

Lyonya, sitting at the wheel in a short brown coat (without a hat—he never wore anything on his head), talked calmly, not allowing his emotions to get out of hand.

"Natasha, please don't be angry. There's no place for God in my head. That's not your fault. Why can't you take me as I am? Am I really so bad?"

Natasha's anger relented. She spoke gently. "I'm not saying you're bad. You're good. But you're an atheist. And so we can never get married."

"What's God got to do with it? A family is one thing and God's another."

"No, it's all the same thing."

"Well, if that's the case, I don't see how you reconcile God with the Komsomol."

"The Komsomol is a different matter."

"That's no answer." Lyonya seized the initiative. "I still want to know how you can reconcile God, the Bible, and the All-Union Leninist Communist Union of Youth, of which you are a member."

"Oh, Lyonya, you never give an inch! How many times have I told you—I joined the Komsomol for the sake of my career. My father's not a minister, or a general, or even a party member. If I hadn't been in the Komsomol, it would have been impossible for me to get into the university."

"But tell me, when it comes right down to it, what if you're asked at a Komsomol meeting, 'Does God exist or not?' What would you say?"

" 'No,' of course."

"And what would the other members think about the gold cross around your neck?"

"When I'm in company I hide it. You know that."

"Oh, Nat, you're a chameleon."

"Yes. I guess I am when I'm at a meeting or in company, Lyonya. Haven't you gotten used to the fact that all of us have two faces—one for show at meetings and work, and the other for one's family and children? Here's what my grandmother says: 'Go to meetings and go to church. Shout your head off at meetings, but bless your soul in church.' "

"Your grandma's like King Solomon."

"She's cleverer," Natasha said with pride. "She says: 'The weakest go to the wall, but you can't live without God.' And that's true, Lyonya. Without God nothing has any meaning. Everything's pointless. You and I can't escape from the Soviet system, Lyonya; we can't go off and live on the moon. But the realm of the spirit, the realm of God, that's ours, and that—"

"God doesn't exist," Lyonya interrupted emphatically. "It's been demonstrated. Last week I met an American scientist, John Critchlaw, who's come to Moscow University for a year on an exchange program. He's a physicist. He told me that in the United States God and religion have been studied scientifically. And they've reached a firm conclusion: there is no God, there's only an illusion of God. It follows that all religion is based on self-deception. The myth no longer works. He said that it has been statistically proven that religion has one foot in the grave, that it's dying all over the world and that rational knowledge is winning. And they, the Americans, are masters at statistics. All in all, what he told me made sense—"

"He's a Communist, this Critchlaw of yours!" Natasha interrupted indignantly.

"Hold on! Don't be so narrow-minded! When he found out that I was the son of Boris Pasternak, the author of *Doctor Zhivago*, he embraced me and whispered in my ear: 'If your father needs to send anything to the West, I'm at his service.' And when I suggested that he emigrate from America to the USSR, because he was full of praise for our scientific centers, he said frankly, 'Alas, Russian socialism doesn't produce enough material comforts for me.' "

"Cretin!"

"Not at all. He's a normal person and a clever one. By the way, he doesn't understand a single thing in the Bible either, and he regards it as folklore or fairy tales. He doesn't take it seriously because it has no scientific value."

"Shut up! God will punish you for saying that."

"You're avoiding a straightforward and logical question: Where does the truth lie? In science or in the Bible?"

"Maybe it's in both."

"Who are you? A medical student or . . . a prim young nun?"

"How do I know who I am?" She began to cry. "I don't know anything."

"Natasha, my sweet, calm down. And don't forget, Eve was created from Adam's rib for his enjoyment. That's according to the Bible. And I think it's disgusting. You're a woman and you're just as much a person as I. I know it's hard for you. Your education, your grandma, an Old Believer, the devil—"

"Don't insult my grandmother."

"Well, stop crying, then. Stop crying or I'll crash into another car. I am the driver, after all."

He turned off Gorky Street onto Tverskoy Boulevard, but before he could proceed farther the engine suddenly died. He coasted downhill and turned into a service road where parking was permitted.

"What's happened now?" Natasha asked, dabbing at her eyes with a handkerchief.

"I don't know. The distributor head must have fallen off again."

Lyonya tried to start the engine several times but succeeded only in running the battery down. After that, putting on leather gloves, he got out, opened the hood and tinkered with the engine. Then he came back to the wheel, turned the key, and pressed the accelerator pedal again, but again without success.

"The distributor cap must have cracked," he said and took off his gloves. "I don't know how many times it's happened already. Everything in our country is so badly made. Now I'll have to spend a whole week looking for a new one. Just a small plastic thing, but you can't get one anywhere in the stores. I'll have to find one in some garage and pay ten times the normal price of course."

"You smell of gasoline."

"What does it matter? Pretend I'm a mechanic. Well, we won't make it to our lecture now. The trolley *crawls* along— it would take a good forty minutes, and the class would be half over. What shall we do?"

"Kiss," Natasha said teasingly.

"Kiss?"

Lyonya looked at her, then embraced her impetuously and began kissing her passionately.

"Lyonya, are you mad? Let go of me, let go of me. Stop

125

it, you stink." But a moment later, with a heavy sigh, she put her arms around his neck.

The only passerby who paid any attention to them was a bandy-legged old man. He tapped on the window with a bent finger and mumbled with his toothless mouth that in Moscow, and for that matter in all of the Soviet Union, kissing on the street or in a car was a violation of socialist morality and that if they didn't stop he would call the police. Neither Lyonya nor Natasha could hear him distinctly, but startled, they stopped kissing. Having 'introduced order,' the old man grinned complacently and went on his way.

"Okay," said Lyonya, "let's leave the car here. It'll be a couple of days before I get hold of a new distributor cap. Let's take the trolley to the university. We've got an hour and a half before the next lecture."

Lyonya locked the doors carefully and tried the handles, and they set off up Tverskoy Boulevard to Pushkin Square. They passed a baker's shop emitting a delicious smell of rye bread, a shoe repairer's, and a dry cleaner's, then found themselves outside a small dingy movie theater, News of the Day, where documentary pictures and newsreels were shown from morning till night.

The opportunity wasn't to be missed, and, after a moment's importuning, Lyonya led Natasha in. Withstanding the scrutiny of a no-nonsense woman ticket taker, they groped halfway down the aisle to two narrow wooden seats. There were three couples in front of them, another two to the left, three to the right, and one or two behind. Few of them were watching the screen. Lyonya and Natasha heard sighs, passionate whispers, unabashed kisses, groans, and shuffling feet. They looked at each other, smiled, and settled into their seats.

On the screen, blast furnaces, conveyor belts, and new tractors were shown in detail; the camera even went down into a mine to film the men working the coal. The commentator's velvety voice, praising love of country, spoke of the fulfillment and overfulfillment of production plans.

Suddenly a bearded man who had wandered in because he felt melancholy got up and said indignantly, "This isn't a movie house, it's a bordello!" And heading for the exit, he added, "Then they complain about alimony."

The mood in the auditorium changed when a newsreel showing the ceremonial session of the Komsomol Central Committee plenum flashed on the screen. Nikita Khrushchev and other party and government leaders were sitting at the presidium table in the famous Hall of Columns of the House of Unions. With his chin propped in his hands and his mouth slightly open, his shirt collar unbuttoned, and his tie askew, the chairman was listening to the report of the Komsomol "boss" Semichastny, a pale, bright-eyed forty-year-old, with deep furrows in his cheeks, who was waving his fist (in imitation of Khrushchev).

The commentator's voice announced: "At the ceremonial session of the Komsomol Central Committee plenum, its First Secretary, Comrade Semichastny, described the unworthy behavior of the poet Boris Pasternak."

Natasha extricated herself from Lyonya's embrace. "Did you hear that?"

Lyonya blinked confusedly, looked at her, and smoothed down her hair. "What?"

"He spoke about your father."

Lyonya raised his eyes to the screen.

Still waving his fist, Semichastny said: "It is well known that in every flock there is a black sheep. In our socialist society this sheep is Pasternak, with his slanderous work. He can't be called a swine, because a swine would never do what he has done. It would not foul the place where it eats and would not turn on the person who feeds it. Why doesn't this 'internal émigré' breathe the capitalist air he seems to regard so highly? Comrades, I am sure you'd all be glad to see the last of him. Let Pasternak emigrate and go to his capitalist paradise. I am sure that our society, our government, will not hold him back. On the contrary, his departure would purify the air . . ."

127

Then Lyonya saw Khrushchev in the foreground. The chairman scratched the back of his neck energetically, sat up in his chair, and yelled loudly in the direction of Semichastny, "Right! Good idea! I support it! More than that, I'll take him to the frontier myself, to Brest or wherever, and then I'll kick the swine in the pants and say: 'Get out! Go and join your imperialist friends!' "

The camera passed along the front rows of the delegates sitting in the Hall of Columns, who, simultaneously, as if on command, began applauding Khrushchev's outburst. Most of them were young people, well-dressed and well-fed representatives of the Komsomol elite.

The people in the theater burst out laughing, not at what Khrushchev was saying but at the speaker himself. Exclamations could be heard on all sides, loud ones, half-whispered, restrained, joking, frightened.

"Sanya, it's our Nikita! Our Khrushchev!"

"He scratches his head like a normal person, shouts, and waves his fist. Stalin wasn't like that. He was always twirling his mustache."

"What a clown."

"Ssh, you idiot. They'll throw you in prison if they hear you saying that. A guy at the station was carried off yesterday for saying something like that."

"Mmm. What we need, Katya, are leaders we don't have to pay any attention to. That would be a blessing. If they'd just leave us in peace."

"The devil take them all. Let's snuggle a bit."

Lyonya leaned over to Natasha. "I'm going to Peredelkino to see my father."

"Right now?"

"No, after class tomorrow."

"Yes, of course, you should be with him. And tell him that I"—she lowered her voice to a whisper—"that I'm an 'internal émigré' too."

Foreign correspondents were working day and night. They sat for hours in their Chevrolets, Citroëns, and Mercedes at the entrance to Pasternak's dacha, waiting for something dramatic to happen, trying to get inside, trying to interview him. They stopped everyone who went in or out, often asking the question: "Does Pasternak believe in God?" Then they dashed off to Moscow, where they searched out prominent Soviet writers, "liberals" and "conservatives," and asked their opinions about the author of *Doctor Zhivago*. They seized on the diatribes in the Moscow press and incorporated them in their dispatches.

By Soviet law all foreign correspondents had to present their articles to the censor of the Press Department of the USSR Ministry of Foreign Affairs. The censor went over them with a red pencil and then stamped them, authorizing their publication in the West. Although the reporters sometimes used illegal means, such as diplomatic pouches, to transmit information to their editors, they usually sent their dispatches from the Central Telegraph Office. The telephone center for foreign correspondents was located on the second floor. Telephones, teletype machines, and typewriters were set up in one large room; a smaller, adjoining room was used by an official of the Press Department of the Ministry of Foreign Affairs. He checked the censor's stamp and gave final permission for the transmission of material abroad.

Since the uproar about Pasternak had begun, the lights had burned late in these offices, and on the night after Semichastny's speech every telephone was in use. A babble of voices filled the room.

"Pasternak is faced with a choice: he must either refuse the Nobel Prize or emigrate from Russia. And why shouldn't he leave, in point of fact, since he's been given permission?"

"The statement by the Komsomol boss Semichastny is a

threat to Pasternak. Khrushchev has approved the idea of expelling the poet from the USSR."

"Pasternak has been accused of cynical individualism. The question arises: What is cynical individualism?" (The censor had probably been uneasy about this statement, but, after hesitating, gave up and left the sentence as it was.)

"Pasternak has been called an antipatriot. This is a dangerous sign."

"Semichastny compared the poet with a swine, in favor of the latter."

"Pasternak has been expelled unanimously from the Union of Soviet Writers, and today's speech by Semichastny is a further blow to the poet."

4.

Another day passed. Lyonya had not found a new distributor cap and so was on the train from Moscow to Peredelkino. Natasha had seen him off at Kiev station, and he had gotten in the third car from the front, where he always sat when he made this trip.

The familiar lights of the Moscow suburbs flashed by the train windows. Lyonya rested his elbows on the armrests and stretched his legs; the seats in front of him and next to him were both vacant. He held an open textbook on crystallography in his lap, but his thoughts wandered and his stomach rumbled, either from hunger or from the anxiety which had not left him since the previous day, when he had heard Semichastny's speech. The newsreel had shaken him. He hadn't believed that the fuss would go so far. His father's expulsion from the Writers' Union had been disturbing, but it had not amounted to a proposal that he emigrate from the USSR. Even now he could not fully grasp the significance of Semichastny's threat and his words "internal émigré." He did know, however, that the secretary's harsh and extreme speech had placed his father in jeopardy.

In the compartment facing the one in which Lyonya was sitting four railway workers, engineers who had come off duty, were "kicking the goat," that is, playing dominoes, on a plywood board balanced on their knees. Seated beyond them in the compartment was a quiet couple, the man tall and blond, in uniform, a junior lieutenant, an ordinary conscript, the woman small, snub-nosed and pregnant. Her head rested on the young lieutenant's shoulder. In an adjacent compartment an elderly man, pockmarked and lethargic, read *Pravda* while a thin woman of about forty, either his wife or a colleague at work, knitted a stocking.

A door banged shut on the platform between the cars.

Lyonya looked at his textbook, but his thoughts remained on his father. Semichastny's speech had made him realize with a pang how dear his father was to him.

Lyonya loved music, which carried him off to an imaginary world. But his understanding of literature was more intellectual, and when he had read *Doctor Zhivago* he had not been moved in any extraordinary way. Indeed, he had found the novel hard to read; there were moments when it bored and even irritated him. Lyonya told himself that he was still too young to comprehend his father's intention and the whole breadth of experience presented in the novel. But at the same time he felt that this was missing the point. Basically, on an important, perhaps fundamental issue, he did not agree with his father. Lyonya regarded himself as a member of the new, young generation that would shape twentieth-century Russia, while his father represented the old, disappearing order that was being swept away. Lyonya believed that his generation would transform the world through science; everything he believed in was subject to the universal power of knowledge. Outside this, he allowed room only for music, and now, perhaps, for Natasha (minus her God).

Lyonya was not emotional, like his father, having probably inherited his even disposition from his mother; he was able to control himself and to substitute rationality for emotion. Thus he was not temperamentally sympathetic to his father's hero, Yury Zhivago. In fact, he saw in Zhivago some of the traits he found irritating in his father—his refined air of detachment, his dreaminess, his poetic nature, and his indifference to material comforts. Yet despite their differences, Lyonya felt an indissoluble tie to his father. His love had been strained when he discovered Olga's existence. At first he had taken his mother's side, but he soon saw that in this sphere he could not and should not be a judge of his father and mother. His half brother Yevgeny had been overjoyed when he found out about Olga, saying that Zina was finally paying for having taken Pasternak from his first wife. Repelled by Yevgeny's malicious delight and by his mother's bitterness, Lyonya had adopted a neutral position. Overall, the rational side of him had won a victory over the emotional (which naturally angered his mother).

The main problem in his relations with his father had arisen almost imperceptibly and was a philosophical one. What, in fact, did his father reject and what did he support? Was he for individualism or for collectivism? Did he support the Soviet system or condemn it? What, for him, was the meaning of life? When he read *Doctor Zhivago*, Lyonya saw that his father, whether intentionally or not, had tried to shake the foundations of the new system and that the novel was an expression of grief over the loss of past values, especially those of Christianity. But Lyonya found it hard to understand his father's world, a world he had never known. He had been born in 1937, had studied in a Soviet school, and had played with children like himself. He had not been brought up in isolation from his environment, and he was therefore basically a product of the Soviet system.

Thus he did not feel the conflict between individualism and collectivism as sharply as his father did. Lyonya's intellect, with its inherent tendency toward logic, could not overlook unjust, stupid, and despicable actions. Nor had he escaped fear both in private and public, the compulsion to do what he did not want to do and the necessity to lie or pretend, to say one thing and think another. But the hardest blow inflicted on him by the Soviet system had been its refusal to admit him to the Bauman Higher Technical Institute, even though he had received top marks in his exams, because on his application form he had indicated he was a Jew. His father had written a letter to the Minister of Higher Education, but the rejection stood.

Anti-Semitism disturbed Lyonya's even temper whenever he encountered it, which was often enough despite the fact that it was officially condemned in the Soviet Union. All the same, he supported rather than opposed the new order. And he regarded his father as one of those impelled to reject rather than accept it. But there were notable exceptions, very typical of the times, when father and son had exchanged roles. Lyonya remembered how his father had called him a philistine because he had wanted, at any price, to buy some nylon shirts made in Czechoslovakia, and how he himself in his anger had shouted, "What an idiotic regime! People can't even get decent shirts."

In fact, Lyonya had been poisoned. Belief in the Soviet system and disbelief in it had been poured into the same bottle; then this strange, wonderful drug had been shaken up so the two were mixed together. This unique poison had been given to Lyonya and many, many others—perhaps to everyone, the whole population. In Lyonya, as in his father, there were many thorny contradictions.

As he tried to sort out his thoughts he became aware of the old man in the compartment opposite reading from *Pravda* aloud: " 'Hero of Socialist Labor, lathe operator from the "Paris Commune" factory, Comrade Kulagin, stated to our correspondent: "I don't know who this poet Pasternak is. I know and love the poet Vladimir Mayakovsky. But anyone who sells himself to Western imperialists, who neglects the interests of Soviet society, who spits on our socialist literature, is an enemy of mine. *Doctor Zhivago* is an insult to the

Soviet system. I fully support the proposal to expel the poet Pasternak from the motherland." ' "

The man wheezed and looked inquiringly at his woman companion. "Did you hear that?"

"Why are they so mad at him? What's Pasternak got to do with them?" she asked.

"We always go to extremes. If an order is given, everyone jumps out of his skin. We've bred lots of heroes."

"Aha, I see, Shurik. Only how did Pasternak make our government angry? What with? A book? What's it about, this book?"

"They say that he, this Pasternak, curses the October Revolution and the Civil War in his book, says they killed people for nothing."

"What does he mean, for nothing? Does he want the czar back? That's a laugh. Even my grandma, Stepanida, wouldn't go that far. This Pasternak is a fossil."

"Listen, here's another, an angry response. 'I, people's poet of Kalmykia, Darma Baly Tundurov, condemn the poet Pasternak for serving the imperialists of Wall Street in America, for cutting himself off from our great people, for not saying a single word in his poems about the wonderful Kalmuck people, for never having tried our wonderful Kalmuck koumiss . . .' " The man laughed. "What's koumiss got to do with it? He's stupid, this Baly-Baly. What an idiotic thing to say!"

"What *is* koumiss, Shurik?" the woman asked, still knitting.

"Horses' milk."

Lyonya smiled.

"But, Shurik," she said, "maybe he's a Jew."

"Who? Baly-Baly?"

"No, Pasternak."

Lyonya heard this as well, but at that moment his attention was distracted by a legless war veteran trundling through the car on a homemade cart pushed by a puny, sullen boy of about fourteen, perhaps the soldier's son, perhaps just a waif. Resting on the man's truncated legs was a forage cap for donations—or rather, for patronage, for the powerfully built, much decorated veteran played a clarinet and played it well, including Strauss waltzes and popular Soviet songs.

As soon as the medley was over, Lyonya put fifty kopecks in the hat—all that he had in his pocket—then moved into the compartment where the elderly man and his woman companion were sitting and, smiling awkwardly, said: "Yes, he's a Jew."

"Who is?" the man asked, looking at him with a suspicious frown.

"Pasternak," Lyonya replied.

"Aha, what did I tell you, Shurik?" The skinny woman seemed pleased.

"But how do you know, lad?" the man asked.

"I'm his son."

Two railway policemen, one freckled and fat, the other swarthy and broad-shouldered, entered the car. Each wore a pistol on the side of his greatcoat. Seeing the legless soldier, the freckled one sternly upbraided him: "What are you doing here again, Yevsei? How many times do I have to tell you, begging is prohibited. It's against the law. Is that clear?"

The soldier looked at him innocently, smiled, and said nothing.

The policeman raised his voice. "Listen, Yevsei, how many times do I have to tell you? It's forbidden to beg."

"I don't beg!" the veteran protested. "I work and get paid. I'm earning my wages. I work harder than you do."

"Let him be," the other policeman whispered, but the first refused to give in.

"Hold your tongue, Yevsei. Or I'll haul you off to the station and you can cool off there."

"What? Haul me off to the station? Damn your station. I don't give a damn!"

"It's against the law to beg!" the policeman repeated loudly. "And it's against the law to play the trumpet and disturb the peace."

"Go put your head down a Turk's pants, you smelly horse's ass!" the veteran shouted.

The passengers exchanged silent glances, condemning the policeman of course. Lyonya was sure that the scene had been played many times before and that it would end peacefully. But the legless soldier suddenly lost control of himself, jumped out of his cart, and, menacing the policeman, yelled at the top of his lungs: "You clumsy oaf, you scum, who do you think you're talking to? Where were you when the Germans came? When did you ever smell death? You sniveling bastard."

The policeman retreated. "I'm talking about the law, Yevsei, the law." And, observing that the train had stopped at Vostryakovo station, he obliged his companion and fled, accompanied by the jeers of the soldier.

"Throwing their weight around, the swine!" he spat after them.

At Vostryakovo a group of rowdy young factory workers—six boys and a girl—piled into the car. One youth played an accordion, while another, tall and thin as a bean pole, ineptly strummed a balalaika. A third, flat-faced and slightly tipsy, brooded sullenly over a cigarette. The girl held a large, freshly painted sign reading "Throw Judas out of our country!"

The ringleader of the gang, a clumsy brute with a hoarse voice, beat his hand on the armrest in time with the music until, not content with their own noise and chatter, he turned to the four engineers.

"Hey, brothers, quit playing your dominoes. We're going to Peredelkino to smash the windows in Pasternak's house."

"That'll shake him up," the bean pole added.

"Screw it. We'll burn the house!" the accordion player shouted.

The nearest of the engineers scowled, looked angrily at each youth in turn, and then asked the ringleader, "What right have you to set fire to anyone's house?" He leaned forward as if to rise.

"Don't get so excited, Pops," the ringleader exclaimed. "Nikita Khrushchev himself gave us the right!"

"Who is this Pasternak?" a second engineer asked.

"God knows," the girl replied. "A poet or something. But who gives a damn? The district Komsomol committee told us to go to Peredelkino."

"We've got the address and a plan of the house," the flat-faced boy added.

Lyonya felt as if he were losing his mind. His heart pounded with rage and fear and blood rushed to his temples. "Throw Judas out of our country!" How could it be? No longer knowing what he was doing or why, he jumped up from his seat.

"Who are you? Fascists?" He took a step toward the leader, who stared back with eyes blind with hatred.

"Stay away from me, you Yid!" He raised his fist automatically.

But before he could advance, the legless soldier vaulted onto the seat next to him and punched him in the face. The boy crumpled as the blood streamed from his nose.

The engineers stood up, ready for a fight, but, in the ensuing standoff, an ice cream vendor pushed a cart into their midst, shouting, "Eskimo-o-o! Ice cream! Eskimo-o-o!" And in the pandemonium that followed, the outnumbered youths used the confusion to cover a hasty retreat.

CHAPTER FOUR

Emigration?

1.

The next evening Lyonya sat at the dining room table with his father, Zina, Nina, and Rosalie, who was by now considered a member of the family. In front of each of them was a pile of letters, some of which, judging by the envelopes, had been sent from abroad, but most of which were from Moscow and other cities in the Soviet Union. Using scissors and kitchen knives, they opened the envelopes, then read through the letters and sorted them into piles according to their contents. In the middle of the floor were two open suitcases, one for congratulatory messages and the other for hostile ones.

With her glasses balanced on the tip of her nose, Nina was smoking and coughing. Zina was smoking too, and now and then she felt a lump in her throat. Lyonya worked like a machine, as did Rosalie, who read each letter intently, sometimes blushing, sometimes turning pale.

Pasternak, wearing a white shirt, tie, and his only new pair of trousers (he looked as if he were dressed for a concert), glanced through the letters and listened carefully to what was going on outside, in front of the dacha. He knew that foreign correspondents were sitting out there in their cars and that KGB agents were trying every possible method to drive them away. He knew that the muffled shouts of the crowd, the sounds of an accordion, the singing of popular songs, were all part of a deliberate plan directed against him. All of this was a "spontaneous" expression of what Fedin had called the "wrath of the people"—their rage against Pasternak, *Doctor Zhivago*, and the Nobel Prize. He tried not to react, but the noise of the crowd drummed through his head and was becoming unbearable. This was the second evening that the dacha had been under siege, and the harassment would probably go on until something dramatic changed the course of events.

Indisputably, the struggle had moved from mere words to action; it had entered its final stage, recalling the confrontation in which Doctor Stockmann, the hero of Ibsen's play, had found himself—except that in *An Enemy of the People* the masses had acted spontaneously, driven by ignorance and greed. Pasternak thought about Stockmann and brooded. There was a certain parallelism, he knew, a tendency toward spiritual isolation, aristocratism, snobbery. According to Ibsen, "I" could be right, while "we," the mass of people, could be mistaken. If this were true, what did it say about the idea of the majority—that is, the idea of democracy? Was the entire system of Western democracy based on a faulty premise? And was Fedin's assertion—that Pasternak was wrong because he was out of step with the people—just so much nonsense? It was convenient to think so, but Pasternak also had reason to believe it was true. It seemed to him quite likely that the majority was not always right, especially when their lower, herd instincts were being exploited, as now.

"Borya, here's one from America." Nina handed him the letter.

He read it with joy and vexation. "It's from John Steinbeck, a famous American writer. This is what he says: 'You're an eagle on a rock. Pay no attention to the mice swarming down below.' Oh, John, John . . ."

"I wonder if he'd be willing to change places with you," Nina said. She opened another letter, containing only a large, crudely drawn swastika.

"Lord, so many threats, so many filthy words," Zina sighed, and crushed her cigarette in the ashtray.

"Zinaida Nikolayevna." Rosalie tried to comfort her. "Don't forget that nearly all these letters were written by order of the district party committees. You know how it's done: people are summoned, and it's suggested to them that they put their signatures under texts that have already been written, or copy them out themselves. There's simply no way for them to refuse."

Pasternak turned to her. "Rosa, dear. You're right. It happened to me. When Stalin decided to get rid of his generals, he staged a trial and had them sentenced to death. On that occasion our 'best' Soviet writers supported the 'leader' and drew up a text for publication in *Pravda*. They sent it to me for my signature. But I refused, saying I was no judge of military commanders. However, the next day, when it appeared in *Pravda*, my signature was there. When I found the person responsible, a writer you wouldn't remember, called Stavsky, I told him, 'You've killed me!' But he said, 'No, we've saved you.' "

"Three to one, Papa," Lyonya declared after a silence.

"Three to one? You mean, bad to good?" Pasternak asked.

"Yes, bad to good," Lyonya replied.

Zina handed her husband a letter containing photographs. "This one seems to be in German."

Pasternak took it and glanced at the contents, then sud-

140

denly laughed. "The first sign of commercial initiative from the West. Frau Ludike, here, from Garmisch-Partenkirchen, wants to sell me her house. According to her, it's not expensive. All included, a hundred fifty thousand marks—West German of course. Two bathrooms. Two open fireplaces. Washing machine and dishwasher. A garden with flower beds. A garage for two Mercedes. She belongs to the Mercedes class, naturally, and so can't imagine having any other kind of car. And there's a stable too. 'If Herr Pasternak and his family ride, they'll be delighted.' I should think so. And why not . . . with millions of people in the world starving?" He passed the photographs around.

"It's an elegant house," Lyonya remarked, "and the garage is first class."

"Your dacha is better!" Nina assured him.

"They won't push us out of it now," Zina added.

"How simple it all is in the West," Pasternak said. "Buy and sell. Make a fortune in the process. Move from one country to another. As simple as that! Provided you've got money of course."

"A hundred fifty thousand marks. How much is that in rubles?" Lyonya inquired, not without interest.

"I don't know, son. I'm not an expert in foreign exchange. But it's probably a great deal of money. After all, I'm supposed to have a million dollars in Swiss bank accounts." He laughed.

"I'm sure you have, Borya," Nina said earnestly. "Maybe even more."

"The BBC reported that you've already collected more than a million, Papa."

"Only it's all inaccurate. Some people love to exaggerate. But in any case the money means nothing to me at all."

Pasternak got up, irritated, and began to straighten his father's paintings, an exercise that seemed to strengthen his courage. "There's no altering the facts," he said at length, returning to the table. "Semichastny, on Khrushchev's behalf, has proposed that I emigrate from Russia. So . . . ultimately a decision has to be made. It's pointless to put it off any longer. They won't give in. And it's stupid to turn into an ostrich and bury my head in the sand. In short, this must be decided. Now. Yes or no? Will we leave the Soviet Union? I put it to a family conference."

Rosalie started to leave but Pasternak restrained her.

"Zina, you're the mother of this family and you have the first say. Tell me your thoughts on this matter." Zina was silent. "Well?"

"I'm the mother of this family? Really?" She put aside the letter she was holding and lit a cigarette.

"Zina, what do you think about us emigrating from Russia?" Pasternak repeated the question sternly.

"Us emigrating? You mean *you*. . . . Well, you've already got a house . . . you won't have to roam around hotels." Zina spoke unhurriedly and without looking at her husband. "Where is it? In Bavaria? You studied at Marburg. Is that far from Frau Ludike's house?"

"Are you suggesting that we—"

"No, not *we*," Zina interrupted. "In my opinion, *you* must go to the West. You've earned respect and fame. You can live out your life in peace there. You'll be free from fear, humiliation, and persecution. There'll be no more lies and pretense."

"You said 'you must go to the West,' and you keep emphasizing 'you.' But we're talking about *us*—about *you*. Do *you* want to emigrate? Either we all leave here together, or—"

"No," Zina interrupted again, picking at the tablecloth with her fingernail and again refusing to look at her husband. "Lyonya and I will stay here, in Russia. We'll have to renounce you of course. Publicly. In the press. We'll be forced to do it, but it'll be an empty formality. You can explain this to people in the West. They're human; they'll understand and won't condemn us."

"You're saying that you want me to go alone?" Pasternak looked at his wife intently, but she did not respond. At

142

length he turned to Nina. "Fine. Now your opinion, Nina. Are you for or against emigration?"

She was confused, as if the question had caught her by surprise. "I don't know what to advise you, Borya . . ."

"But many of your fellow countrymen emigrated to France in 1921, after Georgia became Soviet. They preferred exile, a foreign country, to the Bolsheviks."

"A lot of Georgians did emigrate in 1921. But . . ." Nina sighed. "They emigrated, and then after a while they started dying of homesickness. They wore little bags of Georgian earth around their necks. Some of them couldn't stand it. They came back and gave themselves up."

"And then there was a new tragedy on top of the old," Pasternak said.

Tatyana entered with still another pile of letters. "Here, these are for you," she said. She put them down on the table. "The postman has just brought them on his bicycle. The event of the evening. Those desperadoes at the gate didn't touch him. It seems they've decided we can get mail. Oh, what masterminds we have in the Kremlin—fancy cooking up a plot against a writer! You'd think they'd have better things to do with themselves."

"But aren't you frightened of those masterminds, Tanya?" Lyonya asked ironically. "Aren't you shaking in your shoes?"

"Not in the least, young master. I've never given a damn about them."

Pasternak smiled, got up from his chair, and, putting his arm around Tatyana, asked, "And you, my dear, what do you say?"

"Say about what, Boris Leonidovich? I said I've never given a damn about those tyrants in the Kremlin."

"No, not about that. Tell me your opinion about whether we should leave Russia or not. It's their idea. And you and I might just take ourselves off to somewhere like Paris. Eh?"

Tatyana was outraged. "What do I want with your Paris? Do you know how people live there, Boris Leonidovich? I'll tell you how: a ruble a hat, soup without fat. Yes, and shoes that squeak, and kasha without butter. Oh, it makes me sick to hear all this idle chatter. You're just an old grumbler. Really and truly. You ought to be ashamed of yourself—you're not a child. If you keep going on like this I'll leave you. I'm sick of it. Sick to the back teeth. I'm in a rut here. Enough's enough!" And she went back to the kitchen, slamming the door behind her.

"Tatyana's against emigration. That's obvious," Pasternak said.

Lyonya laughed. "My nanny's a Russian—and proud of it. She thinks anyone who's not is. a savage."

"And you, son? What's on your mind?"

"Nothing, Papa. Do you really believe Semichastny and Khrushchev are sincere?"

"You mean you think all their ranting is intended simply to scare me?" A shadow of doubt ran across Pasternak's face and he looked at Lyonya intently, as if he were trying to understand not just the meaning of his words but also how and why this had occurred to his son when it had not occurred to him. Yes, it could all be a sadistic charade. Did he have any reason to believe that the Soviet leaders would play fair?

Deep in thought, Pasternak went over to the window, half opened the curtain and peered out into the dusk. Almost immediately he caught sight of two burning torches; someone was walking around with them on Pavlenko Drive. By the gate he could see a small crowd of perhaps twenty or thirty people, but no one had ventured through the gate into the yard of the dacha. Shouts could be heard, but the poet was unable to make out the words. Some people in the crowd held placards with slogans or cartoons on them. To the left were three cars and a small truck. A police whistle sounded somewhere, which meant the authorities were controlling the course of events. Suddenly the strains of an accordion were interrupted by two muffled shots, or perhaps it was the sound of a car backfiring. No, they were definitely shots; someone close to the dacha had fired a gun. Tobik and Bubik barked frantically.

"Why is Yury Mikhailovich wasting his cartridges again?" Zina mumbled. "He's found someone to frighten. The crowd?"

"The crowd, Mother. Otherwise some hooligan might ignore orders and try to break into the yard."

"He's just trying to keep us safe," Pasternak said, continuing to observe the activity on the drive.

"They won't try to set fire to the house?" Nina asked.

"No, I don't think so," Rosalie replied hurriedly. "The police wouldn't let them. After all, it's a state dacha, not a private one."

"In a situation like this it's good not to have anything of your own," Zina remarked, pursing her lips.

Pasternak closed the curtains, returned to the table, and sat down. "Dear Rosa, it's bad for you too now. You can't do much walking any more. It's like living in a beseiged fortress. What if they cut off the electricity or turn off the water supply?"

"The water wouldn't matter; we've got a well," Zina observed.

"Yes, and you know, Rosa, maybe they did have a purpose after all in sending you here." Pasternak frowned. "But let's forget about that. Tell me what you, Rosalie Naumovna Zaak, think about emigrating from Russia?"

Rosalie had been waiting for the question and had tried to prepare an answer, but she was still undecided whether to say everything she felt or only a part of it. "Honestly, frankly, absolutely everything?" She turned bright red.

"Of course—how could it be otherwise? Or are you afraid that . . . no, no, there aren't any microphones or tape recorders here, I hope." Pasternak smiled, openly and trustfully as usual.

"And this will remain between us, right?"

"Yes, yes, you can count on me, on all of us. Isn't that so, Zina?"

Zina did not reply. She was smoking. Nina was also smoking, and trying to stop coughing.

Rosalie began confidently nevertheless. "Boris Leonidovich, I was born in Moscow and studied in Usachevka, at the Medical Institute. I left there a doctor. I have a mother. My father was arrested in 1937 and . . . disappeared. I also have an aunt. She lives in . . . Israel. And now I'll tell you my secret. I would love to leave for Israel. It's a dream that I've had for a long time. When I was a child I noticed how people stared at me strangely. I recognized long ago that I was a Jew. A *Jew*. I was forced into recognizing this. And it's a good thing. I'm grateful to our Soviet anti-Semites for this. They force Jews to acknowledge that they are Jews and so arouse national feeling in us. They aroused it in me too. Of course they won't let me go to Israel. They'll say to me: Why Israel? Is it really that bad in the USSR? And what will I answer?

"I've never dared talk about this before. But now I've told you, Boris Leonidovich. It's the dream of my life. This dream and my love for poetry and the theater are what give my existence meaning. Work is just work. I'm talking about spiritual meaning. I'm far removed from all things Soviet. Inwardly, that is. On the outside we're all patriots. Yes, my native language is Russian, and that's the Soviet language, for good or ill. But in my soul . . . I'm a Jew, and I'm proud of it. I feel it in myself, in my blood. It's a special emotion, not like anything else. And I think that every Jew who feels this in him . . . every one should aspire to go to his homeland, to the land of his forefathers. Isn't that so?" She faltered and then lowered her head.

Pasternak was struck speechless. He stared helplessly at the young woman, with the limp and the mustache, and for the moment he entirely forgot his own misfortunes. He stood up and went to her and, taking her hand, said with unrestrained warmth and tenderness, "Rosa. My dear, good, marvelous Rosa, thank you for being so pure and gifted." He abruptly dropped to his knee. "I bow down before you. You're a human being. A great and wonderful human being."

146

2.

Yury Mikhailovich was standing in the yard not far from the dacha's gate. He was a strong man of about forty-five with a simple, kind face, his eyes calm and resolute. He wore a leather jerkin, high boots, and a cap with earflaps. In his right hand he held an old shotgun. Intently he watched the activity outside the gate. Tobik and Bubik, grown tired of barking, sat quietly by his feet.

The Komsomol activists were still holding their "meeting" on the drive. One of them had gathered dry leaves and sticks and had started a small fire. Boys and girls were whirling and dancing around it. Someone sang a sentimental song to the accompaniment of an accordion. Having hung around Pasternak's dacha for two or three hours, the young people seemed to have forgotten the purpose of their visit and were just having a good time. The organizers had also relaxed. Nevertheless the order to go back home had not yet arrived. The foreign cars, which had been in constant attendance, were beginning to leave.

Pasternak came out of the house in an overcoat and cap. Noticing the fire, he tugged at his nose and went over to Yury Mikhailovich.

"I like the smell of leaves burning. Don't you?"

"It's all right, nothing special. Where are you off to at this hour, Boris Leonidovich?"

"I feel like a stroll." Pasternak spoke self-consciously, knowing that Yury Mikhailovich had probably guessed where he was going.

"Is it worth the risk? Maybe you should wait until tomorrow. The ruffians are still having fun."

"What will you do, Yury Mikhailovich, if these 'ruffians,' as you call them, try to come into the yard?"

"What will I do? Very simple—I'll fire at them. Honestly. Not up in the air, but right at them. Yesterday, before it all started, I told them, 'You'll get in here over my dead body,

147

no other way.' I told them I worked for the poet Pasternak as a driver, stoker, and guard. I told them you pay me twelve hundred rubles a month. Other writers have offered me two thousand rubles, but I'd rather have the twelve hundred. And I told them, the ruffians, that in addition I'm a candidate member of the Communist Party. I also told them I was guarding the house in which *Lenin* lives."

"That's going a bit far, my friend. The parallel is rather farfetched, you know."

"I'm talking about honesty. Lenin was honest. And you're honest. Anyway, it's better to exaggerate than underplay things with these thugs. I know their kind, Boris Leonidovich."

"Mmm . . . Are the police still on duty outside the gate?"

"Yes, they're still hanging around. They're no better than the hooligans they're supposed to be watching."

Pasternak was silent for a moment, then he went off toward the back of the dacha. Having climbed over the slanting fence that separated his dacha from that of Vsevolod Ivanov, he cut to one side, emerging on the path that led into the gully and then uphill to the dam.

Looking after him, Yury Mikhailovich shook his head in disapproval and said to himself softly, "Gone to *her* again . . ." He did not like Olga and was on Zina's side.

3.

Fedin was lying on his sofa, wrapped in a tartan blanket, his head buried in a red pillow, trying to escape the noise on Pavlenko Drive. He did not wish to hear any of it. He wanted peace and quiet.

He wanted to stop thinking about Pasternak and all the unpleasantness of the last few days. The threat to expel the poet from the USSR, announced publicly by Semichastny, had dumbfounded him; he thought it was excessively cruel and even barbarous. He was convinced that for Pasternak exile would mean death and that he would therefore not agree to leave Russia. But Fedin was afraid that the Soviet government and Khrushchev would not stop with threats. No, they would not arrest Pasternak or put him in prison; it was simply no longer possible (world opinion had already been stirred up), but they might decide to organize something in the nature of a "lynching." An "infuriated" crowd might burst into the poet's house and break his skull. Then the papers would write about "the people's wrath," the very thing he himself had warned Pasternak about. But while Fedin had talked in vague generalities, what was going on now was all too real. Fedin was afraid that Pasternak's stubbornness (a quality that he secretly envied) would lead him into terrible danger. Fedin feared the very worst—murder. He remembered the Jewish artist Mikhoels, who had been run over and killed on a Minsk street. It was now officially admitted that this "accident" had been carried out on the direct orders of Stalin. And hadn't there been several such murders in the past? What about the murder of Trotsky in Mexico? And why should it be thought that Khrushchev totally rejected the past? Wasn't political murder regarded as a necessary, if extreme, part of the revolutionary struggle?

But what could he do? Write to Khrushchev or Suslov, saying that poets shouldn't be murdered, even if they were ideologically mistaken? The very idea was ludicrous.

Someone touched his arm. He shuddered and jumped up as if he had been stung. His grandson Nikita was standing in front of him, looking concerned, perhaps even pitying.

"Come and have tea. Mama's calling."

"What? Tea? Oh, yes . . ." Fedin smoothed his hair, rubbed his eyes, forced himself to smile. "Well, if it's teatime, let's go and drink some tea."

4.

Pasternak walked briskly along the narrow path leading down into the gully. A wooden bridge without handrails, put up about half a century before, stretched across the dry stream bed. On the right, through a leafy thicket, the lights of a workers' township glimmered in the distance. The sky was velvet black and the stars shone brightly. He was always amazed at how clear and near they seemed in the fall. Walking on, he found himself alone again with nature and realized that he was painfully attached to it. Everything around him attracted his attention and was enhanced by his imagination. He felt particularly sharply that he had come out of nature and would return into it, into this root here, this leaf, this birch tree, this firmament of stars. Often when he was in a forest he cupped his hands around his mouth and called, "I! I! I!" And the forest gently echoed, "I! I! I!" This "I," no longer just Pasternak's but also the forest's, seemed to him to symbolize the essential unity of his soul with that of nature.

Nature gave him solace. In difficult times he would pour out his thoughts to the trees and bushes, the squirrels leaping from cone to cone, to streams, or at nighttime to the stars, choosing the brightest as a confidant. He liked talking to the stars; he felt that each one seemed to say to him: "Talk to me. I'm bored. I want to express myself. People are callous and are only interested in me during the hours of love play, but I have millions of years of experience behind me. I have a story to tell."

As he walked he felt released. His face was freshened by the dew, and the evening air cooled his mind. He felt all around him the invincible universe of the eternal world spirit. No dictator or tyrannical regime had ever been able to get the better of this creative force. Poets and lovers had always been in harmony with it. And so too were holy fools, of whom there were few in heaven or on earth.

Pasternak suddenly thought: What makes Peredelkino so important to me? This gully and dried-up stream with its wooden bridge could be somewhere in Bavaria. And don't birch trees like these grow in France? He shivered. Why was one so attached to one's homeland? Was man, for all his intelligence and sensitivity, driven by the same force that made fish fight their way upstream to their ancestral breeding places? But the Jews, scattered all over the world by history, had managed to retain their national identity. Was it really necessary to remain attached to a single spot on the globe, to the place where you were born, where you lived with your father and mother, where you loved and were happy? Wasn't the human spirit wider and all-embracing? Didn't these stars in the sky shine as brightly in the West as they did here?

Pasternak remembered a friend of his father's, a Jew called Levitan, who was a very talented landscape painter. Although he suffered from the anti-Semitism that was rampant in Russia before the October Revolution, the painter was Russian through and through. His passionate attachment to the land of his birth sustained him. Pasternak then thought: But what about my father? Born a Jew, he was also filled to overflowing with the Russian spirit. Why had he emigrated to the West and died in chilly England?

Which was more important, he asked himself, freedom or one's motherland? He had begun to think that there was no simple answer. His very existence seemed to be threatened. If he chose Russia rather than freedom, he would perish, just as he would if he found freedom but was deprived of his native land.

While dwelling on this, Pasternak heard someone walking behind him. He was not frightened; carried away by his thoughts and feelings, he had escaped from everyday cares. Nevertheless he stopped and turned.

"Who's there?"

"It's me, Papa."

Lyonya had been running and he was panting.

"Has something happened at home?"

"No. Mama told me to come with you. Don't worry, I won't get in the way."

"Your mother was probably afraid I'd be attacked by those thugs."

"Probably."

They walked together, side by side, in silence. Then the

path became narrower and they walked in single file, father in front and son behind. On the left was a small pond. A fir tree struck by lightning the previous year lay next to it, its branches already grown into the earth, perhaps starting a second life. Pasternak had quickened his pace, but now he stopped and sat down on a tree stump covered with moss.

"Lyonya, if the opportunity to leave the country were real and without danger, would you take it?"

"Maybe, but there's only one place I'd want to go—Africa."

"Why Africa?"

"I've always wanted to be a big-game hunter."

Pasternak smiled at his son's impetuousness.

"Papa, I want to have a talk with you."

"Fine. What's on your mind?"

"I don't know how to begin. I want to talk about the most important things in life. I've been waiting for the right moment for a long time but . . . I'd rather begin with a few questions. Is that all right?"

"Of course. Go ahead," his father said. He assumed that Lyonya's first question would concern Olga, and he prepared himself to be completely frank.

"Papa, tell me what made you write *Doctor Zhivago*?"

Pasternak was startled and took a deep breath before answering. They had talked about this subject before, although not since the Nobel Prize had thrown them all into such chaos. Pasternak now detected a new note of urgency in his son's voice.

"Lyonya, it's very difficult to say why an artist is compelled to create a certain work. As I've already explained to you, my novel had its beginnings in the dim recollections of my youth. I started with these memories and then I followed my inspiration—"

"Inspiration?" Lyonya laughed ironically. "Inspiration might give you a poem, but it's not quite enough for a novel. A novel demands a plan, a clear idea."

"Some novels certainly do, but I wrote *Zhivago* the same way I write poetry."

"Without thinking about what you are for and what you're against?"

"Well, almost . . ."

Lyonya felt that his father had not admitted the truth to him, perhaps had not admitted it even to himself. His father seemed determined to ignore the social and historical judgments he himself had found so obvious when he read *Doctor Zhivago*. He pressed him. "All the same, didn't you express your attitude to the Soviet system in *Doctor Zhivago*?"

Pasternak smiled. His son still saw the world in blacks and whites, whereas he himself instinctively tried to avoid defining his political philosophy. "Nina once told me an amusing story. There was an old revolutionary in Georgia, a famous Bolshevik called Mikha Tskhakaya—I met him once, by the way, he was a very nice person. After the formation of the Soviet government he telephoned his wife in Paris. She was an actress and was staying with a rich sister in France. Mikha, without even saying hello, yelled into the phone: 'Lelechka, if you're for the Soviet system, come back. If you're against, stay there.' "

"I'm not interested in Lelechka but in you, Papa," Lyonya said.

Pasternak hesitated and then said quietly, "Lyonya, I am against the Soviet system because it is *inhuman*."

Lyonya dropped into a squatting position; after all the prevarication, his father's direct answer, at long last, pleased him precisely because it was direct. "That means you're against Marxism too?"

Pasternak wanted to smile again but restrained himself. His son's intensity touched him, and he saw how important the conversation was to him. Like most sons, Lyonya had grown away from his father, and Pasternak sensed that this evening was a turning point. If he opened himself, they might find a new closeness; if he turned away, they might gradually become strangers. Pasternak wanted to leave more of himself in Lyonya, or rather more of what was dear to him. Lyonya had to be won over from the "epoch," seized from the influence of the present. But how could this be done in a single conversation? And wasn't it already too late?

Pasternak realized that he faced the eternal dilemma between fathers and sons: how does the past talk to the present? His son had caught him unawares, at the most difficult time of his life. But their conversation perhaps was more important than *Doctor Zhivago*, the Nobel Prize, even emigration from Russia. Tonight could determine Lyonya's future.

Pasternak resolved to join the battle, armed only with the truth as he saw it. "In my opinion, Lyonya," he began, "Marxism long ago became a worn-out phonograph record, a cliché. But don't misunderstand me, Lyonya; I don't reject Marxism in favor of capitalism and philistinism. I'm against monopolism in any form, including monopolism of ideas. Lenin was the first real monopolist of thought."

He paused, questioning his last statement. For wasn't Christ also a monopolist of thought? Doesn't the great Christian ideal of brotherhood and equality monopolize, that is, a single thought? Was dissidence allowed, say, in the Bible? Ultimately, wasn't God a monopolist of thought?

Lyonya seemed to perceive his father's thoughts.

"Do you believe in God?" he asked.

"I wrote about that in *Doctor Zhivago*, son."

"You wrote a lot about Christianity, but—"

"Wait." Pasternak interrupted him. "Let me ask you a question. Do you believe in God?"

"Crystals are my god, Papa."

"That's a dead god, a god without a soul."

"You admit the possibility that a live god exists?"

"Lyonya, everything that's alive embodies God. You, I, our passions, judgments, labor, our joys and sorrows . . ."

"That sounds wonderful, but it's impossible to understand what it really means."

Lyonya had urged his father on, and now Pasternak felt hurt, particularly as he was not just mouthing high-flown words. He was sensitive on this point because he had often

154

been accused of favoring eloquence over sophisticated thought. But tonight he believed he was speaking clearly, from the heart.

"The legend of Christ did not arise accidentally," he said, expanding on his thought. "Christ, a simple man in rags, fitted easily into everyday life and yet he became perhaps the most important figure in history. I'll leave aside that some people took him for the son of God and others for an imposter. The most important thing about Christ for me, Lyonya, is that he wanted to bring man closer to spirituality, to a higher life, by lighting up his petty world with goodness and love."

It was Lyonya's turn to interrupt. "You talk about Christ and spirituality, but in my view the very idea of God is a total denial of God as a supernatural authority—and yet he can't be anything else."

"Why's that? Why is he a denial of himself?"

Lyonya got up and began walking to and fro along the planking. "You see, Papa, eternity is certain movement. You won't disagree with that, I hope. It means matter constantly changes, and this process is inevitably measured by time. And this vastness, called time, is a denial of God, because he, God, is an obstacle to time. God is static, he can't be measured, he's outside time—in short, he's a foreign body in the sphere of infinite metamorphoses. He's a brake on the whole structure. God lacks inner development. As far as I can understand, he's arbitrary. He is something completely outside the system of scientific perception of the world, which is part of our age. My brain . . . demands continuity in everything. Without continuity life is unthinkable."

Pasternak frowned, then looked at Lyonya almost coldly. "There was a time when I was carried away by philosophizing," he said quietly. "I was studying in Germany, under Professor Cohen . . . but when I was your age I wasn't as opinionated as you are."

"Don't you understand, Dad, there has to be something

after God, beyond God, higher than him or before him. There has to be a god who created God, who in turn was created by another, and so on."

"A chain of gods?" Pasternak smiled ironically.

"Like the system of cells in our organism."

"Dostoyevsky said through the mouth of his Kirillov, 'God does not exist but he ought to.' Ought to. That's why it seems to me the hardest death is the death of an atheist. To die with what thought? With what? If nothing exists. If there is just darkness and emptiness, which you measure, all the same, by time, why bother to measure them? For whose sake? You deny the human spirit, Lyonya, the spirit . . ."

Lyonya refused to back down. "The idea of heaven is just a sop for old women."

Pasternak hesitated, then smiled with sudden warmth. Lyonya had changed, discovered his talent, learned to cope, judiciously, seriously. He stood up and went to Lyonya and put his hand on his shoulder. "You've grown up, son. And I hadn't noticed it. You've become clever. Thought plays in you as it did in Socrates."

"That's irrelevant, Papa." Lyonya spoke as if to an equal. "We consigned Socrates to the archives long ago. He said that he knew that he didn't know anything. Science today is fired, not by the names of individual scientists but by a whole complex of knowledge."

"Yes, yes, all that's changed as well. You've got me cornered. Disarmed me on all fronts. Ah, Lyonya, you're a hopeless materialist. Your whole generation is hopelessly materialistic. And that's a catastrophe, because a materialistic philosophy is as one-sided as an idealistic one. It's the eternal argument. Spirit and matter. There is both harmony and antagonism between them. Your intellect, son, demands an exact answer, an unqualified answer. But doesn't it seem to you that everything exact only lengthens and, maybe, even destroys the path to the truth?"

"I'm sorry, Papa, but I think you're being vague and poetic again. It seems obvious to me that the phenomena of life, both material and spiritual, can be understood only through logical knowledge."

"But what about the heart? Where's the language of the heart, son, where's love?"

"What's love got to do with it?"

"Love? In the Bible it's described beautifully. I remember the passage by heart. Listen. 'Love suffereth long, and is kind; love envieth not; love vaunteth not itself, is not puffed up, doth not behave itself unseemly, seeketh not her own, is not easily provoked, thinketh no evil; rejoiceth not in iniquity, but rejoiceth in the truth; beareth all things, believeth all things, hopeth all things, endureth all things. Love never faileth: but whether there be prophecies, they shall fail; whether there be tongues, they shall cease; whether there be knowledge, it shall vanish away.' "

"That's nonsense. Knowledge will never vanish. Anyway, what kind of love are you talking about? Love for Tobik? For the moon? For a woman?"

"For everything. Christian love is limitless. And I'm talking about love for a woman. Yes, my dear Socrates, for a woman too. Love turns us into romantics; when we feel love we become blessed creatures unfettered by logic, by the logical 'how' and 'why,' freed from the captivity of worldly calculation, advantage, and the most terrible thing of all—total egoism, egoism that destroys us. Love is like a fragrant breeze from heaven, Lyonya."

"That's a fantasy, you know. A fragrant breeze. Does heaven really have a scent?" Lyonya smiled condescendingly. "Oh, Papa, you're a poet through and through, even if you transcended the poet in yourself in *Doctor Zhivago*."

"But, Lyonya, haven't you lived in the worlds of music and poetry since childhood? Don't they contain a lot of love?"

"I don't know . . . perhaps . . . but science demands—"

"Science is a disaster when it *demands*!" Pasternak broke in. "It's a disaster when you make it an absolute, which is what you're doing. Then there is no humanity in it, a quality all of us need if we're not just to be freaks, cattle, scoundrels, and sluggards."

Lyonya interrupted him. "You're not explaining anything, Papa. You quote the Bible and you express hackneyed ideas in a pretty but incomprehensible way. Humanity and love are outside logic."

"Forget about logic!" Pasternak exclaimed. "The most important ideas aren't contained in logic. Study crystals—they're intriguing and probably have a significant role in our world system—but don't give up music, don't stop reading literature and going to the theater. If religion is going into a decline today, then literature can and must take its place. People need literature and art more than bread and water. They are the wellsprings of profound wisdom."

"Everything you have just said, Papa, is arbitrary and disputable. You turn literature and art into objects of worship. I don't deny the necessity of either of them, but science plays the decisive role in twentieth-century life. That, for me, is indisputable."

"Let us assume that what I have just said *is* arbitrary and disputable. But I'm not a machine, Lyonya. And I'm not logical. Everything human in me is opposed to logic."

"But we *are* machines, Papa. We're very complicated machines."

"Good or evil ones?"

"You want machines to be good?"

"People are good. Good is within us, Lyonya. It's given us by nature. Like sight and smell. You just have to nourish it within yourself."

"Are you good?" Lyonya asked.

"Me? Not always . . . not in everything . . ."

"Papa, you often put money in your coat pockets, as well as candy, cookies, and all sorts of other goodies, and set off for a walk to the village of Choboty. The poor kids from the collective farm surround you as if you were Santa Claus. Then you give them all treats. Grown-ups, mainly the very old women, get ruble and three-ruble notes shoved in their hands."

"Is that bad?"

"Is it a manifestation of good, in your opinion? You think it's a way out of the situation because it corresponds to Christian precepts about charity. But don't you think, Papa, that contemporary society, with its enormous scientific achievements, is capable of organizing our life so that there will no longer be any need for you to go to Choboty and hand out candy to the children?"

"Do you . . . suppose it's possible?"

After a moment's silence father and son began walking again. The path rose steeply to meet the road from Peredelkino to the Minsk highway. At the junction Pasternak stopped to catch his breath. Then he spoke serenely.

"You know, son, there's a poem of mine whose first line reads something like this: 'Logic? It's like the moon for the lunatic. We're friends, but I'm not its vessel . . .' " Then he added: "Thanks for walking with me. And for the conversation. Watch your step on the way home."

"Don't you want me to wait for you here?"

"What for?"

"For Mama's peace of mind. Please don't think I'm . . . on her side. I'm not on anyone's side. You've got your own life and no one has the right to interfere with it. Even your son. I don't blame you for anything, Papa, believe me. I'm not a saint either. But, Papa, I want to say that despite all our disagreements, I'm . . . proud of you. I'm proud that you dared to write what you wanted to write. And I'm proud you're the first Russian writer to be awarded the Nobel Prize —if you don't count the émigré Bunin."

"Thank you," Pasternak said.

Lyonya approached him and kissed him on the cheek; he could not remember the last time he had done it.

"Thanks," Pasternak repeated quietly.

"And I also want to tell you that—" Lyonya broke into a

smile that made him look surprisingly like his father, an embarrassed smile, somewhat childlike.

"What, son?"

"Well, Papa, I'm . . . I'm in love."

Pasternak was delighted that Lyonya had finally taken him into his confidence. "Really? But that's wonderful. Congratulations. It's about time. At your age I'd already had my heart broken three times."

"Actually, Papa, we've been seeing each other for a few months, but now . . . now I feel that I really love her. There's only one thing I can't seem to straighten out between us . . . she believes in God."

Pasternak beamed. "How old is she?"

"Nineteen."

"That's wonderful. And most remarkable. What's her name, Lyonya?"

"Natasha."

"What a marvelous name!" Lyonya seemed to him to grow younger, as if some boyish innocence had been restored to him. Pasternak embraced him, filled with joy and a sense of promise. He was close to tears. He said, "Well, when are you going to introduce us?"

5.

The corner of the old log house loomed. Its roof was dilapidated, but there were decorative carvings above the windows and at one time the house had probably looked snug and sturdy. Masha's husband, a railway switchman, had inherited from his father the skill of wielding an axe and had built the house himself in the twenties. Five years ago he had been killed in a drunken brawl, hit on the head with a brick, and now Masha was alone, having lost her only son, Gavril, at the battle of Stalingrad. A withered, hunchbacked old lady, with a wrinkled face like a dried apple, she was pious and tenderhearted. She lived on the "sparrow's" pension that the

160

government paid to aged widows, and occasionally she made some extra money by renting two rooms to Moscow writers, who liked to spend the summer in the country. It was these two rooms that Olga had rented for three hundred rubles a month when she had moved to Peredelkino to be close to Pasternak.

The furniture in the rooms was old-fashioned: a high iron bedstead with three pillows piled one on top of another, a squat painted chest of drawers, a decrepit wardrobe whose door squeaked, a square kitchen table, used for eating and working, and embroidered homespun curtains. The walls were dotted with colorful pictures cut out of the journal *Ogonyok*. The first thing one noticed on entering was an icon with a candle burning under it; it had been put up so long ago it seemed to have become part of the wall.

Olga had made herself at home. She had brought some things with her, among them a good Persian carpet, a table lamp with a green shade, a typewriter. A large framed photograph of Pasternak hung on the bedroom wall. At the moment she sat in the other room at the table, using the old Singer sewing machine that belonged to Masha. She wore a housecoat, and her hair hung loose down her back; she sang to herself and kept glancing at the grandfather clock in the corner. Pasternak had promised to come at nine, but he was sometimes late. No matter. Ever since it had become clear that he might have to emigrate, Olga had been in a state of nervous excitement, elated by the possibility that *at last* she might be able to live openly with her lover in the West.

Her eyes sparkled as her fingers moved skillfully. She loved to sew, to make clothes for herself, her mother, and her daughter. Sewing, in fact, gave her as much pleasure as writing poetry and doing translations.

When the clock struck the half hour Olga got up from the table, went over to the window and lifted the curtain. A moment later Pasternak came in.

"Borya, my dearest, at last . . . Why are you so late?" She embraced him and kissed him. "I was so worried I was counting the minutes, what with those villains camped out around your dacha. . . . Take off your coat."

She helped him off with his coat and hung it on the wall by the entrance, where a few nails had been hammered in for the purpose. He sat down, and she took a place at his feet, gazing up at him lovingly.

"Tonight they were even wandering about with flaming torches. Romantic and effective," Pasternak said with a smile. "And they built themselves a campfire from dead leaves."

"They're getting bored. The idiots!"

"But they let the postman in with a pile of disgusting letters. Without any fuss."

Olga stood up. "Ah, Borya, it's all nonsense. You know the motive behind it. You're not bothered by that crowd, are you?"

Pasternak rubbed his forehead. "Olga, I've already had one heart attack because of them."

"My knight!" she exclaimed.

"I don't want to have another one, my princess."

"Don't be stupid! You don't know your own strength. You're spiritually strong, and that's the main thing. You don't know yourself, Borya. I'm the only one who knows you."

"Yes, it's true." He smiled. "What are you making?" He nodded toward the sewing machine, where she had left a piece of velvet.

"It's a secret. I'll show it to you when I've finished. In the meantime . . ." She took a candle from the chest, lit it and put it in a glass. Then she switched off the electric light and said, "That's better," and added softly, " 'The candle on the table burned, the candle burned.' "

" 'The candle on the table burned, the candle burned,' " Pasternak repeated.

Olga went over to him and clasped his head against her breast. " 'As they drove through Kamerger Street,' " she recited from *Doctor Zhivago*, " 'Yury noticed that a candle had melted a patch in the icy crust on one of the windows. Its

162

light seemed to fall into the street as deliberately as a glance, as if the flame were keeping a watch on the passing carriages and waiting for someone. "The candle on the table burned, the candle burned," he whispered to himself—the confused, formless beginning of a poem; he hoped that it would take shape of itself . . .' "

" 'But nothing more came to him.' " Pasternak finished the sentence.

"It did come! It did!" Olga clung to him. "The poem is you and me, Borya. You and me! It's us! Do you remember what Lara said in *Zhivago* before she left for Varykino? 'Yury, my darling, how clever you are, you know everything, you guess everything. Yury, darling, you are my strength and my refuge, God forgive me the blasphemy. Oh, I am so happy. Let's go, my darling, let's go . . .' Do you remember that passage, Borya?" Tears shone in her eyes.

"I remember, Olga."

"You are my strength and my refuge, Borya, my darling . . ."

His face still rested on her breast; her body, warm and strong, was trembling with excitement as her hands moved softly over his shoulders. Pasternak felt the thrill of her move inside him and checked it only momentarily with four recollected lines of verse.

> "Take your hand from my breast:
> For we are both high-tension wires;
> Look out, or we may yet again
> Be thrown together unawares!"

He embraced her waist, then looked up and drew her head down to his.

6.

Later they lay in bed in calm contentment. She ran her fingers over his chest; he placed his hands behind his head.

"Olga . . ."

"What, my darling?"

"You know, today the first lines of a poem took shape inside me at last. I've been carrying it around in my head for days. It's been a difficult birth . . ."

" 'The Nobel Prize'?"

"Yes . . . maybe. Those Komsomol youngsters and all that song and dance helped me." He recited in a melodious voice:

> "I've fallen beastlike in a snare:
> Light, people, freedom, somewhere bide:
> But at my back I hear the chase
> And there is no escape outside."*

"That's all so far. I'm waiting for what will come next."

" 'And there is no escape outside.' It's a concise idea, but stylistically it's not Pasternakian at all."

"Precisely." And he laughed softly. "Surkov could have written it, right?"

"No, Surkov couldn't have, simply because he does have an escape outside. And the sound of the chase isn't at his back. He runs with the hounds, not with the hares."

"Do you think it's too simple, too direct? There's nothing sophisticated about it. Yes . . . something is happening to my poetry. It seems to be losing its intricacy, its refinement. Ha, I'm taking the road to 'socialist realism' or to the 'short change' of the customer, as your Markov put it. But, Olga, poems ought to be unsubtle, like . . . well, like building a fire is unsubtle, or looking after a garden, or something of that kind. One should definitely not play intellectual games. One should believe in the earth and, of course, also not turn out a vulgar newspaper like *Pravda*."

Olga kissed Pasternak's hands. "I love your hands so much."

"Mine are quite ordinary. Lyonya has beautiful hands."

Olga felt a pang of jealousy but went on. "Borya, how

---

* In *In the Interlude: Poems Nineteen Forty-five–Nineteen Sixty*, trans. Henry Kamen (London: Oxford Univ. Press, 1962).

wonderful it is that people have the gift of dreaming. Only people can dream."

"Lyonya says that science can make machines dream."

Olga again swallowed her anger. "Borya, let's dream."

"What about?"

"About happiness. How would you define happiness?"

"Well, for me it seems to be inseparable from unhappiness. In any case, I feel bad when everything's going well. Thank God, I've never been spoiled by happiness."

"That's Slavic . . . nothing without suffering! Even happiness."

"But hasn't everything real in life been born from suffering?"

"Maybe. But man aspires to well-being, joy and contentment. It's in his nature. I think you believe that only the bourgeoisie search for happiness. But not everyone is born a Shakespeare—or a Pasternak. Sometimes you're a bit of an intellectual snob, Borya. I don't think happiness is bourgeois; in fact I long for peace and quiet and contentment."

"Ah, Olga, there'll be plenty of that in the next world, in eternity. But on earth everything's a struggle."

"You sound like Marx. Didn't he write, 'Life is a struggle'?"

"Yes. And on that point I agree with him."

"Borya, let's forget about the real world. Let's dream about what is not possible. Only a dream that can't come true is really enticing, don't you think?"

"Sometimes I dream about trivialities, about a glass of tea, for example."

"Fine, fine, you'll get your tea. But just imagine now, Borya, that you and I suddenly found ourselves in . . . Paris, or in . . . London . . ."

"My two sisters live in London, or rather, in Oxford."

"Oh, if only we were in London! You'd be welcomed with open arms. We've got so many friends there—writers, critics, journalists, remarkable Englishmen. You translated *Hamlet* brilliantly, Borya. You're a Westerner in spirit. Don't deny it. You know European languages, you know European culture. Oh, Borya, we'd find ourselves in a world of real human values. We'd go to Italy, settle in Venice . . . for a month or two." She sat up. "Remember, Borya, how Pushkin cursed Russia. 'It was the devil's idea to have me born in Russia with talent and a soul!' "

"Olga, he wrote lots of other things in praise of Russia."

"And Tolstoy? At one time he was on the point of selling his estate in Yasnaya Polyana and moving to England. It's a fact. And didn't Turgenev spend most of his life in Germany and France? Look truth in the eye, Borya. We're slaves here. I'm not afraid to say it, because it's true. We live in a land of masters and slaves. We obey every new dictator. And we've never been without one; dictatorship seems to be our historic destiny. For thirty years Stalin jeered at millions of people, trampled on their souls, killed them. Did anyone protest? No, everyone accepted tyranny as inevitable. We were all quiet as sheep, pathetic little mice. Some of us even glorified the 'great helmsman.' "

Pasternak caressed her. "Olga, there are periods when nations go haywire. Vile acts are committed—in the name of the people. 'The people.' What a strange concept. For me the Russian people are Ivan, Pyotr, Alexander, and Granya. I could love each one of them individually. But how can one love all of them en masse? How can one speak of them as 'the people' when they are all so different? But at the same time 'the people' do exist. 'The people' lead each one of us out of the abyss of loneliness and futile emptiness. And without 'the people' there would be no religion, no culture, in fact no society at all."

Olga brushed off his words with a wave of the hand. "You're full of contradictions, Borya! You're a heretic and a sheep, both at the same time. I know that now you'll declare, 'Russia is my homeland!' But what's a homeland? I think 'the people' is a boorish lout. All these Ivans, Pyotrs, Alexanders, and Granyas are faceless nonentities that scoundrels like Nikita Khrushchev manipulate magnificently. Homeland!

What does it mean? The birch trees near Moscow? The church of Basil the Blessed in Red Square? Homeland for us means concentration camps, prisons, barracks with stinking stoves and a stench of vodka in every room, and brutalized Ivans, Pyotrs, and Granyas, dim embodiments of the spirit of the 'axe and the icon.' Borya, you must tear yourself away from this inferno. Yury Zhivago has already started to walk through the world with his head held high, and you must follow in his footsteps. He has opened the way for you, and you must become a citizen of the world, not a Russian or a Jew but a citizen of the world, a man with divine spirituality."

"Olga, there is a whole sea of spirituality in Russians."

"Nonsense! Home-baked patriotism! Pretentious idealism! Quotations from Dostoyevsky." She laughed coarsely. "First you quoted Marx, and now you're quoting Dostoyevsky. But in reality the belly rules everything. Borya, don't you understand? God himself is helping you. It was God who sent Nikita to you. Under Stalin you'd have been rotting behind barbed wire long ago. He would have put you in prison without batting an eyelid, even before *Doctor Zhivago* had appeared in Italy. Oh, Borya, you haven't been in the camps. You don't know what it's like, but I tasted it; I know."

"That means you're for emigration too?"

"Of course. But why 'too'?"

"Because Zina's 'for' as well. Only she wants to stay behind with Lyonya."

"That's interesting. For once the old hag has had a good idea."

"Don't call her a hag. I've asked you not to more than once."

"Sorry."

"Suppose I do leave, Olga. They'll take action against you and against your daughter too."

Olga hesitated. "So we'll have to leave together."

"How can we leave together?"

"Tell Khrushchev you won't leave without us."

"But I'm certainly not in a position to dictate conditions."

"He'll agree. The most important thing for him is to be rid of you. Listen, Borya . . . I love you, I live for you. But that's not all. You're not just a human being, a poet and a man for me. You're everything to me—my ideals, my labor, my battles with life, my soul, all that I am. Under Stalin I was arrested for a careless remark. During the search they confiscated your photograph, which was hanging on the wall in my Moscow apartment. I spent five years in exile. Before that they drove my husband, the father of my children, to insanity. Don't you see, I have the right to hate the Soviet system with every fiber of my being. They gave me that right. I know *them*. I know this system. Maybe it sounds paradoxical, but it's *my* system too. Yes, yes. I created it with my enthusiastic Komsomol shrieks, my calls for a radical reconstruction, for freedom, equality, and brotherhood. But this system, my system, taught me hatred as well. It degenerated from the great hope of mankind into a bloody tyranny. One lot of scoundrels has been replaced by another. It's strange, but this system, which took God away from me, returned me to God. Now the time has come to settle scores. The final scores. The first payment has been made—*Doctor Zhivago*. That book's mine as well as yours, if only because I typed the manuscript three times. And if it hadn't been for me I don't think you would have dared hand the novel over to Feltrinelli. I was the one who insisted. And I deserve some reward."

"London?"

"London."

"Paris?"

"Paris."

"Ah, Olga," Pasternak said, raising his voice, "you see only one side of the West. You ignore the other, which lives solely by commerce. Literature and art there are fettered by philistine sentimentalism, which plays on the lowest instincts of the herd and makes a huge profit from it. And all this filthy business is carried on under the aegis of democracy."

Tears came to Olga's eyes. "Borya, Borya, how cruel you

are! How egotistic you are. Can't you give me even a moment of perfect happiness? Just the opportunity to dream? I realize it's all an illusion. You'll never abandon Zina; you'll never abandon this terrible country. But it's impossible . . . impossible to live without illusions."

At length they got up and started dressing. Pasternak seemed oppressed, then merely quiet.

"What do you want?" he asked.

"Decide," she said.

"Fine. We'll leave. Get your typewriter. I'll dictate a letter right now . . . to Nikita Khrushchev."

CHAPTER FIVE

The Poet and the "Leader"

1.

The next morning Pasternak went to Moscow with the letter
Olga had typed. In it he asked Khrushchev for permission to
emigrate to France and to take Olga and Irina with him.
Before leaving he told Zina and Nina that he was going to see
his brother Shura and to pay the rent, electricity, and telephone bills for their Moscow apartment (where Lyonya now
lived). Yury Mikhailovich drove him in the family Pobeda
despite a head injury suffered the night before when one of
the crowd at the gate had hit him with a rock.

As the car moved quickly along the Minsk highway, building sites with tall cranes, new factory plants, industrial de-
pots, and apartment blocks standing like matchboxes flashed

by. In the distance the skyscraper of Moscow State University, one of the monuments of the Stalin era, stood out in the haze, through which the sun had begun to break.

Yury Mikhailovich interrupted the silence. "The authorities brag about their achievements, but the people ask, 'Will there be any thefts under communism?' And answer, 'Only if there's anything left to steal.' " He laughed uproariously, but Pasternak did not respond, perhaps because he had heard the joke before. Yury Mikhailovich tried again. "Everywhere you look, Boris Leonidovich, it's smash and grab, people swiping things. If it's not yours, it's the state's—so go ahead and steal it. My brother's an accountant," he continued. "At his factory they've just elected a joint soviet-party committee to control thefts. They've merged all these committees now, another Khrushchev innovation. Anyway, they elected thirty-two people, and they've only got two hundred fifty workers altogether. And what is the product they're guarding so zealously? Bricks!"

"Do people really steal bricks?" Pasternak smiled ironically.

"Well, what do you expect? When the workers get only seven hundred forty rubles a month? And however hard they work, they can't get any more, because the factory can't raise their pay. If the workers produce more than the quota, they don't get anything over; the bosses just raise the quota. That's what you get for trying. So whether you like it or not, you swipe whatever you can find and try to make some extra on the side."

"You're such a grumbler," Pasternak said, "just like Tatyana—and Nina and Zina too. Look around you, Yury Mikhailovich. The Bolsheviks have transformed the face of Russia. In the old days when you came into Moscow all you saw were church cupolas, hundreds of them, but now . . . Look how much has been built!"

"The Bolsheviks had nothing to do with it, Boris Leonidovich. In fact, if there hadn't been any Bolsheviks, maybe more would have gotten built. And has all this building improved the people's lot? Or has the government just put up a lot of Potemkin villages? Look over there—three dozen television aerials on the roof of a barracks. Do you see?"

"Yes."

"What does it prove? That many people in our country own television sets?"

"What else?"

"You think just like a foreign tourist. Can't you see that if there's a forest of aerials on a roof, it means that families live one to a room in that house? Four or five people live in one room in our country. The government tells us that each person should have six square meters of living space; that's the standard they've set. Is that adequate? And most families don't have their own kitchens and bathrooms. Is that human?"

"No, it's not," Pasternak said. "But look over there, to the right. That's a respectable house, not a barracks. And there aren't many aerials on its roof. Doesn't that mean that each family has its own apartment?"

"Probably. But you can be sure that building's for the elite. I'll tell you what I think, Boris Leonidovich. I think our leaders, all these Khrushchevs and Mikoyans, are terrified of people living in separate apartments. What if a conspiracy should start? How could you keep an eye on it? When people are crowded together they inevitably control each other and there are always informers to be found. So action can be taken at the first sign of a conspiracy. Have you heard the new song?"

"What song?"

" 'Not stokers are we, not carpenters, not engineers, not doctors, not executives, our job is to squeal.' "

"To squeal?"

Yury Mikhailovich nodded and laughed.

"Why are you laughing?"

"Do you want to hear a story about a man who had his own apartment with a bathroom?" Without waiting for Pasternak's reply Yury Mikhailovich continued: "A successful

172

worker, Comrade Pupkov, came home to his apartment, undressed, sat down in the bath, and said aloud, 'Goo-o-ood!' A minute or two later he remembered everything that had happened at the factory that day—the meetings, the squabbles, the trivia—he remembered it all and bellowed 'To hell with it!' and slapped the water.' "

Pasternak laughed.

"Boris Leonidovich, do you know what an American has in his head? Business. In his heart he has dollars, and in his liver, Cuba. What's in the head of a Soviet person? Marxism-Leninism. In his heart he has socialist emulation, and in his liver reorganization."

"Yury Mikhailovich, I can guarantee you, you'll never be elected a full member of the Communist Party."

"That's no skin off my ass. I became a candidate member because of Lenin, and there's nothing left of him. I know this dog's life inside out. Don't think I just discovered all this yesterday. A bump on the head is nothing, but a bullet in the brain—that's serious. I slaved for twenty years on the production line—I was a seventh-grade lathe operator and turned cams. I waited in line for an apartment for years. I did everything the right way. Then one fine day I said 'To hell with it!' and became a driver. Thank God, you took me on. Now I'm a sort of private trader, a petty bourgeois."

The Pobeda approached the intersection of the Minsk and Rublyov highways, and Yury Mikhailovich slowed down. Beside the road by the traffic lights stood a highway patrolman in a glass booth, and nearby were several KGB captains and majors dressed in police sergeants' uniforms. Such details, employed to clear traffic for passing government limousines, are commonplace around Moscow, and the Pobeda's occupants took no notice until the light suddenly turned red and the KGB men flagged traffic down.

The Pobeda stopped at the light, and a tail of cars rapidly formed behind it. A small truck, carrying two men of about twenty, pulled up on the right, and across the intersection a tourist bus and two trucks filled with workmen led the line of stopped vehicles. The intermittent "cuckoo" of police sirens could be heard in the distance.

"Some god or other is coming," Yury Mikhailovich remarked. "Probably the Lord himself."

"Khrushchev?"

"Could be."

The workmen across the intersection jumped off their trucks and spread out along the edge of the highway, looking intently down the road for the government car. Nearby drivers and pedestrians joined them. The excited bustle of the highway patrol left no doubt that it was "he."

Pasternak straightened his cap.

Presently the black limousine of the First Secretary of the Central Committee and Chairman of the USSR Council of Ministers came into view, followed by two cars carrying his bodyguards. The windows of the limousine were tinted green, indicating they were bulletproof, but one of them had been lowered to reveal none other than Nikita Sergeyevich Khrushchev himself. The highway patrol snapped to attention and saluted and the bystanders cheered, whereupon Khrushchev ordered his driver to stop and back up.

The excited crowd started yelling, "Long live Comrade Khrushchev! Hoo-rah!"

A moment later Khrushchev emerged from the limousine, took off his felt hat, and bowed, for all the world like an actor acknowledging applause. His bodyguards, their hands thrust deep into their pockets—to be nearer their pistols—appeared swiftly by his side.

Pasternak stared in disbelief. He had never seen Khrushchev before, or any of the "leaders," for that matter, at such close quarters. He stared at Nikita's thick neck, the color of a pumpkin, and his glossy skull, which looked as if it would ring like a bronze bowl if he flicked his finger against it. He thought Khrushchev looked surprisingly elegant in his fashionable gray coat and his felt hat with its broad dark-green band, all obviously foreign-made. Khrushchev's manner, slightly noble, even ecclesiastical, was strikingly familiar; Pasternak had known many well-born churchmen in his youth. But above all Pasternak was struck by Khrushchev's eyes, bright little buttons that reminded him of cockroaches. The smile and the warts on Nikita's face were worthy of Dostoyevsky, he thought, but they had no place in his own work.

Khrushchev took a final bow and decamped, and as his cavalcade departed, Pasternak suddenly wondered if the incident had been staged. He looked around to see if there was a movie camera. But instead he met the gaze of the young man at the wheel of the small truck next to them. The youth winked at him and sang out unabashedly:

> "We've overtaken America
> In production of milk.
> But we haven't overtaken them in meat.
> Khrushchev was gored by the bull!"

His companion choked with laughter at the parody of the government's radio and television farm-production campaign, and then both vehicles moved on the green light.

"He wants to be another Stalin," Yury Mikhailovich remarked. "His picture has already been put up in every hairdresser's in Moscow, just like Stalin's when he was boss."

But Pasternak, brooding on his missed opportunity to deliver the letter to Khrushchev in person, didn't reply.

2.

"Where are we going first?" Yury Mikhailovich asked when they had left the highway and entered an avenue in Moscow.

"To the Kremlin," Pasternak answered without thinking. Then, immediately correcting himself: "To Manezh Square. I'll get out there, and you can wait for me. All right?"

175

"That's fine with me." Yury Mikhailovich did not appear surprised.

Pasternak remembered how, twenty years earlier, he had come from Peredelkino to Moscow with a letter in his pocket. At that time he did not own a car, so he had traveled by train and had taken a cab from the station to Manezh Square. He had then walked to the Historical Museum and entered the Kremlin commandant's office by the Kremlin wall. Every detail was alive in his memory: the massive door, the low ceilings inside the building, the glossy walls with tiny windows through which passes were handed out. It was here he saw the huge box for "workers'" letters to Comrade Stalin *personally*. My God, the number written to him! Millions. And no one knew if any of these letters was read. Pasternak had dropped a letter into this box in 1937. Yes, in that ill-fated year when Titsian Tabidze and so many others had been seized. Among those arrested had been the husband of the poet Anna Akhmatova. In tears, she had rushed to Pasternak's dacha and had pleaded with him to write a letter to Stalin. Pasternak had done it and had taken the letter to the Kremlin himself. And, amazingly, Akhmatova's husband had been released shortly afterward. But whether this had happened because of his letter or for some other reason, no one knew.

It had been no accident that Akhmatova had come running to him. She knew many brilliant and famous people, and she was famous in her own right. But not long before this a sensational story had spread throughout Moscow: Stalin himself had chatted with Pasternak on the telephone. And the story had been true. The call had resulted from Pasternak's attempts to help a fellow poet. Before the arrest of Titsian in Georgia, Osip Mandelstam had been arrested in Moscow merely for criticizing Stalin in an unpublished poem. Mandelstam was a man of unshakable convictions, and in his poetry he called a spade a spade. He was not a close friend of Pasternak's, although they knew and respected each other. But as soon as Pasternak learned of Mandelstam's arrest he went to the editor of the newspaper *Izvestia*, Bukharin, an intellectual who admired his poetry. He told him that Mandelstam's arrest was a terrible blow to the whole of Soviet poetry. Bukharin was then close to Stalin, and he promised to help. A day later there was a phone call from the Kremlin to the apartment of Pasternak's brother, where the poet was living. Picking up the receiver, Pasternak heard a voice say tersely, "Comrade Stalin on the line for you." A few seconds later a conversation began between the poet and the leader.

Stalin asked the poet, "Why do you defend Mandelstam with such enthusiasm?" The poet replied, "He's one of the best Soviet poets." Then the leader asked the poet, "But do you know his work?" The poet, knowing how disrespectfully Mandelstam had spoken of Stalin in his last poem, replied boldly, "Of course." Stalin replied shortly, "I'll look into it." Pasternak then said, "Joseph Vissarionovich, I'd like to meet you and have a heart-to-heart talk." "What about?" The leader was interested. Pasternak declared, "About life, eternity, death . . ." After a brief pause Stalin hung up.

Recalling this conversation, Pasternak was no longer ashamed that he had wanted to meet Stalin. Instead he felt wryly amused both by himself and by human life in general. A sparkle brightened his eyes. While talking to Stalin on the telephone, hearing his rather impure Russian speech, he had been able to picture the leader's face, his cheeks scarred by smallpox and his twitching mustache. The great leader probably did not like thinking about eternity and death, having hidden himself in a shell (or the armor) of "revolutionary" pragmatism. Nevertheless, after this telephone *pas de deux* the official attitude toward Pasternak had changed abruptly. For some time many orthodox writers and officials from the Union of Soviet Writers had been avoiding him, afraid that he was about to "burst at the seams" and be suppressed; he had been viciously attacked in the press, and his lyrics had been ignored by the publishing houses. But now there was a complete change of heart. Everyone suddenly started smiling at him, vying with one another to shake his hand, and in the restaurant of the House of Writers it was even suggested he eat on credit.

The poet and the leader!

This phrase brought Pasternak back to the tormenting question: Why did Stalin spare *me*? He had not glorified him in his poems (although he had not cursed him either), and his poetry in no way responded to the demands of the party of Lenin and Stalin. For a short time Pasternak had thought well of Stalin, and during this period he had agreed to sign a eulogy published by the Union of Soviet Writers to mark the death of Stalin's wife, Nadezhda Alliluyeva. (He had not known at the time that she had committed suicide; in fact, he knew nothing at all about Stalin's private life.) But any admiration he had felt for the leader had vanished long before Titsian's arrest.

No, I've never betrayed my beliefs, Pasternak thought. He had always rejected any leader who wanted to subjugate others, to hold absolute sway; in this respect there was a touch of the revolutionary in his nature.

"The poet and the leader are incompatible!" Pasternak said to himself. Yet Khrushchev, despite the fact that he was Pasternak's enemy, Pasternak's adversary in a duel, did not arouse in him the same hostility Stalin had. This puzzled him, as he firmly believed that if it proved necessary, Khrushchev would go to the same lengths as Stalin. Hadn't Khrushchev already proved this in Hungary and Georgia, where Soviet soldiers had shot defenseless people on his orders? Nevertheless the man seemed ridiculous rather than terrifying. Perhaps his clownishness led people such as Zina and Nina to think there was a human warmth in him, which had not existed in Stalin.

Pasternak suddenly yearned to live in a country in which, on the street, within earshot of everyone, he could loudly call a king or a president an ass.

178

Yury Mikhailovich parked the Pobeda in the center of Manezh Square. Pasternak turned up the collar of his jacket and pulled his cap down over his forehead before setting off toward the Historical Museum. He drew his head down and tried to change his walk slightly. He wanted to drop his letter into the same box he had used twenty years earlier. Only now of course the box held letters addressed to Comrade Khrushchev rather than Comrade Stalin.

Walking uphill toward the museum, he again remembered the commandant's building, with its gray-enameled walls and small barred windows where passes were handed out. He walked past buildings reminiscent of courts and other official institutions. Their monolithic exteriors made him feel like a character from Kafka. A wave of revulsion swept over him. Suddenly he stopped and looked around. Was Yury Mikhailovich following him? No, he was reading a newspaper.

I can't bear to go into the commandant's building, he thought. I'll just have to mail the letter. I've wasted the morning on this trip, but there's no help for it. He turned sharply to the left and, after going downhill toward Okhotny Row, began walking quickly up Gorky Street. As before, he kept his shoulders hunched, the collar of his jacket concealing his nose and chin. Then it occurred to him that he might attract attention because he was behaving like a criminal or escaped prisoner hiding from the authorities. He boldly turned down his collar and raised his cap.

Pasternak saw portraits of Khrushchev in several shop windows and realized that Yury Mikhailovich had not been exaggerating when he said that pictures of the "corn czar" had started to appear in hairdressers' salons.

Finding himself amid the stream of Muscovites eternally hurrying up and down Gorky Street, Pasternak felt a kind of exhilaration. He ordinarily avoided crowds, because he was repelled by their herdlike behavior. But today the sensation of being swallowed up in a group made him feel glad and even excited. It made him feel good to be a part of a crowd that was rushing to get everyday tasks done.

Crossing to the other side of the street, he started up the stone steps to the entrance of the massive Central Telegraph Office, one of the sights of the new, postrevolutionary Moscow. Halfway up, someone suddenly touched his arm. He shivered and stopped. In front of him, as if they had sprung out of the ground, were a girl of about twenty, wearing ordinary city clothes, and a boy of the same age in a ski jacket and ski cap. She was short, plumpish, and decisive, while he was thin, lanky, and timid.

"Excuse me, please," the girl said in a whisper, "are you the poet Pasternak?"

Pasternak, confused, shook his head in halfhearted denial.

"No, please don't deny it. Andryusha and I have been following you from Okhotny Row. I've got your photograph, and so has he. But I recognized you first. I've got sharp eyes. We're students from Moscow University. From the Literary Faculty. I'm Svetlana Petrova and this is Andrei Kurochkin."

Pasternak smiled uneasily and nodded.

Svetlana went on, with renewed confidence. "Excuse us for bothering you, Boris Leonidovich, but we were so happy to see you on the street. We want to say that we—many of the students at the Lit Fac—support you openly and do not agree with what is unfortunately being published in our central press. Right, Andryusha?"

"Right," the boy agreed shyly.

"We love your poetry, Boris Leonidovich, even though we sometimes find it difficult. It's real, everything in it is sincere and profound. And Andryusha thinks that real poetry should be a bit difficult to understand as it affirms individuality, and individuality is always a bit difficult to understand. Right, Andrei?"

"Right."

Looking around, Svetlana lowered her voice even further. "Unfortunately we can't read your new novel *Doctor Zhi-*

vago, but we will read it one day. We promise you. By the way, Boris Leonidovich, Andryusha is a poet too."

"Really? That means we're colleagues."

"He writes a lot! At night. The Muses only visit him at night. The only trouble is he's hopelessly shy and bashful. You can see, he's just like a young girl. But, Boris Leonidovich, if you'd like, he'll recite something he's written, something short."

"Here? Right now? Mmm—would that be wise?"

"The police can't bother us. It's not against the law to recite poetry."

"Then please do."

"Go on, Andryusha!"

The boy shrank with embarrassment, wrung his hands awkwardly, then suddenly stood up straight and started reciting:

> " 'It's unbecoming to have fame
> For this is not what elevates,
> And there's no need to keep archives
> Or dote over your manuscripts.
>
> Creation's way is—to give all,
> And not to bluster or eclipse:
> How mean, when you don't signify,
> To be on everybody's lips!
>
> But life must be without pretense;
> Conduct your days that finally
> You may indraw far-distant love
> And hear the call of years to be.' "*

"Oh, you coward," Svetlana exclaimed, "that's not one of yours!" And turning to Pasternak, she added: "That's your poem, Boris Leonidovich. We agree with you that there's too little modesty in Soviet literature and too much bragging. Andryusha and I were just arguing over who was the most

* In *In the Interlude: Poems Nineteen Forty-five–Nineteen Sixty*, trans. Henry Kamen (London: Oxford Univ. Press, 1962).

modest man in history. Who would you choose, Boris Leonidovich?"

"Christ."

"Really? I thought Lenin. And Andrei said Chekhov. But
that's not the point. I want to explain to you why Andrei's
not himself. Of course he was born shy, but he's in the middle of a family crisis right now. Right, Andrei?"

"Right."

"He's fallen out with his father once and for all and he's
come to live with me in the hostel. He's living there with us
like a stowaway. His father's an official, a bureaucrat in the
ministry. He's like a Japanese mouse, which sees the world
only horizontally. But Andrei and I see it vertically too. Andrei's father claims that everything in our country is just
great and that we should be proud to be Soviet citizens. But
in reality Andrei's father is deceiving himself, most likely for
the sake of his career. If you look critically at our everyday
life, then you have to admit that everything is far from great.
Right, Andrei?"

"Right."

"Andrei's father calls himself an unsung hero. But what
sort of hero is he? He only sees things horizontally."

Pasternak laughed. "You know, I have the same sort of
problem with my son. One of us sees everything horizontally
and the other vertically." They reminded him of himself as a
boy, when he had defied the composer Scriabin, who used to
visit his parents' house. No doubt it was good to have heroes
or idols when one was young. He recalled how he had also
worshiped the German poet Rilke, and with his friends, students at Marburg University, idolized the professor of philosophy, Hermann Cohen, going to his lectures as if to a festival,
wearing his Sunday best. But remembering Scriabin, Rilke,
and Cohen, Pasternak felt suddenly embarrassed by his earlier excitement in the crowd. "The people" was just a fiction,
generated by the desire for a mediocre community.

He was about to tell them what he had just thought when

Svetlana, her eyes flashing, said passionately, "Please don't go to the West. You're ours . . . ours . . ."

4.

The high ceiling of the main hall of the Central Telegraph Office was supported by two rows of square columns. Copper tubes of the pneumatic dispatch system crawled along the walls, catching light from the large windows and from overhead oblong neon fixtures. Modern tables were placed end to end down the middle of the hall, and, flanking them across a corridor, a low-lying wooden partition guarded each side wall, a shield of thick frosted glass broken by small windows protecting the enclosure from sight. On the right were a savings bank and a post office. On the left was a telegraph office, with signs hung over the first three windows saying "International Telegrams."

As Pasternak entered the noisy hall his eye fell immediately on two wooden postboxes at the near end of the line of tables. Both were larger than the one in the Kremlin commandant's office. One was marked "Letters" and the other "Printed Matter." Pasternak hesitated in front of them. All he had to do was slip the letter into the appropriate box and this world would probably be replaced by another.

He put his right hand into his breast pocket and felt the letter. He was about to draw it out, but suddenly he turned, unsure whether he had heard the voice or not. He looked around, expecting to catch sight of the girl who called herself Svetlana. She was not there.

Upset and ashamed, he began walking around the hall, looking. The hall was jammed; there were no free places at the tables. He leaned against a column and closed his eyes; he felt numb and weak and fell into a semitrance. And there he remained for several minutes until a young man's voice roused him: "Citizen, this place is free. You can take it."

Pasternak sat down at the table and picked up a pen. But he realized he had not gotten the form to fill in.

5.

The wall clock read 10:45.

Khrushchev had told Alexander Tvardovsky to come to his office at eleven, and he had called Mikoyan and asked him to be present at the meeting.

The office of the First Secretary of the Party Central Committee was on the sixth floor of a building on Staraya Square. It looked out over the capital north of the Moscow River. Below, the boulevard stretched toward Nogin Square, a complex of government buildings. The boulevard was lined with old residential houses, which had been restored so as not to offend the top leaders of the Central Committee.

This had been Stalin's office, although he had rarely used it during the last years of his life, preferring his office in the Kremlin and his dacha. Khrushchev had made a few alterations. He had removed the "dressing room," that is, the closetlike room in front of the entrance, which almost all important party and government officials had had built into their offices to guard against being overheard. He had hung the head of a deer, which he had shot in the Crimea, on the wall and added a portrait of Yury Gagarin to those of Marx, Engels, and Lenin. A model of the first Sputnik stood on the conference table. Stalin's four old-fashioned telephones had been replaced by new white ones. But his massive inkstand remained, as did the glass on the large desk, under which a list of important telephone numbers was kept. Khrushchev had ordered the map on the wall decorated with dried ears of corn. A poster proclaiming the slogan "Through corn to communism!" also hung on the wall.

Khrushchev, wearing a dark, single-breasted suit, with two small stars designating him Hero of Socialist Labor, was pacing up and down his office. He had been disturbed by two telegrams that had arrived the night before—one from the King of Belgium and the other from the Queen of Holland—asking Nikita to treat the poet Boris Pasternak indulgently. And earlier that morning he had read in the "white"—that is, the secret—TASS bulletin about a press conference held by the Prime Minister of India in which Nehru had stated: "The Soviet approach to Pasternak to a certain extent inflicts pain on us too, since it is absolutely contrary to our approach to such phenomena. This writer, even if he does express a point of view that opposes the prevailing one, should nevertheless, in our opinion, enjoy respect and freedom of speech." The swine! The goddam sonofabitch! That meddlesome Hindu in white pants should be put in his place! But what could he do? He had publicly called Nehru "my friend." He had been his guest in India, and photographs of him embracing Nehru had been printed in newspapers throughout the world.

Nikita was desperately trying to avoid a controversy that would undermine his policy of "peaceful coexistence." But he was equally concerned about maintaining control inside the Soviet Union. He had gone almost too far in attacking Stalin, but he had checked himself in time. Now he was afraid of being overzealous in dealing with Pasternak. His cunning peasant mind groped for firm ground somewhere in the middle. He had been advised to stick to the middle ground, incidentally, by that old imperialist bulldog Winston Churchill, with whom he had had dinner recently in London.

The Pasternak affair stuck like a burr in his mind. He could not bring himself either to shrug it off or to put it in Suslov's hands. It was too serious a matter. He had to act firmly and expeditiously to prevent the spread of Pasternak's poison. But he had to take care not to alienate the intelligentsia.

Accordingly, Khrushchev had invited the popular poet Alexander Tvardovsky for a talk. In Nikita's opinion, Tvardovsky had the same important qualities as himself: Communist inflexibility and moderate liberalism. Besides, although he hoped he could still force Pasternak to refuse the Nobel Prize, Khrushchev did not exclude the possibility of his accepting it. If this occurred, more rigorous measures would have to be taken against him. Tvardovsky's thoughts on this could perhaps be helpful.

Pausing at one of the windows, Nikita pulled back the curtain and watched the tiny figures on the boulevard—tiny faceless pawns. He wondered if their well-being was really a matter of such great concern to him. Without doubt he had done a lot for the people, but at the same time, hadn't he really been acting in his own interest? Concern for the people, concern for himself—which came first? Who could say whether what he had done for himself was, in fact, necessary for the people? A doubt troubled his mind. All things considered, did he honestly believe that society could be reconstructed on the basis of equality and brotherhood? Was it a real possibility? Or was it merely a convenient pretense that allowed him to enforce his own will? Hadn't he seen much hypocrisy in Stalin? And in Lenin as well?

And in the rest? Khrushchev thought about his "companions" and "comrades." Did they speak the truth at the Politburo meetings where the fate of the country, of millions of people, was decided? Or did they equivocate, influenced by all sorts of personal considerations? Was it not possible that self-interest had gradually become their new faith? He turned away from the window.

Khrushchev was proud of his achievements. But had they rather than chance put him in this office? That is, chance assisted by his own shrewd manipulations. Try as he might, he could not isolate one element that explained his success. Chance had certainly played a part. He had been able to work with Stalin, and Stalin had turned him into a leading party official. But on the other hand, after Stalin's death he had seen his opportunity and seized it. Spurred by his resentment, even hatred for the "leader of the peoples," and by his determination to restore Leninist principles of party morality, Nikita had revealed Stalin's crimes—and thereafter succeeded to his throne.

But what of his own government? It was far from perfect. Take the conflict of the rich and the poor. Hadn't the revolutionaries in 1917 believed that they had all but eliminated it from Russia? But wasn't Russian society still torn apart by class conflict? Didn't ordinary Soviet workers, in their hearts, hate the party bosses, ministers, academics, and the like? And wasn't it true that a union minister received 25,000 rubles a month and a messenger 400 rubles a month? And a minister also had a magnificent apartment, a dacha, a car, servants, all kinds of special allowances, the Kremlin hospital, and so on. What did a messenger have? He was empty-handed.

And what about all these Soviet generals with their adjutants and servants? When they retired, the state guaranteed them servants till they died, the same lackeys as they used to have in the czar's army.

And what about millionaires—Soviet writers and scientists? They'd done all right for themselves on equality and brotherhood! Khrushchev had suggested reducing the salaries of generals, taking away servants from those who had retired, and lowering playwrights' royalties. Oh, what a stink they had kicked up! And were party officials any better?

And what about himself, Nikita? In what way was he better than these others? Didn't he live like a landowner or prince? Apartment, dacha, servants, everything he wanted was at his disposal. Didn't he go out to hunt hares just as the czars had? Yes, this was all true as far as it went. But the apartment and the dacha were not his own property, and if he was booted out tomorrow, he'd be back where he started. The same fate faced every minister and big shot—provided, of course, his wife had not made a fortune buying precious stones, gold, and the like on the black market. But as long as he stayed in office, there was little difference between a Soviet minister and a Western millionaire. The millionaire had his own money and the Soviet minister had the state's. But they both spent it just as they pleased. And they both lived well. But what about the pawn? How did the pawn live? How did the messenger live or the woman without a husband on a collective farm?

Such thoughts were crowding in on him when Mikoyan entered the office, also wearing a dark, single-breasted suit, but with only one star, as Hero of Socialist Labor, on his chest.

"Listen," Nikita asked his trusted shooting companion when they had shaken hands, "what if we took away all the privileges our ministers and party bigwigs have—their dachas, cars, servants, and so on—and introduced a maximum party salary of, say, fifteen hundred rubles a month? What if we made our party and government aristocracy knuckle under? What if we knocked them into the middle of next week? Greed makes a man heartless, Anastas."

Mikoyan looked at Nikita warily. He scratched his mustache. "Then the party and government aristocracy would rebel and make Soviet power knuckle under."

Nikita persisted. "Don't you see, Anastas, we've gone too far. That Yugoslav renegade Djilas was right when he accused us of spawning a new class. Yes, and Mao, that fat sonofabitch, hit the nail on the head too when he called us bourgeois and revisionists." Khrushchev seethed. "But what can I do? It's all Stalin's fault. He gave them too much—ranks, dachas, privileges, titles, rewards, prizes. It's enough to turn anyone's head. I'd rebel too—"

"Don't go to extremes, Nikita," Mikoyan said, interrupting. He sat down in an armchair and lit a cigarette. "It's no accident that in capitalist countries they elect rich people to government posts. It's presumed they won't take bribes—because they've got enough money already."

"But that's nonsense. The rich will always take bribes. Money attracts money." Khrushchev rubbed his hands. "What we have at the bottom of it all is a Thermidor! A real one! A regeneration! What would Lenin say if he could see the state we're in? And it all started wih the cult of Stalin."

"All right, let's put the question to the Politburo. A maximum party salary. I'll support you myself."

They looked at each other. Both laughed. "You comrades-in-arms," Khrushchev said. "You can all go to hell! I've had enough of putting on airs. I'll desert my family. I'll run away to join the people. I'll live on a collective farm somewhere. Hell, I climbed out of the people; now I'll climb back into them. What a splendid idea! When Tolstoy was eighty he ran away from home, even gave up his title."

"But he didn't knock Stalin," Mikoyan said, and they both laughed again.

With ten minutes left until the meeting with Tvardovsky, Khrushchev suggested they move into the small inner office that served as his study. During the war this room had been furnished with a bed, small table, sofa, two armchairs, a cupboard, and a sink. (Stalin, however, had never slept here.) Khrushchev had added a television set and, on a bedside table in the corner, a stuffed hare.

Seating himself on the sofa, Nikita told Mikoyan about the telegrams from Belgium and Holland, calling both monarchs lousy little tin-pot czars.

Anastas had already read about Nehru's speech in "white" TASS and agreed with Khrushchev that they had to continue to stand firm on the Pasternak matter. He too felt that a conversation with Tvardovsky would be useful. "The class struggle inside the country isn't over. Stalin saw right to the heart of the matter in that respect."

"I'm a fool," Khrushchev said. "Not long ago I said in a speech that classes no longer exist in the USSR—only working people."

"That's correct too." Mikoyan smiled. "We're creating life anew, but people are so reluctant to part with the rotten past."

"It's the influence of the West too, of course."

"Of course, that too, Nikita. You won't get far from Stalin there either."

"No, you won't."

"But we must, Nikita."

"No doubt, Anastas."

"It's impossible to keep the people in constant fear."

"Of course it's impossible . . . only it's a vicious circle, that's what." With a sigh Khrushchev added, "The old man was great; we'll never leap as far as he did."

Khrushchev's assistant, Lebedev, a neat bespectacled man about forty-five, entered the study. "Tvardovsky has arrived, Nikita Sergeyevich," he said. "Shall I have him wait or will you receive him at the appointed time?"

"Show him into the office, Comrade Lebedev. And take all my calls. But if Serov phones, put him through."

6.

Alexander Tvardovsky was tall and slim, with bright blue eyes, a small Slavic nose, and full cheeks. He did not have much hair, but such as there was was curly and naturally light brown. He looked no more than fifty, and was decently but not fashionably dressed.

"Good day, Nikita Sergeyevich," he said, offering Khrushchev his hand. "How do you do, Anastas Ivanovich?"

Nikita shook his hand vigorously and, without pausing, dispatched Lebedev to fetch some tea. "Have a seat, Alexander Trifonovich," he said.

Tvardovsky and Mikoyan sat in the armchairs, and Nikita sat behind his desk. He joined his plump hands, his large fingers intertwined.

"Last time we met was—what, two years ago?—in the Pine Trees rest home near Moscow at the government meeting with writers there. Do you remember? I jumped on all of you and butted you around like a bull? Ha, ha, ha! I'm a quick-tempered person, Comrade Tvardovsky. And stubborn. Such a nice fellow! Eh?"

"How could I forget it, Nikita Sergeyevich? You swore

190

you'd bury all vacillators so far underground that no one would ever find them."

"Did I really? What a clumsy oaf I am. To tell the truth, I'd had a drop to drink at lunch. To summon up courage . . ."

Mikoyan grinned. "And you and I went out on the lake in a boat, Comrade Tvardovsky. And Ilya Ehrenburg."

"Yes, I remember. We were both very impressed by your rowing, Anastas Ivanovich."

"And I got very worked up," Khrushchev interrupted. "Not by Ehrenburg, but by those writers who were demanding total creative freedom. If we want to put filth in the Soviet system, don't stop us, they declared. We are creative individuals; we can do anything we like. Don't touch us. Goddam sonsofbitches!" he sputtered. "And it was raining. Do you remember? Well, that's not important now." He paused. "I want to consult you, Comrade Tvardovsky—Mikoyan and I, that is. The thing is—"

Lebedev returned with a document in his hand, followed by two stewards in white aprons carrying tea and buns. Khrushchev read the document and signed it and, dismissing the stewards and Lebedev, invited the others to join him at the round table in the corner. As always, he drank his tea unadulterated, from a saucer.

"You like it merchant-style?" Tvardovsky smiled.

"Uhuh," Khrushchev snorted.

Tvardovsky and Mikoyan put sugar in their tea and drank from glasses.

"You're from peasant stock, aren't you?" Nikita inquired after a pause. Tvardovsky nodded. "I'm also from peasant stock. So you and I, Alexander Trifonovich, know that the most important and most difficult problem in our country is agriculture. Agreed?"

"Agreed."

"But why? Why such a problem?" He leaned forward. "Because psychology is all mixed up in it, the devil take it! The instinct of the property owner is alive and well in the peasant. Lenin saw it and he was right. So, Alexander

Trifonovich, I've just signed a document—" He suddenly checked himself. "Top secret, you understand?"

Tvardovsky nodded.

"All right, I'll tell you something about agriculture, Comrade Tvardovsky. Actually, there's no great secret about it." He hesitated again. "Some time ago I decided to carry out an experiment. At the beginning there were no objections in the Central Committee. We took one of the agricultural districts of the Altai and organized something like a homestead economy there. We gathered some peasant collective farmers together and said to them: 'Forget about collectives for a while. Here's some land—take as much as you want. Organize yourselves in whatever way suits you. Join together in brigades; collect the members of your family, your friends, whoever you like. Then make your own calculations—how much you can produce from the plot of land you choose, given its size and type. And tell the state what you need—how many machines, how much seed, equipment, and so on. Then draw up your own production plan.' That's what we told them. We made sure they understood that only one thing was important to us: deliveries of fixed amounts of produce to the state. 'What's left over is yours, and you can do what you like with it.' That's what we said. No control. Right, Anastas?"

"It was your idea, Nikita, so you can sort out the mess," Mikoyan responded dryly.

"You see, Alexander Trifonovich, even Anastas wants to wash his hands of it. Yet he and I agree on most things. You can imagine what the others think of it. Anyway, the experiment was a success. A group of Altai peasants got organized, worked everything out, went out into the fields—and gave the state more than it wanted. They didn't do badly for themselves either. Production *tripled*. Tripled! No joking. So we've made a documentary film, and all sorts of papers have been written. We're still writing them. And I'm giving a report at the next Central Committee plenum. But all to no purpose, you may be sure. Nothing will come of it. I know in advance my proposal will fail. And I'll be cursed into the bargain and accused of dragging the country backward toward capitalism. The goddam sonsofbitches!"

"When you proposed opening up the virgin lands," Mikoyan protested, "I supported you. Did I not, Nikita? I also supported wider dissemination of your beloved corn. But as you know, my old friend, I opposed the Altai experiment from the start. It flies in the face of the whole socialist system."

"You hear that, Comrade Tvardovsky? They talk about principles and systems, but they don't mention our starving Soviet peasants."

"Nikita, we're all trying to work out a solution. But a homestead economy, based on private property, would only land us in new difficulties."

"You see how far all this talk gets us, Comrade Tvardovsky. Yet theoretically I agree with Mikoyan. Only, behind all these theories we've stopped paying any attention to the common citizen. He scorns theory. He wants to be free to eat his fill, to own a car—in short, to live like an average American. That's our era for you, Alexander Trifonovich."

"In a hundred years historians will call it the Khrushchev Era," Mikoyan said with a reassuring smile.

"Maybe . . . and maybe not," Khrushchev morosely replied.

"Nikita Sergeyevich," Tvardovsky broke in. "I've heard about the Altai experiment. The world is full of rumors, you know. And I agree in particular with Anastas Ivanovich's criticism of it. But still, if you summon me to the Central Committee plenum, I promise to defend your idea."

"Thank you, Alexander Trifonovich—only you and I will be in a beleaguered minority. They'll eat us up for supper. I've already considered it from every angle. You can't beat the party machine." He shrugged. "Well, then," he said at length, "let's move on to today's business. . . . First of all, Comrade Tvardovsky, you're a literary man. Tell us, as an honest party man, is Boris Pasternak a good poet?"

Tvardovsky placed his unfinished glass of tea on the table. "Do you think I'm a good poet, Nikita Sergeyevich?"

"Of course. That's why I invited you here. Your 'Vasily Tyorkin' is like Tolstoy's *War and Peace*. Imagine—a poem about an ordinary Soviet soldier helped destroy Hitler. I read you in the trenches myself. You're a remarkable poet, Comrade Tvardovsky."

"Seconded," said Mikoyan.

"Let us suppose you're right. Then, in comparison with Pasternak, I'm . . . I'm just like this, you see . . ." He showed Khrushchev his little finger.

Khrushchev eyed him skeptically. "What's so special about him?"

"He's a great poet, Nikita Sergeyevich, believe me. His talent is highly original. Vladimir Mayakovsky called him an 'overseas wonder.' "

"Aha, *overseas*, not ours."

"How can I put it . . . Poets can't be divided into ours and not ours . . . not great poets. You see, Nikita Sergeyevich, Pasternak has the gift of constant poetic invention. He lives in a unique imaginary world, as if he's actually in contact with the spiritual values of the universe."

"Fine, fine," Khrushchev interrupted. "I'm not much good at understanding the spiritual values of the universe, but you tell us, you personally, are you against *Doctor Zhivago*?"

"Yes, I'm against it."

"Why?"

"I've read the novel, and despite Pasternak's genius, I can't accept his view of history. But you see, Nikita Sergeyevich, Pasternak is complex and contradictory. Two epochs, two worlds, two ideologies have crossed in him. He has the *past* in him. He's not entirely on the side of the Soviet system. But he's not a criminal and he's not a saboteur. Everything he does comes from the heart and is therefore authentic." He paused thoughtfully before continuing. "I'll show you one side of his character. In 1937 two famous Georgian poets, Titsian Tabidze and Paolo Yashvili, were liquidated. Pasternak was a friend of both. Well, ever since 1937 he's sent fifteen hundred rubles a month to each of their wives, even though he often had to tighten his belt. Fortunately his own wife made a little money transcribing music."

"When I was little," Khrushchev replied with irony, "my mother taught me: 'Nikita, love thy neighbor as thyself.' "

"Nikita Sergeyevich, Pasternak isn't a poseur or a hypocrite."

Khrushchev got up and walked around his office. "So you're defending him, Comrade Tvardovsky? 'Tightened his belt,' did he?" He turned abruptly. "Are you aware that Pasternak's mistress, that Olga bitch, has been working hand in glove with Western correspondents? That any day Western royalties for *Doctor Zhivago* will start being transferred into their account? And those payments won't be in dollars or in marks, my friend, or in pounds sterling, but in dear little Soviet rubles. Where do you think they come from? They're bought on the black market, in Paris and Rome."

"And you think Pasternak knows about this? He's not interested in money. He's already turned down foreign royalties."

"You're right. Last year, when the first pile of money, all *foreign* currency, came in, Pasternak, under pressure from us, refused to accept it."

"So I understood."

"Yes, but that was *last* year. Now things are different. Now you can't make head or tail of all the intrigues. But I assure you, the KGB will sort it all out. Olga will get what she deserves. Sweet little Olga . . ."

"I can't vouch for Olga, Nikita Sergeyevich."

"All right. Fine. But now, Comrade Tvardovsky, dear Alexander Trifonovich, I'm interested in one thing. I want you to understand that I'm kindly disposed toward Soviet writers. I'm not bloodthirsty like Stalin. Nevertheless, Comrade Tvardovsky, I'm concerned about the effects of certain movies and plays and poems that have recently appeared—and books, the great and small *Doctor Zhivago*s. I—that is,

Anastas and I—we're for everyone's having the necessary creative freedom. But there's a limit to everything. And that's really why I invited you here. You know the popular saying, 'Two minds are better than one.' Or 'Many hands make light work.' Well, I—that is, we decided to consult you before taking any serious steps in regard to Pasternak. Surkov is one thing. You're quite another. I want to know what *you* think, the poet Tvardovsky, the Communist Tvardovsky. I repeat, I'm not Stalin. Nevertheless, Alexander Trifonovich, I'm a Communist like you. And I'm telling you, my hand will not falter if the core of Marxism-Leninism is threatened! Do you remember Hungary, Comrade Tvardovsky? Do you remember what happened there? It all started with writers and 'creative freedoms.' But the USSR isn't Hungary, Comrade Tvardovsky. We won't have it!"

Khrushchev's manufactured hysterics didn't appear to scare Tvardovsky in the slightest, but Mikoyan had seen the leader's calculated tantrums get out of hand. "Don't get excited, Nikita," he entreated. "Hungary is behind us. But the USSR isn't Hungary. You're right. We won't have that."

"Won't have it? Have you forgotten about the uprising in Central Asia? Have you forgotten about that insolent demonstration in Georgia?" Nikita shook his jowls furiously. But the effort was wasted; Tvardovsky, although appalled by the spectacle, maintained his composure. Nikita fell silent, then rubbed his sweaty face with the palm of his hand, twitched his lips, and laughed as if nothing had happened.

"Did I frighten you, Alexander Trifonovich? I sometimes get carried away. Don't pay any attention to it. What do they say about me in your writers' circles, eh?"

"Only good things on the whole."

Khrushchev was suddenly interested. "What, for example? Well?"

"One writer calls you a pathfinder."

"Really! Do you hear that, Anastas? And what other nonsense, Comrade Tvardovsky?"

"Well . . . another compared you with Jaurès."

"Who?"

"The French revolutionary, Jaurès."

"Oh yes, I remember, we did a course on him at the Communist Academy. Do I look like him? Did he have a big belly?" Khrushchev burst into laughter. "Have I been compared with any other leader besides this Jaurès?"

"Well, no . . ."

"Are there any good jokes about me going around? Don't be afraid, Alexander Trifonovich; I like jokes. Tell me. Tell us one. As an example. Just one. I don't ask for more."

At length Tvardovsky unwillingly agreed. "But don't forget," he added, "I didn't make it up myself." He tried vainly to begin. "I'm not much good at telling stories."

"Fine, fine. Tell it, then."

"All right," he said. "Here goes. Two Muscovites meet. 'Petya, have you heard, Khrushchev has been awarded a third star as a Hero of Socialist Labor.' 'Really? What for?' 'What do you mean, what for? Valery Brumel cleared two meters and eighteen centimeters.' "

Mikoyan laughed, but Nikita missed the point.

"Now let me tell you one," Khrushchev said. "Do you know what 'cult-light' is?" Khrushchev watched him with a sly glint in his eyes.

"Cult-light?"

"Yes. What is it? Do you know? You keep quiet, Anastas. I'm not asking you. I'm asking him. Well, Comrade Tvardovsky?"

Sensing a trap, the writer shrugged and hesitated. "Generally speaking, in our Soviet terminology 'cult-light' means cultural enlighenment."

"No-o!" Khrushchev chuckled with delight. "It's a shaft of light between two cults. So, if I started a new cult, the period between Stalin and me would be called 'cult-light.' "

"Out of date, Nikita . . . that's an old joke. I'll tell you a good one. There were two shoe repairers in a workshop—"

"Tell me, Comrade Tvardovsky," Khrushchev interrupted, "did Pasternak really suppose he'd be able to publish *Doctor Zhivago* in the USSR?"

"In my opinion, Nikita Sergeyevich, Alexei Surkov made a mistake in turning this affair into a *cause célèbre*. And Comrades Suslov and Polikarpov from the Central Committee were wrong to have supported him. Of course *Doctor Zhivago* shouldn't have been published in a mass-circulation magazine like *Novy Mir*. But why couldn't the novel have been issued by the publishing house Sovetsky Pisatel in an edition of, say, three thousand copies? No one would have paid any attention to it. I assure you, Nikita Sergeyevich, it's not a book for the people, for the masses. It would have passed unnoticed. Then Western scribblers wouldn't have been able to kick up such a fuss."

Khrushchev sat down in an armchair. "Nina told me the same thing."

"Who?" Tvardovsky asked.

"My wife."

"She's like Catherine the Great, Nikita, only you don't give her a chance," Mikoyan remarked.

Khrushchev agreed and returned his attention to Tvardovsky. "I supported Suslov and Polikarpov, Alexander Trifonovich, and Surkov too, that fop in a foreign suit. So there's no going back. What do you think will happen, Alexander Trifonovich, if we really do deport Pasternak or put him on trial and send him to Tartary?"

"There'll be an outcry, Nikita Sergeyevich! In the West they'll—"

"Fuck the West!" Nikita shouted. "Do you think the Central Committee of the Communist Party cringes every time some lord or senator or Rockefeller lickspittle makes a protest? Capitalist opinion holds as much interest for us as last year's snow."

"And rightly so, Nikita," Mikoyan agreed.

"What about our foreign friends who hold the same views as we do—Western Communists?" Tvardovsky asked.

"It's always better to avoid a scandal of course." Khrushchev was disarmed by Tvardovsky's earnestness. "And I ask you once again, Alexander Trifonovich, to tell your colleagues that Khrushchev's 'thaw' is still going on and that the attack on Pasternak does not indicate a return to Stalinism. Not at all. But I just want to emphasize, Comrade Tvardovsky, that if the situation calls for action, then—as I've already told you—my hand will not falter. The USSR isn't Hungary, but in Hungary everything started from that Petifo circle."

"Petöfi," Mikoyan corrected him.

"What's the difference!" Khrushchev exploded. "Whatever it was, they were goddam sonsofbitches! And that's all there is to it."

"But, Nikita Sergeyevich," Tvardovsky ventured, "Don't you think that, although we gained, we also lost in Hungary?"

"Without a doubt. Of course we lost. But it's stupid to think only in terms of winning or losing. The most important thing is to get the best deal possible, which is the whole basis of my policy of peaceful coexistence."

Lebedev entered the office. "Nikita Sergeyevich, Serov is on the hot line."

"Fine, Comrade Lebedev. I'll speak to him." Khrushchev moved quickly to the small telephone table, lifted one of the phones and, stretching his neck like a goose, said, "Hello, Ivan, what news have you got for me?"

Mikoyan whispered to Tvardovsky, "I love Nikita, Alexander Trifonovich. His temper is outrageous, but he's a live human being. He doesn't fit into any mold, and that's a good thing. Stalin was very cunning, you see, but Khrushchev wears his heart on his sleeve. Of course he makes mistakes. We all make mistakes. Sometimes even the party makes mistakes... *sometimes*..."

"I understand, Anastas Ivanovich."

Khrushchev, still talking on the telephone, stamped his foot enthusiastically. "Fine, Ivan, fine," he said. "Let me have the text. Dictate it slowly. Like that." He wrote several lines on a pad of foolscap, barely containing his excitement. "Thanks. And say thanks to your boys, Serov. Well done." He replaced the phone and yelled at the top of his lungs.

"What happened?" Mikoyan asked.

"Guess! You're not stupid." Khrushchev drew closer to Mikoyan and Tvardovsky. "The ice has cracked. That was the Chairman of the KGB on the phone, our socialist Gestapo. Serov knows absolutely everything. And Ivan's got a brain, even if he does seem to be a simpleton like me." Khrushchev hooted again. "Dear Alexander Trifonovich, I've outsmarted your Pasternak. Yes, outsmarted! Yes, indeed. Just like that. I've tied him up in knots. Now he won't escape from my grasp. Now he's mine, mine . . ."

Tvardovsky stared at him incredulously.

"Nikita, stop being mysterious," Mikoyan said.

"All right, listen. Comrade Tvardovsky, I'll be frank with you. The intrigues of battle—" He popped a sugar lump in his mouth and cracked it with his teeth. "While we were sitting here consulting, I was waiting for Serov's call, like manna from heaven. You see, this morning, Alexander Trifonovich, Pasternak left Peredelkino for Moscow. Serov's people were following him. I authorized it. Intrigues of battle. We have to know everything about him. Goddam sonofabitch! So Serov reported to me this morning that his highness had left for Moscow—but no one of course could predict where he was going. But now we know. A complete capitulation."

"What kind of capitulation?" Tvardovsky asked.

"Guess!"

"There's no stopping him now." Mikoyan sighed and looked at Khrushchev reproachfully.

"Well, Nikita Sergeyevich, I suppose that Pasternak sent a telegram to Stockholm refusing the Nobel Prize."

"How did you know?" Nikita exclaimed, disappointed.

"I didn't know. I guessed."

"Well, you guessed right, dammit. You certainly are a shrewd one. More tea?"

"No, thanks. I was convinced that Pasternak would take this course in the end."

"We helped him. Spurred him on. Now I'll tell you what he said in his telegram." Khrushchev went back to the phones and picked up the sheet of paper. " 'To Andres Esterling, The Swedish Academy, Stockholm. Because of the importance attached to your award by the society to which I belong, I am obliged to refuse the undeserved distinction conferred on me. I beg you not to take offense at my voluntary refusal. Pasternak.' "

"Very good!" Mikoyan exclaimed.

"Yes . . . well phrased . . ." Tvardovsky muttered.

"Shall we drink to it, eh?" Nikita could not restrain himself.

"Drinking's not permitted during working hours," Mikoyan said.

"True, true. If Suslov found out, there'd be hell to pay. The monk. Doesn't drink, just plays a few hands of cards at night. But I've heard you aren't indifferent to brandy, Alexander Trifonovich. I like brandy myself. However, right now I'd prefer champagne." He hesitated, distracted. "I've just had an idea. What if we send this Nobel laureate on a creative field trip. Say . . . to Baku. Let him live there, smell the fuel oil, talk to working people, write a novel about Soviet oil. What do you think?"

"You're in too much of a hurry, Nikita," Mikoyan said.

"Quiet, Anastas, I want to know Tvardovsky's opinion. He's a poet. But who are we?"

"Nikita Sergeyevich," Tvardovsky pleaded, "we were talking about freedom. Poets don't like party tasks, even if we do go along."

"You don't like party tasks? But if the creative field trip should take you to Paris, you wouldn't mind, would you?" Khrushchev waved Tvardovsky aside and went back to the telephones. He picked up the "Kremlin phone" and dialed a number.

"Comrade Suslov? This is me, Khrushchev. Has Serov phoned you? Then you know about Pasternak. Well, this is how we'll help things along. Keep the pressure on. He's taken the first step. Now we have to force him to take the second. Keep printing 'angry responses' in the press. Tone them down a bit, though. Is that clear? And keep printing letters demanding that he be deported. Yes, and don't let the Leninist Komsomol give him any breathing room at the dacha. Let the boys go on with their meeting there. What? Overdoing it? Don't worry about that. Comrade Tvardovsky is here. The poet Tvardovsky. Yes. He's on our side. In principle. He's going to explain to his colleagues in private that I'm not Stalin. . . . Precisely. That's right, Mikhail Andreyevich. So long."

He replaced the phone and looked at Tvardovsky. "Alexander Tvardovsky, I think it's scandalous that the imperialist sharks and their lackeys in the Swedish Academy have overlooked our titan Mikhail Sholokhov, with his *And Quiet Flows the Don*. I'll force them, yes, I'll force them to award the Nobel Prize to him next year."

Tvardovsky demurred with a skeptical smile.

"No? Just wait and see. They're all scared to death of us in the West, like the devil fears incense, because we're their gravediggers, because the banner of communism is already raised over half the world. There's no hiding from it. Their only defense is to play for time. That's why they're making such a fuss over me, hoping to cajole me, to arouse a petty-bourgeois instinct in me. But we'll make fools of all of them, Alexander Tvardovsky. I'll replace our ambassador in Stockholm. Listen, Anastas, what if we send Mikoyan there, Anastas Mikoyan? Like every Armenian, he's a master of deception. You'll twist them all around your little finger, lead the Jews by the nose. And Mikhail Sholokhov will be a Nobel laureate!"

CHAPTER SIX

Renunciation

1.

The light burned in Olga's room. She took a few steps backward from her mirror in order to inspect her new black velvet gown. It fitted snugly and reached to the floor. She turned left and right, acknowledging her beauty, then picked up a comb and began arrranging her hair, which was gathered at the nape of her neck. She smiled, fancying herself a lady of leisure in her Paris boudoir.

The door creaked and her mother entered. A strong, energetic old woman, with a weathered face and sharp, birdlike nose, she wore her outdoor clothing and carried two shopping bags. She placed the bags on the table, took off her coat, and caught her breath, then looked at her daughter and said with irony, "Just like a French queen."

"Oh, Mama, does it really look that bad?"

"The dress, you mean? The dress looks fine." Her mother sat down on a stool. "Only your France is in mourning, Your Highness."

"What do you mean?"

"Mourning, weeping bitter tears."

"I don't understand, Mama. What are you getting at?" The old woman stood up, wiped her nose with a handkerchief, and started unpacking the bags. "Mama, why don't you finish what you're saying?"

"I met Jean at Kiev station, as we planned, yes?"

"Yes, and so?"

"Your hero, your Borya . . . has refused the Nobel Prize."

"What? You've . . . you've gone out of your mind."

"Jean told me. I would hardly make it up. Your Borya sent a telegram to Stockholm. It's already been broadcast worldwide."

"It can't be."

"You've been sitting here at home all day while he—"

"Nonsense! You're lying!" Olga cringed. "I don't believe you. Who told you this?"

"Have you gone deaf? Jean, Jean told me."

Olga seized her mother and shook her hard. "I don't believe you! You're playing tricks on me."

"Why would I play tricks on you? You've finished your dress and now you're trying it on, getting ready for your journey to Paris. But he, if you please, that knight of yours, has gone and sent a telegram—"

"Mama!"

"Listen, Olga. I met Jean at Kiev station, by the baggage counter. You made the appointment yourself. He said the foreign radio stations had just reported a telegram was received at the Swedish Academy—yes, from Pasternak."

"It can't be true. Khrushchev must have sent the telegram and signed it Pasternak."

"Really?"

"Borya went to Moscow to deliver a letter to the Kremlin commandant's office, a letter requesting permission for all of us to emigrate." She clasped her hands. "Could he really have lost his nerve?"

"Yes. He lost his nerve."

"Oh, it's so like him!" Olga almost screamed. "He and his tormented Zhivago—spineless, vacillating, endlessly changing his mind. Slavic souls, forever grabbing within . . ."

"Slavic souls? He's a Jew!"

"Miserable, pathetic, neurotic intellectuals . . ." Olga wheeled on her. "But I typed the letter to Khrushchev myself." She began to pace up and down, biting her lips and wringing her hands.

"And another thing, Olga: now I know for sure we're being followed."

"Who by?" The response was automatic.

"Who by? Use your head. By our guardian angels from the KGB."

Olga looked at her coldly. "Who cares? What's the use of crying over spilled milk?"

"They could arrest you for currency dealings."

"Let them."

"Put you in prison."

"Yes, prison."

They stared at each other.

"What can I get you for supper?" the older woman asked.

Olga sank into a chair and looked at her indifferently. "Do you want to stay overnight?"

"Can't I? It's too late for me to go back to Moscow."

"Fine, stay. You may as well put some potatoes on."

"Is he coming?"

"He should be."

Her mother took a square parcel from one of the bags, unwrapped it, and put three large packets of money on the chest. "From Jean. Twenty thousand rubles."

"Did you count it?"

"How could I? At the station? Jean's never cheated us."

"What size bills?"

"One-hundred ruble."

"Did you bring the mail?"

"Here." She gave her daughter several letters and newspapers and began straightening up the room.

Olga went over to the chest, picked up the bundles of bills as if she were weighing them and with a careless gesture shoved them into one of the drawers. She opened the mail, glancing at each letter before she put it aside, and then quickly looked through the French newspapers.

"Jean also noticed we were being followed," her mother said. "He's terrified. He could be expelled for what he's doing. Other journalists—"

"They'll deport him and make a big stink. And rightly so." Olga smiled maliciously. "The whole of his brilliant career will go to hell. But he'll get deported to France, Mama, while we'll go to Kolyma somewhere."

"You're a strange creature. What are you smiling for?" She waited for a response. "He said we shouldn't meet for a while."

"Oh, wonderful, marvelous! What brilliant conspirators you are!" Olga suddenly lost patience. "What a fool I am, fool, fool! I believed in him, my knight, my Borya . . ." She trembled with inner rage, then fell back into her chair. "Where's Irina?" she asked at length.

"With her student at the French hostel in Moscow."

"Maybe he'll marry her."

The old woman spat with contempt. "Frenchmen are pimps. She's a fool and you are too. He'll have a time for himself and then he'll be gone with the wind. I'm surprised your daughter hasn't got herself pregnant yet. And your son . . ."

"And what of him?"

"He's bought himself a motorcycle."

"You gave him the money?"

"He helped himself. I told him no, but he said, 'Shut up, you old witch, or I'll have you and Mama locked up by the

KGB for your shady deals.' Threatened me, he did. He'll grow up to be a crook."

"The spirit of the times, Mama, the spirit of the times." Olga stood up again. "I'd strangle him with pleasure."

"Your son?"

She went to the window and, pressing her brow against the pane, stared vacantly into the night. A lone bulb hung on a post by the tavern, casting a ring of light. She turned, then quickly went back to her mother, gathered up the letters and newspapers, and put them out of sight.

"He's coming," she said, glancing in the mirror and smoothing her hair. "Go to Masha's, Mama, and don't come back."

Olga stood opposite the door, alone, when Pasternak entered. He appeared stooped, his left shoulder lower than his right, and he seemed tired. His smile suggested preoccupation, perhaps resignation, until he looked up and saw her, "Oh . . . how beautiful you are tonight," he said.

"And how beautiful you were today," she replied. She didn't move. "With your white flag."

"So you know everything."

"The whole world knows!" she said.

"You think I surrendered."

"I think Steinbeck's 'eagle' crashed."

Pasternak shifted from one foot to the other, waiting for her to ask him to sit down.

"Olga, my dearest, let's not quarrel. You once said that I had two sides—a heretic and a sheep—and you were right. Yesterday I rebelled. Today I gave in. But I must follow my own best judgment. It's the only defense I have. No one forced me to do anything. I went to Moscow to deliver the letter to Khrushchev. But then . . . something changed my mind."

"And that something was *fear*!"

"No," he insisted. "May I sit down?" He sat down and unbuttoned his coat. "No, Olga, it wasn't fear. It was something deeper. The same thing happened to me in Marburg fifty years ago when my philosophy teacher, Cohen, tried to persuade me to settle in Germany. He promised me a brilliant future and I agreed, and then one day I went home to Moscow. I know it sounds pretentious, Olga, but I can't give up my native land. Whether I want it or not, I have it; whatever it is, it's *mine*. I have a son, a family, friends—a people, a great and tragic people. And I have you. It's all indissoluble. All of it—"

"Rubbish," she interrupted. She had not moved. "You can forget about me. I helped you with all my strength to fight against yourself. I tried. But the rotten cowardly sheep, the weak, insignificant *Soviet* Yury Zhivago won."

"Olga, don't talk like this."

"They called you an 'internal émigré.' What kind of 'internal émigré' are you? You're a sellout!" She abandoned her pose. "What's the point of pretending a sellout is something exalted—a patriot or whatever? The truth is, you deserve your old hag and your Georgian princess."

"Olga, why do you insult Zina and Nina? They had nothing to do with it."

She paced about the room, shouting. "You suffer because Stalin didn't touch you. But the tyrant knew what he was doing. You mourn because your friends died in the camps and prisons. Osip Mandelstam was honest, straightforward, and courageous; that's why he died. But you? Stalin didn't kill you, because you're a coward, a coward."

Pasternak struggled to his feet.

"You're a coward! A coward!" she repeated.

"Olga, stop it."

"No! No power on earth can stop me now. I'm going to speak. I made you into a hero. But in this vile life heroes don't exist. The emperor has no clothes. When the time came to act decisively he scampered into the bushes, complaining of a stomachache. Lord, what lies Yury Zhivago wrote in his poems!

> " 'And never for a single instant
> Betray your true self, or pretend,
> But be alive, and only living,
> And only living to the end.' "*

"Olga! Stop it. Stop it."

"To the end! To the end!" she screamed.

Pasternak could not take his eyes off her. He was riveted, appalled by her. How had he loved such a woman, such a grasping petty bourgeois. For all the world, she reminded him of the women hucksters at the market—loud, impudent, brazen, calculating. Goaded beyond bearing, he lost his restraint.

"Olga, is this what you were planning to wear in Paris?"

"What? What did you say? Yes, this—"

"It suits you. The President of France himself would not rebuff you. You're a perfect cliché."

His words stung her into frenzy, but the revulsion shown in his eyes made her congeal inside. Transfixed for the moment, she burst into sobs and, turning her rage inside, began to tear at her clothes. The gown had become her disgrace, and, hysterically, she seized it in her teeth and, managing a first rent, tore the remainder to shreds. Scraps of velvet lay scattered all over the room when she was done. She collapsed in her chair, her naked shoulders trembling with her crying.

Pasternak watched her but did not approach her. He watched as from across a divide, understanding that the qualities he had loved in her were the same he now despised. He had long ago recognized them and had fought against them, but at the same time he knew and had known that her untrammeled passions were a healthy check to his own. She brought him down to earth. But what a mass of contradictions she was—a talented poet and translator, a truthful woman, a petty bourgeois, and an egoist. He had loved this combination in her; the wedding of good and bad that made

* From "It's Unbecoming to Have Fame," in *In the Interlude: Poems Nineteen Forty-five–Nineteen Sixty*, trans. Henry Kamen (London: Oxford Univ. Press, 1962).

her alive and attractive. He had even loved her vulgarity. And now he felt terribly sorry for her. He stepped toward her and placed his hands on her shoulders, then leaned down and kissed her hair.

He thought of the lines he had written in *Doctor Zhivago* about his heroine Lara: "One fine day Lara went out and did not come back. She must have been arrested on the street, and she vanished without a trace and probably died somewhere, forgotten as a nameless number on a list that afterward got mislaid in one of the innumerable mixed or women's concentration camps in the north."

Olga remained silent, but she had stopped crying.

Pasternak squeezed her shoulders. "No, Olga, you must live. Your turn hasn't come. Wipe away your tears." He waited. "I want you to sit down and type what I tell you to. Olga . . . did you hear?"

She wiped her eyes and then her whole face with a towel, got up from the chair and put on a housecoat. She placed the typewriter on the table and slid a sheet of paper into it, then sat down and prepared to work. She moved mechanically, like a robot.

" 'To Nikita Sergeyevich Khrushchev,' " Pasternak dictated, " 'Central Committee of the Communist Party of the Soviet Union. Respected' . . . no, just 'Dear Nikita Sergeyevich, I am addressing you personally, the Central Committee of the Communist Party and the Soviet government.' " As he spoke he walked about the room picking up the pieces of velvet.

" 'From the report of Comrade Semichastny it has become known to me that the government "would not put any obstacles in the way of my departure from the USSR." This is not possible for me: I am bound to Russia by birth, by my life and my work. I cannot conceive of a life separate from and outside that of Russia. Whatever my mistakes and aberrations have been, I could not have imagined that I would find myself at the center of the political campaign that is now being waged around my name in the West.' . . ."

He sat down in a chair and said quietly, "It's the truth, Olga. If they had appreciated literature in the West, their press would never have started this orgy. There was no need to turn me into a martyr. The Western press has used me—that's the main fact."

Olga remained silent, staring at the typewriter.

He stood up and started to pace again while he dictated the final sentences. " 'Now that I have become aware of all this, I have informed the Swedish Academy of my voluntary refusal of the Nobel Prize. Exile beyond the boundaries of my native country would be equivalent to death for me. Therefore I beg you not to take this extreme measure. With my hand on my heart, I swear I have contributed to Soviet literature and can still be of use to it. Boris Pasternak.' "

When she had finished, Olga pulled the sheet of paper from the machine and offered it to him. He took it, folded it, and placed it in his breast pocket. Her silence annoyed him.

"That's only the beginning, Olga. I'll have to write to *Pravda* as well, repenting all my mortal sins. And I will, I will repent, whether I have committed the sins or not. No, Olga, dear, it's not cowardice and it's not apostasy. It's not weakness either. It's necessity. Better men than I have gone through the same thing. It's one of the hazards of the age. To be proud and to die without bowing one's head at sixty-eight is probably not that difficult, especially if there is a possibility of, say, leaving for Europe, where you've got money in the bank. But to humble oneself at that age, to renounce one's own self, that's terrifying . . ."

"I'm tired, Borya," Olga said through clenched teeth. "Spare me."

"There's a price one must pay for living one's own personal judgment."

"Take the letter and go," Olga said. "It's late."

"Fine." Pasternak put on his cap. He stopped at the door and turned to her. "I'm asking you to break off all your dealings with foreigners. I've put up with it until now. But I've had enough. I don't want any more. No more newspapers and letters from abroad. And the main thing: no money. If you receive any illegally again, give it back."

Olga went to the chest, took out the bundles of cash and put them on the table. "Here's your money," she said. "Take it. Give it back. Do what you want with it. Only leave me in peace." She raised her eyes to his, unrepentant.

"Give it to Masha," he said.

Olga's mother came in as soon as Pasternak had left. "I heard everything," she observed energetically. "Don't be upset, Olga. He'll come back. He can't manage without you." She picked up the currency and put it back in the chest. "What an idea! A widow's pension for Masha. The whims your Borya has! He's a fool. I hope he doesn't come back. To hell with him; who needs him anyway? Don't grieve, Olga, you've still got his will . . . and the blank sheets of paper with his signature."

Olga frowned. "What did you say, Mama?"

"About his will. You can rewrite it. If you've still got his signature."

Olga suddenly slapped her mother across the face with all her might.

2.

Nina was laying out a game of solitaire on the table, while Zina idly arranged the liqueur bottles on the sideboard.

"A lot of berries and not much juice," she muttered, and shook her head. "Someone is having a drop on the sly. That's a fact. And it's not the first time it's happened. It's either Tanya or Lyonya. But just try and catch the thief. Lyonya says it's Tatyana, and she says it's Lyonya. A fine pair!"

"What's the time?"

"What's worrying you? He often stays late with her, Nina."

"Those hooligans are still wandering around." She spoke angrily. "Borya's refused the Nobel Prize. What more do they want?"

"They'll calm down. On orders from above."

"On Khrushchev's orders?"

"No doubt."

"Whatever did you and I admire in him?"

"He promised to erect a monument to Stalin's victims."

"True."

Zina sat down opposite her and lit a cigarette. "How's the game going?"

"It's not working out."

"You know, Nina, I got used to Rosalie, to Rosalie Zaak with two *a*'s. Now that she's gone I feel . . . something's missing. She was sensitive. Isn't it marvelous how well the state machine works? In the morning Borya sends a telegram to Stockholm and by three o'clock they've already taken her away. It's no longer important whether Pasternak hangs himself or not. The deed has been done. According to their calculations, he's hardly likely to hang himself now."

A shot rang out and the dogs began to bark.

"What's Yury Mikhailovich wasting cartridges for?" Zina stood up, intending to go outside, but then she waved her hand in frustration and sat down again.

"Where's Tanya?" Nina asked.

"She's sleeping. In her room. She's tired of it all."

Nina shuffled the cards. "To be honest, Zina, as soon as Borya refused the prize, I felt better. I realize it wasn't an easy thing for him to do. He's still upset, no doubt, but all the same . . . in my opinion, the immediate danger has passed."

"Most likely."

"And the most important thing is that Borya will stay in Russia. Isn't that true? Here. With us. With you, Zina."

"With me? What difference does it make to me, Nina? Whether he's in Paris, London . . . or Peredelkino? We're strangers. It's true that I objected when he decided to give *Doctor Zhivago* to an Italian publisher. I was worried about the family, about Lyonya." She brightened. "But to tell the truth, Nina, I have felt better since Borya refused the prize.

People are funny. He goes to his mistress every day, and here I am, still concerned about him."

"Because you love him."

"No."

The door from the kitchen opened and Pasternak came in. He looked depleted, spent, and when Zina and Nina saw him, they clasped their hands.

"Borya, are you all right?" Nina jumped up from the table.

He looked at both of them as if he had just recognized them. "The Komsomol are drunk," he said.

"Did they attack you?"

"Are you hurt?"

Pasternak shook his head. "They didn't see me," he said. "It was all so ordinary. So ordinary and everyday. They attacked one of their own and killed him, I think." He shuddered. "Oh, what do I know about my people, about humans in general, their lives, their morals? Poet! Prophet! Philosopher! Nonsense! I don't know a thing. Everything I wrote, it was all . . . the hothouse suffering of a Narcissus."

"The people are rough, Borya," Nina commented. "And that's how you portrayed them in *Doctor Zhivago*. The people are stupid . . ."

"Nina, you say the people are stupid, rough, and malicious. You say that's how I portrayed them in *Doctor Zhivago*. But is it true? Are they really like that? Maybe my imagination led me astray. The people—a wild animal? Is it true? No, no . . ." The book that Rosalie had been reading lay on the table; he picked it up and looked at the title. "And *Anna Karenina* here . . . a satiated lady of leisure, tormented by intellectual and sexual dissatisfaction, 'enslaved' by social injustice . . ."

"Borya, what are you saying?"

"While millions of simple Russian women were dying just because there was no one to help them during childbirth."

"But why oppose the one to the other?" Nina objected.

"Where, Nina, where is the real hero of our time?" Pasternak said without listening. "Where is he?"

He put the book back on the table, then silently went upstairs to his room, where, without switching on the light, he collapsed on his bed.

Of course he had not meant what he had said. His mind was such a tangle of contradictory arguments. He did know the people; he loved and hated them at the same time, and he had made that clear in *Doctor Zhivago*. And despite what he had just said about Tolstoy, he believed that Tolstoy too had known the Russian people. His criticism of *Anna Karenina* was just a form of self-defense. Olga was right when she called the people a "mob." And he had portrayed this truth in *Doctor Zhivago*, but the human being in him found it difficult to accept. He had often reminded Olga that "a sick and unhappy child is dearer to his mother's heart . . ."

He got out of bed and switched on the light and went over to the photograph of Tolstoy.

"Here you are, great writer of the Russian soil. Do Anna Karenina, Pierre Bezukhov, and Natasha Rostova really represent our people? No, they are weaklings, aristocrats with white hands, who indulge in spiritual agonies, in elevated introspection . . . they're the same type as my Zhivago . . ." He shook his head. "But where, oh where is the *real* hero of our time?"

3.

The house had finally fallen asleep when Pasternak sat down and copied out the cherished lines from *Doctor Zhivago* on a clean sheet of paper. The lines, which Olga had recited as they walked from the station, seemed to explain everything.

"Russia, his incomparable mother, famed far and wide, martyred, stubborn, extravagant, crazy, irresponsible, adored, Russia with her eternally splendid, disastrous and unpredictable gestures."

The words contained not a hint of the stupid and coarse Russia, of the "mob." They were the key to Pasternak's soul.

215

And as he thought about himself and the people, about Russia, a creative ecstasy moved in him, and poetry began to form on his lips.

He took another sheet of paper, on which the first quatrain of "The Nobel Prize" was already jotted down, and within half an hour he had added another three quatrains.

Then he got up from the table with the sheet of paper in his hand and recited aloud:

> "I've fallen beastlike in a snare;
> Light, people, freedom, somewhere bide:
> But at my back I hear the chase
> And there is no escape outside.
>
> Darkest wood and lakeside shore,
> Gaunt trunk of a levelled tree,
> My way is cut off on all sides:
> Let what may, come; all's one to me.
>
> Is there some ill I have committed?
> Am I a murderer, miscreant?
> For I have made the whole world weep
> Over the beauty of my land.
>
> But even at the very grave
> I trust the time shall come to be
> When over malice, over wrong,
> The good will win its victory."*

He repeated the lines "For I have made the whole world weep over the beauty of my land." He liked them, but at the same time he found them disturbing. Although beautiful, personal, they were weak, because there was a definite strain of vanity in them. "I have made the whole world weep." Wasn't it simply too grandiose? And the phrase "beauty of my land"—wasn't it too abstract? Pasternak felt that in *Doctor Zhivago* he had moved beyond the confines of his "land,"

---

* In *In the Interlude: Poems Nineteen Forty-five–Nineteen Sixty,* trans. Henry Kamen (London: Oxford Univ. Press, 1962).

returned to his poetic past, to the pantheism still alive in him, perhaps still the most important part of him. Maybe this was what had estranged him from his son and what had attracted him to the West.

For some reason he recalled a concert at the Moscow Conservatory, a performance of Scriabin's works. The composer himself had conducted the orchestra, and Pasternak could still visualize him as if he were alive—a handsome, vigorous, serious man, wearing an elegant tailcoat over a starched collar and cuffs, with his hair streaming across his forehead and his body moving in time like a slender birch tree in a storm. The youth had looked at the maestro spellbound and dreamed that one day he too would bow to an enraptured audience. He had dreamed of being famous. Was it vanity? He questioned now. No, he hadn't wanted glory; he had wanted fame as a vindication of his work. He had never worn a tailcoat in his life.

Nor would he now. He imagined a huge baroque hall, brightly lit by crystal chandeliers, with gilded moldings on the vaulted ceiling and walls. The hall, filled with chairs and armchairs covered in red plush and paintings by Italian masters, opened into another, where a trio played Scriabin. A Swedish dignitary, superbly dressed, was speaking to the guests, all of them luminaries of European culture—writers, artists, painters, professors, architects. Immediately before him sat the laureates themselves, men in tailcoats, with starched collars and cuffs. And among them one empty armchair.

Pasternak rubbed his brow. It was an unworthy dream. Had he not written: "It's unbecoming to have fame"? And when he met the slightly sullen gaze of Leo Tolstoy, he felt ashamed. Tolstoy, Leo Tolstoy, had not received the prize. Nor had Anton Chekhov either. Who was he beside these men? The prize was not worth having.

He thanked God that he was in his own home and that he no longer needed Frau Ludike in Garmisch-Partenkirchen.

PART TWO

CHAPTER SEVEN

Exile to Georgia

1.

The full Council of Ministers of the USSR had met at nine in the morning, and three hours later it was still in session. All the union ministers and chairmen of committees attached to the Council of Ministers were present. The only one missing was the Minister of Foreign Affairs, Andrei Gromyko; he had gone back to his office at ten, with Khrushchev's permission, because an important message had arrived from London about the official visit to the USSR in March of the Prime Minister of Great Britain, Harold Macmillan.

Nikita was presiding; Mikoyan was next to him, and beyond him, seated in order of rank along the wide table covered with dark-blue cloth, were the other wielders of executive power—well-fed, clean-shaven, fashionably dressed in the

Soviet style, and, all in all, each one remarkably like the next.

Khrushchev felt sick; his head was aching, his feet were swollen (he had slipped his shoes off), and his heart occasionally missed a beat. All this of course was a result of yesterday's government reception in the restaurant of the Sovetskaya Hotel on the Leningrad highway. Three thousand guests had attended. About 100,000 rubles had been spent on the food and the rest. It had been a splendid affair, and today the world press was undoubtedly raving about "Khrushchev's feast." Those Western correspondents, goddam sonsofbitches, if you gave them fresh caviar and plenty to drink, they'd praise whatever you liked. They were happy so long as the tables were laden with fine food and good liquor. Well, fine, let them blast away. The scoundrels! Even though they were so good with words, they were all beasts, beasts. Well, at least capitalists everywhere would realize they were dealing with a great power. Only a great power could throw a real banquet, with fresh caviar straight from the Caspian Sea, the devil take it! And although it was paid for with socialist money, all those foreigners were ready to swallow it down by the mouthful, enjoying it without a second thought.

Oh, how sick he felt . . .

What a fine state of affairs! He'd gotten drunk on champagne yesterday. He'd polished off ten glasses and chased them with a large glass of brandy. The two had gotten mixed up together, and during the night he had been sick, groaning and giving Nina no peace. He had fallen into a fitful sleep around three, and then had to jump up when the alarm went off at eight, in a rush to shave and leave for the Kremlin. He had no valid reason to postpone the session of the full Council of Ministers, and despite his discomfort, he was determined to sit through it.

Nikita yawned. His distorted mouth attracted the attention of one of the ministers. Goddam sonsofbitches! They had all been at the reception yesterday, but not one of them had gotten drunk; they had gone home early and slept well of course, not like him. And not one of them had said anything he shouldn't have to the foreign correspondents, but he, Khrushchev, had talked a lot. Now he could remember what had happened. Americans were lousy, all of them. They were insolent, pushing in everywhere and not letting anything get in their way. Not on their life! They were democrats, the devil take them! The swine had heard that the Soviet premier liked to wet his whistle at receptions and talk about "life," so from the very start they hadn't left him alone, forming a tight circle around him and vying with one another to throw leading questions at him. Some of them didn't need interpreters, and they gabbled at him in Russian. The champagne had loosened his tongue, and he had bragged to them that "we Bolsheviks will lull you capitalists to sleep with peaceful relations, then—wham!—we'll hit the whole bunch of you over the head." During the night the press department of the Ministry of Foreign Affairs had telephoned all the foreign correspondents with an official denial of this statement.

Ugh, he felt sick . . .

A bottle of Narzan mineral water stood on the table in front of him. Next to it was a large nickel-plated bowl in which Nikita saw a distorted reflection of the whole conference hall. If he looked closely he could see the scene outside the window—the battlements of the Spassky Tower, covered in snow, the snow-topped roof of the GUM department store on the opposite side of Red Square, and even the pigeons strolling about on the window ledges.

Khrushchev thought again about the American correspondents who had found his weak spot (what he called his "weak string") and exploited it to the full. Although he cursed these large receptions, calling them a "pointless business," he enjoyed them and took great personal interest in their preparation. Before every reception he went over the cost estimates. He encouraged lavishness, and if the reception's budget was 100,000 rubles, he would usually increase it to 120,000, thinking to himself, "Better too much than too little." The restaurant in the Sovetskaya Hotel was especially to his liking. In czarist times it had been famous as the Yar, and merchant millionaires had held extravagant parties there. Someone had told him that naked women had bathed in champagne fountains at these galas. What fun and games! The little beauties howled. What a picture, eh? Just splendid! "Proletarian morality" prohibited such attractions, which came from the capitalist menu, but Nikita found it pleasant to see Soviet lackeys—waiters, that is—hovering around him and trying to please the "boss" in every possible way.

Khrushchev turned his attention back to the meeting. Beshchev, the USSR Minister of Railway Transportation, was reading his report. He was solidly built, as if cast in bronze, and seemed as durable. He had occupied his post for many years under Stalin, had held onto it during the interregnum, and was still sitting there now, under Khrushchev. Nikita called him the "bronze tower." He knew it was impossible to find fault with Beshchev; his reports were always excellent and his percentage indicators constantly wavered between 105 and 110. What more was there to say?

Khrushchev recalled that yesterday, at the reception, Beshchev, in his ministerial uniform (which he never took off), had eaten without stop, as if he were starving. Since he kept busy with the ham, he didn't have time to drink and chat with foreign correspondents. You can't talk with your mouth full. That was clever. Yes, he had traveled by every route. He knew that if you enjoyed ham, you'd stay alive.

Yes, I have to give up drinking, Nikita thought. First, because of my health. One day I'll just collapse from it, and that'll be the end of me. Why go off to join your ancestors before your time is up? His feet throbbed and his heart beat out a strange rhythm. And then, no good ever came from drinking. That red Jesuit, Suslov, was clearly collecting evidence to use against him. That morning Khrushchev had spoken to Serov on the hot line and the latter had reported to him that Suslov intended to propose that the Central Committee Politburo pass a resolution forbidding the First Secretary of the Central Committee of the Communist Party to consume alcohol. The Politburo had already recommended that he abstain from vodka. He had switched to champagne, but this had not altered the situation.

Khrushchev wanted to gulp down some Narzan, but he stopped himself; if he did, everyone would gloat and spend the whole week whispering that Nikita "had had a drop too much," then sobered up on Narzan.

No one was listening to Beshchev of course, but they were all pretending that his arithmetic interested them.

Oh yes, Stalin had been a lucky fellow! In the last few years of his life the "old man" had assembled his ministers only when he felt like it, for his own entertainment, in order to bully them and set them on "the right path." Stalin could say, "I am the Council of Ministers," just as some French king had once said, "I am the state," because Stalin decided everything himself. But Khrushchev had to put up with collective decision making and sit through these long and often absolutely fruitless talk shops.

Nikita turned his head toward Mikoyan; the latter threw him a sly look that said, "Feeling sick, brother, eh?" But Khrushchev did not want to admit to this and wrote on a sheet of paper, "Beshchev is the perfect bureaucrat, eh?" and held it out to Mikoyan. (The custom of exchanging notes during meetings had been introduced by Stalin and had become entrenched.) Anastas looked at the message and immediately added, "On whom we depend and shall depend, Nikita, old fellow." Then Khrushchev wrote, "Was it really like this under Lenin?" To which Mikoyan replied, "Definitely. Only Stalin increased it tenfold." Khrushchev chewed his lips and scribbled, "And what are we doing?" Mikoyan answered, "We're doing the same—*so far*."

It was the drop that made the cup overflow. Khrushchev began to fidget. His general indisposition and hostility toward Beshchev were heightened by a sharp pain in his buttocks. He suddenly interrupted the speaker by tapping on a glass with his pencil.

"Your report is impressive, Comrade Beshchev, but passenger trains still run as late as ever."

His comment was irrelevant, since Beshchev had been talking about the new system of control administration on freight lines.

"Don't distract me, Nikita Sergeyevich, or I'll get off the point!"

A smile passed across the faces of those present and Khrushchev realized that he had blundered and that Beshchev, aware of his own invulnerability, had just shaken off a remark of the Chairman of the USSR Council of Ministers. But it wasn't worth taking a stand on, especially since Khrushchev knew little about railway transport. Yet at the same time he believed that Beshchev was talking gibberish. His ministerial reports were models of bureaucratic prose, but year in and year out the trains were always late.

At that moment Nikita felt painfully alone in this great conference hall, as if he had been dropped by parachute into the wastes of the Sahara. He felt sorry for himself and remembered his school hero, the Spanish knight Don Quixote, who fought windmills and who was laughed at by everyone. Wasn't he himself laughed at for refusing to accept the gigantic socialist bureaucracy? Even he could see the humor in his situation. He was, after all, a respected part of the bureaucracy he was attacking, and at times, especially under Stalin, he too had gone on like Beshchev here, not just for thirty minutes but for an hour or two without stopping, and about nothing in particular, just beating the air. All his attempts to improve administration met with resistance. Or worse, the changes he proposed seemed to enlarge the bureaucratic web, embellishing it with new intricacies. He wanted to put life into a soulless machine, but he was blamed for increasing the machine's power. Serious criticism had been directed at his efforts to reorganize the party structure—for example, at his decision to split district committees of the party into district committees for industry and district committees for agriculture, in the hope that more attention would be paid to the

Soviet countryside and to the needs of the peasantry. But as a result the bureaucracy had grown, and the wits circulated an epigram: "Did you hear that a second queen has been crowned in England? The first one is for industry, and the second one for agriculture." A new system of regional economic councils that he had proposed also had been criticized, as had his plan for increasing the cultivation of corn.

To hell with all their objections! He wanted to bring the apparatus of power closer to the people; he wanted to increase personal responsibility and reduce centralization. In short, he wanted to encourage initiative. Because he traveled about the country visiting factories and plants, collective and state farms, talking to workers and collective farmers, he was ironically called a "populist" and an "actor on tour." Bureaucrats at both the top and the bottom cursed him for his mania for reform and for his desire to break up the Stalinist machinery, to which they had grown accustomed. It was hard to believe, but things had gotten to the point where *every* new conveyor belt at the Gorky automobile plant had to be approved by Gosplan and the USSR Council of Ministers; and as a result, Soviet cars were at least twenty years behind American ones.

Khrushchev felt a sudden urge to get up from his chairman's seat, let his pants down and display the two red spots on his buttocks that he knew had been caused by sitting for so long.

Having guessed how Nikita was feeling, Mikoyan passed him a note: "It will all work out for the best."

Mikoyan's words calmed Khrushchev down. The leader looked at his first deputy and smiled. Mikoyan knew how to make him feel better. The Armenian was right of course. He must arm himself with patience; it would all work out for the best. Well said. Said by the people. He allowed himself a glass of Narzan, and wrote back to Mikoyan: "Ugh, I feel sick, Anastas, sick." Mikoyan took him literally and answered, "You should stop drinking." Khrushchev replied, "I won't drink anymore. *Ever.*"

He looked around at the impassive ministers, wondering if anything had changed since Stalin's time. Despite his many sincere and passionate attempts to break loose from the Stalinist legacy, he still did not have the strength to free himself, and he had left many things as they had been under Stalin. He recalled a joke Serov had told: "Stalin gave Khrushchev two wills and ordered him to open the first one on his death and the second one a few years later. After the 'great one' died, Nikita opened the first will, which read: 'Blame it all on me.' Then a few years later he opened the second will, which read: 'Now do everything the same way I did.' "

Khrushchev was constantly tormented by a particular doubt. What if the fault lay not in Stalin but in the idea of a communist society? In other words, was it inevitable that everything noble and humane would vanish as soon as practical action began? Did communism itself necessarily involve the destruction of life? He had no answer. Perhaps if he had been able to act on his own, as Stalin had, he would have discovered the truth. He envied Stalin's independence.

At half past twelve, after the debate on Beshchev's report had started, Gromyko returned. His fleshy face with its thin lips and dull eyes seemed more dour than usual. He sat down and immediately wrote a note to Khrushchev: "Nikita Sergeyevich, it has just been reported to me from London that the Prime Minister of Great Britain, Macmillan, has told one of his retinue that he will attempt to meet the poet Boris Pasternak during his stay in Moscow. I think it should be remembered that Macmillan is the owner of a large publishing house and therefore might undertake such a step in hope of commercial gain. They're all businessmen over there, even the Prime Ministers. What if he offers Pasternak a contract for a new novel? And how can we refuse to allow a guest of high rank to meet with Pasternak?"

Khrushchev read the note and almost shouted. "That Jew again!" He had recently consoled himself that the whole affair had more or less died down. True, Serov had reported that someone in London was planning to make a film of *Doctor Zhivago*, but that was beyond his control. However, if Macmillan were allowed now to meet Pasternak, there would be endless troubles. A horde of Western correspondents would follow the Englishman to Peredelkino, and dozens of articles and commentaries would appear. And who knew what Pasternak would say to the Prime Minister? Gromyko was right of course. The businessman Prime Minister would try to wheedle another anti-Soviet work from the author. But how could Macmillan be refused? Gromyko had seen right to the heart of the matter. The Englishman will be a Soviet guest. How can a guest be refused? What should he be told if he asks for a meeting with Pasternak?

Khrushchev scratched the back of his neck and scrawled down one side of Gromyko's note, "Anastas, what do you think?" Mikoyan looked at Gromyko's message and Khrushchev's question, then flared his nostrils and wrote, "What if we announce a smallpox quarantine in Peredelkino?" The suggestion made Khrushchev laugh, but he thought it astute. He scribbled another question on the note—"Ivan, what do you think?"—and passed it down the table to Serov. The general read all three men's notations and, after glancing at each correspondent, wrote without pausing for thought: "Nikita Sergeyevich, I think we should make sure Pasternak is not in Peredelkino during the week of Macmillan's visit. Why not suggest to him that he go and visit his friends in Georgia, have a rest there with his wife?"

The KGB chairman's idea was most appropriate, and Khrushchev felt more serene. A splendid fellow, he thought. He slipped his feet into his shoes, got up, and, without saying a word, left for the Council of Ministers' secretariat. No one was startled by his departure, as, since Stalin's day, the Chairman of the Council of Ministers had had standing authority to leave for the secretariat without warning or explanation.

Calling Suslov, Nikita reminded himself that he had to get hold of some compromising information about "the theoretician" in order to forestall the latter's scheming. Nevertheless his voice was calm as he told Suslov the details about Macmillan and Pasternak.

"Get Surkov to 'advise' Pasternak to go to Georgia for two weeks," he added. "Let him and his wife have a rest there. We'll take financial responsibility. Is that clear? Surkov must make Pasternak understand that he is to say nothing about Macmillan; otherwise it'll leak into the Western press that I exiled Pasternak to Tbilisi because of the British Prime Minister."

2.

Faded violet saddlebags hung on the flanks of a scrawny, rust-colored donkey; they held clay pitchers containing matsoni, a homemade yogurt fermented in the surrounding villages and sent for sale to Tbilisi, the capital of Soviet Georgia. A frail old man trudged behind the beast, wearing a black felt cap and a worn-out linen shirt, which in characteristic Georgian style had tiny balls of cloth for fasteners instead of buttons; he had a long gray mustache and held a gnarled stick. Every hundred feet or so he shouted at the top of his voice: "Mats-oni!"

All her life Nina had awakened to the cry of "Mats-oni!" And this morning was no exception. She got out of bed, put on her dressing gown, and opened the window. It was still cool outside, but the sun was already shining and the sky behind the high peaks of Mtatsminda Mountain was perfectly clear.

Looking at the donkey and the old man, she smiled. She remembered donkeys and old men like these from her childhood, when she had lived in her native town of Telavi; she had encountered them again in Tbilisi when she married Titsian, and they had even survived the upheaval in 1937. Yes, life had changed swiftly, but some small, insignificant details from the past remained. Thank God, she thought, Soviet power hasn't abolished them yet!

She lit a cigarette and began to cough, then made her bed and went into the dining room. The apartment, which she had received after the posthumous rehabilitation of her husband, consisted of four rooms and a verandah overlooking a courtyard. The front of the apartment faced the street on the first floor, but the veranda was on the third, as the four-story writers' residence stood on the slope of a hill. She switched on the electric kettle and listened attentively. All was quiet.

Her son-in-law, Alik, a young doctor of small but athletic build, had left for the Institute of Cardiology; Nitochka, her lithe, agile daughter, had left for the technical school, where she was a secretary; her lively grandson, Giviko, who slept on the verandah year round, had, as usual, jumped out of bed before everyone else, done his exercises, and, without having breakfast, run off to school, where he was in the seventh grade. The only other person in the apartment was Alik's old nanny, an invalid of devout Russian Orthodox faith who stayed in a tiny room off the kitchen.

Nina drank a glass of tea and then went onto the verandah, which overlooked the whole of Tbilisi. The city, spread out in a shallow valley, was covered with a light morning mist. Nearby, behind a high wooden fence, government residences could be seen. The top party and government officials of Georgia lived there, and the "palace" of the First Secretary of the Central Committee, Mzhavanadze, was directly opposite Nina's verandah. Nina often observed what was happening in this "czar's" territory, with its tennis court, swimming pool, garden, and spacious servants' quarters. Sometimes she caught a glimpse of the proprietress, the wife of the "boss," a very portly Ukrainian woman with a lively face. Rumor in Tbilisi had it that the proprietress, also known locally as "the Cossack," had her husband firmly under her thumb, even beat him occasionally. Madam Mzhavanadze, as Nina always called her, liked to walk in the garden with her fifteen-year-old daughter, who covertly watched Givi exercising on the verandah. Sometimes Nina saw the "boss" himself; he was also very fat and had a large Georgian nose. He had been appointed to his post on the personal recommendation of Khrushchev, who had gotten to know him in the Ukraine, where Mzhavanadze had spent the greater part of his adult life as a political officer in the army, ultimately reaching the rank of general. Nina had been told that the portly bureaucrat had all but forgotten his native tongue and conducted Politburo sessions of the Central Committee of the Georgian Communist Party in Russian. Generally speaking, the Tbilisi intelligentsia despised Mzhavanadze as a "hireling," but at the same time was afraid of him and especially of his friend, Inauri, another general who had served in the Ukraine and who was now Chairman of the Georgian KGB. Inauri had been a cavalry officer, and it was said that he was cruel and given to cutting people down without mercy. Perhaps this was true and perhaps not.

The government residents were still asleep, so Nina could enjoy without distraction the view of the beloved city. It had grown so in the last several decades that it was impossible to take it all in, and it indisputably had lost much of its charm in becoming an industrial center. All the same, she adored Tbilisi, home of her youth and of the terrible seventeen years she had spent as the ostracized wife of an "enemy of the people." Nina had suffered more than a few misfortunes here, but she still thought of Georgia and the Georgians as very special. And she felt that Soviet power was not as oppressive in Georgia as, say, in Russia. When people here addressed each other, even in party circles, they still said *batono* or *calbatono*—that is, "mister" or "mistress"—and rarely used the androgynous Russian term "Comrade."

Nina was about to make Givi's bed when she was interrupted by a knock at the front door. It was probably the milkman, she thought, and cursed Alik for not having repaired the doorbell. But on opening the door she discovered the postman, Yagor.

"Good morning, Calbatono Nina." He pronounced each syllable distinctly and smiled cheerfully. "There's a telegram for you. From Moscow. I was in such a hurry I almost tripped on the stairs. No doubt something important. You don't send telegrams for nothing."

Nina hesitated in alarm and confusion but took the communication from him and signed a receipt for it. Then, retreating momentarily to the bedroom, she returned with a ruble tip and thanked him.

Yagor smiled even more broadly, nodded his handsome head, and took off his uniform cap. Moving backward toward the staircase, he almost fell again. "Thank you, Calbatono Nina, thank you . . ."

When Nina closed the door she reproached herself for her abruptness. Nitochka would have invited Yagor into the dining room and given him a glass of Kakhetian wine. But Nina had no time for him. She was agitated—a telegram from Moscow. Who could have sent it? She hesitated again before opening it. What if the state publishing house had decided against publishing Titsian's collected poetry? But a publishing house would hardly be likely to inform her of its decision by telegram. News from Borya? The thought troubled her. She had received a letter from Pasternak only a week before, and he had indicated that life in Peredelkino was more or less back to normal.

She returned to her room and sat down on a low Caucasian ottoman, then placed an embroidered velvet cushion behind her back, and lit another cigarette. Finally she opened the telegram and read: "Arrive 16th, flight 37. Meet airport. Borya, Zina."

Borya was well. She sighed with relief. That was the main thing. More than anything else, she had feared he was ill. When she had left Peredelkino she noticed he was much weaker, and she knew that the events of the preceding weeks could not have failed to take a toll of a man almost seventy.

But why had they suddenly decided to fly to Tbilisi? Her joy at the prospect was mixed with suspicion. There had been no talk in Peredelkino about such a trip. And Pasternak had not said a word about it in his letter. No, something was wrong. Something had happened. And why were they flying? Borya hated planes.

Forcing herself to think of the reunion, Nina sat down at a table and began listing everything she had to do before the Pasternaks' arrival. They'd probably stay a week or two, or maybe even a month. Lord! She wished they'd stay forever. The last time they had been in Georgia must have been in 1935, more than twenty years ago. Oh, what wonderful news, what a boon for the Georgian poets!

As if summoned by her thoughts, the telephone rang and she heard the stammer of Irakly Abashidze, a poet famous in Georgia. Although he was a member of the younger generation, he was a great admirer of Titsian's work; he was also First Secretary of the Union of Soviet Writers in Georgia, a deputy of the USSR Supreme Soviet and a member of the Politburo of the Central Committee of the Georgian Communist Party. Yet, notwithstanding his high position, Irakly had treated Nina with respect even during Stalin's reign; he had tried to help her in every possible way, and in private conversations had not been afraid to call Titsian Tabidze an "outstanding Georgian lyricist." He had openly and publicly assisted Nina after Titsian's rehabilitation, assigning her an apartment of four rather than three rooms. And when it was announced that five thousand copies of the one-volume edition of Titsian's poetry were to be printed, he had seen to it that the number was doubled.

Immediately after Irakly's words of greeting, Nina started to break the news that she had just received a telegram from Pasternak.

"Yes . . . Nina, I know about it," Irakly interrupted.

"What? You know about the telegram?"

"No, not about the telegram but about Pasternak flying to Tbilisi."

"How?" Nina's heart beat faster. There you are, she thought, my intuition never lets me down. I knew there was something more to Borya's visit.

234

Ignoring her question, Irakly asked her not to mention the telegram to anyone but her family. He gave no reason but invited her to lunch the next day, saying that he had something important to discuss. He let her understand that the subject was not suitable for the telephone.

"Believe me, Nina, it'll be best this way," he said. "And please don't tell anyone about my phone call either. Let it remain a secret. All right? I'll call for you at one o'clock."

Irakly's tone was insistent rather than pleading, and Nina, knowing that he was not given to dramatizing trivialities, agreed to the secrecy and to lunch.

3.

The next day Irakly Abashidze arrived at one o'clock precisely. Nina had put on her best dress and had even used a little lipstick. Tall, thin, and bald, he appeared comparatively unobtrusive. As they set out in his green Volga, they chatted about neutral things, then sat in awkward silence. But when Nina saw that Irakly was driving beyond the city limits, she spoke again.

"Where are you taking me?"

"To Kodzhori," he replied.

"Why?"

"To have lunch." He sighed and added: "Nina, please listen to me. We're going to General Inauri's dacha. We'll be having lunch with him. This may seem strange to you, but it's our life; it's reality. Titsian would condemn me of course . . ."

"What? Inauri? Of the KGB? You're mad."

"He invited both of us. Together."

"Irakly!"

"Nina, I know you can hold your tongue, so I'll be frank with you. Believe me, this isn't an easy mission for me, but I couldn't refuse to do it. Someone has to do it. And if there'd been a complete villain in my place, it would be far worse for all of us."

"What are you talking about?"

"Nina, Inauri phoned me the night before last. By the way, my dear, he speaks Georgian well, unlike Mzhavanadze. He called and said that Pasternak would be flying to Tbilisi on Wednesday with his wife and that they would be staying with you for a week or ten days. He said that in connection with this visit he wanted me, on his behalf, to invite you to have a . . . chat with him. Nina, I swear on my honor, I don't know why Pasternak is coming to Georgia. And I didn't ask Inauri about it. I think the conversation will be about *what* you should do when your guests arrive."

"But why didn't you mention Inauri yesterday morning?"

"On the telephone? No, my dear, you don't mention such things on the telephone."

"But what if I don't want to have lunch with the Chairman of the KGB?"

"Nina, you're doing it for Pasternak."

Their eyes met. Nina realized that Irakly was right.

"All right, I agree," she said. She smiled ironically. "Under Stalin I had a chance to be taken to the Soviet security 'organs' in a prison van. And now, under Khrushchev, you, Irakly Abashidze, whom I love, and whom Titsian loved, are taking me to Inauri's dacha to have lunch. He'll probably treat us to roast chicken or Karsky shashlyk. Yes, times have changed."

"Changed, but only a little," Irakly said. "Nina, don't get upset. It's not easy for poets to live in this world, but we have to live, we *must*."

"I'm not a poet, Irakly."

"You're the wife of a Georgian poet and the friend of a Russian poet."

"What do they want from me?"

"The KGB? I think Inauri wants just one thing—and that's probably on orders from Moscow—that Pasternak's visit go off quietly and without fuss."

"But why, why is he coming? And how does the KGB know about it?"

"Oh, Nina, you still haven't gotten used to not asking questions."

4.

Inauri was not at all as Nina had imagined him. Of average height, heavy but well built, with a fine military bearing and slightly bowed "cavalryman's legs," he wore an elegant general's uniform with several rows of ribbons on his chest. His expressive hazel eyes and aquiline nose were striking; his voice was loud but pleasant, with velvety intonations, and he spoke pure and intelligent Georgian. Nina noticed his beautiful fingernails (they were oblong, like Titsian's) and his highly polished officer's boots, with their small clinking spurs (he still wore them out of habit). When she was in high school she had seen men like him among the officers of the czar's army—friends of her elder brother, who came, of course, from the Georgian aristocracy. Inauri was from the *glekhi*, the peasantry, but he carried himself like an aristocrat.

Inauri's state dacha had been built in Kodzhori by German prisoners of war. Nina could remember passing through the place and seeing the prisoners working. At that time, like most Georgians, she had felt sorry for them because they had been torn from their country, homes, wives and children. Georgia had suffered very little from the fascist invasion and so the Germans were not hated there. On several occasions Nina had taken packages of bread, cheese, and cigarettes to the Germans working on the construction of the Medical Institute in Tbilisi. And now she was going to have lunch with the Chairman of the Georgian KGB in the dacha they had built. She wondered at the surprises of history.

The table was set for a typically Georgian meal. There was a feast of fresh produce—cucumbers, tomatoes, salad greens, radishes, and spring onions—and four or five plates of cold hors d'oeuvres and tornispuri (Georgian bread), which, together with several bottles of Khvanchkara, the slightly sweet Georgian wine, completed the spread. Lunch began with grilled Sulguni cheese. Then chicken Satsivi was served, followed by roast beef and, to finish, Karsky shashlyk. A meal fit for a czar.

Inauri acted in true Georgian fashion in playing the role of toastmaster, or head of the table. He proposed several toasts and was, as custom required, very eloquent. The first he devoted to Titsian Tabidze, calling him a "giant among Georgian lyricists." Nina was stunned when he concluded by reciting some lines of Titsian's verse.

> " 'Though tears are hopeless,
> Your sobs do not cease.
> A melodious pipe
> Sings to you of love.
> You reach out toward it.
> Thus a poet is born . . .' "

Irakly applauded. He was equally amazed. For this was Nina's favorite passage, and Pasternak adored the lines. Perhaps Inauri had learned them just for the occasion. But who on earth could have told him? Was it possible that he genuinely cared?

According to the custom established by fathers and forefathers, a few songs were sung at table. Despite his stammer, Irakly joined in. Inauri sang like a professional—almost all Georgians sing well—and Nina remembered that Stalin too, according to eyewitnesses, had had a small but pleasant tenor and also liked to sing Georgian songs at the table. Her feeling of hostility and revulsion gave way to surprise and curiosity. This general was not at all like the usual party bosses.

During the meal Irakly was mostly quiet, but he did take an opportunity to talk about the publication of Titsian's work. "Nina Alexandrovna is disturbed, comrade General, that the State Literary Publishing House in Moscow has delayed publication of the one-volume Russian edition of Titsian."

"Really?" Inauri frowned. "That's a disgrace. We'll have to put pressure on the publishing house through the Central Committee. Calbatono Nina, I promise to help you. Russia must read your Titsian. I'll phone my colleagues in Moscow. Do you have any other difficulties? Don't be shy, tell me everything. I'm your friend. I'm at your service."

"Thank you, but . . . I no longer have any difficulties," Nina replied.

And not a word about Pasternak. For two hours absolutely nothing was said about Pasternak and his arrival in Tbilisi. Nina thought that this must be the new KGB style—not to talk about business. However, after lunch Inauri invited her into his study and, having offered her an armchair, sat down at his desk (which gave their meeting a different, clearly official tone). Then he said, "And now, Calbatono Nina, about Pasternak."

"Yes, General."

"He's arriving to stay with you on Wednesday, with his wife. You already know about this since you've received a telegram. Whether he stays a week or ten days, we would like his visit to be a strictly private one. You yourself can understand that after the whole *Doctor Zhivago* business and the award of the Nobel Prize, the very fact of his arrival here could provoke an undesirable reaction. To be brief, sad though it may be, today he is a very dangerous figure. Forgive me for being blunt, but it's my official duty. Personally I love Pasternak's poetry, but questions of state security are more important to me. In short, Calbatono Nina, you must give me your word, the word of Princess Makayeva"—he smiled when he addressed her by her maiden name—"that Pasternak's life here will be organized in such a way as to avoid unnecessary talk in Tbilisi—you know that the people of Tbilisi have a weakness for gossip. Specifically: the poet should not go to concerts, to the opera, or to the theater. It would be better if he avoided public social events altogether. I would not like him to meet strangers. I hope that he himself has no such plans. But a lot depends on you. Don't make any such suggestions to him. And please restrict his encounters with young people. Our youngsters are already too 'freedom-loving' and wayward. I repeat, this visit must not get any publicity. I don't object to meetings within the confines of the family. Do you understand me, Nina Alexandrovna?"

"Yes, I understand, General," Nina replied. His request—"you must give me your word, the word of Princess Makayeva"—still rang in her ears. Princess Makayeva . . .

"It will be best if he stays entirely within your family circle, as I've already said. Please limit your guests and make sure they're trustworthy individuals. Naturally, I won't object to a meeting with Leonidze and Chikovani. They're old friends, and I've already had a chat with them. And another thing: please, not too much noise at the airport. We Georgians love noisy meetings and send-offs."

"My daughter and her husband will be going to the airport, and my grandson."

"Fine. Finally, if any unforeseen circumstances arise, call me right away, without fail, through Irakly. It'll be better for you that way. But I have to be kept informed of events and make a daily report to Moscow."

"General, may I ask one question?"

"Yes, of course."

"Tell me, why is Pasternak coming to Tbilisi?"

"According to my information . . . he wants to have a rest."

"Where did you get this information?"

"Nina Alexandrovna, that's a second question." Inauri laughed. "And besides, I simply can't disclose the secrets of how we work." He became serious. "It would be good if Pasternak stayed at home during the day and went out for walks only at night. He shouldn't go alone of course; your daughter or son-in-law can go with him."

5.

They drove back in silence. Nina's head was buzzing slightly from the wine. She was remembering how Titsian had sometimes praised Stalin. This had come to mind because during lunch with Inauri she had seen once again how difficult it was in this Soviet life for a poet to stand his ground. The poet, the artist, the scientist, the painter—any intellectual who fell into the clutches of these Inauris—was not immune to the "charms" of the powerful. And this attraction, combined with the pressure exerted by fear, still endemic to the epoch, could subjugate them without their even noticing their fall. Nina was ashamed to admit to herself that during lunch she had fallen a little in love with the general. He had won her over not only because he had a gallant bearing (she had adored such types ever since her girlhood) but because he seemed to be a cultured, well-educated, clever man. And when he talked to her about Pasternak she had been able to see his point of view. It had seemed reasonable to her that the Soviet system should protect itself from "unnecessary" rumors and any type of demonstration. (She could also understand now how Titsian had occasionally succumbed to Stalin's appeal, although more often than not he had cursed the "leader of the peoples.") Nevertheless her hostility toward Inauri had returned when he placed on the round table in front of her an agreement, drawn up and typed out in advance, by which she was bound to keep their conversation secret. Her name, "Nina Alexandrovna Tabidze," had already been written in ink on the agreement. General Inauri's name did not appear in the document; instead he was referred to as the "acting official of the KGB attached to the Council of Ministers of Georgia." The last paragraph stated

241

that in the event of the agreement's being broken, criminal proceedings would be instituted against the transgressor.

"Thank God, Inauri didn't suggest that I inform on Pasternak and other friends of ours," Nina murmured, more to herself than to Irakly.

Irakly turned pale, and after several moments said with a marked stammer, "I've never informed on anyone, Nina. But I'm on their side—yes, I am—because I'm a member of the Communist Party and I share the ideals of communism." She started to protest, but he went on. "I try to do nothing that would harm our Georgian writers, but sometimes, whether I like it or not, I do harm them of course. Do you think I don't hate myself for having signed the statement condemning Pasternak? I hadn't even read *Doctor Zhivago*, even though you offered me the manuscript. Do you know"—Irakly lowered his voice—"that before I agreed to sign I thought many times of . . . suicide. I've got a pistol; I could have shot myself. Alexander Fadeyev had the courage to put a bullet through his heart. I didn't. But, then, it wasn't simply a matter of bravery. I'm a Georgian, Nina, and I love Georgia, and I love Georgian poetry, even if its hands are tied. I came to the conclusion that by making a compromise I could be of use to our culture. The main thing is that it should continue to exist. No matter if it's stunted for a time, the main thing is that it should live. And since I have some influence on Mzhavanadze and Inauri, I decided that I should live and help Georgian culture survive."

Nina looked at Irakly and felt terribly sorry for him. She was touched by his need to justify himself to her. She was not only the wife of his idol, Titsian Tabidze, but also a victim, a witness of the vile and evil actions that had been carried out under Stalin, the same leader Irakly had glorified in verse. Looking at him, Nina realized that the compromise to which he had long ago agreed awaited her too. No, she had already risen to this historic level by trying to restore to Titsian all his poetic and civil rights, and . . . by having put her signature on that foul bit of paper, and by smiling as she left him.

My God! What would she tell Pasternak about all this?

6.

The TU-104, a jet aircraft recently introduced on the Moscow-Tbilisi route, covered the 1500 kilometers between the cities in two and a half hours. The propeller plane that had previously flown the route had taken five hours, in part because it had to fly around the Great Caucasian Range. The TU-104, however, could fly over the peaks of the range, and it stayed above the clouds for most of the trip.

It was true that Pasternak did not like flying. If it had not been for Surkov's advice and Lyonya's persistent persuasion, he would have gone to Tbilisi by train. So when he boarded the airliner his heart was already heavy. The very fact of being torn from the earth and viewing it from far above seemed to him unnatural, although he always liked to observe the flight of birds and in his youth had been entranced by the legend of Icarus. His confused feeling about flying was another manifestation of the dualism that shaped his mind. On the one hand, the mythical Antaeus, who drew his strength from contact with mother earth, lived in him. And on the other, since Pasternak exalted the innovative powers of the intellect, the mythical Prometheus, who gave man fire, was alive in him. Pasternak recognized that technology and science had long since become an indispensable part of everyday life, but at the same time, as he often had indicated in conversations with his son, he feared that man's most vital attributes—his spirituality, divinity, mystery—would be enslaved by technology. Although he used an automobile, he would have preferred a horse and carriage; he disliked the airplane, and he disapproved of all the Sputniks, cosmic rockets, and the like. Like Rousseau, he had a passion for nature in its pure state, for what was created by nature itself and was untouched by man's amendments. He did not have much admiration for the technological achievements of America; he suspected that instead of playing with their dolls, American children disemboweled them, anxious to discover what was inside.

Perhaps his conservatism had its roots in his attachment to what was stable, to what had surrounded man for thousands of years, and, especially, in his passion for antiquity. Pasternak looked more to the past than to the present. Indeed, in many ways he preferred the old Russia, a patriarchal, peasant country, to the new Soviet state. All in all, he looked unfavorably on what was novel, and perhaps, if it had been in his power, he would have attempted to put a brake on time.

Sitting in their aircraft seats, Pasternak and Zina, in their old-fashioned clothes, looked as if they were a museum exhibit. They didn't seem to belong in the modern plane, with its well-dressed stewardesses—one of them a Georgian, the other perhaps an Estonian—and its prosperous passengers, the vast majority of whom were from the Soviet elite.

Pasternak still felt a weight inside him. He had not told Zina about his meeting with Alexei Surkov, and so she did not know that the trip to Georgia was being undertaken on Surkov's insistent "advice." Pasternak had simply told her that he wanted to spend some time in Tbilisi and visit Nina; he had promised Surkov not to disclose the reason for the trip. He was also disturbed by this particular aircraft, the first jet in which he had flown. Lyonya had been right—as soon as the machine reached its cruising altitude, the shaking and tossing from side to side stopped, and Pasternak felt that the plane was simply hanging motionless in space. Only the slight vibration of the fuselage and the rumbling of the two jet engines reminded him that they were moving at six hundred kilometers an hour.

Yes, Lyonya was right—science was becoming the organizing force in human life. But why, Pasternak thought, did he himself oppose it so vehemently? He imagined what would happen if an essential screw in the machine came loose. A catastrophe would follow. The machine, together with all the people in it, would crash to earth. There was no escaping the great law of gravity. The same law existed, most likely, in the spiritual realm; in any case, it seemed to exist in Pasternak's spirit. There were certain subjects—among them death—that inexorably attracted him. And when he thought about death he often found consolation in picturing the cemetery in Peredelkino, where he dreamed of lying for all eternity. No, he did not want his body cremated and his ashes cast upon the Volga. Timidity or audacity? He wondered. At times he felt ashamed of his attraction to the earth—of which, incidentally, there was little in his poetry.

After lunch Pasternak occupied himself looking down at the clouds and mountains. Despite himself he was captivated by the sight of the fantastic peaks of the Great Caucasian Range. He forgot about Antaeus; Prometheus stirred inside him. His distance from earth no longer frightened him; on the contrary, he was delighted. He saw another jet, probably flying from Tbilisi to Moscow, and almost began clapping.

All his distrust of technological advance seemed to fall away from him. He recalled a line from *Faust*: "Stop a moment, you're beautiful!" It was addressed to a group of workers and glorified man's labor and intellect. Perhaps Lyonya was right. Perhaps only the powerful human intellect, armed with knowledge and *logic*, could force nature to open wide. Looking down at the earth from ten thousand meters, he cried out with delight.

The Georgian stewardess smiled as she passed by. A few minutes later she returned and, on instructions of the captain, invited both husband and wife to the cockpit. There followed a quarter hour of the most intense excitement as Pasternak, confronting the universe from beside the copilot's seat, inspected the countless knobs, levers, light signals, and arrows that the four crew members so expertly read and handled, precise and efficient in their movements, clear-eyed and sure of speech. Pasternak thought that they indisputably held the machine in their hands and it submitted to them. Here man triumphed over machine. He said so, and the crew members all thanked him effusively, aware of the fame of their guest.

Pasternak returned to his seat as the aircraft began its descent, but suddenly he felt ill. His left arm became heavy and a sharp pain invaded his shoulder blade. His heart began to beat in short unrhythmical bursts and a bitter taste arose in his mouth—the same symptoms that had preceded his heart attack five years before. He let his head fall back and clutched the armrests tightly, then closed his eyes and began breathing deeply. A thought flashed through his mind: Am I dying? He had been waiting for a second attack ever since the Swedish Academy had announced the prize. He wasn't afraid, just helpless. Neither Faust nor Prometheus—nor a belief in the boundlessness of the human intellect—was of any help to him now. The most unpleasant part was the waiting. When would death come? And what would happen to him then?

Zina noticed his pallor. "Borya?"

"I feel . . . bad."

She hurriedly opened her bag, and, removing some tablets, pressed one onto his tongue. "Ach, I told you you shouldn't travel by airplane, and you've . . . gotten excited again."

7.

Pasternak lay on a cot at the airport for half an hour and the incident passed. And once recovered, he found life at Nina's bliss. He was surrounded by care and affection, his every desire anticipated. Nina was thoroughly in command. When he slept after lunch, his usual forty minutes, she made sure the apartment was quiet. Alik or Givi even forestalled commotions in the street, advising passersby that there was a sick man in the house.

Pasternak woke in the morning, as Nina did, to the cry of "Mats-oni!" And also like Nina, he threw open the window and breathed in the clean air, gazing with joy at the donkey and the old man. Later in the day he watched one-legged Gabo, the shoemaker, take up his post under a rough wooden shelter on the corner opposite the house and argue noisily with his clients, gesticulating wildly and frequently reaching for his bottle of clouded peasant wine. And almost every evening the poet listened to neighbors gathered on the street under the windows, talking and singing beautiful Georgian songs.

In the mornings Pasternak worked in Nina's room on some translations of English poetry that he had begun in Peredelkino. Nina and Zina meanwhile looked after the house, and in their spare time sat at the dining room table and played cards, as usual smoking one cigarette after another.

Pasternak had been won over by Alik's cheerful energy, and he privately nicknamed him "the beaver." Alik had taken charge of his medical care after taking him to the Institute the day after he arrived. An electrocardiogram had indicated that he had not suffered a heart attack, and Alik and his superior, Professor Truidze, had concluded that his heart was not in such bad shape after all. (But Professor Truidze still recommended that he go back to Moscow by train.)

Thus Pasternak was in good spirits. Every morning he and Givi did their exercises together on the verandah; true, he could not sit on his haunches like the sixteen-year-old, who was determined to become the best fencer in Georgia, but he enjoyed spending time with the youngster anyway.

9.

Two days later Alik took Pasternak to the sulphur baths in the old part of town, which the local residents still called by its former name, Maidan. Traditionally, guests, especially from Russia, were taken to the baths. Tbilisi, which literally means "warm springs," had been built around natural sulphuric springs, and its hot baths had been renowned for centuries. Pasternak had first visited them with Titsian in 1935, when he had been struck by their Oriental style: walls decorated with brightly colored mosaics, low-vaulted ceilings, marble tubs sunk into stone floors. He remembered the long corridors and the strong smell of sulphur.

In this part of the city, despite the plan of socialist reconstruction, which had already been largely carried out, there was still an atmosphere of antiquity. The Moslem mosque dominated the area around the tiny Viri bridge, and the mullah read prayers from the minaret every morning. All around there were traders with baskets full of trinkets. On almost every corner there was a *chaikhana* (teahouse), where luli-kebabs were grilled before the customers' eyes.

Alik wanted to take a private room, but Pasternak preferred the communal bath, where, finding himself among several dozen naked men, he observed the hallowed ritual. Hiding his nakedness within a cubicle, he sat down on a marble bench and, smiling shyly, inspected the faces around him.

For an additional fee Alik meanwhile was washed by a masseur. In Georgia masseurs are highly respected professionals; they are the heirs of masseurs, the skill passed from one generation to another. Alik's was very strong, with a curled mustache and a long nose; his hands were pink from warm water and soap and looked like old wet rags. All of the masseurs wore wooden clogs and short oilskin aprons.

Alik lay on a special shelf, covered with suds, which the masseur worked up with a bag filled with soap. The only other tools of his trade were his hands and, on occasion, his feet. He worked over Alik for forty minutes, pummeling every part of his body, until Alik's voice finally rose in protest. For a moment Pasternak thought they were having an argument. But as Alik explained later, the masseur had *demanded* to be allowed to walk on him, while he himself had stubbornly refused.

No, it never gets to the point of a fight in Georgian baths.

In the cubicle next to Alik's a masseur climbed onto his

client and began to walk all over him; the client groaned and then burst into cheerful song. The masseur joined in.

After Alik had emerged, all bright and pink, from the bath, he said something to his masseur in Georgian about Pasternak. The Georgian burst out laughing and slapped Pasternak on the shoulder. The slap was so loud the poet's ears rang.

Alik's experience in the bath left him sleepy. He dozed as they rode the streetcar from the old part of the city to Lenin Square, named Beria Square until Stalin's death, and before that simply Yerevan Square. Alik had wanted to take a taxi, but Pasternak insisted on the streetcar. As they left the baths Alik had remarked that as a boy he had gone there with his parents in a phaeton drawn by two horses. Pasternak recalled that he and Titsian also had driven about in a phaeton. Alas, there were none of them left in Tbilisi now.

At Lenin Square, Pasternak prodded Alik and suggested that they take a stroll along Rustaveli Avenue, the capital's main street. As they passed the iron gates of the Alexandrov Gardens Alik said quietly, "If you like, Boris Leonidovich, I'll show you where I hid during the uprising."

Nina had told Pasternak in detail about the Tbilisi uprising, and word of it had even spread to the West. (Lyonya had heard about it on the Russian-language broadcast of the BBC.) It had all started in 1956, on the third anniversary of Stalin's death, when a small group of "patriots" assembled at the monument to Stalin beside the river Kura in the center of the city. Nationalistic sentiments were running high. The crowd had begun by shouting anti-Khrushchev slogans, because in their opinion Khrushchev had defamed "the great leader." The demonstration had then grown into a protest against the Soviet government, with the demand that Georgia be given independence. With tears of laughter in her eyes, Nina had told Pasternak that the leader of the demonstration as it turned out, had been a Russian Jew.

Khrushchev's hand had not faltered. The protest, supported by thousands of Georgians, mostly young, had ended in bloodshed. On Khrushchev's personal command, troops had massed on Rustaveli Avenue and, after a warning volley, had submachine-gunned the entire crowd. About seven hundred people were killed or wounded, Nina said.

Alik had been among the demonstrators, and when the shooting began he had run into the Alexandrov Gardens. A gazebo stood just inside the gates, and he had thrown himself down in the high grass beside it, where he lay motionless for thirty minutes, listening to the bullets whizzing over his head.

Now he showed Pasternak the spot and said with self-conscious pride, "That's the sort of people we Georgians are! Defiant!"

10.

The next day, a Saturday, Pasternak was shown a demonstration of Georgian defiance when Nitochka, Alik, and Givi drove him to Mtskheta despite Nina's efforts to dissuade them from the trip. (In discouraging them, Nina was of course carrying out Inauri's orders.) They went in a red Moskvich that belonged to Doctor Dumbadze, a friend of Alik's.

The town of Mtskheta is situated twenty kilometers from Tbilisi where the river Aragvi flows into the Kura. Its most remarkable feature is the excavated remnant of an ancient city, with burial grounds built, according to archaeologists, about a thousand years before Christ. The city, once the religious capital of Georgia, was famed for its magnificent but austere cathedrals, Sveti-Tskhoveli and Mtsyri, and a nunnery.

When Pasternak entered the cathedrals he lost all sense of time. Antiquity had always fascinated him and fed his imagination. He scrutinized the frescoes, touched the slender columns, breathed the "'air of ages past." Nitochka shared his wonder, but the others, especially Givi, followed along out of sheer politeness. At one point Givi began to whistle, and

Nitochka scolded him. Lyonya was just the same, Pasternak thought. Antiquity did not interest him. Young people looked to the future; they were always in the thick of what was going on, never caring about the past. How many times, Pasternak thought, had he told Lyonya that without the past there could be no present, that without love for the past one could not understand the present and put the hullabaloo, vulgarity, and narrowness of the time into perspective. Knowledge of the past revealed the essence of life, for the past was eternal, while the present and future were ephemeral. Without the past there was no culture, the only yardstick by which mankind could be measured.

He recalled how at the beginning of the Second World War, when the fate of the Soviet Union hung in the balance, Stalin, not by accident, had invoked Alexander Nevsky and Anton Chekhov in his appeal to the Soviet people. It always irritated Pasternak when the ancient past was denied for ideological reasons, as when the Italian Renaissance, for example, was thrown from the scales of history because it had witnessed the birth of the bourgeoisie. It was true that toward the end of his life Goethe had become a disgusting grandee, but did that diminish the genius of *Faust*?

After standing for a few minutes by the burial ground, thousands of years old, Pasternak thought that in another thousand years people would stand like this looking at the surviving monuments of twentieth-century life. Would they respect the people of today? Would they respect him? And what would he mean to them?

As Pasternak left the monastery a young Georgian in a velour coat and felt hat stopped him and asked in Russian, with a marked Georgian accent, "Excuse me, but aren't you, by chance, Boris Pasternak?"

"Not by chance, quite the opposite," Pasternak replied. The answer was clear enough, and the news spread quickly through the crowd of tourists—mostly students from Tbilisi, but also visitors from Kutaisi, Rioni, Gori, and even Batumi. Thereafter, on the road back to Tbilisi, the red Moskvich was surrounded, both in front and behind, by an escort of Pobedas and Volgas as well as a packed yellow school bus, all honking their greetings to the famed Russian poet. The vehicles moved back and forth, overtaking and falling behind, while their occupants waved, cheered, and shouted encouragement from the windows.

Alik, who was sitting behind Pasternak, was delighted by the demonstration. He clapped his hands and exclaimed: "What a people we are, we Georgians! Recalcitrant!"

11.

On Sunday evening Pasternak went for a walk along the Tbilisi esplanade from Vera bridge to Chelyskinsky bridge, where a large new building had been built for the circus. With him were Nitochka and a friend of hers, Rezo Kipshidze, a small, pink-cheeked but fiercely mustachioed and excitable Georgian. He had completed his master's degree in Moscow and spoke Russian with scarcely any accent. He wore horn-rimmed glasses and conspicuously Western clothes and made no secret of his deep hostility toward the Soviet Union notwithstanding the fact that he taught its history at Nitochka's technical school. He had read the manuscript of *Doctor Zhivago* at Nina's apartment and found it brilliant, and thereafter pressed her to introduce him to its author.

Rezo looked at Pasternak as at a creature from a higher order, but at the same time he was determined to talk to him intelligently and absolutely frankly about the *main* issue. The occasion soon presented itself.

Pasternak began praising the Bolsheviks. During his last visit to Tbilisi before the war, he said, the area between the two bridges had been used for dumping the city's garbage and the bank of the Kura had been in a state of total neglect. But now there was a magnificent esplanade of concrete and asphalt, and several small squares, lit up in the evenings by round, frosted-glass lamps on tall metal pillars.

"What have the Bolsheviks got to do with it?" Rezo objected. "If it hadn't been the Bolsheviks, others would have done the same, perhaps rather better. Life doesn't stand still. I think capitalists would have built a fashionable resort here. And why not, Nitochka?"

Pasternak remembered that he had heard something similar from Yury Mikhailovich when they were driving from Peredelkino to Moscow on that famous day.

"The Bolsheviks base their actions on what does *not* prevail in human nature, or, if you like, on what is unnatural," Rezo continued.

"You mean the ideal of collectivism?" Pasternak asked.

"Yes, precisely," Rezo said, adjusting his glasses, which had slipped down his nose. "In my opinion, Boris Leonidovich, man begins from his own 'I.' Without this 'I,' there is no man, only a beast. Man is indisputably an egoist. I use the word in its best sense. In order to love your neighbor, you must first love yourself. What is dearest to man is what belongs to him alone."

"I'm not disputing that, Rezo, but the Bolsheviks are reshaping human nature, directing man toward a better future."

" 'Reshaping.' " There was irony in his voice. "Yes . . . or to be more precise, they're crushing human nature, deforming it. And what comes of all this? Nothing, except terror and bloodshed. Oh yes, they want to replace individualism with collectivism. What nonsense!"

"You see, Rezo, I'm not convinced there isn't a tendency toward collectivism in human nature—"

"Of course there is!" Rezo interrupted. "If I, an individual, wish, at my own discretion, to cooperate with someone in building a house, then that's excellent. I may even want to live in a hostel. There are such fools. Voluntary collectivism is a rational phenomenon. Sometimes, in extreme circumstances, it may even be obligatory. Well, during wartime, for example."

Nitochka burst out laughing.

"Uncle Borya, you won't stop him now. It's his favorite hobbyhorse. By the way, he promised me he wouldn't talk too much."

"Nito dear, I'll shut up if you like," Rezo said, pretending to be offended.

Pasternak laughed. "No, no, Rezo, go ahead. I'm very interested in what you have to say. Because I agree with you about many things. And your thesis, put philosophically, is the alpha and omega of contemporary life. The future of all mankind depends on this question."

"Without a doubt, Boris Leonidovich," Rezo said. "And you spoke out in defense of individuality in *Doctor Zhivago*."

Nitochka said something to Rezo in Georgian and then turned to Pasternak. "Let's talk about poetry instead. That's what I said to him."

But Pasternak was determined to continue the discussion. "The question is this: Is it necessary to refashion the nature of man and replace 'I' and 'my' with 'we' and 'ours'?"

Rezo answered excitedly. "The capitalist system proves that individualism, as the only source of initiative and private enterprise, as the most productive organization of the labor process, gives people a thousand times more than communism and collectivism, with their lack of personal responsibility and their generalized—that is, *no man's*—production. That's a fact, and statistics prove it. We, here in the USSR, pride ourselves on the fact that in forty years we have created a powerful people's economy. But people in our country don't have enough to eat. And at the same time West Germany, for example, which was destroyed during the war, has in fifteen years reached an economic level we can't even dream of. And German prosperity is based on capitalism. Right?"

"Mm, yes, maybe."

"Why mince words? When a man works for himself, he

gives himself to it totally. If it's a matter of his own personal plot of land, the peasant in the countryside lies awake at night thinking about what he should cultivate. But he's not concerned with the collective-farm harvest—that is, *no man's* harvest. People don't give a damn about fine words like 'communism,' 'socialism,' 'collectivism,' 'the new era,' and so forth. People don't live for words. People want to be happy in *this* life—the only one they have. They want to have houses, cars, yachts—"

"You know, Rezo, Christ did without yachts."

"Well, and so what?"

"Uncle Borya, don't talk about Christ. Rezo's an atheist."

"I'm a . . . pragmatist."

Pasternak looked at him intently. The young Georgian seemed almost comic, almost pompous, as if he were straining to climb a mountain far too rugged for him. Yet Pasternak saw in him the same sincerity and thirst for knowledge that Lyonya showed during arguments. But Rezo and Lyonya would not have agreed on basic issues, because Lyonya was an apologist not for capitalism but for science.

"Fine, Rezo, I'll put just one question to you. Should the man who thinks about life pragmatically ignore *ethical* considerations? Do you claim that the social system under which a part of society is very rich and the other part very poor is just?"

"That system is just, Boris Leonidovich, that grants everyone free and unrestricted opportunity. What comes after that depends on the individual himself. He who fails has only himself to blame. One man works hard, while another is lazy from birth. Capitalism encourages the talented and leads to dynamism, but collectivism encourages idlers and leads to screwing around—excuse me."

"Yes, but under capitalism this 'free and unrestricted opportunity' gives rise to terrifying competitiveness, which wears men out and fosters greed, cruelty, and, of course, egoism. Under capitalism every man must be prepared to commit any crime for the sake of money. Whether he succeeds or not is a matter of luck. But is mankind not capable of building a more intelligent society, a society where people are equal, a society in which there will be no reason to destroy one another?"

Rezo burst out laughing. "Did you say equality? Equality is a pipe dream, Boris Leonidovich. And besides, in such a society there would be no place for your *Doctor Zhivago*, just as, incidentally, there would be no place for him in a society *without* equality—that is, our own Soviet society. There will be no place for individuality, for my 'I,' in a society that mandates equality, because people will be numbers instead of names and surnames. Equality is fine for skeletons and rotten corpses."

"And so, in your opinion, Rezo, the best society is one based on capitalism? But don't you think that self-sacrifice and love for one's neighbor are higher and nobler than egoism, and that the latter is a base instinct in our nature? And doesn't it therefore seem to you that capitalism, even when it gives many material blessings, at the same time degrades human worth, especially when it rejects the possibility of equality or calls it a pipe dream?"

"We don't live in an ideal world, Boris Leonidovich! Utopia will never exist on this earth," Rezo stated with irritation.

"But all the same, shouldn't we measure any existing society by the standards of an ideal society?" Pasternak asked mildly.

"In general, I'm not so much for capitalism," Rezo said, retreating slightly, "as against *false socialism*."

"That's not true!" Nitochka exclaimed angrily. "You're for capitalism, because you dream about having your own private yacht. And besides, your father is a professor of microbiology, and has two private houses, one in Tbilisi and the other in Batumi. And you're afraid that sooner or later the authorities will take them away."

"Nita, that's nonsense! How can you say such stupid things? What's a yacht got to do with it?"

"You wouldn't be angry if I hadn't hit a sore spot," Nitochka blurted out, blushing deeply. In her look Pasternak caught the familiar and to him very precious glint of Titsian's eyes.

"Rezo," he said, "Russian thinkers started criticizing the West, with its capitalism and bourgeoisie, more than a hundred years ago. Herzen, for example, who lived in England for quite a long time, wrote that the petty bourgeoisie constituted the definitive form of Western civilization."

"And we should learn from the wise petty bourgeois of the West!" Rezo exclaimed. "People in the West work in order to live, and here we live in order to work."

The evening had become chilly, and the esplanade was nearly deserted. In the squares one or two couples sat wrapped in embrace. The conversation with Rezo, and Nitochka's comments, had absorbed Pasternak, especially as Rezo was concerned with the same problems Pasternak himself had been pondering for years, what he called the "alternatives of the century." True, Rezo had a firm position. He had chosen a side and did not have any doubts, while Pasternak still did not have a definitive answer to the question of how to combine in a single human creature the ideas of "I" and "we." He was bedeviled by the paradox of capitalism, which gave people freedom and at the same time limited it by the dictatorship of money and philistinism. And he could not embrace communism because he believed that by imposing its moral code it limited freedom and individuality, and also led to "socialist" philistinism.

Rezo and Nitochka had begun to squabble in Georgian, and their dispute presently attracted the attention of two policemen in a passing car. The Pobeda stopped and a hefty sergeant got out and, touching his cap, admonished them politely. "Excuse me, citizens, but it's not proper to argue in public." The sergeant smiled and departed.

"There you are," Rezo said to Pasternak, "collectivism in action. It's not 'proper' to argue. What rights do we have? If I try to drown myself in the Kura and I'm dragged out alive

I'll be convicted for having committed an antisocial act. I'm not even the master of my own body. It belongs to the state, to a great idea."

Before parting outside Nina's house, Rezo took Pasternak aside, so that Nitochka could not hear him, and said in a whisper: "Despite the fact that I respect you very, very much, Boris Leonidovich, I must tell you that in your place I wouldn't have sent a telegram to Stockholm and I wouldn't have written letters to *Pravda* and to Khrushchev. No! Not for anything!"

His reproach made Pasternak's ears burn.

12.

After dinner Pasternak told Nina and Zina about his argument with Rezo. (The next morning Nina reprimanded Nitochka for taking Kipshidze along without asking.) He did not mention Rezo's last words to him.

"I'm not convinced of anything of course," Pasternak said, "although it still seems to me that the property instinct in people is debasing. Rezo didn't agree with me. In my opinion, egoism is evil. And I'm inclined to think that collectivism in theory, or even in practice, is close to the idea of Christian communion. It seems to me that it is essentially a new stage in the history of mankind." He stopped suddenly. "Am I boring you?" And then he burst out laughing.

"I've always thought you were a Communist without a party card, Borya," Zina said seriously.

"What do you mean, Zina?" Nina was indignant. "Borya's a Christian; he can't be a Communist. Communists don't believe in God."

"Borya has his own God."

Later, lying in bed, Pasternak reconsidered what Rezo had said. He wondered if the younger man had mistaken cynicism for pragmatism. Rezo's arguments had been persuasive. But Pasternak regretted not having asked him straight out whether or not he advocated restoring capitalism in Russia. He regretted not having told Rezo that it was indecent to be a property owner, to own land. The land belonged to nature. It was a crime to trade in nature. Once again he thought of Christ, who came to earth and left it without owning a thing. Shouldn't He serve as an example for every man? Why was private property necessary? In America, for instance, there were millionaires who owned whole towns. And the happiness of those entire communities depended on the millionaire's mood. And there was another question Pasternak had forgotten in his argument with Rezo: Hadn't Marxism and the idea of communism come to Russia from the West? Hadn't they arisen there as forms of protest against the injustice and oppression of capitalism? It was ridiculous to regard communism as a conspiracy directed by a few highwaymen when half the world had already flocked to its banner.

Nevertheless, as he considered the arguments against Rezo's position, Pasternak saw the strength of the younger man's claims. It was true that in the West, in capitalist countries, people did not experience the spiritual bondage and physical fear that were familiar to Soviet citizens. That was indisputable. And in the West people had the right to move around freely. Just try and move permanently from one Soviet city to another! It was impossible without the permission of the state. And maybe, from the point of view of everyday life, Western democracy really was the highest form of political development, despite its negative aspects and imperfections, particularly the crushing power of money.

Characteristically, Pasternak could not find precise and definite answers to his questions. He sensed that he was dwelling on them in order to avoid the most terrifying and wounding thought of all.

Ever since he had refused the Nobel Prize and had sent letters to Khrushchev and *Pravda* he had lived in constant expectation of reproach. He had not been surprised by Rezo's parting shot any more than he would have been by a new outburst from Olga. The blow from Rezo, the first since that unforgettable evening with Olga, reminded him of her taunt: "You're a coward! A coward!" Wasn't she right? Wasn't Rezo right? Was he not in fact a coward, disguising his weakness with rhetoric and sophistry? And wasn't it for that reason that he had censured the West so vigorously? In order to justify his renunciation? His decision to follow Surkov's advice and fly to Tbilisi seemed conclusive. And yet he did not judge himself too severely, because after the events of the last few months he had little interest in meeting the British Prime Minister. Certainly less than in staying with Nina.

Pasternak lay awake for a long time. The last thought that flashed through his mind was the thought that Bernard Shaw had lived as an individualist but had advocated socialism. So had Picasso, Sartre, and others. Who had remained on the right? Were there any artists who had taken up a position on the right? Artists were always on the left. All, that is, but the author of *Doctor Zhivago*.

13.

The day before Pasternak returned to Moscow the poet Gogla Leonidze invited him to his dacha for the day. Leonidze's friend Simon Chikovani, another noted poet, was also there. Both of them were from Titsian's generation and both had been close to him. They had escaped Stalin's arrests, probably, because the Georgian had been pleased by their works. Leonidze had written *The Childhood of the Leader,* a long poem about Stalin's youth, for which he had received a Stalin Prize, while Chikovani had written several poems praising the leader. God had blessed both Leonidze and Chikovani with poetic genius, and Pasternak loved them and had translated much of their work into Russian. In his heart he thought they were both Petrarchs, worldly poets who loved life, had families and children, and needed money. To be sure, both were vain, greedy for recognition and fame, but both had achieved a deserved renown. Leonidze had become an academic and director of the Literary Museum of Georgia. Chikovani had lived to see his works regarded as classics.

For their parts, both Leonidze and Chikovani secretly envied Pasternak for having reached a clear confrontation with reality, albeit toward the end of his life. They both understood that the true poet was always engaged in a fierce conflict with reality and as a rule perished at the hands of the executioner—power. Like Titsian, Pasternak was an unanswerable reproach to them. They both felt shame, and both preserved it in wine.

The day at the dacha passed quietly. The three men walked, read aloud their own poems and the poems of Titsian, Paolo Yashvili, and other poets who had perished (including a few works that had been suppressed), and reminisced about the past. At times they fell into a somber silence. Neither Leonidze nor Chikovani mentioned *Doctor Zhivago*, although they had both read the novel at Nina's apartment. Pasternak himself was not eager to touch on the subject. He thanked God that both Leonidze and Chikovani had been able to avoid signing the official petition calling for his explusion from the Writers' Union and for his deportation from the USSR.

The table was spread with the inevitable Georgian feast, which Peputsa, Leonidze's wife, of whom Pasternak was very fond, had prepared. Leonidze proposed a series of toasts, each more colorful than the last. And, although Nina had forbidden both Georgians to prime Pasternak with wine, all three, after a few hours, were drunk. By the end of the day Pasternak had sung Georgian songs, kissed and embraced everyone, and talked excitedly without a thought for what he was saying.

In the evening Leonidze and Chikovani took Pasternak home and delivered him to Nina, who exploded when she saw his condition.

"Gogla, I told you that Borya is not allowed to drink. He's

had a stroke. And what do you do? You drink like fish your-selves and think that the meaning of life can be found only in wine."

"Nina, you've forgotten that I've had a stroke too."

"So have I," Simon added.

"Titsian drank like a fish too," Leonidze added.

"And of course the meaning of life lies in wine. Where else would we find it?" Chikovani said.

They were all drunk, all three.

Laughing, Pasternak embraced Nina and kissed her, then tried to embrace Zina as well, but she pushed him away, whereupon he fell to his knees and began recounting his childhood as a foundling and his later conversion to Chris-tianity. He insisted that he did not belong to "the noble Jewish family" of the Pasternaks, that he had been found by his adoptive parents under a gate, and that his real father and mother were the coachman Yakov and the cook Anastasiya, who lived in the servants' quarters in the Pasternaks' court-yard.

Nina put him to bed and waited until he seemed to fall asleep. But a few minutes later she discovered him in the vestibule off the kitchen embracing Alik's nanny, telling her too that he was a foundling and a convert. When Nitochka, Alik, and Givi came home from the movies, he burst into tears and started embracing and kissing them. As he kissed Nitochka he said with great emotion that she was like her father, like Titsian. When he kissed Alik, on his bald head, the young doctor responded with a bewildered smile and tried to feel his pulse. They urged him to lie down and rest, but he spurned all appeals. Still crying, he started kissing the doors, the tables, the chairs. Nina and Nitochka tried to re-strain him, but he broke loose and, running into Nina's room, kissed the photograph of Titsian and then the walls, saying over and over again: "I'll never ever be here again. Do you understand? *Never*. Can you understand the meaning of this word? *Never* . . . This is my last joy. Do you understand?

I'm saying goodbye to all of you. I'm saying goodbye to wonderful Georgia, to Titsian . . ."

Pasternak spoke so pathetically that Nina and Nitochka both began sobbing. Givi, standing in the doorway, also burst into tears. Then Zina entered the bedroom, looked at all four and said to Alik, who had followed her, "Give them all aspirins."

<h2 style="text-align:center">14.</h2>

Nina and her family, the wives of Leonidze and Chikovani, and three friends of Alik and Nitochka came to see the Pasternaks off at Tbilisi station. (Rezo had wanted to come, but Nina asked him not to.) Alik, as always, occupied himself with practical matters. He put the Pasternaks' luggage on the rack in the sleeping compartment, found a place for the two bags of food (the journey took four days) under the table between the seats, checked to see that the toilet and washbasin were working, and had a word with the Georgian conductor. He then joined Pasternak and Zina and the rest of their party on the platform.

Zina was holding a bouquet of flowers given to her by Alik and Nitochka's friends.

There were still fifteen minutes before train time. Pasternak tried to smile although his head was spinning from the previous day's wine.

"Borya . . . let's go for a little walk," Nina said. She took his arm and they strolled along the platform until at length she asked the question that had been avoided throughout Pasternak's stay in Tbilisi. "Borya, what made you come . . . so unexpectedly . . . to stay with me?"

Their eyes met and instantly his shifted in confusion. "Nina . . . but . . . well, I just wanted to see you . . . and I wanted to make one last visit to Georgia. You know the place it occupies in my heart. I came to say farewell to this promised land." Pasternak considered the lie and found in it a kernel of truth. "You know, Nina," he went on, "when our General Secretary Sasha Fadeyev decided to put an end to his life, he spent a month saying farewell to the places that he loved. He went home to the Far East and trod the paths he had known as a child and a young partisan. Then he said farewell to his beloved nature, to the trees, every one of which was dear to him. Then he said farewell to things—the houses and the station at Peredelkino—and finally to the people he loved." Tears welled in Nina's eyes. "But didn't anyone talk to you . . . before my visit? Didn't you get any instructions about how to receive Boris Pasternak?"

It wasn't easy for Nina to lie, but she did. "What do you mean, Borya? Of course not."

The railway bell sounded twice, signaling the train's imminent departure. They hesitated momentarily, then, summoned by the others, returned to the car, which Pasternak and Zina boarded without delay, still clinging to the hands of their friends on the platform. The train lurched just as Pasternak caught sight of Irakly Abashidze dashing from the government waiting room, a bouquet of tearoses in his hand. Irakly jumped onto the train steps, handed the flowers to Zina, and embraced Pasternak, stammering, "Boris Leonidovich, don't be angry with us . . . we're with you in spirit . . ." And before Pasternak could answer he was gone.

The electric locomotive hooted and the train picked up speed. Alik and Givi ran down the platform smiling and waving.

"Come again," Alik yelled, "we'll go to the sulphur baths again!"

CHAPTER EIGHT

Easter

1.

April came, but winter lingered and Peredelkino was still snowbound. The snow had lost its virgin whiteness and was covered with dust and soot.

Midnight was approaching and with it the celebration of the Resurrection of Christ—Easter. The bells of the white church with golden cupolas and narrow barred windows were ringing loudly and triumphantly. On the hillside below the church the monuments of the cemetery were visible in the cold moonlight.

A religious procession moved slowly around the outside of the church. Orthodox believers, dressed for the holiday and holding candles and cheesecloth bundles containing sweet cream cheese, Easter cake, and painted eggs, followed the church servants, arrayed in all their Easter finery. Most members of the congregation, apart from the simpletons, cripples, invalids, and beggars, were peasant women or factory workers from Moscow. The senior priest, handsome and portly, with a long beard, walked at the head of the procession holding a cross and a lamp. Two lanky deacons swung censers, leaving a pungent cloud of incense in the air. The Gospels and icons of the Resurrection were borne by priests. The congregation sang, "Your resurrection, Christ the Savior . . ." Banners unfurled like huge eagles over the devout.

It seemed as if time had stood still in holy Russia, as if the October Revolution had never occurred. The procession barely differed from those under Ivan the Terrible. To be sure, below the church, at the side of the highway, were two dozen cars, including two new Volgas. Chauffeurs sat in several of them, indicating that the wives or mothers of important Moscow bureaucrats had come to the ceremony. Indeed, people were still coming on foot from the Peredelkino station to the Church of the Patriarchal Residence.

A pockmarked woman of about thirty-five, wearing a coat made of otter, high laced boots, and a deerskin cap, obviously a Soviet office worker, turned to her friend, a mannish woman who was startlingly homely, and said, "Did you know, Raika, they say Khrushchev himself is planning to come here tonight?"

"To exchange a triple kiss," her friend commented ironically. "He should be good at that. He slobbers over everyone he meets and then talks a lot of nonsense."

A chestnut-haired man with large red ears heard her comment and retorted: "Right! Nikita looks like he knows how to hold his tongue, but he's really a blabbermouth."

"I hope he shows his face here," a third woman said. "It's time someone took him to task. You have to stand in line all night for wheat flour. How are you supposed to bake Easter cake? He's a fat Antichrist, a good-for-nothing who wants people to wolf down corn. What kind of Easter cake can you make from corn?"

Masha was in the procession as well, accompanied by two small nieces who had come to live with her after her sister's accidental death on a collective farm near Moscow. They followed their aunt docilely, holding two small cheesecloth bundles, but they regarded the crowd with wary eyes.

Olga and her mother moved several paces behind them, both dressed in winter clothes. Olga as usual had nothing on her head; her hair was gathered at the nape, her features set in a strong, self-possessed expression. Her mother carried a bundle of Easter cakes and painted eggs.

Olga pushed a man who had jostled her, perhaps deliberately. "What's your hurry, worker?" she snapped. "If you keep at it, we'll all be crushed."

"We won't get crushed, my lovely," he answered jovially. "We're a tough race!"

Zina and Tatyana also were near Masha and her nieces in the procession. Tatyana carried a large cheesecloth bundle with both hands and sang the hymns with great fervor. Zina, wearing a black cloth coat and an old-fashioned hat, had become even more bent since the trip to Georgia.

Suddenly appearing among them, Yury Mikhailovich pushed his way through the crowd, searching for Zina and Tatyana. He stumbled upon Masha and her nieces and asked them if they had seen Zinaida Nikolayevna. Masha pointed her out and asked, "What's the matter? Has something happened to Boris Leonidovich?"

"Yes . . . his heart." Yury Mikhailovich turned away hurriedly.

Olga heard his words and followed him anxiously with her eyes. He approached Zina and touched her elbow.

"Boris Leonidovich has had another heart attack," he said. "He's in a bad way. Lyonya is with him. I phoned Moscow from the writers' hostel and called an ambulance."

Zina pursed her lips but remained calm, thinking about what to do. "Let's go home, Yury Mikhailovich," she said at length. "Tanya, you stay here."

Word of Pasternak's illness spread through the crowd.

Those who came from Peredelkino and Choboty and other nearby places, and who knew Pasternak, murmured, "Boris Leonidovich is dying. It's his heart."

Hearing the news, a skinny woman with a wrinkled face frowned and said loudly: "They drove him to it! Khrushchev and that . . . viper, Olga, who tried to break up his home. There she is, circling about, hoping to atone for her sins. We all know she's guilty. She settled here to cause more trouble."

The woman's outburst triggered an argument among the women, some of whom took Olga's part while others denounced her. The thought that "Boris Leonidovich is dying" was momentarily forgotten, as Easter was forgotten, and also the religious procession—although it was continuing, growing in numbers as it went along. Those who knew nothing about Pasternak and Olga were bewildered by the dispute and asked questions, to which those in the know did not reply, believing there was no reason to involve outsiders from Moscow or Vostryakovo in the controversy.

A man of about fifty with a crooked nose said in a deep voice: "Why is she a viper? Olga, I mean. She's a beauty—she's got a good body. And she fell in love with Boris Leonidovich. You can't legislate that, friends."

"Love's all very well," a fat woman called Dusya, a cleaner from the writers' hostel, retorted, "but it's wrong to interfere with a family. She's not his wife. Zinaida Nikolayevna is his wife. No one should come between a husband and his wife."

"It all starts with the man. It's always the husband who wags his tail, or something else," another woman called out.

"No, it's the woman," a man replied. "It starts with her. She's bewitched by the devil—woman is a seductress, Lord forgive her!"

"Olga's the one who's sinned." The skinny woman with the wrinkled face would not let go. "She's a viper! She's got no sense of duty. She lives by hook or by crook."

Her words reached Olga, who felt the hostility of her neighbors in the crowd but ignored their prying eyes; she despised these people, the "mob." "Mama, what if Borya . . . dies?" she said quietly. "You heard—it's his heart again. The driver came for the old hag . . . but I . . . I can't help him . . . I can't even enter his house." Her eyes glinted angrily.

"He won't die," her mother said consolingly.

The undercurrent of hostility became louder, and Olga found it difficult to ignore it. "Viper," "home wrecker," "villain," rang in her ears. She heard the skinny woman repeat her abusive words—while the man who was dearer to her than anyone in the world was dying, dying without her. She despised these women with their trivial slander, their pea-sized brains. Zina, whom she hated, had gone to the dacha, while she, who adored the man, remained behind. She rushed at the skinny woman, fighting her way through the crowd, and shouted hoarsely, "Go on, then, hit me, hit me for breaking up a family! Hit me!"

The head of the procession had stopped at the church doors and the senior priest intoned, "Christ is risen from the dead! He has crushed death with death and granted life to those in the grave!"

The communicants repeated the chant three times while the doors of the church opened.

"May God arise from the dead and his enemies be scattered . . ." the priest continued.

And the people replied, "Christ is risen from the dead." The devout began crying, embracing and kissing one another three times. "Christ is risen! He is risen indeed!"

The skinny woman with the wrinkled face embraced Olga and kissed her three times.

"Christ is risen, Olga," she said.

CHAPTER NINE

The District Hospital

1.

Pasternak's first day in the hospital was very different from
the quiet days he had enjoyed at home. He did not choose the
hospital himself; the ambulance delivered him to the first
one that had room for him. Although he had suffered a serious heart attack, he was put in a corridor, because both wards
for heart patients were full. However, he did have a bed
(some patients lay on mattresses on the floor), and the corridor was spacious, with a high ceiling and large windows
overlooking a park. There were more than a hundred com-
parable hospitals in Moscow, some slightly better, some
slightly worse.

Despite the threat of renewed agony if he made the slightest movement, and notwithstanding the familiar, acrid taste

in his mouth, Pasternak observed everything going on around him. At times his surroundings seemed so unreal that he thought he must have died, but in fact the vivid details of the hospital routine helped bring him back to life.

To his right, in the depths of the corridor, he saw the small table of the attending physician, its desk lamp under a green shade; nearby he noticed a galvanized tank containing sterilized water and on one of the walls, painted the obligatory pale yellow, a rasping radio loudspeaker. He was surprised that there were no portraits of Communist leaders. Instead there was a slogan, written in red gouache on pasted-together sheets of white paper: "A healthy body means a healthy mind!" The message amused him, sounded poetic; it had artistic expressiveness and laconic brevity, he felt.

A pungent smell of carbolic acid assaulted his nostrils. When he closed his eyes he imagined himself transported to the morgue, where he saw corpses piled on top of one another on high metallic tables, parts of the bodies already decomposed.

But life still went on around him, and he found it strangely comforting. The nurse responsible for both wards and the corridor was sixty-year-old Matryona, a heavy-set woman with coarse features who wore a worn white coat and homemade cloth slippers. On the second day after his arrival she won his heart. She and the hospital orderly, a morose, elderly man wearing a lilac coat covered by a rubber apron, were carrying out the sheet-wrapped corpse of a patient who had died. Ibragim, a husky, black-haired Asian clothed in hospital pajamas tied with a military sash, half rose from his mattress and blew a whistle at them.

"Wait, Sbruya," Matryona said. They lowered the body to the floor and she turned to Ibragim. "Hey there, Turk. You going to give me that whistle or not?"

"I won't give it up until you fix my hernia!" Ibragim jeered, and added cheerfully, "Dear comrades, I've had enough." Half standing on his mattress, waving his left arm, he spoke with a heavy Tatar accent. "This hospital is a disgrace. I've been kept here for a whole week, in the section for heart patients, and I've got a hernia. A big one. I need an operation and they give me aspirin."

"Will you hand over the whistle or not?" Matryona repeated.

"No, I won't. You'll have to kill me to get it, Mom."

"Damned policeman!" Matryona exclaimed. "Where did the whistle come from anyway?"

"My wife brought it in." Ibragim grinned. "Hey, Mom, to hell with you. If you won't fix my hernia, then at least you could scratch my back. My wife always scratches my back. I've gotten used to it. All right, Mom?"

"Not for you, Eskimo," Matryona barked.

Sanko, a fair-haired lad with a pale, gentle face, who lay in the bed to Pasternak's right, looked up. "I wish you'd make up your mind, Matryona Kharitonova," he said. "First you called him a Turk, now he's an Eskimo."

"Shut up, you Komsomol brat. Stick to your books, broaden your mind." Matryona wheeled on the orderly. "Hey there, Sbruya," she shouted. "Stop sleeping, you tapeworm! Wake up!" The orderly opened his eyes and yawned. "Let's get the body to the morgue."

"Who was he? A Jew or what?"

"The devil only knows. Death's all the same anyway, whether you're a Jew or not. Okay, lift!"

Ibragim continued his complaint. "It's a madhouse. I need an operation and they've put me with heart patients."

"These things happen, comrade policeman," Sanko said. "A misunderstanding. Be patient."

"What misunderstanding? It's incompetence."

"These things happen . . ."

"Will you scratch my back?"

"I've got decompensation of two mitral valves."

"Decompensation?"

"Yes."

"How do you . . . with your wife?"

"I can't," Sanko said embarrassedly, lowering his eyes.

"Oh . . ." Ibragim shook his head and lay down.

Pasternak was too weak to laugh or cry. But he couldn't help reacting to the life seething around him. He liked Sanko. Ibragim seemed to him a character out of proletarian comedy, and Matryona assumed the dimensions of a heroine, even though the attending physician, Nadezhda Sergeyevna Rudakova, was more nearly suited to the part. She was thirty-five and had tired eyes and graceful movements. She wore a doctor's coat tailored to fit her slim figure, a white cap, and high-heeled shoes that made an insistent tapping sound that was punctuated by brusque commands, such as, on one occasion: "Ibragim, cover yourself up."

The Tatar immediately covered himself up, and when Rudakova had disappeared into the near ward, remarked with respect, "She's a good woman." Then, hearing "Greetings, Murka, my dearest!" addressed to the doctor by a patient in the next room, he added, "Who haven't we got in here, eh? Even a sex criminal has appeared." He burst out laughing.

"It is a district hospital, comrade policeman." Sanko returned to his book.

"What are you reading?" Ibragim asked.

"*How the Steel Was Tempered.* By Nikolai Ostrovsky. For the third time."

"Ah . . ."

"It's about the part the Komsomol played in the Civil War. Pavel Korchagin, the hero of the novel, is my hero," Sanko explained, realizing that Ibragim had not read the novel. "It's a good book."

A small worn-looking bald man in the bed beyond Sanko's got up, in a short muslin dressing gown, and staggered toward the wall on which the clamoring loudspeaker hung. He raised a withered white hand and switched it off, then returned silently to his bed and covered his head with his blanket. Thereupon a huge red-haired man emerged from the near ward in his underpants, a Turkish towel draped around his neck. "Who's the swine who's throwing his weight around? I'll bash his head in!" he bellowed. "They're broadcasting 'The meaning of rationalization and socialist emulation in the peat industry.' The radio brings knowledge to the people. It has to stay on. Is that clear?"

Rudakova, who had come back into the corridor, answered him. "Patient Nechayev, how dare you walk around without a dressing gown? Get back in your bed."

"I'm sorry . . . madam . . ." He smiled strangely, stressing the word "madam," switched on the loudspeaker, and went back to his ward.

The small man writhed under his blanket as if he were fighting a demon.

"Nechayev's mad, totally crazy," Ibragim said.

Pasternak's face was ashen, but his eyes burned with curiosity. For him life in the corridor was a twilight zone between vaudeville and hell, a caricature of Gogol. But this was his world, he thought, his people, his country. It was life unvarnished, real.

He lay on pillows and sheets brought by Zina, now seated in a chair beside him. The blanket covering him also had been brought from home, after she had overcome the bureaucratic obstacles by confronting the hospital director and the head doctor. He looked at her. She had not slept all night—another privilege dearly won—and she was now dozing, her head drooping toward her chest. Occasionally the cries and groans from the wards caused her to shudder and stir. Pasternak felt immeasurably grateful, and sorry for what he had done to her.

Forty minutes passed. At length the head doctor, Luchnikov, looked in on Section Three. Portly, clean-shaven, and suavely handsome, he wore shoes polished till they gleamed, immaculate trousers, and a silk doctor's coat with a stethoscope in the pocket.

"Good day, comrade heart patients!" he said, and a few minutes later, approaching Pasternak, "Hello, my dear poet." He bowed to Zina, who had risen. "Good day, Zinaida . . .

Nikolayevna, if I'm not mistaken. How did you sleep here? Not very comfortably, I'd guess." And without waiting for an answer, he continued, "Well, what have I to say to you? The patient looks superlative, fit as a fiddle." He felt Pasternak's pulse. "Your pulse is leveling out. Excellent. Excellent. I studied your cardiogram carefully, Boris Leonidovich, and the X-ray, and all the test results of course. There's nothing to worry about. All that's needed is time, my friend. And rest. Complete rest. Zinaida Nikolayevna, one moment please . . ."

He took her over to the window and said quietly: "Mmm, you see . . . your husband's condition is quite serious. The attack affected a large part of his heart. And his heart was weak to begin with. In short, he needs very careful watching. Given the conditions in this hospital, I cannot guarantee the outcome will be successful. The slightest blunder and . . . You understand, my dear, I'm being frank with you because Pasternak is a name. He's not an average worker for our glorious motherland. You must make an effort to have him transferred to the Kremlin hospital. Appeal to the government. Today."

CHAPTER TEN

Fedin, Khrushchev and Others

1.

Dressed in slacks and a blue sweater with a pattern of white deer on the front, Fedin sat in his rocking chair worrying a string of beads in his hands. Although he looked fit, the Pasternak business had engraved several new lines on his forehead. (The day before, while shaving in front of the bathroom mirror, he had inspected them and declared, "Borya's work.")

Zina sat on his sofa smoking a cigarette. She still wore her hat and coat, having refused to take them off when she came in from the district hospital about a half hour earlier. She held a bronze ashtray cast in the shape of a lion.

"Perhaps you'll have some tea after all, Zina?"

"No, thank you, Kostya," she repeated. She had been trying without success to keep the conversation on one topic—the necessity of having Pasternak transferred to the Kremlin hospital.

"You see, Zina, we knew all about Borya's relationship with Olga. And I personally think that Olga should bear the blame for everything that has happened—with *Doctor Zhivago* and the Nobel Prize, I mean. She's a malignant influence. Borya is too compliant, too easily swayed; he's full of vacillation and doubts. He always has been. She put pressure on him, constantly pitted him against the system. Zina . . . may I ask you . . . perhaps it's not tactful on my part, but . . ."

"Ask me, Kostya."

"I don't understand . . . how it happened?"

"What?"

"How did Olga gain so much control over him? You and Borya were so much in love, and everything between you was so good. And you—your intellect, your heart—are so far superior to her . . ."

Zina looked livid. Fedin, she knew, had no right to pry. But she needed his help, and because he had been close to her in the past, she resolved to tell him the truth.

"Most likely I'm the guilty one, Kostya," she said, although she was convinced she was not.

"Why?"

"Well . . . it was in 1946 . . . I found a letter from her, from Olga, on Borya's table. My eyes were opened, and I finally saw how close they had become. A few months before that Borya had introduced me to her—at the editorial offices of *Novy Mir*, I think."

"Yes, she used to work there as a secretary."

Then Zina told Fedin about the death of Adik, her first son by Heinrich Neuhaus. When the Germans were approaching Moscow, she said, during the war, she and Lyonya had been evacuated beyond the Volga, to the town of Chistopol. Adik stayed in the capital, and Borya was in Peredelkino. Adik could not be moved because he was gravely ill with tuberculosis of the bones. Borya visited him in the hospital every day and did everything he could for him. But his mother was far away. She had news of Adik only from Borya's letters; she knew that her first-born was dying, but the war kept them apart. It was an intolerable situation and it broke her heart.

"You lost Dora, Kostya, you know what anguish one goes through."

After Adik died, she continued, she was devastated, near suicide. If she hadn't had to take care of five-year old Lyonya she would have killed herself. Her only comfort was work, to which she devoted herself twelve, sometimes sixteen hours a day, caring for children of soldiers at the front. She lost herself in the children, seeing her own Adik in each one. After the war she returned to Moscow, but continued to work with children, taking a job at an orphans' home in the Zamoskvoretsk district. She wanted to adopt a lame boy called Eddik, but his parents were suddenly found. She disappeared for days and nights, spending all her time at mothers' meetings in the Zamoskvoretsk district.

"And so, Kostya, gradually, imperceptibly, I moved away from Borya. The mother in me, the sorrowing mother, took over my soul. Those womanly qualities so important to Borya were drowned."

"I understand, Zina."

"And that, I think, forced him to seek someone else. When I found out about Olga, I broke with him once and for all."

"Didn't he seek a reconciliation?"

"Yes. But I'm ruled by pride. I can't help myself."

"Pride is a dangerous thing, Zina."

"I know. But it's all I have. Oh, Kostya, it's such a tangle. Maybe . . . maybe I'm inventing and complicating things. The story about Adik's death, about the woman in me having died. Maybe it's all nonsense. Maybe I need all that so I can justify myself somehow, so I won't be simply another abandoned wife. Perhaps I just grew old and was retired from the scene. And Borya took himself a younger woman, glamorous —even blond. Everyone seems to be doing it. Old generals, academics, writers, other members of the 'elite'—they abandon their wives and become infatuated with girls. Someone told me that Khrushchev decided to fight the trend—and decreed it illegal to change wives more than three times. Borya is human; he fell right into the trap."

"No, Zina, Borya isn't like that, no . . . he has a big heart and a genuine one."

"Kostya, a man is still a man, even if he has a big heart."

"Oh, Zina, life is never so simple. But let me tell you one thing, the most important thing." Fedin got up from his rocking chair and paced the room. "It's true that Borya and I are no longer close friends. Ideological differences are complicated too, and decisive sometimes. I don't think either of us is petty or narrow, but our principles and ideas have clashed. But all the same, Zina, I'm not his enemy. I love Borya as a man and as a poet. He is my youth; I carry him inside. I swear to you that I love him still."

Fedin's eyes smarted with tears and Zina saw her chance. "If you love him, you will save him, Kostya. You must get him away from that place. Do you understand? Every minute is precious. We can't sit here talking about our troubles while he's lying in that squalid district hospital. I've described it to you. He's lying in the corridor."

"Yes, yes, I understand, and I'll call the Union of Writers, I promise you."

"No!" Zina interrupted. "There's no point in calling the Union. Surkov has gone to Belgium for a congress of 'progressive world activists.' Call the Central Committee. Now. *Now*—while I'm here. The head doctor, Luchnikov, told me that Pasternak is a name."

"You want . . . you want me to call the Central Committee? Right now?"

"Yes, Kostya, now. This minute. Otherwise it will be too late. Do you understand?"

"Of course, of course. And you're right—Pasternak is a name. Or rather Luchnikov is right. Pasternak is a name, and a big one. But what's the time? Will they be gone for the day?"

"No, it's not five o'clock yet."

Fedin hesitated for a moment, then went to the telephone on his desk. "All right. I'll talk to . . . 'Uncle Mitya.' Polikarpov, that is." He smiled. "A lot depends on him. I think he can transfer Borya to the Kremlin hospital. Just a minute." He looked through his telephone book. "By the way, Zina, when exactly did Borya have his attack? Was it yesterday?"

"The night before last."

"On the eve of Easter? How sad. You're religious people . . ."

He found the number, dialed it, and, clearing his throat, prepared to talk. "Hello. Comrade Polikarpov's office? Good day, this is Konstantin Fedin. The writer Fedin. I need to talk to Dimitry Alexeyevich. Urgently. On *important* business. What's that?" He recoiled. "Really? Oh, how unpleasant. I had no idea. But please tell me. How is he now?" He shook his head at Zina. "Thank God. Let's hope he will soon be fine. Yes, yes. Thank you. Goodbye."

"What, has he had a heart attack too?"

"An angina attack. What an amazing coincidence. He was admitted to the Kremlin hospital yesterday. Maybe it's something in the atmosphere. Heart patients are very sensitive to changes in the air. In fact, my chest is aching a bit too."

"Kostya, call Suslov."

"But Zina, he's . . . Secretary of the Central Committee."

"So what? Pasternak is famous throughout the world. Why should Polikarpov go to the Kremlin hospital and Pasternak to some horrible dump? What if they find out about this abroad? What if I write to Borya's sisters in Oxford and tell them how he's being treated? What if I report it to foreign correspondents in Moscow?"

"No, no, Zina, don't do that. Then you won't get out of the mess so easily. Don't dabble in international politics. I beg you."

"Then call Suslov."

"You . . . insist?"

"Yes, Kostya, I insist."

Fedin looked at Zina intently. Her face was beautiful in its menacing grandeur and determination. No, she was not asking. She was demanding. And Fedin had to submit.

"All right, I'll call Suslov."

"Now. While I'm here."

"All right. I've got his office number somewhere." He smiled awkwardly and searched in his telephone book again. "You're right, Zina, we're talking about the life of a great Russian poet. Ideological differences don't matter. If you remember, Zina, Stalin saved Anna Akhmatova's life when she was dying of typhoid in Tashkent, even though she was never considered a proletarian poetess. He helped her with medicine and food. That is, he saw to it that—"

"Kostya, stop wasting time," Zina interrupted. "And if Suslov has had a coronary, call Khrushchev."

"What? Zina, how can you joke at a moment like this? Anyway, Khrushchev runs a greater risk than any of us of facing apoplexy." Fedin dialed a number and cleared his throat. "Hello? Comrade Suslov's office? Good day. This is the writer Konstantin Fedin speaking. Please put me through to the Secretary of the Central Committee. I'm calling on very *important*—no, *urgent*—business. I ask you to inform Mikhail"—Fedin hesitated as he tried to recall Suslov's patronymic— "Mikhail Andreyevich that Konstantin Fedin is calling. Yes, yes, please." And covering the mouthpiece of the phone with his palm, he winked at Zina and whispered, "Seems my name has some weight too."

"You're a marshal in literature, Kostya," Zina said.

Suddenly Fedin stood straight. "Comrade Suslov? Good day, Mikhail Andreyevich. This is Fedin. Sorry to trouble you. But it's an urgent matter. I phoned Comrade Polikarpov, but unfortunately he's in the Kremlin hospital. I'm calling to tell you, if you haven't already heard, that Boris Pasternak had a heart attack the day before yesterday. It's the second one he's had. He's in very serious condition, in an *ordinary* hospital in the Mozhaisky district. It's so overcrowded that the poet is lying in a corridor. Yes, in a corridor. It seems to me that it would be unfortunate if the

Western press got wind of this. Will you give instructions for Pasternak to be transferred to the Kremlin hospital? What? Yes, of course. The head doctor of the district hospital told the poet's wife that he won't vouch for his life if he is not given the right treatment. I understand, Mikhail Andreyevich, that our district hospitals present a complicated and acute problem, but nevertheless . . . What? My health? I'm still a bit under the weather. Thanks. Yes, yes. Very good. Thank you, Comrade Suslov. Many thanks. And excuse me once again for troubling you. Goodbye, Comrade Suslov." Fedin replaced the phone and sighed with relief. "Phew, I'm all in a sweat."

"What did he say?" Zina started to get up from the sofa.

Fedin wiped his forehead with his handkerchief. "Well, Zina, the deed is done. The leader—well, the half leader, or one-third leader—has uttered the magic words: 'Measures will be taken.' That's their style: 'Measures will be taken.' That's how they talk. Machine language. But to hell with them! No, I don't mean that—we'd be lost without them." He smiled mischievously. "A magic carpet will appear and whisk Borya to the splendid Kremlin hospital."

Zina went to him and, bending down, kissed his hand. "I shall be indebted to you for the rest of my life, Kostya."

Fedin turned red and then pale. "What are you doing, Zina?" he gasped. "You ought to be ashamed of yourself. What for?"

"Thank you, Kostya."

"Stop it! I know—I'm sure that everything will be fine now. Don't worry. There are excellent doctors in the Kremlin hospital. And Borya has immense spirit. Death backs away from such people."

"God willing." Zina quickly retreated to the door, and then turning, said: "Kostya, it would be dishonest of me to go away without telling you that, after your last conversation with Borya, he forbade me to enter your house. And he made me vow that if he died before me, in case of extreme need I would turn to Surkov, not you. He told Nina and me that the Russian intellectual in you was dead."

"Ah, Borya . . ." Fedin dropped into an armchair and covered his face with his hands.

"But I think he was mistaken. The Russian intellectual in you is *still* alive, Kostya." And so saying, she left.

2.

Khrushchev was clearly "under the influence." He hadn't touched liquor for almost a month, and the choice brandy had gone straight to his head. His eyes sparkled like glow-worms on a summer night; he waved his arms like a bird flapping its wings, threw out his stomach outrageously, then suddenly froze with his arms akimbo, in the pose of a mata-dor confronting a bull. The alcohol clearly had excited him, but he was also stimulated by the curious, even enraptured gaze of a woman.

Nikita was wearing a new dark-blue suit, made in Italy, over-elegant, with drain-pipe trousers, soft shoulders, and short sleeves; his Ukrainian shirt, with embroidered front and ribbons tied at the neck, could be seen underneath. He paced up and down his office in the Central Committee building, occasionally turning to his visitors from the Central Commit-tee of the French Communist Party.

The guests were seated on the sofa and in armchairs: five men and a woman, who also acted as interpreter. The latter was no more than thirty-five, slim and attractive, with au-burn hair. (Because of her black eyes Nikita had christened her the "mouse.") The men were middle-aged ordinary Frenchmen with rather coarse but good-natured faces. The first wore no tie and had left the collar of his shirt open; the second wore an engagement ring as well as another ring; the third had eyes that slanted downward toward his nose; the fourth had heavy, fleshy hands (Khrushchev guessed he

had probably once been a metalworker or a blacksmith), and the fifth was well dressed and precise, rather like a mathematics professor.

On the round table were two bottles of brandy, Narzan mineral water, a variety of glasses, and dishes of crackers, fruit, roasted nuts, and the like.

Leonid Brezhnev, Khrushchev's newly promoted protégé, sat near the windows, in front of their lowered blinds. He had thick eyebrows overhanging his heavy eyes like cliffs, and he looked as if he had just swallowed a plum. His eyes never left Khrushchev, and his smile was obsequious if restrained. He was conscious of his appearance and kept smoothing his thick mane of hair. Nikita had recently made him a secretary of the Central Committee and placed him in the central apparatus of the party, hoping thereby to limit Suslov's power. Khrushchev knew Brezhnev was a single-minded careerist and encouraged his ambition, thinking it would make him his man; he had even thought of appointing him Chairman of the Presidium of the USSR Supreme Soviet—in other words, making him President. But that ultimately had proved an unwarrantable trust.

The French guests had drunk several toasts, and their faces, tanned by the Black Sea sun, were flushed and sweaty. Nikita had just finished telling them an amusing story about Stalin, and the Frenchmen were still laughing. The First Secretary of the Central Committee paced up and down as if building up steam; he was like a spoiled actor, addicted to applause.

"Nikita Sergeyevich is our expert raconteur," Brezhnev remarked deferentially.

The tall Frenchman with the blacksmith's hands addressed Khrushchev through his colleague, the interpreter: "Comrade Nikita, my friends and I would like to know, confidentially, how the Politburo of the party's Central Committee . . . mmm . . . dealt with Stalin's right-hand man, the boss of the secret police, Marshal Beria . . ."

Khrushchev answered without hesitation. "We snuffed him out."

"What, without a trial?" The "mouse" asked the question herself.

"Goddam sonofabitch! A trial would have been only for the press. You can't treat a bandit with kid gloves. If we hadn't killed him first he'd have sláughtered us all. Like chickens—yes, like chickens. Bang, bang. The capitalist monster. He raped young girls and left a whole tribe of bastards behind him. That crook had the whole of the state security apparatus in his grasp. You call them the secret police. Fine, have it your own way. There isn't much difference anyway. Oh, he was cunning, that Beria, to be fussed over and treated well."

"Who . . . killed him?" the Frenchman who looked like a professor asked.

The "mouse" translated his question.

"I did!" Nikita said heartily.

"You?" The "mouse" gasped.

"Yes. I! That's right, isn't it, Leonid Ilich?" Unnoticed, Khrushchev winked at Brezhnev.

"Quite right, Nikita Sergeyevich," Brezhnev answered quickly.

"All right, comrade Frenchmen. I know you have a yen for stories of this sort. Although you're communists, you were born and you live in a country where everything starts and ends in murders, rapes, bank robberies, and so forth. Only the Americans outdo you in that kind of business. So I'll tell you in detail how I did away with Beria. But on one condition. You must swear it will all remain, as you say in France, *tête-à-tête*. Between ourselves. Do you swear?"

The "mouse" quickly translated for her comrades, then raised her arm enthusiastically and answered on behalf of them all. "We swear!"

"I know you, I know," Khrushchev laughed. "I know how well you hold your tongues. If I tell you something sensational today, tomorrow it will be all over the world. I know you, my foreign brothers."

The visitors understood without benefit of translation and smiled uncomfortably. But none of them protested, probably because they could see that Nikita himself was impatient to tell them his story.

Khrushchev went over to the desk, opened the middle drawer and took out a steel-blue pistol.

"Here you are, you see!" He turned to his guests and showed them the gun. "A Browning. I've had it since the Civil War. I shot bourgeois with it like pigeons. A time-honored weapon. For me it's like a cross around the neck of a believer. If any of you secretly believes in God, please forgive the comparison." After laughing and pausing to let the "mouse" translate his words into French, he went on: "I can't do a thing without this Browning. By the way, Stalin never parted with his Browning either. And Brezhnev here has a Browning in his pocket. Right, Leonid Ilich?"

"I've got a Nagant," Brezhnev replied in confusion.

"Well, a Browning or a Nagant. What's the difference? Carrying a pistol is part of our Bolshevik heritage! Yes, comrade Frenchmen, it was this very Browning that blasted the skull of that vile Georgian prick—Beria, that is. The goddam sonofabitch! The Monster." He smiled ingratiatingly. "Do you want to hold my pistol? It's a historical heirloom. Perhaps after my death it will grace a museum, alongside some dried ears of corn: 'A relic of the revolution.'"

"And of the Khrushchev Era," Brezhnev added.

"Yes, *my* era . . ." He removed the magazine and, checking the chamber in the light, offered the weapon to the "mouse." It passed quickly from hand to hand.

"This is how it happened . . ." Khrushchev gulped another glass of brandy and popped some roasted nuts into his mouth. "Leonid Brezhnev here won't let me tell a lie. Actually, he was still in short pants then, but he knows all about it. So, two years before his death our mustachioed helmsman—Stalin, that is—realized that Beria, his Georgian henchman, might try to send him to join his ancestors, and so he decided to chop off Beria's hands. He took away the state security apparatus from him and transferred it to Mikoyan. It's our procedure that every member of the Politburo is in charge of a group of ministries or committees. So Anastas took over the KGB. Stalin put Beria in charge of the armaments industry and rarely saw him after that. He clearly preferred the chatterbox Malenkov, with the elephant legs. I was held back. Right, Comrade Brezhnev?"

"Right, Nikita Sergeyevich."

"Well, then. After the old man breathed his last, Malenkov and Beria seemed to come to an understanding, even though before that they'd been like cat and dog, and they started to lure Molotov into their gang. And that Civil War hero— Voroshilov, I mean—who—"

The telephone rang, and Khrushchev, angrily breaking off in mid-sentence, went to the desk and picked it up. "Khrushchev. Hello, Alexei. What do you want? Not yet. Objections have been raised. Come to the dacha this evening and I'll tell you. How's Rada? Fine. I'm busy now, Alexei. I've got guests from France. So long."

He returned to the Frenchmen. "That was my son-in-law on the phone. Adzhubei. In Moscow they say, 'One doesn't need a hundred friends, but one needs to marry the way Adzhubei did.' Ha-ha-ha! He's the editor of *Izvestia*. You've heard of him of course. I forgot; he's already been to France. He likes traveling, so he never gives me any peace. He also uses his family connection to shower me with advice. Between us, he dreams of becoming Minister of Foreign Affairs. Now, what was I telling you about, comrades?"

"About Beria," the "mouse" reminded him.

"Aha. That bandit, that monster. Well, then . . ." He took his Browning from her, inserted the magazine, and placed the pistol in the pocket of his pants. "Well, then, although Malenkov and Beria appeared to come to an understanding, *I* knew that a life-and-death struggle was going on between them. I was sitting on the Central Committee, and I knew that Beria wanted to arrest all of us and take full power into his hands. The security forces were still loyal to him at that time. However, Beria's deputy, Ivan Serov, was my boy. He reported everything to me. Now, it so happened that this Georgian prick, this scum—who, by the way, had two chief bodyguards, one for his own body and the other for his mistresses' . . . Excuse me for such intimate detail." Khrushchev made a low bow to the "mouse," who blushed but had not lowered her eyes.

"Well, then . . . it so happened that this ruffian left Moscow for a three-day inspection tour of the Ukraine and the Baltic republics. It was the right moment to get organized and take the necessary steps. I took the initiative into my hands. I had a talk with Malenkov and Molotov. And then I went to see Voroshilov. When I told him what I was planning, the old fool burst into tears and embraced me; he wanted to get rid of Beria but was terrified of him. I established a link with the army. Marshal Konev was more reliable than the rest. He surrounded Moscow with troops. Meanwhile Marshal Moskalenko and a group of senior officers took up key positions in the Kremlin. All this was done before Beria's return to the capital. When he arrived at the Central Committee for the Politburo session, all the Moscow railway stations were under army control. Konev's tanks, ready for battle, were positioned in the central squares.

"Only one thing had not been definitely decided: which one of us was to shoot Beria? An accurate shot was needed. Among the members of the Politburo, Mikoyan and I were good shots. Anastas never missed at close range either. So we decided to toss a coin. Heads or tails. It fell to me to shoot. So I—wait, I'll show you how it all took place." Khrushchev grabbed the Frenchman who looked like a professor and sat him down in another seat. "You take Beria's place," he said. "The rest of you, imagine that the Georgian gangster is sitting right here. Don't forget—I'm only showing you. Well, and I was here. Which means Malenkov, who was conducting the Politburo session, was there. The rest were sitting to the left and right around an oblong table. We discussed economic problems and something else; then Malenkov said, 'The only other business on the agenda, comrades, is the question of the antigovernment activity of Lavrenti Beria.' As soon as he said that, in a slightly quavering voice—he was a coward, Malenkov—I got up, like this, and put my hand in my pocket, like this. Then, without the swine noticing, I went around behind him—like this. Don't look around, comrade professor, don't look around. Beria didn't look around. He started shouting something, jumped up, and shoved his hand into *his* pocket. Now, I knew he always carried a Mauser, but I didn't falter. I pulled my Browning out and let him have the whole magazine in the back of the neck. He didn't make a sound. The Georgian crow . . ."

Khrushchev lowered the pistol, and the Frenchman turned his head, smiled abashedly, and babbled something in French. His colleagues appeared almost equally uncomfortable, especially as the Browning was loaded again. After the "mouse" had finished translating Khrushchev's story they began coughing and talking agitatedly among themselves.

"Fantastic!" Nikita exclaimed. "He didn't make a sound, the goddam sonofabitch! And Marshal Moskalenko and his officers, armed with machine guns, mowed down Beria's bodyguards in the next room. Then in a couple of weeks we cleaned up—what are they called?—the Augean stables, and pulled up Beria's satraps—I love that word 'satrap'—by the roots. The swine had craftily placed them at key points all over the country. Some of them we stood against walls and shot, some we exiled to the hinterland."

Nikita interrupted himself when he saw Suslov enter the room. The latter went to the party leader and whispered in his ear. Nikita frowned, then nodded to Brezhnev and set off toward his study. Brezhnev and Suslov followed him, entering the study in that order.

When the French Communists were alone, the one wearing the engagement ring laughed with relief and said, "In my opinion, our corn Marat is a bit like Baron Munchausen."

"Did he make it all up?" the "mouse" asked, her eyes wide with astonishment.

Meanwhile in the study, where the three had sat down, Suslov reported Fedin's call.

"Well, what shall we do, comrades?" Nikita asked, looking at Suslov and Brezhnev in turn.

"Nikita Sergeyevich, I think Pasternak should be transferred to the Kremlin hospital," Suslov said.

"Seconded," said Brezhnev.

"Fine. Give the order, Mikhail Andreyevich." Khrushchev hesitated and then grinned. "Wait . . . What if . . . Yes, yes . . . what a wonderful idea! . . . Your Polikarpov, Comrade Suslov, who nearly gave up the ghost as well, he's in the Kremlin hospital too, isn't he?"

"Yes, he's in the Kremlin hospital." Suslov did not understand what Khrushchev was getting at. "So what?"

"Why don't we put the two in together? The Communist and the nonparty sheep in the same room. Eh? What about it?"

"I agree," Brezhnev said immediately.

"Excuse me, but what for?" Suslov asked.

"What do you mean, what for?" Khrushchev paused—he had got up and started walking around the room, waving his arms—and looked at Suslov with irritation. "To let them get to know each other better, to let them exchange ideas. It might do both of them good. Ha-ha-ha! On the one hand, an important party boss, an ideologue of collectivism and communism, the head of the culture section of the Central Committee. On the other, a poet, Narcissus, ideologue of individualism and capitalism. What a pair—the ram and the ewe! Ha-ha-ha! There won't be any escape. Enclosed by four walls. They'll lie there side by side, surrounded by smiling doctors in white coats. Both of them sick, afraid of dying. What a scene! What a marvelous idea!"

"That's right, Nikita Sergeyevich, a wonderful idea," Brezhnev agreed.

"You hope Polikarpov will reeducate Pasternak?" Suslov cracked his knuckles.

"Or the other way around!" Nikita exclaimed.

"But they're both seriously ill, Nikita Sergeyevich," Suslov insisted. "They shouldn't argue. One's got angina and the other's had a heart attack. An experiment like the one you've proposed might cost them their lives."

"Don't worry so much. Let's just let them argue a bit under the doctors' care." And to let Suslov know that the subject was closed, Nikita abruptly changed it. "I had no idea, Mikhail Andreyevich, that you played whist. You should invite me for a game. I like whist. I learned how to play at the front. We can play together." Glancing at Brezhnev, he thought: This cockroach puts on airs and doesn't play cards, but according to Serov's information he's interested in women; he's slept with all his secretaries.

Khrushchev turned back to Suslov and said sharply: "I entrust you, Mikhail Andreyevich, with the task of phoning the Main Treatment Center at the Kremlin and instructing them that Pasternak be placed in the Kremlin hospital, in the same room as Polikarpov. We'll consider the matter settled. Leonid Ilich, let's return to our Frenchmen. My God, they're such geese—they'll believe anything." He moved toward the door. "Now I'm going to tell them how we threw Stalin's body out of the Lenin Mausoleum. At first we triumphantly put the man with the mustache next to Lenin, but then we changed our minds, and wham!—out he went, head first . . ."

"But that's the truth."

"Do I *always* tell lies, Lyonya?"

CHAPTER ELEVEN

The Kremlin Hospital

1.

The next day Polikarpov was transferred from a single to a double room and a new patient was put in the bed next to him. The condition of the head of the Central Committee cultural section was still unsatisfactory, and at first he did not notice who his neighbor was. Pasternak remained in critical condition; he lay motionless and absolutely unaware of his surroundings. They both were under constant surveillance by doctors and nurses.

The Kremlin hospital was wonderfully equipped and luxuriously furnished and had first-class personnel, but even here, as in the chaotic, understaffed district hospital, there were different floors and different wards for patients of different status.

Their room, classified as deluxe, was set aside for the top ranks. There were silk curtains over the two windows and thick drapes of expensive brocade. In the middle of the mirrorlike parquet floor was a large Turkish carpet. A polished mahogany wardrobe stood in a corner. The beds were foreign-made, with all kinds of medical appliances; on bedside tables next to them were white telephones and bells for calling the nurses at any hour of the day or night. A chandelier hung from the center of the ceiling. There were also two armchairs and two floor lamps with shades made of crocodile skin. A door on the right led into a private bathroom. In short, the room looked as much like a lady's boudoir as it did a hospital room.

A week went by and both men improved. Polikarpov was allowed to get out of bed and walk slowly around the room, and he spent several hours a day sitting in an armchair reading his favorite Dumas. He wore fine blue woolen pajamas, brought from home, and soft red leather slippers. Pasternak was still in bed, but now he was able to sit up and talk without discomfort. His eyes had become clearer, his face had some color, and his lips were no longer like a corpse's.

Another week passed before the inevitable philosophical dispute occurred.

"Here's an example for you, Boris Leonidovich," Polikarpov said while sitting in his armchair. "A historical example. Paris and Leningrad. Two cities. Two symbols."

"I don't understand." Pasternak pulled himself up in his bed.

"When Hitler's hordes surrounded Paris, the city did not defend itself; it simply capitulated. The French did not even consider defending their honor at the price of destroying the treasure-house of world culture. Their decision was above class, above ideology. At that time, for rich and poor alike, Paris was above war, above the national fate of France. Do you agree with me?"

"Well . . . let's assume I do."

"But what happened in Leningrad? This city, also to a

293

certain extent a treasure-house of world culture, was destroyed pretty thoroughly during the war when the Germans —yes, the same Germans, the Nazis—surrounded it and shelled it. Leningrad defended itself to the last, and won. The people won, the heroic Russian people, the great Soviet people. And this, from my point of view, is more significant than all the architectural monuments and museum collections in Paris. I was in Leningrad when it was under siege; I saw death hover over the city. But if Leningrad had capitulated, Boris Leonidovich, then a flag with a swastika would probably be flying over Paris today. And the same fate would probably have befallen London. Would you go to a Louvre that was named after, say, the traitor and fascist Knut Hamsun?"

"I don't know."

"Paris and Leningrad—they show the absolute differences between two worlds, two philosophies, two approaches to human existence, and last, two moral codes. Without a doubt, you regard me as a party Talmudist and bureaucrat, in love with Marxist dogma, and yet this is the second week that I, like you, have been staring death in the face."

"And so?"

"Well, when one is looking death in the face it is impossible to deceive oneself and engage in political propaganda. We Communists, Boris Leonidovich, are the only people to put the ideas of equality and brotherhood into practice. Literature and art cannot be above this historic mission. You can't be one of those who hide behind illusory and, forgive me, cowardly petty-bourgeois ideals—no, not of individualism but of egocentrism. Do you remember what the great Russian critic Belinsky said? He said that a great poet must inevitably live in society; he is a social animal, he expresses the spirit of his people and his time. But if he sings only about himself, he is just an unthinking bird. Enormous changes are taking place in the world today, Boris Leonidovich. The spirit that Paris embodies can no longer save us. Age-old values have become museum exhibits. That's all they're good for. The model for contemporary life is Leningrad. It resisted and acted. *Acted*. And won. We live in an epoch of resistance and action. This has not yet penetrated the consciousness of the Western masses, who are poisoned by philistinism, but it will become obvious to them in the end."

"Dimitry Alexeyevich, you discount Paris so easily. But can you toss off the thousand-year past of Russia so cavalierly?"

"There's no similarity between the two. We glorify our past, although of course today is more important. We are building a new life. You're a snob, Boris Leonidovich. You allow yourself luxuries in a world that is ready to endure the most terrifying deprivations so that justice can prevail."

"What luxuries are you talking about?"

"Living for the beauty of one's inner world, enjoying the rarest nuances of one's gift. In our age those are luxuries."

Pasternak remembered that the same thought had occurred to him not long ago.

"Maybe you're right," he said.

"I've read everything that you've written," Polikarpov went on. "I've read *Doctor Zhivago* twice. And I'll tell you frankly: your talent is enormous and indisputable. But it's turned in the wrong direction; it's turned inward. Its light can be seen only by you and a handful of people like you."

"Fedin said almost the same thing," Pasternak remarked with a gentle smile. "That evening you were sitting at his dacha in Peredelkino."

"You think like your Yury Zhivago, Boris Leonidovich, like a traditional turn-of-the-century Russian liberal. This type could acknowledge the greatness and importance of the people only as long as he occupied a position superior to theirs. Safe on his lofty perch, he could admire the brightness of his own spiritual originality. He, this liberal, would never have agreed to become just a man in the crowd, one of the millions, gray and colorless, if the struggle for a just cause had so required. A liberal of such persuasion was always above the people. This was the position he wanted and sought to attain. In order to enjoy his spiritual beauty and originality, he was even prepared to call out, 'Revolution, you're a wonder!'—just as you did in your time, Boris Leonidovich."

"I see you really have read everything I've written."

"It seems to me that if you had emigrated to Europe or America and had been given the millions of dollars you've made from the sale of a *Doctro Zhivago*, you would have started to donate your money to good causes. You'd probably have sent some even to us, for the enlightenment of Russia. Those terrible Bolsheviks are ignoring the poor people, so let's open a literary museum somewhere, say in Voronezh. Is that a fair estimate of what you'd do?"

"Yes, I'd say so."

"And wouldn't it have occurred to you at the time that by doing this you would be deeply insulting the country you regard as your motherland?"

"Insulting? Why?"

"It's the theme of Paris and Leningrad again. Ah, Boris Leonidovich, if you would just once make yourself think really deeply and genuinely about this. For example, some Rothschild, trying to redeem his countless sins before God, gives a poor writer a hundred thousand dollars, and this money allows the writer to create a genuine work of literature. Is that good or bad?"

"Good, of course."

"In other words, it's not important from whom you receive the money, just as long as you receive it."

"I don't understand."

"In my opinion, it's bad; it's base and amoral."

"But why?"

"Because . . . no, I'm not saying this as a Marxist or as an official of the party Central Committee, but simply as a human being, an *honest* human being. Hasn't the idea occurred to you that the age of philanthropy, of patronage of the arts and charitable deeds by the rich—of everything that expresses the superiority of one man over another, of everything that is dependent on the good will, or ill will, of a boss, patron, or possessor of capital, on his egocentric or ostentatious humanism—that such an age is drawing to a close? People no longer need or want crumbs of charity or noble gestures. People want lawful social equality and life without philanthropy. And they deserve it. They want a little literary museum, or better still a proper museum in Voronezh, to be opened on *their* earnings. They don't need your crumbs. Maybe they still live poorly and don't have much; maybe from time to time they grumble, get angry, and express their dissatisfaction with some defect in the system, some mistake or even individual abuse of power. But all the same, they know there is no boss over them, no higher creature, no rich man to determine their fate. And it's not important whether he's a humane Christian, this rich man, or an out-and-out villain."

Listening to Polikarpov, Pasternak remembered his arguments with Olga and Lyonya and his recent discussion with Rezo in Tbilisi. It was interesting how much of what Polikarpov said had come from his own mouth in those arguments; but when he himself voiced these sentiments, it seemed to him that they sounded completely different. Had he not denied the validity of the "boss and worker" paradigm? What was it that troubled him in the ideas Polikarpov expressed? He thought the party man simplified, vulgarized, and thereby utterly distorted an important philosophical question. The society Polikarpov was advocating could be achieved only by destroying or suppressing individuality and spiritual freedom, by increasing the power of the state, by subordinating the individual to the will of the state machine. That is how it was in practice, although in theory Polikarpov never swept aside individuality but merely called it "socialist." (Rezo was right about that.)

Polikarpov took off his slippers and lay down on his bed.

After a while Pasternak said thoughtfully, "Paris and Leningrad."

"What?"

"Paris and Leningrad."

"What . . . has it got you thinking?" Polikarpov could barely conceal his satisfaction.

"Yes, it's got me thinking. You're right. There are deep meanings hidden in this comparison. It was no accident, Dimitry Alexeyevich, that the struggle at the time was between Hitler and Stalin. Two extremes. Two historic evils." Pasternak spoke quietly, but distinctly, unconcerned by Polikarpov's obvious pique. "Your philosophy is the philosophy of extremism. It is nothing but vulgar sociology. You think the salvation of the world lies only in your party and government reforms. But the world is far more complicated. Wait! It has to be reshaped not only from the outside but from the inside, within the soul of every man. Without this inner change your reforms are pointless—harmful and perhaps even fatal. I'm for a just society without wealth and poverty. More than that, I'm against private property, because I'm a Christian. But your Marxist ideas are too specific and utilitarian to become a universal panacea for order on our planet. And because you—"

"Aren't we for spiritual change?" Polikarpov objected, his hand fretting at his chest.

"Wait! Let me finish what I was saying. . . . And all the garlands of revolutionary romanticism and creativity that you drape over your clichés can't disguise the poverty of your thought. You are intending to establish equality by *enslaving* man with the *dogma* of equality, forgetting that if you succeed, equality will become an empty word signifying nothing more than a swarm mentality." Polikarpov started to protest but recoiled in pain. "And that inevitably leads to *totalitarianism*. The USSR is the most flagrant example. Besides, Dimitry Alexeyevich, your definition of spirit as a higher form of organized matter is probably correct, but in my opinion matter, in acquiring its higher form, becomes the antipode of matter. No, you Communists don't believe in the greatness of the spirit and so you don't believe in the greatness of man. For you he is just an object of your social experiments, a piece on a chessboard, which you are free to move here or there as you wish. You're a rich man too, Dimitry Alexeyevich, but instead of money you've got the power of dogma in your pocket, which generates fear, fear of the octopus—the state and party machine. You have chained all of us to dogma. You have destroyed the soul of Russia; you have banished God, and you've turned literature and art into debased vehicles for your devilish propaganda. Oh, you've surpassed Goebbels! You've surpassed everyone! Look around at what you've done! Around you now are not people but shadows, spiritually castrated monsters . . ."

Polikarpov tossed in anguish, but, oblivious, Pasternak pressed on.

"You, Dimitry Alexeyevich, have killed literature and art by killing what is miraculous, ingenuous, and benevolent in them—in short, everything that ennobles people. That is why rudeness, greed, philistinism, careerism, and other disgusting vices are now rampant in Russia. And what equality, in fact, are you talking about? You, in your Kremlin hospital here; you, the ants' boss, crowned with privileges; you, with your dachas, special rations, service cars, special pensions, sanatoriums, and a host of lackeys around you. Are you and your fellows the ones to judge what is good and what is bad? Are you the ones to denounce Rothschild? You are no less evil than he is. If he tries to subject the world to himself through the force of money, you try to achieve the same through the force of your Marxism. You justify all your bloodlettings by citing lofty historical goals, which you impose on the Soviet people. Who authorized you to do this? Did someone elect you, freely and without compulsion? Did anyone vote for you of his own free will? All your elections are performances of *Petrouchka*, yet you accuse the West of dirty dealing."

"How dare you!" Polikarpov was gasping, his face blue from lack of oxygen.

"You are the apostles of destruction! You foster everything corrupt in man. You debase him almost scientifically, reducing life to a struggle for a crust of bread. You say that your goal is the elimination of envy, but in practice you spread its corrupting influence by creating new classes of privileged citizens. You are insensitive, heartless bureaucrats! If your neighbor were in trouble, nothing could make you help him, because according to your philosophy all the troubles of mankind should be abolished, first and foremost, by your social reforms. You . . . you . . .''

Pasternak tried to go on, but, overcome by sudden weakness and gagged by the repulsive taste in his mouth, he fell back and lay still.

Polikarpov meanwhile had managed to slip three nitroglycerin tablets under his tongue, and within a minute both men were still—exhausted and asleep.

2.

Zina did not know why, but she had been in a cheerful mood all day. Perhaps because there was a smell of spring in the air (the snow in Peredelkino had vanished in the last few days) and the sun had a warm glow. Or perhaps because at the station, where there was a small market, she had bought a bouquet of violets, the scent of which she adored.

Yury Mikhailovich dropped her at the All-Union Lenin Library at noon. She got out of the Pobeda and, crossing Kalinin Street, headed for the large, gray, six-story building that housed the Kremlin hospital. The building could be distinguished from those around it by its wide windows, balconies, and rooftop solarium.

The vestibule of the hospital was spacious, bright, and clean. A marble staircase in the middle led to the second floor. On the left, behind some columns, was a cloakroom, where Zina checked her coat and requested a white hospital smock.

"Whom are you visiting?" the female attendant asked.

"Boris Pasternak," Zina said.

"Of course, of course . . . the aviator. I mean, the general, eh?"

"No, he's a poet."

"Of course. Of course." She wracked her brain. "In room fourteen. Oh . . ."

"What is it?" Zina asked.

"You'll have to wait." She checked her list. "He's got a visitor right now."

"A visitor? Who?"

"His wife."

Blood rushed to Zina's head. "*I* am the wife of Boris Pasternak, and I have been for thirty years."

The attendant shrank with embarrassment but did not relent. "I'm sorry, citizeness, but rules are rules. You'll have to wait. Otherwise you'd be two visitors in the room at once, and that is not allowed. Please take a seat at the table. There's a magazine there for you to read."

For the next fifteen minutes Zina stewed, leafing mechanically through *Smena*, with the violets in her hand. All her cheerfulness—the feeling of spring, the delirium of the violets, and the catlike desire to warm herself in the sun—had vanished. Olga was the woman upstairs, without a doubt. Yes, Olga was in the habit of calling herself Pasternak's wife. Zina had even heard that when she passed Pasternak's dacha in Peredelkino she assured people that she lived there. There was no limit to the woman's effrontery, but Borya was still loyal to her and forgave her everything; he still visited her when he was well, and she was in his life even now when he was ill. What was there for him to say about his old wife? Zina's cheeks were ablaze, as if she had been slapped across the face. Nor did they fade while she waited.

At length Olga appeared on the staircase. She wore a new dress with short sleeves, over which she had thrown a white coat. She walked calmly, even majestically, as if she had long ago gotten everything she wanted out of life. At the cloakroom she pushed a three-ruble note toward the attendant, who started fussing over her, not revealing that she knew Olga was the second, not the first Mrs. Pasternak. Unaware, Olga then tossed her a careless goodbye and headed toward the exit. She stopped when she saw Zina, then changed course decisively and went over to her.

"I was visiting Borya . . . as his literary secretary," she said.

"I thought it was as his lawful wife," Zina replied without looking up.

Olga stammered momentarily.

"Leave me in peace," Zina added.

"No. We have to have this out. I did lie. I told the attendant that I was his wife. Punish me if you like. But it won't change a thing. Yes, I love your husband and I regard myself as his wife."

"He's yours. Take him."

"No, he's not mine and I can't take him."

"I'm not stopping you."

"Listen, Zinaida Nikolayevna, you and I should find a common language. Stop ignoring me. We love the same man and so we're in the same boat. Borya is not capable of leaving you, just as he is not capable of abandoning me."

"We've got nothing to talk about." Zina stood up.

"You're wrong there. I take care of all his financial affairs and I have his will in my house."

"Is this blackmail?"

"No . . . but . . ."

"Trash." Zina went to the cloakroom, took a white coat, perhaps the same one that Olga had just taken off, and disappeared up the stairs.

3.

On Pasternak's bedside table there were some strongly scented white roses. Zina noticed the flowers and realized that Olga had brought them. She was confused, not knowing what to do with the violets, but presently she placed them on the bed at her husband's feet.

"How are you, Borya?"

Pasternak barely stirred and his voice was a whisper: "Zina, my dearest, save me! You mustn't abandon me to the tyranny of fate. I'll die here. I want to go back to the district hospital, to the corridor, to *life*."

"Why are you so upset, Borya? What's happened?"

"Talk to whomever you have to. You know how. Convince them. Let them take me back, back . . ."

"But it's hell there!"

"No, no, it's hell here! It was wonderful there!" He smiled pathetically. "You can't imagine what it means to be here, in the same room with . . . this dying party monster."

Pasternak nodded toward the bed next to him, where Polikarpov lay, with his eyes closed, his face pale, his lips bluish purple, pretending to be asleep, enraged but too feeble to bleat.

CHAPTER TWELVE

Life Goes On

1.

It was a sunny day in Peredelkino. The scarecrow, in his weather-beaten checked jacket, had returned to the kitchen garden. The potato beds were freshly turned. Lyonya and Tatyana were playing Ping-Pong, although the table, from which everything had been cleared, was still damp. Wearing a gray herringbone overcoat and a cap, his right arm in a sling (since his heart attack it had been partially paralyzed), Pasternak sat on the steps leading into the kitchen, serving as referee. Tobik and Bubik lay at his feet.

Tatyana was winning easily. Lyonya, in a bad mood, missed one easy shot after another. Tatyana taunted him and smashed the ball, almost like a professional. Pasternak, helplessly amused, tried to hold back a smile.

"Forty-fifteen. Game," he announced. "No, Lyonya, you're no match for Tanya. Tatyana is a champion. We'll have to send her to China to show up Mao Tse-tung."

"She practices for hours every day," Lyonya complained.

"What nonsense!" Tatyana was indignant. "Who have I got to play with? Tobik or Bubik, you mean? I'm slaving in the kitchen all day and cleaning up the house. Who's got time for hitting little balls? No, young master, you're the problem, not me. You're a chemist *in love*, that's what. And love has addled—"

"Don't be stupid!" Lyonya cut in.

"You can't put your mind to anything. Who forced me to learn how to play Ping-Pong? Who? Who, Boris Leonidovich?"

"Lyonya."

"I resisted. I said I didn't want to. But he kept badgering me, 'Come on, come on.'"

"That's true. Admit it, son. Tatyana's right for once."

"I'm always right, Boris Leonidovich."

"Come on," Lyonya said disgustedly, "let's play another game."

"Some other time. I've got work to do. What's the point in my wasting time with you? You'll only lose again. You're in love, Lyonya. And I've got lunch to make." She went into the house.

Pasternak hesitated before intruding. "Lyonya? How's Natasha?" For the last few evenings Lyonya had been staying at the dacha instead of going to Moscow. "Has something happened?"

Lyonya stared at his feet. "We had another argument, Papa," he said at length. "Everything's a mess."

"What did you quarrel about?"

"It's always the same thing! She tries to force me to read the Bible. To enlighten me."

"And so? Why won't you read the Bible a bit for the girl you love?"

"I try, I've tried . . ." Lyonya fretted momentarily and

then sat down on the step beside his father. "On my own. With her. We've gone on trips together and read it out loud." He struggled dejectedly. "It just doesn't sink into my brain, and that's all there is to it."

"But it does into hers."

"Papa, religion is best digested in childhood, with mother's milk. Natasha's grandmother is an Old Believer, who dragged her off to church when she was tiny and taught her to wear a cross round her neck. She hammered the Bible into her head, like fairy stories. That's how she mastered it."

"Without going into the meaning of it?"

"Of course."

Pasternak stroked Bubik's head. "Might be. . . ."

"But Natasha refuses to acknowledge it. She's stubborn and says she can't love an atheist. Yet she's a physicist herself. It's all such nonsense. She's a fool, and that's all there is to it. I'll find myself another girl—without a cross around her neck."

"Lyonya . . ." Pasternak's eyes scanned the sky. "There's something else I wanted to ask you. During the war, you know, the Germans surrounded Paris. The city had to choose between fighting and capitulating. If it had fought, the Germans would have destroyed it. But Paris is the capital of the world—the Louvre, Montmartre, the priceless architectural monuments. So, if it had depended on you, would you have ordered the French to fight to the last or to surrender?"

"Surrender," Lyonya replied immediately.

Pasternak frowned. "But if you think about it more deeply?"

"There's nothing to think about. Any civilized man would make the same decision. Why destroy when you can create and preserve what's been created? As a result, Paris is still Paris today and not a heap of ruins."

"Yes, but at what price? For a long time the swastika flew over Paris. And then, doesn't it seem to you, Lyonya, that our Leningrad, by defending itself, by surviving the siege, may have in fact saved Paris?"

"What has Leningrad got to do with it?"

"It *didn't* surrender, even though part of the Hermitage was destroyed and hundreds of thousands of people died. Why didn't Leningrad capitulate?"

"Because . . . because the commander at that time was Stalin, who was uncivilized."

"That means you would have preferred that Leningrad surrender?"

"You see, Papa . . ." Lyonya hesitated. "How can I explain to you . . . I don't know . . . I'm not sure . . ."

"But if Leningrad had surrendered, today we might be living under a Nazi regime. Or more likely, I'd have been liquidated at Auschwitz long since."

"Papa, Leningrad is our city . . . you said it—*our* city. It's a Russian city, and the Russian people are different. We're not Europeans."

"You're backing down."

"Papa, if we lived in Paris, we Russians, we probably would not have surrendered it to the Germans. But we're different. We're not the French."

"But your first reaction was: surrender. A straightforward human reaction, not Russian and not European. You talked about being civilized. Paris had to surrender. Right?"

"They're . . . humanists there. For them the most important value is the preservation of life."

"And for us?"

"And for us . . .?" Lyonya smiled. "We're certainly Asians, Papa. And we're Soviet as well. That means we can't live without an idea, without honor, without—"

"Lyonya, if you don't condemn Paris for surrendering, then you ought to, yes, you ought to read the Bible, and then you'd understand what is written there. That's what it's about, Lyonya, about what *should be* our conduct toward people—about good and evil, and *how* to achieve the good."

"Papa, you've talked to me about this before."

"Hold on, I just want to remind you. In one of Yury Zhivago's poems, 'Gethsemane,' there's a verse:

'Peter resisted the murderers,
Struck off an ear with his sword.
"Steel cannot decide a quarrel," he heard:
"Put back your sword in its scabbard." ' "

"That's straightforward, Papa. But everything in real life is more complicated. The world is doing integral calculus, while the Bible is about arithmetic exercises. By the way, Papa, Natasha wants to read *Doctor Zhivago*."

"Well, there's a good excuse for making up with her. Give her the book."

"I haven't got a copy. The last one was passed around in the district hospital."

They both looked up suddenly. Yury Mikhailovich, at the wheel of the old Pobeda, had returned from Bakovka with the mail—a neat oblong parcel and a telegram. "The telegram's from Tbilisi," he exclaimed. "Must be from Nina Alexandrovna. Who else would wire you from Tbilisi?"

"Yes, yes, of course it's from Nina." Pasternak tore at the seal and read it. "There you are," he said delightedly. "She's arriving on Tuesday at three forty-five. The plane lands at Vnukovo."

"Who's the parcel from?" Lyonya asked Yury Mikhailovich.

"I think it's from America," he replied. "I think it's a book."

"A book? Yes, it would be a book. You open it, Lyonya. Who will go and meet Nina? You and I, Yury Mikhailovich, yes?"

"If Zinaida Nikolayevna agrees," the driver replied evasively.

The package contained a copy of *Doctor Zhivago*, published in Russian by the University of Michigan Press. Lyonya handed it to his father, who leafed through it and then sniffed the paper.

"I love the smell of printer's ink . . . Nicely done, isn't it? It's amazing our censor let it through."

Months earlier the same press had sent Pasternak a complete collection of his works in four volumes; but only three volumes, those containing his poetry and some of his prose, had arrived. The fourth, containing *Doctor Zhivago*, had been lost on the way—or so he was told at the post office in Bakovka. Now another fourth volume had arrived from Michigan, in response to a letter stating that the first had been missing.

"Well done! Well done!" Pasternak repeated in raptures. "Even if it is published with imperialist money. Lyonya, here's the copy for you to give to Natasha. And tell her that I advise her not to give up in her fight for the Bible. Every intelligent and *civilized* man, whether he believes in God or not, should read the Bible." He got up. "And now I'm going to make your mama happy with this telegram."

2.

Zina was skillfully wielding a hoe in the garden, laying manure under strawberry plants and gooseberry bushes and singing softly to herself. She was wearing flannel pants of Lyonya's, a working jacket of Pasternak's, old leather boots.

As Pasternak approached her he waved the telegram and shouted from a distance, "Nina is flying in on Tuesday!"

Zina looked up, wiped the sweat from her forehead, and smiled. "I've missed her, Borya."

Coming nearer, he said, "That means things are going well for her. She wrote that she would come if the publication of the new edition of Titsian's poetry was approved and if his anniversary celebration was fixed up."

"Who'll go to meet her?"

"I will."

"No, you can't. It's too soon. The doctor forbade you to go to Moscow, so . . . no, Borya, you can't. Let Lyonya go with Yury Mikhailovich."

"Zina!"

"No, no, you can't."

"Oh, you're a—" He burst out laughing.

"What are you laughing at?"

"I'm just looking at you with that hoe . . . and remembering how you fooled me once years ago."

"I never fooled you."

"No, no, I'm not complaining. I just remembered you going out one evening to some neighbors—the Trenevs, I think—to play poker. You came back at six in the morning. I'd just awakened, and I looked out the window and saw you. 'Mama, why are you up so early?' I asked. And you, not wanting to be found out, grabbed a hoe, this same hoe, and pretended you were already working in the kitchen garden."

Zina held back a smile with difficulty.

"It's true you fooled me then. You felt awkward admitting you had been playing cards all night."

"Yes . . ."

She went back to work. Pasternak watched her arms moving capably and confidently. Immediately he recalled a much younger Zina, kneeling and washing wooden floors in the dacha in Irpen, when she was Neuhaus' wife and he himself was still living with his first wife. It was then that she had first made an impression on him with her broad and, as he called them, "sensible" movements. He had recognized in them the eternal, creative force that recently he had noticed again in the movements of Matryona Kharitonova, the nurse at the district hospital.

A minute went by in silence.

"Zina . . ." Pasternak spoke in a quieter voice. "I give you my word that I'll never . . . see Olga again. I haven't much time, and I want to die at home. It's the most important thing for me now. I want to return to my family. But I know that to do this . . . you'll have to forgive me for the past . . ."

Zina threw a quick glance at him, and her eyes, grown warmer after reminiscing about the "trick," became cold and impenetrable. She continued working silently. Pasternak waited for her to speak. Planes were flying overhead; the roar of their engines could be heard from Vnukovo, where they were coming in to land.

"Zina, we loved each other. Our love was lofty, unique, boundless as the sky, and . . . immortal. How many of my poems were dedicated to you and inspired by you?"

"Stop it, Borya."

"Zina, remember how our love blazed? From the moment we met. You went to my reading with your friend. She fell in love with me, and I fell in love with you. And do you remember, on the trip to Irpen in the Ukraine . . . do you remember how on the way back we stood almost the whole night between the cars of the train? The wind was blowing through your hair. Your husband and my wife were asleep in the compartment, but we talked and talked to the sound of the wheels. You were so divinely beautiful, so open and trusting, a dream—"

"Stop it," Zina interrupted angrily.

"Zina . . . just promise me . . . that you'll think about it . . ."

"I've got nothing to think about," she said dryly.

Pasternak sighed; he was near tears, but he knew his grief would not move her.

3.

Olga set the table for tea. A housecoat clung snugly to her body as she moved quickly, energetically. Pasternak sat in a chair watching her hair, which fell in waves over her plump shoulders. His right arm was still in a sling. He looked pensive and tired.

"Imagine, Borya. It was so unexpected. The editorial board of *Molodaya Gvardiya* sends me six poems by a new Czech poet to translate. He's not bad either. I've already done a rough translation. And they've promised to pay me five rubles a line."

"That's the top rate."

"I know. It's even cheered me a bit."

"It's recognition of your standing as a poet. It's about time."

"Maybe it's too late. Sit down at the table."

Pasternak moved to the table. Olga joined him and poured the tea into glasses. They stirred their tea, then looked at each other and smiled. For the first time something had come between them, a tension that seemed about to snap and reveal the pain underneath.

"What are you thinking about, Borya?"

"About us, Olga."

"I'm thinking about us too."

"What are you thinking about us?"

"What are you?"

"Everything in the whole world is approaching a climax. Sooner or later the curtain will fall. Here's a good old Russian proverb: 'However much string you have, it can't last forever.' Human life is ending, creativity is ending, love—"

"That's not very new, Borya."

"It's as old as the world. But it always seems new to him whose time is running out. It's ahead of us too, Olga. The farewell. The time has come to say the last . . . the last . . ."

"But I've already said goodbye to you, Borya." Olga spoke calmly. "It's strange, but it happened when I came to see you in the Kremlin hospital. Afterward I went to the Lenin Mausoleum with Misha Markov. I told you about it."

"Yes."

They both sat stirring their tea.

"But we can be . . . friends, Borya. Can't we?"

"Of course. No one will ever take that away. Only I must do everything now to return to my family. I must die with them. With my son and wife. And I must win her forgiveness. My conscience gives me no peace. 'Conscience, the sharp-clawed beast, tiresome company.' That's how Pushkin described it. I've inflicted so much pain on Zina. I must repent, forever repent. My soul is tormented by sinfulness, Olga. I can't live, or die, without forgiveness."

"But will she forgive, Borya?"

"Zina? Will you?"

"Why me?"

"Will you forgive me?"

"Forgive you for what?"

"Perhaps I've shattered your life too. I've wronged those I loved most."

Olga got up from the table and walked around the room. "Oh, Borya, Borya, what are you saying . . ." She stopped by his chair and kissed his hair. "God gave me the happiness of meeting and loving you and being near you. You revealed the world of beauty to me. My dearest, I forgive you for everything, everything, because you are the best thing that ever happened to me. You are a profound and talented man, and your sins are the sins of a profound and talented man. Untouched by vulgarity or filth." She sank into her chair and began crying.

"Olga, don't. Let's part nobly, without tears."

"They're tears of happiness, Borya." She looked up. "Forgive me. They're tears for the happiness we had, by some miracle, for so many years. Imagine. Here we are together, dying, disappearing, talking like this, parting. Yet I can almost hear the beating of your heart. We've won, Borya. I've triumphed over the jealous, merciless, domineering predator that was me. There was such a woman inside me."

"And she was the woman I loved."

"I know, Borya, I know, I know. We were fiery lovers. But you said that it couldn't last. And here we are, bidding farewell to our past, our stormy, burning, passionate past, that wore us out and led us to ecstasy." She stood up, then went to the chest and, opening the top drawer, held up two packets of money. "This is the last thing that oppresses me, Borya. This money."

"Then get rid of it. Send it to Paris or Rome."

"Yes, but we're still alive physically. Our perishable bodies still exist. You may need it. We're not spirits yet, Borya. Who knows what might befall us."

Pasternak got up and put on his coat. He took the notes

from her and returned them to the bureau, then embraced her and kissed her forehead.

"Farewell, Lara, my love," he said.

"Farewell, Yury Zhivago, my unforgettable knight," she replied. "I'll be left with poetry and with God. You won't find a more selfless person praying in the Patriarch's Residence than I." She wiped away her tears with her hand. "My only allies."

Pasternak smiled. "We are like children playing at being grown up, performing a tragedy by Corneille or Racine."

"Yes, yes, you're my Romeo, and I'm your Juliet . . ." she said.

After Pasternak had gone, Olga went into the bedroom and lay down on her bed. She lay for an hour or two without sleeping. Then suddenly, enraged by her stupidity, she leaped up and began crying hysterically. Only now her tears were malicious, joyless, without charity, without any beauty at all. She laughed harshly, remembering all the ridiculous, childish, high-flown, false words she had said, full of cheap sentimentality and vulgarity. There would be no such "farewell." She told herself that life was *continuing*, was to be lived; that she would grasp everything she could from it; that she would not give up Borya to Zina for anything, even if he was dying; that she would fight for him to the end, cut Zina's throat, kill her, him, herself, before she would accept this loss.

And, marvelously, she felt better. The tirade brought back her energy and seemed to balance her. She went into the dining room, drank some cold water, and picked up a comb and mirror. But as she looked into the mirror she caught sight of the icon, with its burning lamp, in the far corner of the room.

What about God? she thought. The question frightened her. Was God always on Borya's side? She felt like a pagan who has espoused the faith but still feels the pagan inside him, constantly stumbling, performing now a good, now an

evil action—now wanting to be selfless and devout, now possessed by stormy passions. Did she believe in God? Or was she
a frightened agnostic? Perhaps, like so many people, she
needed God only to maintain a moral framework, so that
when she violated the morals she could beg forgiveness.

Olga put the mirror on the table, sat down, buried her face
in her hands. Her cheeks were burning. "What shall I do?"
she murmured. Then, a moment later, she rushed to the icon,
fell on her knees, and began crossing herself frantically. She
whispered a prayer, a jumble of words lacking any cohesion.
But they expressed her inner fears.

4.

It was warm and the May bugs had already appeared. Pasternak's dacha could be entered from the small open verandah
three steps up from the garden. In front of the verandah
apple and cherry trees were in bloom, covering the marble
slab in the grass under which the ashes of Zina's first-born,
Adik, were buried.

Zina and Nina sat at a long table, rudely constructed but
covered with a white tablecloth, on which were set a bowl of
fruit, plates of Georgian sweetmeats, and a clay jug filled
with wine. The women were smoking, and Nina was coughing. She had put on weight, but her hair was tidily, even
fashionably done, and she was wearing a new, well-made
dress. Zina had on her everyday dress—the brown one with
the lace collar.

"Yes, it's true, he did ask me to forgive him. He said he
wanted to die peacefully, in the family. He thinks about
death all the time now. He even gave me his word that he
would never see Olga again." Zina spoke with calm detachment, just as if she were discussing some purchases she had
made in Moscow.

"You . . . what did you say?"

"I didn't say anything."

"Oh, Zina, how could you? You're killing him and your-self."

"What *could* I say? Should I have thrown my arms around him? You don't know how many times he's made that prom-ise, and broken it within days. As soon as we heard that your plane was delayed, he went to see her—though of course he told me he was going to work in the library of the writers' hostel."

"Perhaps he was telling you the truth."

"Nina, I know Borya like the back of my hand. He went to see her. Anyway, he . . . he's afraid of death, and I think that's the reason he wants to return to . . . the family, to me. His conscience is tormenting him."

"Naturally."

"Well, let it."

"Zina!"

"If I offer my hand to him, Nina, then—don't you see?—then I'd be depriving myself of everything, I'd be renouncing my human dignity, everything . . . There'd be no reason to live . . . I'd be empty . . . Yes . . . I know it's not Christian, but there's nothing else I can do." Her eyes flashed with deter-mination.

"Zina, Zina, come to your senses! Are you really so hard? Oh, God, your pride is awful. You're such an egoist. You think only about your own suffering. It's stupid—forgive me —but it's nonsense, just as if you were seventeen and your Romeo had deceived you. You get pleasure from it. There's a sadist hidden in you. Yes, it's true. And if Borya broke his earlier promises not to see Olga, then I'm sure you were to blame. Anyway, Borya was younger then, but now we're all . . . You say he's afraid of death. Aren't you afraid of death? I'm afraid. It's only human. And when life is drawing to an end, naturally we all—"

"No, I can't." Zina was obdurate. "I know you're right. I agree with everything you've said. But I can't, Nina. My feel-ings are too strong for that."

"God, how terrible."

"Yes."

"That means you and he . . . will go to the grave . . . without forgiveness?"

"Yes." Zina began talking intensely. "Sometimes I hate how I'm acting, but this situation has trapped me. It hasn't lasted just for a day or a year, Nina. He's been humiliating me for a decade. And I've gotten used to it and worked out a defense."

"An eye for an eye and a tooth for a tooth?"

"Oh, Nina, it's so good to talk to you . . ."

"I know. But, Zina, people must change with the years. You and I can no longer dance the night away. The time for that has passed. It's the same with marriage. A husband and wife in their old age can't be as they were in their youth."

"Don't preach to me," Zina snapped. "I'm not a schoolgirl."

"I'm not preaching—I just think we've reached the age when the most important thing is to be able to forgive. When you're young it's very difficult, but when you're old . . ."

"The thought of it makes me even more angry. I'm unhappy, Nina, but I don't have the strength to change."

Pasternak appeared from the direction of the gate. Nina saw him first.

"Borya's coming," she said, getting up from the table, and, it seemed to Zina, immediately forgetting all about their conversation. She cupped her hands to her mouth and, with joy on her face, shouted, "Bor-ya! Bor-ya!" Then she ran down the steps to meet him. Looking at her, Zina could not help thinking, as she had so many times before, She can't live without him either.

"Nina! My dearest!"

They embraced and kissed three times in the Russian manner. Pasternak smoothed her hair and looked at her with tender affection.

"Your flight arrived late. Was everything all right? In the air, I mean?"

"Oh, yes, everything was fine. The plane was delayed in Tbilisi because of a storm."

"Yes, yes, Lyonya phoned the airport from the writers' hostel."

"So we're together again, Borya."

"It's a banquet for Zina and me. But, Nina, forgive me. I was held up. I was at the library and then dropped in to see a friend." He turned to Zina as they walked toward the verandah. "So Nina's with us again, Zina. Here we all are together again. Isn't it wonderful, Zina? Oh, Lord, what a stupid question!" They went up the steps to the verandah. "Nina, let me look at you properly. You've changed for the better. You've grown prettier, younger. Hasn't she, Zina? And you haven't got as many gray hairs. Your dress is elegant. And your shoes. Some money has clearly appeared."

"I'm catching up with the fashions, Borya." Nina burst into girlish laughter.

"And why not? In the words of the popular Soviet song: 'It's too early to die, there are still things to do at home.' Right?" He took off his coat, placed it on a bench and, with Zina's help, put his paralyzed arm into the black sling.

"It seems the Soviet government has adopted me, Borya. Yes, some money has appeared. I received a substantial royalty from the State Literary Publishing House."

"Wonderful! That means that everything's settled and they'll be publishing a volume of Titsian."

"And a new collection in Georgia. And an anniversary evening of Titsian's work on May 24 in the Rustaveli theater." She laughed again, notwithstanding the fact that none of it could have been accomplished without the invisible hand of the Chairman of the KGB in Georgia, General Inauri.

"How lovely! In the Rustaveli theater. That's marvelous! An anniversary evening of Titsian Tabidze. Zina, hoorah! Let's drink some wine to it!"

"You can't drink wine, Borya. Not a drop," Zina said tersely. "As you can see, Nina, his right arm has been par-

318

tially paralyzed. And the doctors have told him that he can work only standing up from now on. I've bought him a work stand."

"Oh, Zina, it's nothing. It'll pass. And I've already learned to write with my left hand. Very well, too. Just a drop, Zina dearest?"

"No."

Pasternak threw a glance at the sweetmeats.

"Then some kozinaks. I love them so much. Kozinaks are allowed. May I?" He took a piece of the roasted nut-and-honey confection and popped it into his mouth: "Oh, what a luxury. Not life but clover . . . Well, Nina, tell us your news. How are Nitochka and Alik? How's Givi?"

"I saw Nitochka and Alik off to a resort in Makhindzhauri. Givi's become the fencing champion of Georgia."

"Really? Just think!"

"Only at the junior level so far."

"That's wonderful, wonderful. Titsian would have been so proud. A grandson who's a fencer, and a champion at that. D'Artagnan. And how are Gogla Leonidze and Simon Chikovani?"

"They send their regards. So do their wives. Gogla and Simon are flourishing. You saw how they live. Like landowners. The Soviet government long ago—"

"Adopted them? And Irakly Abashidze?"

"Him too."

"The devil take it, how wise it is, our precious Soviet government. It tried to adopt me too—and there was a time when it almost succeeded. That's well put—a system of adoption. The kozinaks are very sweet."

"Nina brought two piglets," Zina said.

"Bringing piglets on planes is forbidden, Borya, but I smuggled them in."

"Oh, Nina, you're incorrigible."

"I can do anything I want now that I'm rich."

"And I too." Pasternak stopped abruptly.

Zina looked at Nina, and in her gaze Nina read: "You see,

I told you he was with her. Where else do you think the money is?" Zina went into the house.

"Borya . . . you don't seriously think that the Soviet government has adopted me? Even though it has, in a way. You know what a complicated tangle life here is. Titsian tormented himself trying to find the proper attitude toward the government. More than once, in my presence, he called Stalin a great man. One day I even slapped him across the face for saying it."

"Titsian told me about it." Pasternak smiled. "He told me his cheek stung for days. I know, I know, Nina. I understand what a complicated tangle life is. You want Titsian to live, but he can live as a poet only in Georgia. In Paris, among the émigrés, it's not the same. But Soviet power rules in Georgia, so you have to learn how to deal with it. Yes . . . things turned out rather differently for me. In some incomprehensible way I survived in 1937. And now I've survived—or almost—in 1958. But the fact that I've become famous in the West means absolutely nothing here, where I'm totally forgotten and isolated. I'm outside official literature and, in general, outside life. My 'colleagues' fear or ignore me. And so on. Why? Because I was *not* adopted by the Soviet government. That's not a reproach to you and Titsian. His creativity was above politics and ideology. He was lyrical and profound in his *national* self-expression. And I also thought poetically about Stalin once or twice. I confess it. It's a terrible thing to remember, because at the same time Osip Mandelstam condemned Stalin justly and boldly, and paid for it with his life. Yes, Nina, yes, it's all a very complicated tangle. Life is much easier if you concede defeat early on. All the same, Titsian didn't, and neither did I. Titsian was torn to shreds, and I've just been crucified. But now I'm for the sovietization of Titsian. It's a compromise. And you did right to agree to it."

"Borya, but can't you give in a bit to Soviet power now that *Doctor Zhivago* has entered world literature?"

"Give in? Haven't I given in already? Oh, Nina, I've given

in too much. You want me to become sovietized? It's too late. *They* wouldn't agree to it now. *They* prefer to keep me silent. Perhaps after my death they'll decide that my work is part of Soviet literature. Just my poetry of course, not *Doctor Zhivago*. Maybe. They're crafty. Now they're trying to introduce that émigré and rabid anti-Bolshevik Bunin into the literature. Sovietization? What would be the point?"

"So that Russia could read you *now*, during your lifetime."

"Oh, Nina, everything that's happened lately has left its mark on me. What would I gain? I'm about to exchange my Spartan bed for a coffin. Don't be surprised and don't protest. In antiquity they prepared for death. The elders slept in their coffins and got used to them. It was easier to think in a coffin, to prepare to leave."

"Stop it, Borya! Stop all this talk. It's premature. You had a heart attack, two. Some people have five or ten of them. You've recovered. Your arm—that'll pass. Gradually. Now you just need to observe the regimen and everything will be fine."

"Nina." He lowered his voice to a whisper. "I'll tell you a secret. The heart attack didn't affect just my heart."

"What else?"

"My soul."

Zina called out from the kitchen, "Borya, will you have some yogurt?"

"Yes, Zina! You know, Nina, the poet of the revolution, Vladimir Mayakovsky, was terrified of old age. The woman he adored, Lily Brik, told me. Apparently he was panic-stricken whenever he discovered a new wrinkle. He wanted to be thirty forever. Lily said that was one reason for his suicide, besides the basic conflict between his genius and our epoch. In *Studies in Optimism* Ilya Mechnikov suggested that, along with the instinct for life, we have an instinct for death—that is, the desire to die. He said that if a man lived to be a hundred, he would dream, yes, dream about death, and he held that our death instinct was part of the structural harmony of life."

"You're still a long way from a hundred, Borya."

"No, it's quite near, really. As Yesenin wrote: 'Too early it fell to my lot to suffer weariness and bereavement.' " Pasternak laughed ironically. "Nina, please don't tell Zina, but it's become hard for me to work. No, not because of my arm, and not because I have to stand up. No, no . . . I've just started a play. The title is good: 'Blind Beauty.' It was suggested to me by a patient in the hospital who mistakenly called the ballet *Sleeping Beauty* 'Blind Beauty.' It stuck in my mind. I conceived a historical drama, but . . ."

" 'Blind Beauty'? Is that Russia?"

"I don't know . . . maybe . . . But I'm feeling a decline in my strength. I'm writing very slowly, without passion. Oh, if only I could find my former strength. If I could, Nina, then I'd rewrite many of my early poems. The intricate, precious ones. They're incomprehensible to the average person. Now I know that loftiness and beauty lie in simplicity and accessibility. But I was accessible only to a chosen few. That's the truth. I was in an ordinary district hospital, Nina, among ordinary Soviet people. And there I realized that they, no less than you and I, need literature to arouse romanticism and a desire to discover good. With my hand on my heart, Nina, I can tell you that I've never had a good word for Vissarion Belinsky. I regarded him as an archvulgarizer, a dry critic. But now I think that he defined the poet's task accurately. The poet who is not understood by his people is a useless creature. The poet who despises the mob is nothing. I think it's a crime to squander one's gift for the aesthetic enjoyment of the chosen few when around you are masses of people thirsting for a real poetic line from you. The gift of the poet belongs to the people, Nina. The poet must be *public* property."

"Borya, you so easily go to extremes."

"That's my weakness, but it's also my strength."

"Is *Doctor Zhivago* for the chosen few as well?"

"No, I wrote *Doctor Zhivago* for the millions."

"But, Borya, all readers aren't the same. Some have perception, some live superficially. Which ones do you want to speak to?"

"I don't want to write for any one group, Nina. I just want to write the truth. Here's a little story for you. When Michelangelo completed the Sistine ceiling, Pope Julius the Second complained that the colors seemed excessively dull. The great master replied, 'They didn't wear gold in those days. The individuals I've represented were not rich.'"

Nina lit a cigarette and started coughing.

"There you go again, smoking like a chimney. And coughing. What do you do it for? Is it really impossible for you to give it up? God, how many times I've asked you to."

"I smoked before they adopted me and dressed me in cloth of gold, Borya," Nina replied with a smile. "And I'll continue smoking now that it's happened."

"Zina puffs away the whole day too. Do you know what a certain woman, known to you, whom naturally you don't like much, nicknamed you both?"

"What?"

"Only don't be offended. All right?"

"Yes."

"'Smoking spiders.'"

"Do you think that's witty?"

"No. She was insulting you. But if I were you, I would give up smoking just to spite her."

"Borya, are you still seeing her?"

"Who?"

"That woman."

"Nina, believe me, it's all over. Believe me, Olga and I have parted. Peacefully, as friends. I'll be frank with you—it happened today. I decided to do it before you arrived. Yes, I saw her today. I've just come back from her. No, I wasn't in the library. It was our last meeting. We're friends now. We have no reason to be enemies. Everything is back to normal. She's accepted the inevitable. But, Nina, you must help me

323

establish peace in this household. I want to return to Zina. But without her consent it's impossible. I'm part of her. I can't die without being reconciled with her."

5.

They set off to shoot hares early on a Sunday morning. To Borodino. The usual complement were there: Khrushchev, Mikoyan, and Serov. Nikita was in high spirits as the black limousine sped along the Rublyov highway. Turning to Serov, he said, "Come on then, Ivan, you eager beaver, tell us what new jokes about 'Khrushch' you've picked up from the people."

"Is it worth it, Nikita Sergeyevich?" the KGB chairman retorted.

"Go on, go on, I'm not Stalin. We're among ourselves here." He looked at the driver. "Old Mitya knows me inside out, and I know him inside out. So no one's going to be shocked. Go on. Tell us."

"All right. I'll tell you one. But it's not that funny."

"That doesn't matter."

"Anastas Ivanovich doesn't object?"

"How can I object if Nikita orders you to? I'm not First Secretary of the Central Committee. He is." Mikoyan laughed.

"That's true. Go on, then."

"So . . . Comrade Khrushchev summoned his assistant, Comrade Lebedev, and asked, 'Well then, brother, do the Soviet people tell many jokes about me?' Lebedev answered, 'Yes, Nikita Sergeyevich.' Then Comrade Khrushchev said, 'Well, then, brother, let these jokesters know that *not only* corn is planted in this country.' "

Khrushchev and Mikoyan burst out laughing. Mitya and the chief bodyguard looked puzzled.

"That's good," Nikita remarked without a hint of embarrassment. "It implies that while corn is planted in our country, you can also get planted in prison for telling a joke. That's a laugh! They say the American President collects caricatures of himself from the newspapers. And I love jokes about myself. Do you know who made it up, Ivan?"

"No, it's anonymous."

"You're lying!"

"Honestly, Nikita Sergeyevich. There's no way of discovering its origin."

"I've heard—not a joke, Nikita—well—how can I put it?—an apt remark."

"What, Anastas?"

"About your son-in-law."

"Mmm?"

"He's been nicknamed 'Czarevich Alexei,' because Czar Peter the First had a son called Alexei."

"Oh, another sly remark directed at Alexei. Goddam sonofabitch! He's been plaguing me to death. Every day he's blathering that the most important thing is for the USSR to establish diplomatic relations with the Vatican and for Nikita Khrushchev to kiss the Pope. He's gone off his rocker. Everything in his head is screwed up."

"The Pope?" Mikoyan asked.

"Alexei," Khrushchev replied.

When they were close to Borodino the conversation turned to Pasternak and Olga.

"Listen, Ivan, has that Olga, the blonde, calmed down, or is she still meeting foreigners and dealing in currency?" Khrushchev asked.

"That sort only calms down behind bars, Nikita Sergeyevich."

"Yes, it's not for nothing blondes have a reputation. The bitch!"

"She's a counterrevolutionary through and through, and she's friendly with all sorts of doubtful characters. She's in regular correspondence with 'friends' in Paris, Rome, and London. Illegally, through embassies of course. By diplomatic channels. She's trying to send out all kinds of material about Pasternak and about Moscow literary life in general. Slandering us in every way possible. We intercepted one account about the poet Markov, the madman we put in a psychiatric hospital for observation. Her daughter hangs around the embassies. She's a slut. Both of them are impossible floozies. And we also know, Nikita Sergeyevich, that Pasternak's will is in Olga's possession."

"Who gets how much?"

"Unfortunately the contents aren't known to the KGB."

"Anastas, what if we put the heat on this Olga? For instance, what if we charge her with currency speculation and put her on trial? What do you think?"

"Not now, Nikita. Let's wait till he dies."

"Who? Pasternak? How long do you think we'll have to wait? He might pull a fast one. They say he almost drove Polikarpov into his grave in the Kremlin hospital."

"No, Nikita Sergeyevich, he doesn't have much time left," Serov said. "I've seen the medical report. He won't be with us much longer."

"Well, if that's the case, let's wait. You're right, Anastas. Touch her now and that riffraff in the West will raise a hue and cry all over again. Let's wait. There's no hurry. Only don't lose track of her, Serov."

"My people know every step she takes—Olga, her mother, and her daughter. Her daughter is chasing a French student who's in Moscow on an exchange. Either on an exchange or by way of the French Sûreté—we still don't know which exactly. She wants to marry him.

"Stupid exchanges! Infernal Sûretés!" Khrushchev sighed. "Listen, Ivan, what about the will? You said that Olga has it. How much money has he got piled up in the West?"

"The Voice of America recently estimated it at seven million dollars," Mikoyan said.

"Really! That much?!"

"I think that's an exaggeration, Nikita Sergeyevich. According to KGB calculations he has about three million."

"All the same, it's a tidy sum."

"And the money pours in daily. *Doctor Zhivago* has been translated into almost every language in the world. It's being made into a film too. There'll be royalties from that as well."

"But the money is ours!" Khrushchev bellowed. "It belongs to the Soviet people. We'll choke the imperialists to get it! Serov, we must make sure that we get our hands on Pasternak's millions. Think the matter over thoroughly and report to me. If necessary we'll put it to a session of the Politburo. No, I won't give up the money to scoundrels, to capitalist sharks!"

"Yes, Nikita Sergeyevich."

"Perhaps we should give ten percent to the family?" Mikoyan remarked.

"All right. Ten percent, but no more."

"Nikita Sergeyevich, to do this, Pasternak's will may have to be rewritten," Serov commented.

"Then rewrite it. It's not my job to teach you how. Haven't you got specialists? It's no crime. You won't be doing it for your own pocket, Ivan, but for the cause of socialism."

They hunted till midday. Nikita hit six hares and was delighted. Serov hit four and stopped there, having long since mastered the role of subordinate. Mikoyan consoled himself with five.

Crossing the field with Serov (the bodyguards followed them at a distance), Khrushchev suddenly asked, "Ivan, have you gotten anything new on Suslov? That poseur will pull the wool over the eyes of all of us."

"Yes—not very much, but something." Serov had been waiting for the question.

"Whist again?"

"No. I have a statement made by his cook, KGB Captain Klavdiya Saveleva. She complained that last Sunday, in the kitchen, Suslov's wife gave her—"

"A coded message?"

"A slap across the face."

"Really? The wife of a Central Committee secretary bashing someone in the chops. Are you joking?"

"No."

"That's a bombshell. A bombshell. Well done, Ivan! Now we've got something worthwhile. Send me the statement by special courier. I'll summon Suslov and I'll have a talk with him. Oh, the sonofabitch! I'll have a talk with him all right. I'll say: 'So, comrade Secretary of the Central Committee, we made the October Revolution to destroy the old life, but your wife is still slapping her cook across the face, and a KGB captain at that.' Well done! Well done, Serov!"

"I really had nothing to do with it, Nikita Sergeyevich. Klavdiya Saveleva wrote the statement and brought it to my office."

"Stop talking nonsense! She would never have done it if you hadn't advised her to. I'll never forget your comradely services, Ivan. As long as I'm in power, you'll be in power. But now I want your advice on something else. This is strictly between ourselves. Understood? It's become known to me—that is, I've heard a rumor that Stalin, when he became General Secretary of the Communist Party Central Committee, ordered a special device to be installed in his office, one that allowed him to listen to telephone conversations of Politburo members. Get it? Some Czechoslovakian Communist engineer installed the device. Get it? And this was probably what enabled the old man to knock his opponents down like ninepins and concentrate absolute power in his hands. So . . . whether this story is true or not, I think that I should have a device like that for eavesdropping. Oh, how I'd like to listen in on what Suslov and Kozlov gossip about. Or on Brezhnev's chats. Of course it would take a lot of time— sitting and·listening to all the conversations. But what if we attach a tape recorder to the listening device, Ivan, and record the conversations? On Sundays we could listen to the tapes together in a secluded spot somewhere, eh? Just keep in mind that this business has to be done very quietly, so that no one knows a thing."

"From the technical point of view, Nikita Sergeyevich, it's possible to carry all this out. That's no problem."

"What's the problem, then?"

"Stalin didn't just listen in to telephone conversations of Politburo members; afterward he also—"

"What?"

"Imprisoned them. He started the *terror*. You can't have one without the other. Eavesdropping without terror is nonsensical."

"You think so?"

"You'll have to put people in prison."

"Mmm, goddam sonofabitch! Maybe you're right . . . No, I mean you're right about eavesdropping being pointless without terror . . . I know that Suslov is saying God knows what about me, but I can't pick him off yet . . ."

They walked in silence for several minutes.

"Forget about it, Ivan." Khrushchev stopped. "To hell with the special device! I don't want to be like the man from Georgia. Times have changed. The terror is over. People die naturally now—at their own discretion." Nikita laughed out loud.

Serov looked at him pityingly as if to say "So what?"

6.

Before going to sleep, as he lay in bed with Nina, Nikita said, "Come on now, lady, lay on the blame."

This had become a ritual, her commenting before going to sleep on everything she had seen or heard about him during the day, a dressing-down, as she called it. Sometimes a heated argument would ensue, ending always in victory for the First Secretary and capitulation for his wife. On rare occasions he would turn his back on her, saying angrily, "You're a fool, old girl, that's what you are!"

Khrushchev liked his wife's criticism because he could understand it. In general, Nina judged life from the same standpoint as he did; she looked at it soberly and in the same framework as the average Soviet citizen. She accepted the basic conditions of Soviet life as inevitable, but at the same time thought they were progressive in terms of the world. She prided herself on this view. But there were times when Nina's opinions contradicted those of the workers, and then Nikita laughed at her, comparing her with their "intellectual" daughter, Rada, and occasionally losing his temper. He could not stand high-blown discussions, especially about literature, philosophy, or art. He believed the people, first and foremost, should be given a well-nourished, well-organized existence, with televisions and bathrooms. He had ridiculed Mao Tse-tung, saying the masses needed bread, not his poetry.

"Well, what can I say?" Nina began. "Today I read a story in *Pravda* about repairs that are being made to a small house in some Byelorussian town. It seems that the job can't be done properly because there's a shortage of skilled workers and materials. So, I thought, what is our Soviet system worth if this is material for the major newspaper of the Communist Party? Does this really have to be reported in *Pravda*?"

"Aha, sticking up for your own opinions again, lady!" Nikita scratched the back of his neck and continued sarcastically. "Rada's just like you, or you're just like her. You women, the devil himself couldn't make you out! You don't care a damn about the everyday needs of the workingman. Don't you understand, you lousy intellectuals, that our people still live in poverty? All their efforts go into getting some food, repairing their houses, buying a bicycle, and so on. But you want to tell them, 'Don't enslave yourselves with material possessions, don't lapse into philistinism, think about lofty matters. You're a citizen of the new communist society.' What do you know about their lives? You live like a princess."

"What are you talking about, you corn planter? I said nothing of the kind! What have you lost your temper for?"

"I know you, old girl; you learned English and now you

330

think you're a lady. And you want to talk about Shakespeare. I wouldn't be surprised if you believed in God."

"Don't get away from the point. I'm a member of the Communist Party. What have Shakespeare and God got to do with it? I'm saying that something's not working properly in our country if such trivialities are written up in *Pravda*."

"Of course something's not working properly. In fact, nothing's working properly. When people here can live like they do in America, with cars and their own houses, then everything in our country will be working properly. But in the meantime we've got a dictatorship. The Bolsheviks are bloodsuckers, and they've got a grip on the people. How can we expect anything to work properly, goddam sonofabitch!" Nina was not sure if he was being ironic or serious, and he laughed at her perplexity. "You're making a mountain out of a molehill, Nina. But when your son-in-law, the scoundrel, wears me down completely with his Roman Pope, you say nothing, not a word. You indulge them, Alexei and Rada. It's the third day she's phoned me at the Central Committee and yelled at the top of her voice, 'Papa, I think your visit to the Vatican will be a high point in the Khrushchev Era!' Alexei egged her on of course. She dances to his tune. Mikoyan told me today when he were out hunting that the Muscovites have nicknamed Adzhubei 'Czarevich Alexei.' One day very soon the red Jesuit Suslov will bring up the subject of nepotism for discussion in the Politburo."

"Nikita, Alexei wants to win five hundred million Catholics over to our side."

"What a family! Opportunists, every one! You, Rada, Alexei, all of you! Just imagine what a picture it would make, lady: Nikita Khrushchev, a former herdsboy and miner, now head of the preeminent Communist state, receiving the blessing of the Pope and kissing his hand. Religion, as Comrade Marx said, is the opiate of the masses. You learned that too, Nina. No, none of you cares that Adzhubei's idea has already been rejected by the Politburo. So far no one in the Politburo has brought up the issue of my favoring a relative—but it will happen, I can see it coming. Serov reported to me that a week ago Alexei went to a meeting with workers at a factory named after Vladimir Ilich Lenin. He was asked, 'Is it true that you're a relative of Comrade Khrushchev?' And he, the idiot, took it on himself to reply, 'But comrades, we're all relatives of Comrade Khrushchev. He's our teacher and father'! The artful dodger. It's not surprising his mother is a fashionable dressmaker, who sews for our Soviet princesses."

"Did he really say that?" Nina smiled.

"You can smile, old girl. In actual fact, that could be my downfall. 'Teacher and father'! Yes, that's what he said. Stalin sent ten million people to their graves in order to become teacher and father. What have I done to deserve the same name?"

Usually they did not get to sleep early. Nina received mail from the most varied of sources. Throughout the country, rumor had it that she was a good woman and had influence with her husband. So she was inundated with letters, many of them handed to her directly at the academy, some even by the children she taught. A great deal of human misery was written in these letters, and Nina spent hours reading them. She brought the most distressing cases to Nikita's attention. Sometimes he agreed to help, but on other occasions he swore at her and forbade her to accept private letters.

"Let them write to the Central Committee or the Kremlin. They'll get reported to me," he would say angrily. "There must be some control in this matter."

"Who will report them to you? Your bureaucrats? You know they'll keep them from you, and there are rivers, whole rivers of human suffering, Nikita."

"Rivers, rivers . . . Do you want to empty them by the hatful?"

Under Stalin, Nina had not felt particular pity for the mass of the Soviet people. She lived with official party blinkers and lied a great deal to herself, just as Khrushchev had done. But now her husband had abandoned Stalin's course, or had tried to (especially at first), and she believed in his good intentions.

"Give people a little more freedom," she would say. "Let them sigh as deeply as they want. They had a hard time under Stalin."

Although no one knew it, it was Nina who had urged Khrushchev on at the crucial moment, giving him the courage to address the party congress in his famous anti-Stalinist speech.

Khrushchev basically agreed with her, but sometimes he would snap, "You're driving me to disaster. You and your 'freedom.' I opened up foreign tourism, and how many of our 'tourists,' the parasites, stayed in the West? And now those lice are barking on Radio Liberty and attacking us in every possible way. Freedom! You wanted a 'thaw,' and now see what's happened. The Nobel Prize was awarded to Pasternak. It's a double-edged sword, you know.

"No, old girl, it's dangerous to be a liberal. It leads back to capitalism. The ideological struggle is still as heated as it ever was under Stalin. But my idea of peaceful coexistence is working just the same. Do you understand? The West gets weaker when we are seen as a peace-loving state. I'm trying to destroy the bogey of the 'red peril.' Because it undermines the growth of class consciousness in the capitalist world and allows the imperialists to consolidate. I'll tell you an anecdote. A Jew handed over his two sons to a Russian priest for a year so the priest could teach them Russian. But a year later, when the Jew came back for his sons, he discovered that they hadn't learned a word of Russian, although the priest was speaking fluent Yiddish."

Nikita laughed out loud and Nina joined in.

"You see, old girl, it's the same with peaceful coexistence. The question is: Who will teach whom his own language— will the West teach the USSR or the USSR the West? Who would have thought that that baptized Yid, that rotten fruit Pasternak, would inflict so much harm? That's what *one* book, yes, just one, can do in the present circumstances, with all these exchanges and contacts. Do you think the *Doctor Zhivago* business has blown over? No, I'll have more hell to pay when Pasternak casts off for a better world—and he'll be in his coffin soon. What will we do then? How shall we bury him? With full honors or on the sly? We can't give him full honors when he's been expelled from the Writers' Union. And we can't bury 'internal émigrés' with full honors anyway. But on the sly won't work either—we can't just sweep him under the carpet. There's no golden mean. Those Western correspondents, the jackals, will hear about his death and they'll descend on Peredelkino and write their lies. 'Khrushchev killed Pasternak! It's his work!' And what if there's a demonstration at the cemetery? Should we call out the troops? Shoot into the crowd? What if Pasternak has planned his own burial rite, including all sorts of religious nonsense?"

"Well, he won't be able to say much about the ceremony once he's dead."

"I won't allow it! Goddam sonofabitch! No burial services!" Nikita bellowed, and then added calmly, "All right. Let them have a service, but it has to be held at home, at night, just for his family. The windows must be covered with blankets, and the deacon, the pest, mustn't rabble-rouse."

"Why not in church?"

"No, I won't allow it. I've got enough on my hands without having Pasternak pictured in the capitalist press lying in his coffin with some bearded priest intoning over him, 'Lord have mercy . . .' "

"If you ban it, it'll be worse. The capitalist press will say that Khrushchev controls religion in the USSR."

"So what? Let them! Let them say what they like. It's like water off a duck's back. You're a great help, old girl. You're a brain—like Catherine the Great, the devil take her. Mikoyan calls you that—Catherine the Great. Mind you, his Ashkhen's got a head on her shoulders too." Khrushchev smiled. "I've got a new joke, Nina. A parishioner calls up the church and asks for Father Filaret. The housekeeper answers, 'Father Filaret is busy, he's at a party meeting.' "

"Don't blaspheme, Nikita. Party cards won't help us in the next world."

"That doesn't worry me. I've looked death in the face several times. The only question is: Which of us will go first? Do you want to?"

Nina suddenly clung to him. "Don't make fun, Nikita. Life wouldn't be worth living without you."

"You'll go first, then."

"I would want to."

"Are you afraid?" He suddenly relented, or appeared to. "Don't cry anymore. You can go first. Find a comfy little place for me. I don't know how they'll classify me there—as an ordinary man or a hero. Come to think of it, I've no idea how they'll bury me here. They could put me alongside Lenin in the mausoleum, or brick me up in the Kremlin wall, or bury me next to Stalin. Or I could be buried somewhere in Novodevichy or Vaganovsky as an ordinary Bolshevik journeyman. Anything could happen. Nina, I've had an idea!"

"What?"

"Well . . . when Pasternak dies, we don't want a mob attending his funeral. So to make sure that his writer colleagues, particularly those in the party, don't go, we'll call a general meeting in the Union of Soviet Writers for that day, and we'll show two French or Italian films with half-naked women—"

"Nikita!"

"They'll love it! Half-naked or completely naked. And that's all right. I'm not against it. Let them occupy their minds with debauchery. If they occupy themselves with debauchery, they won't be interested in politics. That's the most important thing for us. In short, naked women will entice them away from the funeral. Right?"

"The things you think up! What are our writers, party members, worth if they can be enticed away from Pasternak's funeral like that?"

"Hey, lady, you're getting all fancy again. Don't you see,

even those most dedicated to the cause of communism, like Alexander Tvardovsky, will want to go to the grave of this Pasternak character. I'm sure Tvardovsky will go—maybe not on the first day, but he'll go later, and stand by the grave and shed a tear. He's not just a Communist, Nina, he's a poet as well. Poets are a special breed. Yes, yes, Tvardovsky himself told me that a poet—how did he put it?—oh yes, 'A poet constantly explores the spiritual values of the universe.' "

"Nikita, if you let life move of its own accord, as it moves anyway, your ideas wouldn't get so mixed up."

"Thanks for the advice, Grandma. But we're called on to change the world. That's the essence of Marxism. *Change.* We're obliged to change it, and not to lag behind. But should we allow a demonstration, old girl?"

"What demonstration?"

"During Pasternak's funeral."

"You've got an irrepressible imagination. The man hasn't died yet and you're already describing his funeral!"

"Right! Right! We'll allow a demonstration, even an organized one. Mao style. Let all our Moscow counterrevolutionaries gather at Pasternak's coffin, and Serov's people will film them. We'll have a clear picture. The enemy will be revealed. Then we'll gradually pull out all the weeds, stalk by stalk, carefully, quietly—students, liberals, malcontents, we'll mow them all down."

"Really!"

"The Chinese system. What's it called? 'Let a thousand flowers bloom' . . . or something like that." He laughed again, maliciously, voluptuously, perhaps as Ivan the Terrible had laughed when as a boy he was taught to pull the heads off sparrows as an exercise in cruelty.

"Laughing again?"

"Yes, I'm laughing. I just imagined how two wives would look in the procession following Pasternak's coffin, among his family and friends. The lawful one and the blonde, both trying to push to the front, to show the world who his real wife was. Then they'd grab each other by the throat. Do you think it'll come to blows, Nina?"

Nina turned her back to him and said nothing. Khrushchev lay for a minute in silence, then said in a gentle, even tender voice: "Don't be angry with me, Nina. I was only joking. Come, Nina, don't sulk. That's all the talk for tonight. We've talked our fill. We have to show some moderation. It's two o'clock in the morning. But let's rather . . . let's remember our youth, Nina . . . Remember what we . . ."

"I don't want to." Nina knew what he had in mind.

"Well, isn't that great! I'm still a man who needs it."

She turned to face him. "It's time to calm down, Nikita, my—"

"Aha, you're giving in! Oh, you women. There's life in the old girl yet. Oh, you, my little beauty . . ."

He switched off the light on the bedside table and kissed her on the mouth.

7.

Pasternak went down into the gully, turned right, and set out along a narrow mushroom-strewn path that led through a birch grove and a glade thick with poppies to the white Church of the Patriarch's Residence. He walked alowly, inhaling the transparent air; his eyes, reflecting nature, shone ecstatically. Observing him, Nina felt glad and sad at the same time. Her heart ached with foreboding.

"Nina, I'm having lots of dreams," he said, sensing her anxiety. "Dream upon dream upon dream. The whole night is spent dreaming. It's never happened to me before. They're all realistic. And for some reason the past is resurrected in all of them. I used to love remembering the past. Now it oppresses me more and more. I'm beginning to be afraid of it—my dreams are so amazingly full of detail, so true to life, so exact. I see the fence that used to enclose our dacha near Moscow, or the corner of the house we lived in on Mokhovaya Street, with its fallen-down drainpipe. I dream of the sideboard in my mother's dining room and its wooden board for cutting bread. And these things, Nina, they become symbols and oppress me. I wake up and realize that now, fifty or sixty years later, the fence around our dacha probably no longer exists, and Mama's sideboard almost certainly fell apart long ago. The number of these dreams is a signal, Nina. The sideboard has fallen apart, which means it's time for me—"

"Borya!"

"The past is tormenting me. It reduces me to despair. If the past dominates, you see—and it's dominating me now— then there's no room left for the present, let alone the future. There's no salvation from the past. It's vindictive. It knows its strength. It numbs the soul. A certain measure of the past in the present is a good thing. But when it replaces the present—"

"Stop it, please, Borya. I have dreams too in which the past—"

"Nina, do you want me to tell you about the dream I had last night?"

"No, I don't want to hear about it!"

"But Titsian was in it."

"All right, tell me, then."

Pasternak stopped by a tall birch tree, leaned back against it, recovered his breath and began: "I was sitting in the office of Comrade Stalin. But for some reason there was a portrait of Hitler on the wall instead of the one of Marx. Stalin was wearing a white Circassian coat and soft Caucasian boots. Didn't you tell me, Nina, that Stalin was rumored to be the bastard son of a Georgian prince, and in the past they liked wearing Circassian coats?"

"Only some of them. And only some of the time."

"And instead of a cartridge belt Stalin had medallions of Marx, Engels, and Lenin on his chest."

"Lord!"

"Yes, imagine. Stalin was very polite to me. He offered me a glass of Kakhetian wine, which he poured out of a red wineskin lying on his desk. Stalin spoke haltingly." Pasternak began imitating Stalin's Russian, which was overlaid with a thick Georgian accent. " 'So, Comrade Pasternak,' he said, 'I know you don't understand why I didn't touch you in the thirties, or later; why I imprisoned others but spared you.' I nodded in agreement. He twisted his mustache and lit his pipe. 'You see, Comrade Pasternak, I'm a Georgian and I love Georgia. And you translated our Georgian poets into Russian so beautifully that I decided to spare your life.' Then, Nina, I suddenly heard Titsian's voice from behind Stalin: 'Borya, don't believe him. He's a fiend!' I jumped up and pushed Stalin aside, and saw Titsian lying on a stretcher, covered with blood. He whispered to me, 'Borya, don't believe any of them. They're all fiends!' Stalin roared with laughter and blew smoke from his mouth, then ordered Marshal Beria, who was standing nearby, 'Give it to him good, Lavrenti!' Beria looked like a huge hog dressed in a marshal's uniform; his chest was covered with awards and medals, but for some reason he was barefooted. Beria struck Titsian on the head with all his might. And Titsian suddenly . . . disintegrated . . . fell to pieces. Someone started to cry in the corner of the room. I turned around and saw Stalin's wife, Alliluyeva, sitting on the floor, sobbing, her fists clenched in anger. I woke up in a cold sweat."

"Lord, what a graphic dream." Nina said quietly.

"Yes . . . yes . . ."

They walked on.

Presently Pasternak stopped again. "Somewhere I wrote, 'Shame has gotten damp and will not burn.' That must have been about our life. But now, right at the end, at the moment before the final curtain, shame has dried out and caught fire in me. Oh, Nina, how the past torments me. There are so many *sins* to account for. My neglect of Zina. My cruel inattention to my eldest son. I was a bad father to

him. I preferred Lyonya. And that's a sin. Then there's Olga
. . . Olga . . . I've sinned against her too."

"You promised not to see her, but you were with her yesterday. Why did you do it, Borya?"

"Nina . . . I can't live without her. I'm sinful. I thought we
had parted peaceably, on good terms, that we would just be
friends, but I was wrong. I'm full of irredeemable sins, Nina,
and I'll carry them to my grave."

"We're all full of sins, Borya." Nina considered her own
guilty passion and wondered if he'd ever suspected it.

They walked up the hill toward the church. Pasternak
laughed quietly.

"What are you laughing about, Borya?"

"It's not new, Nina, but sometimes I think man *needs* to
sin. It's an important part of his diet, full of calories. Sin,
deceit, lies, hypocrisy, treachery—they're essential amino
acids. If everyone were like Christ, life on earth would be
unbearable. No, Nina, that is nonsense, absolute nonsense."

They stopped at the top of the hill and turned. Peredelkino looked as if it could fit in the palm of a hand. Pavlenko
Drive, the transformer box, Fedin's dacha, Pasternak's dacha,
the Ivanovs' house next door, and, to the left, the writers'
hostel—all were like tiny jewels. The field below was already
green, and in the distance a dark wood stood out against an
endless sky without a cloud in sight.

Pasternak led Nina to a small rise in the cemetery where an
immense maple tree stood proud and alone, its branches just
coming into leaf. Pasternak had visited the spot often, falling
more and more into the habit of wandering among its graves,
reading the tombstone inscriptions, even addressing the dead.
"Did you love your wife, Grigory Lukich? Tell me honestly.
You don't have to lie now." He was pleased by the graves of
old men and old women and moved by the fraternal grave of
the communard Bolsheviks—twenty young men who died in
the battles for Krasnaya Presnaya during the October Revolution and who for some unknown reason had been buried
on the slope of this hill.

"This is my spot, Nina," he said at length. "I want to be buried under this tree."

"Oh, Borya, for God's sake, stop talking about death!"

"All right, then, I won't say another word." He smiled affectionately. "I'll make hay while the sun shines. 'Oh, how sweet to exist, how sweet to live in the world and to love life!' Remember? In *Doctor Zhivago*? But, Nina, right now while I look at my native Peredelkino, where the best years of my life have been spent, I'm trying—not for the first time either—to formulate in a single thought the meaning of everything that has happened to me since the day when I was eight and suddenly asked my mother, 'Who am I?' And, Nina, you know, it's amazing, but I can feel myself returning to the very point I started from. Like Pythagoras. Pythagoras claimed that history moves in never-ending circles. I feel like the scientist who evolves an earthshaking formula, having spent almost his entire life on it, only to discover, unfortunately, that he has returned to the starting point. It can be a disturbing thought. Has life been lived in vain? But I think not, Nina, because the wisdom of life lies precisely in this. A friend of Tolstoy's, the painter Gay, called one of his philosophical-religious pictures 'What Is Truth?' For me, Nina, as I suspect for him, truth is nonacceptance of evil and affirmation of good, a testing. It's not original. It's simple Christianity—elementary but final. Too much evil has accumulated in the world: social inequality, national prejudice, egoism, and obscurantism. But when Christ came down to earth he called people to self-sacrifice, to love, to goodness. And if I had to answer the question 'what is truth?' by example, I would offer my hatred of money, of force, of petty narrow-mindedness."

Nina looked at him. His eyes were alight with passion. To her he was a man gifted with a finer vision, rarer feeling, more profound understanding, a man blessed with the most complex and precious thing given to human beings: the capacity to think, feel, and participate in life and pronounce one's *own* judgment on it. She saw a demonic strength in

341

him, and for a moment she ached to stop him and say, "I love you, Borya, and I haven't got the strength to hide it any longer."

"Nina, in your opinion," Pasternak continued, "if Christ were to visit our sinful earth today, which side would he be on—communist or capitalist?"

The question brought Nina back to earth. "Not communist, certainly."

"Why?"

"Why? Because . . . communism lacks a human face."

"What did you say? Lacks a human face? That's well put, Nina."

"It's the truth. Just take the concentration camps. And the KGB. And closed borders."

"But will communism ever have a human face?" Pasternak answered his own question: "I don't know. Probably not. All the same, Nina, it seems to me there would be work, plenty of work for Christ in both communist and capitalist societies. *There* and *here*. In both worlds. Yes, the world has been divided in two. Fedin isn't wrong about that. There are two worlds, Nina, theirs and ours. I feel suspended between them, as if I had cast off from both. That's probably the most tragic situation for an individual—to be in between. Two irreconcilable worlds. And yet, Nina, that's how it was, that's how it is, and most likely how it will be for a long time to come. There's no place for truth anywhere."

Pasternak brooded momentarily on the meaning of pluralism, so valued in the West. All in all, the idea of pluralism seemed to him to have no validity; in the struggle between the leading ideas of the epoch only one would win and only one would become the idea of a whole generation. Pluralism was fine in discussing which sausage to buy in a shop or which suit was best for autumn weather, but it was worthless as a political criterion.

"Great, conscious freedom and great, conscious choice inevitably lead to good and to love between people. That's what I think. In the West, Nina, a sort of freedom flourishes

342

that cannot and does not wish to restrict the terrible power of money. And that's a plague! In our world, in the USSR . . . belief battens on disbelief. One part of our society believes in the dogmas of Marxism-Leninism, another actively rejects them; but many millions, the vast majority of our people, are interested only in getting by, in living as best they can. And that's a plague too! Both worlds have reached an impasse, Nina. Nina, dear . . ."

"What, Borya?"

"Can I recite one of my poems for you? Rather, one of Yury Zhivago's poems?"

"Of course."

Pasternak paused and then began in a singsong voice:

"The noise is stilled. I come out on the stage.
Leaning against the doorpost
I try to guess from the distant echo
What is to happen in my lifetime.

The darkness of night is aimed at me
Along the sights of a thousand opera glasses.
Abba, Father, if it be possible,
Let this cup pass from me.

I love your stubborn purpose,
I consent to play my part.
But now a different drama is being acted;
For this once let me be.

Yet the order of the acts is planned
And the end of the way inescapable.
I am alone; all drowns in the Pharisees' hypocrisy.
To live your life is not as simple as to cross a field."

He had scarcely finished when the bells in the bell tower started ringing—at first the small ones, young and frisky, then, one after another, the "wise old men." The peal of the big bells plunged them both into trepidation and bliss.

Nina started crossing herself. Pasternak looked up, and seeing the bell-tower pigeons, which had taken wing and begun
circling overhead, he crossed himself too, slowly and deliberately, three times, his face majestic.

"I want to receive Holy Communion before I die," he said.
"I want a burial service to be held over my body. I want
Tchaikovsky's Trio to be played, as it was at my birth. Above
all, I want you to promise me that you'll be here, Nina, in
Peredelkino. Promise me, Nina."

"I promise," she said.

Epilogue

Pasternak died a year later. In the early summer of 1960 he took to his bed and lay ill for only a few days. At first the doctors supposed he had suffered another heart attack, but, paradoxically, he died of lung cancer.

He spent his last days confined to the music room, with branches of lilac peeping in through the windows. Zina, Lyonya, his eldest son, Yevgeny, his brother, Shura, and Nina were all at his bedside throughout.

Once it was clear what the outcome would be, Zina suggested that Olga be called. "She's kept a vigil at the gates from morning till night, Borya," she said.

But Pasternak wouldn't countenance the intrusion. "I want to die with my family," he whispered.

Near the end he looked like a skeleton, with taut yellow skin, but the spark of intelligence still glimmered in his eyes.

"It's good that I'm dying," he confided to Nina. "I could never reconcile myself to the injustices that exist here . . . and there . . ."

On the day of his death Nina defied religious convention and gave him communion. As she sprinkled the holy water on him, he repented his sins. Death followed a few minutes after eleven o'clock that night. Zina counted his last breaths, agonizing but still unable to forgive him for his unfaithfulness. That night Tobik and Bubik bayed, and other dogs in Peredelkino were said to have bayed also.

The authorities gave permission for a funeral service conducted by a priest and deacon. But they insisted that it be held at the dacha at night, with curtains drawn and only the family and others living in the house attending. (The Western press learned of the ceremony only long after the event.)

During the service Tatyana could not stop crying. Yury Mikhailovich was plunged into gloom, foreshadowing an even further darkening of his already dark temperament. Lyonya attended with Natasha. His father's death had stunned him, and he seemed numb and disoriented. He followed Natasha everywhere and did everything she told him.

During the requiem, works by Chopin and Beethoven and Tchaikovsky's Trio were played, and afterward the poet was buried under the spreading maple tree at the top of the hill overlooking Peredelkino.

Despite special measures taken by the authorities—a party meeting was, in fact, called in the Union of Soviet Writers and the roads leading from Moscow to Peredelkino were blocked by KGB cars—about three thousand people gathered for the burial. In the crowd, among others, were all the foreign correspondents accredited in Moscow.

At the grave, in front of the coffin, Olga sobbed uncontrollably, and notwithstanding her earlier insistence on walking closest to the poet, frantically entreated, "Borya, forgive me! Borya, forgive me! Borya . . ."

Nearby, Zina stood motionless, without a trace of emotion, and beside her was Nina, supporting her by the elbow.

Shouts could be heard from the crowd: "Khrushchev killed Pasternak!" "*Doctor Zhivago* belongs to us! We'll read it!" "Quiet. Show some respect for the dead."

And then the KGB moved in, quickly nailed down the cover of the coffin and lowered it into the grave.

The newspaper *Literatura i Zhizn* carried a short obituary notice stating that a member of the Literary Fund, Boris Pasternak, had died.

2.

Two weeks later Olga and her daughter, Irina, were arrested by the KGB and put on trial for illegal currency dealings. Olga received a penalty of five years and was exiled to the Kirov district in the northern part of the country; Irina escaped with a few months in prison.

Four years later Nikita Khrushchev was "overthrown." As he had anticipated, it was mainly Suslov who intrigued against him and Brezhnev who played the principal supporting role. In his absence on vacation they gained the support of the Politburo and scheduled a special plenum of the Central Committee, to which Khrushchev was summoned to answer charges of "voluntarism" and foreign-policy mistakes and account for a host of other sins. It was a knife in the back. Khrushchev defended himself furiously; his speech at the plenum lasted four hours. But his camp proved to be in a minority. Even Mikoyan deserted him at the end. (Serov was by then no longer in power.)

Khrushchev retired to his dacha (which was a bit simpler than the one in Barvikha), enjoying the perquisites of one Volga and one bodyguard, a Major Borodavkin, whom he called "Lanky." Nina continued to teach at the academy, and so Nikita was often left alone. The whole world, it seemed, had forgotten him. Only in the West was his name occasionally mentioned, a fact he discovered by listening to BBC and Radio Liberty broadcasts. At best, he could expect to be buried in Novodevichy Cemetery, as an old Bolshevik. There was no thought of Red Square anymore.

One winter's day, while browsing at the bookcase with

nothing better to do, the stooped and considerably aged former party leader happened on a volume of *Doctor Zhivago*. The copy, published in West Germany in Russian, was the same that Nina, years earlier, had read at his command. For lack of anything better to do, he decided to have a look at it, a luxury he had had neither time nor inclination to indulge at the time the novel appeared.

Perhaps because the interval had softened his prejudice against Pasternak, and perhaps because his fall from power had darkened his view of the Soviet system, the novel so enthralled him that he read it throughout the night, disdaining even to respond to Nina's ironic questions. But when he had finished the book, during dinner with Nina and Borodavkin the following evening, he gave his opinion.

"It's a wonderful book, this *Doctor Zhivago*! You ought to read it, Borodavkin, and think it over. There's nothing *harmful* about it. It's about the fate of real people, and it's wonderfully true. You were right, old girl. We should have published it, let people read it. Only good would have come of it. I'll never forgive Surkov for proscribing it! The idiot! Raised such a scandal! Goddam Stalinist! And those lice Suslov and Polikarpov supported him too. They wanted blood. Savages! Goddam sonsofbitches!"

"Goddam sonsofbitches!" Nina repeated. "Only it's a bit late in the day for you to have changed your mind, my beloved, Nikita-the-fool."